D1559159

PLAYED TO DEATH

BOOKS BY BV LAWSON

Scott Drayco Series:

Played to Death
Requiem for Innocence
Dies Irae
Elegy in Scarlet
The Suicide Sonata
False Shadows, Eight Scott Drayco Short Stories

PLAYED TO DEATH

A Scott Drayco Mystery

BV Lawson

Crimetime Press

Played to Death is a work of fiction. All of the names, characters, places, organizations, and events portrayed in this novel are either products of the author's imagination or are used fictitiously. Any resemblance to actual events, locales, or persons, living or dead, is entirely coincidental.

Copyright © 2014 by BV Lawson.

Published in the United States of America.

For information, contact
Crimetime Press
6312 Seven Corners Center, Box 257
Falls Church, VA 22044

Hardcover ISBN 978-0-9904582-2-7
Trade Paperback ISBN 978-0-9904582-1-0
eBook ISBN 978-0-9904582-0-3

In Memoriam, Sherman B. Vanaman II

Acknowledgments

Many thanks to the lovely folks on the Eastern Shore of Virginia who helped inspire some of the sights and scenes in this book. Both Cape Unity and Prince of Wales County are purely fictional and an amalgam of various towns and counties on the Delmarva Peninsula.

The English translation of Bohdan Zaleski's poem "Mgła mi do oczu zawiewa złona" is by Professor Mieczyslaw Tomaszewski of the Warsaw Academy of Music.

Special thanks to Michael Garrett for his editing assistance with an early draft of this novel.

Most of all, I have undying gratitude, to infinity plus ten, for my beloved family (my parents, my brother Ben, my very special in-law "adopted" family) for their encouragement and patience especially my astoundingly patient husband Charles, who is also my beta reader and supporter-in-chief.

Part One

My heart is heavy, my eyes full of sorrow,
Darkness creeps over me.
I can no longer sing of tomorrow,
For I am dumb with grief and weeping.

—From the song "I want what I have not," poem by Bohdan Zaleski,
music by Frédéric Chopin

1

It was a helluva welcome to a town. More a raw wound on the landscape than a sign—with large red letters weeping down the front of muddy plywood: *Cape Unity, Home of Real Americans! Developers and Other Devils Turn Back Now!* Scott Drayco hoped to take in some sights near the waters of the Chesapeake Bay, but this wasn't what he had in mind.

The overlook next to the sign was deserted except for Drayco in his vintage Oldsmobile Starfire, its indigo paint coordinating like bruised skin with the amber sky. He climbed out and looked toward the Bay. The Atlantic Ocean on the opposite side of the Peninsula lay hidden from view by barrier islands, but it wasn't hard to imagine long-ago European immigrants in fragile ships catching sight of these shores. Perhaps he shared more in common with those exhausted pilgrims than he cared to admit.

The cold wind blew stinging sprays of saltwater into his eyes, but it felt good. One way to know he was no longer hemmed in by an urban metropolis. Not to mention that unmistakable shore aroma, Eau de Seaweed with a pinch of fish market. He had to keep pushing wind-swept hair out of his eyes, his fingers pulling away dark strands. His barber said mid-thirties was a bit early to go bald, just lay off the stress and "you'll be fine." Maybe next lifetime.

Looking at his watch, Drayco heaved a deep sigh and slid back into the driver's seat. The rumble of the engine's eight cylinders probably sounded like a sea monster to the native wildlife. He followed the scribbled instructions on the piece of paper on his passenger seat and finally pulled in front of his destination. Snippets of Beethoven's "Pathétique" sonata flashed through his mind—dark, moody, rueful—as he stared at the Opera House in front of him. He was in unfamiliar territory, in more ways than one.

Drayco climbed out of the car to get a better look at the Opera House building, a fading snapshot of better days as it loomed in the flash of morning twilight. He studied the façade, a true stylistic schizophrenic. Patterned shingles and weathered copper rosettes flanked the gables above. The orange brick walls sported contrasting white stone highlights. Dingy windows remained intact, but cracks crept along the front steps, and peeling paint resembled a pox, fallout from the sea air he could almost taste.

A gust of the unsettled March winds startled him. He jumped back when a piece of cornice blew off the Opera House roof line, landing at his feet. An omen? Drayco squinted up at what remained of the cornice, hoping it held together.

He had two reasons for being here and hadn't asked for either. One of those reasons, the potential client he'd agreed to meet here, was nowhere in sight. Was this all just a huge joke at Drayco's expense? If so, the mystery client was a great actor, his voice on the phone agitated, insistent. No, likely just late.

Deciding to take a look inside and using the key his attorney gave him, Drayco paced down the hallway over the faded carpet. Once likely a brilliant-red color, it was now more a salmon pink. Two shuttered box office windows stood as mute sentinels questioning who dared disturb their musical mausoleum.

As he approached the auditorium, Drayco stopped short, listening. The building hadn't been used in years, yet it was as if he heard faint strains of piano music and applause. He reached out to open the door, but his feet felt glued to the carpet. He'd moved past all that, hadn't he? What's done was done? Standing up straight, he pushed into the pitch-black hall, his flashlight revealing row after row of ghostly seats and the faint silhouette of the piano on the stage.

He picked his way down the aisle to the front and fumbled around for a light switch. When his fingers landed on one next to the stage, he flipped it on. The lone bulb cast a dim, amber glow, but it was enough for him to see something there that didn't belong.

With a knot forming in his stomach, Drayco was grateful for his long legs as he hoisted himself over the apron's footlights, strode to center stage, and stopped. If this was the mystery man he was supposed to meet, the man wasn't just late for his appointment.

The body lying on the stage had a gunshot wound to the head and a pattern carved on the chest where the shirt was cut away. A wilting red carnation was pinned to the lapel of the man's coat, the blood and carnation forming a grotesque collage. But it was the man's wide-open eyes that were the most disturbing. Eyes frozen in surprise? Terror?

From the dried condition of the blood, he was murdered a few hours ago. Just in case, Drayco listened for sounds the killer was lurking nearby. Not hearing anything, he dialed 9-1-1 on his cellphone, the unfortunate dead man and the piano his only company.

As Drayco waited, his breathing formed vapor tempests in the cold and silent space, the swirling breath-clouds echoing back to him. He resisted an overwhelming urge to touch the piano, to play it before the spotless keyboard got covered in black fingerprint powder. Instead, he blew on his hands, trying to warm them up. If only he could reach down and close the dead man's staring eyes.

Drayco knew anyone else would balk at arranging a meeting with a stranger at a dilapidated Opera House at seven in the morning. But in his line of work that passed for normal. So did the unsmiling face of the man in a sheriff's uniform who strode down the aisle only eight minutes after Drayco's call.

"You're Drayco," the sheriff stated, tilting his head up.

The quarter-moon paunch and balding pate of this particular sheriff didn't make the man appear threatening, until one noted the piercing brown eyes and hulking shoulders worthy of an offensive lineman. Drayco nodded down at the officer and looked at his nametag, "Sheriff Sailor." No deputies, just the head guy himself. The scale of everything was different in a small town.

Sailor took one look at the body and uttered, "Jeez," then joined Drayco in studying the deceased. A pair of pince-nez eyeglasses like those favored by Teddy Roosevelt lay beside the body. The glasses were intact but smeared with blood from the bullet hole in the man's forehead, the likely cause of death despite the pattern slashed into the flesh.

Drayco said, "I doubt the victim carved up his own body before he shot himself. And no gun or knife in sight."

"Or did you hide them?" Sailor wasn't joking, watching Drayco's reactions closely.

Rather than take offense, tendrils of sympathy wrapped around Drayco's brain. He'd walked in the other man's shoes far too many times. He replied, "As I said, murder by a person or persons unknown, not suicide."

The sheriff said, "The victim's wife, Nanette, would agree with you about suicide. Fifteen minutes before you called, she phoned to say her husband was missing. Didn't leave a note, suicidal or otherwise."

"Would that be Mrs. Nanette Keys? Assuming our victim over there is Oakley Keys."

"That's him. You never met him before?"

"I'd never heard of him until he called yesterday and said he wanted to hire me."

"So you know of absolutely no reason he'd want to hire a detective right before he's found murdered—on said detective's own property?"

Drayco sucked in his breath and chose his words carefully. "Keys arranged a meeting early this morning but wouldn't give details. I'd planned on coming to town soon, anyway."

It was supposed to be so easy. Quick trip over to the Eastern Shore, quick trip out, just long enough to decide what to do with the Opera House. Drayco's Opera House. He would never get used to the sound of that. It had to be a world record for unusual bequests by grateful clients. When his attorney called to say Horatio Rockingham had left Drayco the place in his Will, he'd looked at the calendar to make sure it wasn't April 1st. "How did you know I'm the new owner?"

"It's my business to know. Little surprised to see you in person. Kinda expected a realtor to handle everything. The boys and I laid wagers as to how fast a 'For Sale' sign would go up."

"Are you that sure I'm going to sell?"

"You'd be insane if you didn't." Sailor looked over at the body again. "Only half past seven. Yet it looks like Keys has been on the floor for some time. Doesn't make sense he'd schedule a meeting with you then sneak in hours beforehand." Sailor examined the blood spatter. "But he wasn't dragged here from somewhere else. He died here."

Drayco pointed to the victim's chest. "What's with the carving? Resembles a letter of the alphabet. 'G,' I think. There are even serifs."

"'G' for gruesome. Strangest damn thing I've seen. Maybe the M.E. in the state's Norfolk Office will pin down more. Along with an approximate time of death." The sheriff locked eyes with Drayco again. "Can anyone vouch for your whereabouts last night and this morning?"

"Fellow drivers held prisoner on the Bay Bridge, thanks to a chain-reaction crash. I left the District at eight last night but didn't arrive here until fifteen minutes ago. Spent the night in my car on the bridge."

"Any corroboration?"

"The emergency crews working the crash didn't take down license info if that's what you're asking."

"Where were you before eight last night?"

"At home alone, but my nosy neighbor and unofficial biographer can give you a detailed account of everything I did." For a microsecond, Drayco thought he saw a flicker of amusement on the sheriff's face. If so, it was gone as quickly as it came.

Drayco weighed his options. As the sheriff guessed, he'd secretly hoped for a quick Opera House sale before heading off on his first real vacation in five years. Although if he were honest with himself, it wasn't so much a vacation as an escape, a chance to banish the nightmares from his last case. Nightmares that left him wondering if it was time to retire from investigative work altogether.

Instead, here he was, trapped in the middle of a legal minefield.

At home, his answer would be to dig into a Bach fugue, sinking into the composer's complex counterpoint for inspiration. Investigations were Drayco's counterpoint, and once a "theme" like

Oakley Keys' murder appeared, Drayco's analysis gears kicked in, looking for motifs, patterns, layers.

He eyed Oakley's mutilated body. The congealed, dried blood spread out on the stage like a demonic child's fingerpainting. Why couldn't the man wait until the time they agreed to meet? And how had he gotten in?

"Are you willing to spot a suspect a few questions, Sheriff?"

Sailor strolled over to the piano, a position that placed him at equal distances from Drayco and the corpse. "Depends on what you ask."

"For starters, have there been similar mutilations?"

"Makes it sound like we've got aliens removing cows' lips." Sailor flicked a piece of imaginary lint off his hat before depositing the hat on top of the piano. "But the answer is no. Although this is my first murder case." He quickly added, "In this town."

"So what would make Oakley Keys a target?"

"Possibly a land dispute. He was David versus a development company Goliath that wants to build condos. No specific threats."

Drayco read about that in the *Washington Post*. A brief article about Eastern Shore development, buried on an inside page. No direct mentions of controversy, but some hints about pollution in estuaries. The awkward, eternal dance between progress and entropy, waltzing onto the shores of Cape Unity.

"Was Oakley Keys wealthy?"

"Not yet." The sheriff pulled plastic gloves out of his pocket and walked over to the body.

Drayco stepped back to allow him to pass. "Not robbery, then."

"His wife said nothing was missing from the house. Except a mask of some kind." Sailor picked up a wallet filled with money and a credit card. "And there's this."

Two deputies burst through the front of the hall and marched down the same aisle the sheriff had taken. With a tilt of the head from Sailor, they went straight to work. It got brighter, and Drayco scanned the stage. Where had he missed a light switch? One of the deputies wore a camera draped around his neck, had a sketchpad in hand, and an evidence kit and some brown-paper collection bags lay at his feet. Everyone must do triple duty in this department.

The triple-duty deputy knocked over an aluminum case, and Drayco winced at the jagged magenta spikes the sound set off in his head. He realized he must have identified them out loud when Sailor tilted his head and asked, "Jagged magenta spikes?"

Drayco started to wave off the question, but he didn't want the sheriff to think he was losing his mind. Or a psychopath. He could see the newspaper headline now: *Deranged Detective Swaps Sleuthing for Slicing.*

He replied, "Chromesthesia. It's a type of synesthesia where people hear sounds as colors, shapes, and textures."

Sailor tilted his head. "Is that so?"

Drayco glanced at the deputy with the aluminum case, the man oblivious to the symphony of fireworks he'd set in motion. Sometimes Drayco envied people who only experienced the world in flat, 2D sound. "My attorney mentioned a caretaker. Is he here?"

The sheriff called out, "Tyler, find Seth Bakely for me. Closest house in back."

The second deputy, a young woman, disappeared out the back stage door for a few minutes and returned with a man in denim coveralls, who lumbered onto the stage. With sepia hair, snowy eyebrows and furrows of wrinkles, his age was hard to guess: anywhere from sixty to eighty.

Bakely stared at Drayco, who was between Seth and the body. "Who's he?" he growled in a liquid sandpaper voice.

"This is Scott Drayco, Seth. The new owner."

Seth Bakely didn't shake Drayco's outstretched hand. "Heard about you. Thought you'd be older." He coughed. "Guess Mr. Rockingham's heirs are glad he dumped this thing. Don't think I saw the man twice. Don't know why he paid me to stay." Seth's forehead crinkled into tighter rows. "Suppose you'll be wanting to hire other people to take over."

"Did you know that man over there?" Drayco moved aside so Seth could see the body.

Bakely blinked his eyes several times and stared at the corpse, then turned away to wipe his mouth on his sleeve. "In this town, you know everybody a bit. What happened? He dead?"

"Very."

"You kill him?"

Funny that Seth voiced the question Drayco expected the sheriff to ask outright. "Do you have any idea how he got in, Seth?"

"Hain't seen him in here. Don't get visitors. Just mice and spiders. Must have come in the stage door. Lock's temperamental. Don't always work." Seth kept shifting his feet in place. "Told you Rockingham never spent a dime on this place."

"Any signs of someone else who didn't belong? Anything out of the ordinary?"

"Just you. And him." Seth wiped his sweating face, which was a shade or two paler than when he arrived.

Sheriff Sailor, leaning on the piano and mostly silent, grabbed that moment to chime in. "What time did you leave the Opera House last night, Seth?"

"'Bout six. Went home and watched TV. With Paddy. Don't start my morning rounds 'til nine."

"And did you hear anything? A gunshot?"

"Ears don't work like they used to. Was watching an old war movie. And there was some rain, pretty heavy. Almost sounded like hail."

Sailor said, "All right. That's it for now, Seth. And don't clean in here until we give the okay."

Bakely swayed on his feet, then righted himself and jerked his thumb at Drayco, "My house is on the street behind. If you need anything, holler." He shambled down the hall and out of sight.

Drayco said, "Garrulous type, isn't he?"

"Man of a thousand words. Just not in the same lifetime. Keeping his son Paddy out of jail doesn't help his attitude."

Surprisingly, the sheriff didn't stop Drayco as he bent down to study Oakley's skin, being careful not to touch the body. "Grayish, signs of advanced rigor in the upper body. With the cold temps in here, it's harder to tell, but likely dead eight to twelve hours, give or take. Which means he arrived, and was killed, before midnight."

He examined the wound on the forehead. "Irregular hole, some powder tattooing and lesions but no searing. An intermediate-range shot."

Drayco did a quick three-sixty view. Lots of clear sight lines, with the wings of the stage and curtains perfect for a stealthy approach. "From the blood patterns, there may be an exit wound. Wonder if the bullet went through?"

The triple-duty deputy called out from the side. "It lodged in a post over here. Only one I've found."

At least that was one tiny piece of good news. Drayco said, "No damage to the lands and grooves on that bullet, if we're lucky. And it'll be easier to remove a piece of post than a whole wall." He got as close to the red carnation as possible without handling it. "I don't see any blood on the pin, which means our carver didn't handle it with his bloody hands or gloves. Keys wore it here."

Sailor folded his arms across his chest. "You act more like a CI than a PI. Was the newspaper wrong? Not that it'd be the first time."

Drayco was surprised. "Newspaper?"

"We do have those around here. And an out-of-town detective becoming the new owner of a historic building is big."

"Not a CI. Not exactly a PI. Call me a crime consultant. Or crime guru, like someone did once. I think it was an insult." Drayco pointed to the victim's jacket. "Strange for him to be wearing lightweight seersucker. It was only a degree or two above freezing last night."

The sheriff shrugged. "Oakley had money problems and wasn't the *GQ* type."

"The wife didn't report him missing until this morning?"

"He was an odd bird. Been on the straight and narrow for a while, but had a history of drinking. And a few other indiscretions. This was old hat to Nanette, who, by the way, is a fine lady. Does a lot for this community." He paused. "It's unfortunate she doesn't have an alibi."

"How do you know?"

"She told me she was alone all last night."

Drayco chewed on that for a minute "Were Oakley's 'indiscretions' arrest-worthy?"

"Last I heard, extramarital affairs aren't illegal."

An affair would increase the odds this was nothing more than a domestic dispute case. Drayco should be relieved by that. But he'd learned never to trust a coincidence—like having a would-be client murdered before he can talk to you.

The sheriff's voice cut through Drayco's reverie. "Crime guru or no, my deputies and I have work to do. I've spotted you a half-dozen questions. More than I ordinarily would." His tone of dismissal came through loud and clear. "I suppose you'll be staying in town a while?"

Drayco saw where this was headed and envisioned his last chance of a quick exit flying out the window. He thought briefly of the nonrefundable plane ticket to Cancun back at his townhouse. "The Opera House has me chained here, anyway. What's a few more days?"

"Plenty of time for the grand tour of Cape Unity. Come to think of it, that might only take a half-day." Sailor's expressions ranged the gamut from A to Blank. The man must be a good poker player if he were the gambling type. Right now, Drayco hoped he was.

Sailor added, "What the hell, if this thing has us stumped, maybe we'll hire you. We're down a deputy to the mumps. Keep you in town longer. Especially if you get the mumps."

"For you, Sheriff, I'll waive expenses." Drayco worked with law enforcement officials of all stripes, and it was always a crap shoot. At its worst, it degenerated into a competition. Egos, one; justice, zero. "Does this mean I have your blessing to leave now?"

"As long as you don't touch anything on your way out. But as a big-city professional crime consultant, that should be SOP for you, right?"

With one last look at the remains of Oakley Keys, Drayco left the building and sat in his car with the engine off, staring at a jagged line of cracked bricks on the Opera House façade. One decaying and unwanted Opera House, one murdered potential client, one wary sheriff, and he'd been in town less than an hour.

Opening up his car window to let in a blast of cold, salty air, Drayco watched the scud clouds swallow up the last traces of the sunrise. He fingered the remains of his breakfast, a PayDay candy bar wrapper. What did their old jingle say? "The nuttiest bar in town." Why stop at just one town? Why not the whole damn universe?

When the universe handed out karmas, Oakley Keys was standing in the wrong line. It was all so easy for people who explained every evil in the world as "God's will," or predestination or whatever credo they subscribed to, comfortable in the belief there is a purpose for everything. Even murder.

He watched the ambulance pull up to the rear door of the Opera House, ready to ferry the newly deceased off to its autopsy. Too early to tell until results came back, but Keys was likely killed a few hours before Drayco arrived. A brutal ending for one in this town, and an uneasy beginning for another.

He replayed the mental image of the body formerly known as Oakley Keys, waiting for his date with the medical examiner. Why did Keys want to hire Drayco? Why did he break into the Opera House, only to be shot and carved up like a Thanksgiving turkey? And why the devil was Keys wearing a red carnation?

2

Armed with tongue-scalding Ethiopian Sidamo brew from a place called the Novel Café, Drayco navigated Cape Unity's appropriately named Main Street. There wasn't a building younger than mid-twentieth century. Some were in good shape, but others were crumbling shells with roofs partially caved in. They were forgotten monuments with holes in the front like staring eyes. Eyes pleading for help. He tried not to think of Oakley Keys' eyes, frozen wide open in rigor.

Drayco continued past a virtual roll call of small town Americana—courthouse, library, post office, and church. Dogwood trees stripped bare surrounded the town square, with tufts of dormant fescue grass in the middle. The few planters were meant to showcase flowers but held only brown Mid-Atlantic dirt, like miniature graves.

He parked in front of his target, the courthouse. If he was stuck in town for a few days, he might as well make good use of the time. Look up records, make copies of documents, whatever would help in selling the Opera House. This part of his trip, at least, should be trouble-free.

The courthouse for Prince of Wales County shared some of the same construction as the Opera House, but grimmer and more institutional. Why did architects seem determined to make government buildings uncontroversial bland boxes? A misguided attempt to prove government wasn't frivolous? The interior matched in tone—standard beige concrete walls, beige stone trim throughout, and a wooden reception window, also painted beige.

It would be a relief to get this chore over with.

A receptionist with a turquoise hummingbird tattoo on her neck reached for a form and asked his name. He'd barely replied "Scott Drayco," when out of the corner of his eye, he spied a figure lunging in his direction.

Drayco jumped out of reach of his would-be attacker, a gaunt-faced man with a jagged white scar over one eyebrow and thin, scraggly hair draped over his shoulders—a living, breathing scarecrow. The man's arms flailed, punctuating his rambling epithets like exclamation marks.

"You goddamn uppity maggot. My daddy earned that building. Cared for it when nobody else gave a rat's ass. Go back where you came from. Or better yet, you go straight to hell."

Drayco kept the man at arm's length. But with the man's face an apoplectic red, Drayco wasn't as concerned the stranger might deck him, as keel over from a heart attack. Two bailiffs jumped on the writhing scarecrow-man, dragging him off into the bowels of the courthouse.

As they manhandled him away, he yelled, "Keys deserved what he got, that maggot. Make sure it don't happen to you."

Drayco debated whether to follow the bailiffs, but was halted by another man whose voice dripped with a surprisingly ugly caramel-colored drawl. "Won't you come this way?" A hand pressed down on Drayco's arm, pushing him toward an empty meeting room. Just big enough for an eight-person table, the space had the sweet chemical smell of fake-lemon polish.

"I overheard your name, Mr. Drayco. Allow me to introduce myself. I'm Councilman Randolph Squier. So terribly sorry about that little incident. Paddy Bakely is not one of our more exemplary citizens, tending heavy toward the drinking."

So that unfortunate scarecrow was the Opera House caretaker's son. The sheriff's comment about Seth Bakely made more sense. Drayco said, "I think I understand."

"In fact, Paddy is due in court on a charge of assault. I hope you won't unfairly judge our town because of him."

Because of him alone? That was doubtful. Cape Unity was no Mayberry. "Every town has its lost souls."

Squier dipped his hands in the pockets of his cream-colored suit and rocked back on his feet. He'd be perfect as the Southern-dandy token in a boardgame of Stereotypical Politicians. "Lost soul is a good moniker for Paddy, Mr. Drayco. He and his father have been down on their luck most of their lives. Paddy's mother died in childbirth. Seth was never the same, nor did he know what to do about his son."

"I met Seth Bakely earlier. Aloof, but sane."

"He's tended the Opera House since he first came to Cape Unity. I'm not certain he intended on settling in town this long. But he married a local beauty, Angel Quillin. And then there was Paddy to take care of, so he's become part of our community."

"Paddy feels Rockingham should have left the Opera House to the Bakelys?"

"A faint dream of theirs, perhaps. But really, though they can do the odd job here and there, what would they know of running and restoring an Opera House?"

Squier arched one eyebrow into an upside-down V. "You're here with a purpose toward that end, perhaps?"

Running and restoring wasn't quite what Drayco had in mind, but he'd play along. "Whatever may help."

"I considered purchasing the Opera House myself at one time. I concluded it was not a wise business investment."

Drayco almost said, "Tell me about it," but held his tongue. "You weren't surprised when Paddy mentioned the murder of Oakley Keys."

"Paddy likely heard it from one of the bailiffs. The sheriff informed the mayor, who in turn, called the Councilmen. It's been the talk of the courthouse this morning. We pride ourselves in Cape Unity on our low crime rate, so such incidents get the tongues wagging. It may make the Washington papers."

Squier seemed gleeful at the idea. Or he subscribed to the philosophy there's no such thing as bad publicity. Murder drew cold-blooded sharks to whatever profitable chum they found, be they ambulance chasers, authors of tell-all books—or someone wanting a marketing gimmick to use in a Cape Unity travel brochure.

Squier added, "People will try to pin this on Oakley's neighbor, Earl Yaegle. He's one of our finer citizens, who owns several businesses in town. Plenty of old-timers might rush to judgment. I fear a symbolic lynching."

The councilman angled his head forward. Drayco thought at first he was bowing. "Is there a way we can make your visit smoother, Mr. Drayco?"

"Access to any Opera House files the courthouse has."

"We don't have much, I fear. But I will get my secretary to make copies for you. And to make up for this unpleasantness, you must join me for dinner at my home."

Drayco hesitated a moment before accepting. Making the rounds of the Cape Unity social set was apparently another burden of his immediate job description. No neckties. He'd intentionally not brought any.

As they re-entered the lobby, a female voice startled him with a "Hello, darling." Drayco swung around, his mouth open, then realized the woman was looking at Squier.

Squier beamed. "I invited Mr. Drayco to dinner with us. Mr. Scott Drayco, this is my wife, Darcie."

For a brief moment, Drayco's heartbeat was loud in his ears, and the walls around him faded into a blurred time warp. Except for being a decade older, Darcie was the twin of Drayco's former fiancée, Tatiana. Darcie wasn't airbrushed perfect, but not for lack of trying. Her plump ruby lips surrounded snow-white teeth that hinted of veneers.

He forced himself to focus on her ring finger.

Darcie grabbed his hand and held onto it for a few seconds longer than necessary, rubbing her thumb over his palm as she pulled her hand away. "How nice," she said. "We haven't had a dinner party in—I don't remember the last time. I hope you said yes, Mr. Drayco. Ugh. That's too formal. Can I call you Scott?"

"I. .. of course." Drayco got a whiff of her perfume, a hint of something familiar. He also didn't miss Squier's lurch closer to Darcie and the brief clenching and unclenching of his jaw. It would appear that the councilman's dinner invitation just got a lot more complicated.

Squier draped his arm around his wife, corralling her back toward his office in much the same way he had with Drayco. Before Darcie disappeared from view, she turned to give Drayco one last megawatt smile.

Realizing he was still staring at the spot where the councilman's wife stood, Drayco switched his focus to a circular Scales of Justice mosaic on the floor. The choice of red and green tile made it look like more like a tacky Christmas ornament. A waste of good tile.

Speaking of a waste—what had he gained from his visit to the courthouse? Nada. And apparently, he'd gotten on the bad side of two more townspeople, Paddy Bakely and Councilman Squier. It was a shame Squier didn't go through with his plan to buy the Opera House. If Rockingham had sold the building a few years ago, it would be easier for everyone involved. Except the Bakelys.

Paddy Bakely's anti-Oakley diatribe, now that was intriguing. Drayco frowned at the thought, trying again to nip his investigative curiosity in the bud. He had plenty to keep him busy, preparing to sell the Opera House. Until the time he was cleared as a suspect—assuming he was cleared as a suspect—he doubted the sheriff would want him kicking up grass on his home turf.

Besides, Drayco needed to refocus on his own practice, no more turning away clients like the last two. He wasn't sure why he'd agreed to meet Oakley when he wasn't ready to take on another case so soon. Had it only been three weeks since the little Cadden twins were buried?

He sank down on a bench in a corner and watched people passing through the courthouse door, wondering what brought those people here today—property tax disputes? Birth Certificates? Marriage? Divorce? Death certificates? The paper-cycle of life.

His thoughts roamed back to the murder scene with the body, the blood spatter, the "G" carved into Oakley's chest. This was no Opera House special-effect dreamed up by a props coordinator, with the actor bounding up from the floor after the curtain came down. Drayco felt like an audience member watching a drama by an anonymous playwright or librettist. He just hoped the murderer wasn't working on a second act.

3

Earl Yaegle ducked into a back entrance next to the dumpster. He'd hoped to avoid dealing with his businesses for a few days, but this new manager was greener than the others and prone to what Earl called "flailure." He wondered what earth-shattering crisis it was this time. It better be good enough to leave his refuge, the one place he didn't feel stares burning holes in his head. It had only been half a day since the news of Oakley's death, but word had spread like a pneumonic plague. People had been calling him all morning.

"Earl! So glad to see you," Randy said. As usual, he was red-faced and sweating, even in the middle of March. A little weight loss wouldn't hurt, but Randy was addicted to cheeseburgers and fried oyster sandwiches and wasn't about to give them up.

"Our supplier for the Winchester 12-gauges lost our latest shipment and said they haven't received our payment. I know I paid them, Earl. Squier's been bugging me about it for the past two days, wanting to get his hands on his new shotgun. If you call the supplier, I know they'll listen to you."

"I'll call them." It was partly Earl's fault, after all. He'd bragged on those guns to the hunt club, and Squier had salivated all over himself at the thought. They weren't cheap, over a thousand dollars, but Squier didn't care.

Randy genuflected in Earl's direction. "Thank you, fearless leader." Then his expression changed to one of concern, eyes big and dewy. He was definitely a heart-on-your-sleeve kind of guy. "How are you holding up, Earl? You know that any talk about you having something to do with Oakley's murder is nonsense, right? It'll blow away. You'll see. Soon as people find some other flavor of the month to gossip about."

Earl looked around for Joel but didn't see signs of the lanky employee until a voice piped up over his shoulder. "But those words you said the other day, Earl. What about that?" Joel's eyes were narrowed, accusing.

Earl promoted Randy over Joel, and Joel hadn't forgiven him. Joel added, "Didn't I hear you say you wished Oakley Keys would disappear? That Oakley needed someone to teach him a good lesson?"

Earl remembered. He was angry with Oakley, sure, but he'd also gotten angry that same day with a truck driver who made a wrong delivery, a utility crew that cut off power to the shop, and a customer who accused him of lying about an order. And none of them was dead. He said, "Words, Joel. Just words."

Randy pointed his finger at Joel. "Maybe you're jealous because you aren't sitting on a property gold mine like Earl is."

Joel threw up a hand dismissively. "Bah. Like it matters. The whole town's going to be overrun soon by artsy-fartsy types. Drive up fuckin' property values so none of us working stiffs can afford so much as a pine shack. That is if the illegals don't bring the values back down. Ride the land roller-coaster while you can before the price of admission is too steep, I say."

Earl had hoped to do just that. It all seemed so easy. But that was before Oakley went berserk and dug in his heels. Now he was dead, and Nanette would likely sell, so the deal would go through after all. Blood money, that's what they'd call it. And Earl had it all over his hands, whether he liked it or not.

Randy looked determined to be cheerful. "Things aren't all bad. You've got your health, your businesses. Say—did you read in the paper about the new owner of the Opera House? Said he's a detective. Maybe you should hire him. The sheriff's a nice enough guy, but this is big-city stuff."

"No detectives. I don't need one." No matter how desperate things might seem, Earl wasn't about to trust some dog-jowled sleazy operator who profited off the misfortunes of others for a living, taking pictures of wayward housewives or snooping through people's dirty laundry. Although Oakley would be prime fodder for that, he had to admit.

Joel countered, "You should listen to him, Earl. You might find yourself in deep slag."

"I can take care of myself." Earl hoped that those weren't just words. That he would feel them, mean them, as much as he wanted to. And soon.

Joel scowled. "Whatever you say, man. It's your neck."

4

Drayco made another quick stop at the Novel Café. He needed to buy a thermos while he was in town, or else spend all his time looking for coffee shops. The clerk refilled his cup for free, rare back in D.C. He took a sip and wrinkled his nose. Good, but a bit sour. Spying a salt shaker near the counter, he sprinkled grains into the coffee. Much better.

The clerk suggested he talk with Reece Wable, president of the Cape Unity Historical Society, which had documents on everything—and perhaps everyone—in town. Hopefully, more than the "we don't have much" Squier hinted about the courthouse archives. If Drayco were lucky, the society's documents might help him decide how to proceed with his Opera Leviathan.

He entered a Victorian house with blue siding, noting the lavish care on pristine displays in velvet-lined glass cases. But an air of the bizarre permeated the place. Loud ticking like a time bomb from a lighthouse-shaped grandfather clock. And a dinosaur skull grinned at him.

"Calhoun is a traitor. Calhoun is a traitor." Drayco followed the source of the voice which had an unusual pattern to Drayco's ears, a greenish cloud with star-like borders. He spied the culprit in a small cage on a stand, a bird with charcoal feathers and a maroon tail.

"That's an African Gray parrot. Name's Andrew Jackson," a human voice said from behind Drayco's back, before coming around to face Drayco. "The parrot's, not mine. President Jackson hated Vice-President John Calhoun. Called him a traitor. Unlike his namesake, this Andrew Jackson likes Moroccan olives and the NASCAR channel."

"I'm more a fan of Sicilian olives." Drayco stuck out his hand. "And my name is Scott Drayco."

Reece Wable was not what Drayco expected. Most historians wore bland, Smithsonian-friendly suits. Wable could have popped out of a vintage clothing store in his gold paisley vest and black swallowtail coat.

Apparently, they had mutual assumptions. "You're that investigator fellow. Guess I thought you'd be wearing a trench coat and fedora, not an aviator jacket. Younger than I expected, too. Longer hair, no buzz cut." Wable leaned in closer, "Are those purple eyes?"

"In certain light, maybe." Presumably from his mother's side, or at least the one picture of her indicated as much. Wable, on the other hand, had a gaze most unsettling. His left eye didn't move in tandem with the right, with subtle color differences between the two. A glass eye.

Wable's good eye inspected Drayco. "The only detective type I ever met was a horrid man who smelled of cheap grape cigars and five-day-old sweat. And he almost got me arrested for a crime I didn't commit. In short, a jackass."

"I'm not fond of cigars, and I showered last night. What crime were you charged with?"

"All a misunderstanding." Reece waved his hand in the air. "So you're the new owner of the Opera House. We have materials dating back to the founding. It has a more interesting history than people realize."

"Is that a fact?" Drayco tried not to sound skeptical.

"Famous musicians performed in its heyday, which ended mid-20th century around the war. God knows it's a podunk town now. Back then, genteel resorts in these parts drew folks during the summer months. That is, when the railroad still carried passengers down from New York. They wanted culture with their sea oats, and the Opera House was born. Violinist Ivan Ostremsky played here,

Ginnie Geddie sang here. And there was poor Konstantina Klucze. You familiar with her?"

"The Polish pianist who fled the Nazis?"

"The same. The last stop on her American tour was right here in Cape Unity. As it turned out, it was also her last concert. Ever. And the last concert in the Opera House before Rockingham closed it down. She died young, after she returned to Britain. Oakley Keys started to do some research for us on the subject, but pickings are scarce—there's only one biography—and Oakley and I haven't spoken in a while."

"Oakley worked here?"

"Oakley volunteered here. We had a disagreement and, well, I shouldn't discuss it. Especially with recent developments. But I guess you've heard since he was murdered in your building."

Drayco looked at his watch. Two o'clock. Only six hours since he'd left the Opera House. He was amazed how news of tragedy spread in a small town, like crabgrass in a neglected yard. Such misfortunes in D.C. barely registered a blip on a more jaded populace. Hardly surprising, when every newscast led off with violence. The Eastern Shore might only be eighty miles from Washington, but in some ways, it was a world apart.

Drayco didn't let on that he'd seen the body. "Word gets around fast."

"STS—Small Town Syndrome. The murder doesn't surprise me. Oakley hasn't made many friends lately."

What had the sheriff said? David versus a developer Goliath? "Because of the condos, you mean."

Reece shuddered. "Ghastly, isn't it? We don't have a single national chain store in Cape Unity. But when those condos go up, in come the chains and out go the Mom-and-Pops. Oakley and I did agree on that issue. It's all Councilman Squier's doing, spearheading the development thing. Made it part of his reelection platform. Got a lot riding on its success."

Reece hunched over and lowered his voice. "Oakley drank. And those affairs, too, including that notorious one with Councilman Squier's wife, Darcie."

So that explained the councilman's cavalier attitude toward Oakley's death. And Darcie's flirtatious behavior. Reasons to cancel his dinner with the Squiers? Drayco wasn't sure he liked that notion or not. "I heard rumors of affairs. No names."

Reece rubbed the back of his neck. "I don't take much stock in rumors. Rumors will fly that you're a murderer, and I'll bat those away, too. I could have forgiven Oakley his philandering, but theft—that's beyond the pale."

Andrew Jackson flapped his wings and squawked. Drayco said, "Your feathered sidekick agrees with you. But theft? You have proof?"

"Oakley denied it. But when the mantle clock went missing, I knew it was him. We were the only two with keys to the building. No one had broken in. Who else would it be? Some say that clock belonged to President James Monroe. I've searched several auction houses, and it's never turned up. An item like it went for sixty grand at Sotheby's."

Reece's arms were stiff at his side, his hands gripping the hem of the swallowtail coat. Injustice, large and small, was like sour, moldy bread. Consumed often enough, it brought on hunger for the meat of revenge. But murder over a clock stolen years ago? That was one ravenous grudge.

The more people Drayco talked to, the stronger his curiosity about Oakley Keys grew, despite his best efforts to stifle it. But it was documents he'd come here seeking. "You mentioned historic materials?"

Reece nodded. "Oakley organized our Opera House files. One of his pet projects. In addition to being an unsuccessful writer, he was a history buff."

"Did his wife Nanette also volunteer here?"

"I wish, but no." Reece rubbed his chin. "Sadly, I never got to know Nanette as intimately as I'd like. Maybe I'll pay her a call."

Reece led Drayco to a reading room and lugged in a box filled with a stack of Opera House pamphlets, letters, and clippings. "Here you are. Oakley had more he was going to add. I have no idea what happened to it all. A shame."

Drayco settled down with the documents, trying not to sneeze from the dust particles the papers released, the freed spores of history. As he flipped through the pages, his mind wandered until he recognized why. He was looking more for nodes of connection between Oakley and the Opera House than the building's past.

He forced his attention back to his original research mission and stopped to read a society column. It detailed lavish parties in Konstantina Klucze's honor at the homes of prominent townspeople. Among them, Maxwell Chambliss, a former town councilman. And Marshall Rockingham, father of Drayco's deceased client, who owned the Opera House before his son.

Reece was right. The Opera House, with its rich musical history, shared a unique synergy with the community. If Drayco sold it, it might be torn down for more condos. But maybe no one cared about history or culture anymore. Perhaps people were content to spend all their free time watching pet videos on YouTube. The Opera House lay unused for all this time, so would it really be missed?

After spending another hour immersed in reading, he found more reasons not in favor of selling the Opera House than for it. Unable to get the stolen clock off his mind, he hunted down Wable. "If Oakley was behind the theft, what was his motive?"

Reece wrinkled his forehead and pursed his lips, forming puffs of air as if making smoke rings. "His writing career was running on empty. And he had a high bar tab."

"Was his wife aware of your suspicions?"

"I'd never do anything to hurt Nanette. That includes letting her know her husband was a cad. His death may be a blessing."

Drayco filed away Reece's worship of Nanette for future reference. "Anything else go AWOL from the Historical Society while Oakley volunteered?"

"Only that. But when I accused him, he stopped coming."

Oakley Keys was no choirboy, but why steal a clock? The sheriff alluded to Oakley's financial problems, and this might be a one-time event—if it happened at all. It was Reece's word alone since Oakley wasn't around to defend himself. If Reece wanted to poison Oakley's reputation postmortem, that said more about Reece than Oakley.

Drayco said, "It's hard to believe Oakley didn't miss the friendships he lost, one feud at a time. Like yours."

Reece stood still, his good eye glazing over, then cleared his throat. "Everyone has regrets when a former friend bites the bullet. Even a bastard like Oakley. Don't they?"

Finding it difficult to separate the murdered Oakley Keys from the Opera House, the impotent failings of the man's life enveloped Drayco in a cloak of gloom. Another statistic for the records, like the yellowed, crumbling clippings in Reece's files. As Drayco was leaving, he heard Andrew Jackson squawking in the background, "Oakley is a madman. Oakley is a madman. Bye-bye."

5

Time to unload his one suitcase, plus he needed to check with his answering service from a landline. Cellphone service on the rural Eastern Shore was spotty. Not wanting to stay at a personality-free hotel, Drayco had made reservations at a place not far from the center of town. He followed the directions from a travel brochure until he drew in front of the Lazy Crab. Or more accurately, the Lazy Cab, the "R" having fallen off the sign. The only other vehicle in sight was a red motor scooter.

The sightline through the front window went all the way back to the kitchen where a woman with Creamsicle-colored hair fanned her face with what looked like a blueprint-paper accordion. Steam geysers wafted upward from a Dutch oven she was barely tall enough to see over. The faint strains of Led Zeppelin danced through the air, and the woman picked up two wooden spoons and tapped a rhythm on the counter. He hated to disturb her by ringing the doorbell.

The woman greeted him with one spoon in hand. "May I help you? I'm one of the proprietors. Name's Maida. Maida Jepson."

"I'm Scott Drayco and—"

Maida interrupted, "We were expecting you late last night."

"Sorry about that. Nasty accident on the Bay Bridge."

She sighed. "Not again. Then we're glad you made it safely. Mister Scott Drayco, you're a celebrity. When you made the reservation, we didn't realize you're the new owner of the Opera House. And call me Maida. I can be Mrs. Jepson when I'm ninety."

He followed her through the doorway. The foyer opened onto a hall with steep circular stairs, a den visible around the corner. The few pieces of artwork were stereotypical beach scenes and the furniture a touch faded. But vases of daylilies adorned a side table with fancy scrollwork and the seat of an antique hall tree.

It was like his great-aunt's house where he was dumped in the summer, spending mornings rescuing stranded starfish, throwing them out to sea. His first taste of the vagaries of life and death. Finding more creatures, often the same ones, beached again the next day, dead and desiccated.

Dead and desiccated. That could describe the Opera House, too. A few other words came to mind. Money-trap. Time-waster. Boondoggle. "You must have read the newspaper article about the Opera House, Maida."

"The whole town's buzzing. Everybody's hoping for great things to jump-start the downtown and bring back tourists."

Drayco hesitated. "There may be structural problems. And it will need repairs." After a glimpse of Maida's hopeful expression, he didn't have the heart to tell her his plans for a quick sale. Perhaps people did care about the fate of the Opera House, after all. Or at least, one person. Was anyone else in town casting him as an urban-renewal savior?

She plunged ahead, undeterred. "Victorians are being turned into art galleries on Atlantic Street. And the Fairmont Hotel's been restored to its former glory. We won't have to refer to our town as Cape Extremity anymore. Of course, there's that condo battle." She grimaced.

Maida's rapid-fire delivery was difficult for him to follow. Being sleep-deprived made it worse. "Cape Extremity?"

She motioned for him to enter the kitchen. "If you look at the entire Delmarva Peninsula turned on its side, it looks like a loggerhead sea turtle. We're on the tail, one of the softer parts of the turtle and not terribly interesting. Unless you're another turtle or a predator. I'll have to cook you up some turtle gumbo."

Drayco smiled, but she only held half his attention. The fireplace was too inviting. Ordinarily, he wasn't bothered by cold weather except for his arm, which was starting to ache. Yet his physical therapist was adamant weather wouldn't have any effect on his injury whatsoever. It was a good thing he didn't play baseball for a living—the only thing worse would be a pianist. He forced himself to relax the fingernails digging into his palm. "Those condos you mentioned. They're a hot topic."

"Oh, they are. But I'll wager you're more interested in a hot toddy to stave off the chill."

Maida ushered him to a wooden armchair that looked like it was carved from a ship's mast, then headed to the stove where she ladled a red liquid out of a steaming pot into a mug. After adding shots from a couple of unlabeled glass bottles, she handed over the mug with the unidentifiable concoction. Was that cranberry and nutmeg?

"I'm famous for these," Maida said, taking a bow. "Secret family recipe. Although the main ingredient didn't come from a still in the backyard like Cousin Harvey's. Every bit as potent."

"Do you have other guests? There's a scooter in front."

"You're our one and only. The scooter is mine. Perfect for short hops to the store, and I can cut corners."

Drayco settled into an agreeable inertia when an alarming warmth crept up his foot. As he looked down, it was impossible to miss the orange-blue flames of a newspaper on fire. He jumped up and stamped out the sparks with his shoe, trying to keep the shoe from catching fire. It didn't, but his foot tingled, and he inhaled a whiff of burned rubber. He barely made out the charred headline on the newspaper, "Manuscript Theft from Library a Mystery."

Maida double-checked the danger was over, looking embarrassed at the lapse.

"Don't worry, Maida, it's nothing major."

"Funny you should say that. My husband's name is Major."

Drayco found himself blinking in a fog again. Must be the drink. "Major?"

"He was in the military, but that's not where he got the name. It's just Major, though folks around here call him *the* Major. He had to go out, but hopefully, you'll meet him soon. At the very least, at breakfast tomorrow. He's always ready at nine for tea and scones following his morning errands, come hell or high water."

"Sounds like an ex-Brit."

"He was born on this side of the Pond, but his adopted parents were originally from Torquay. He'll be dying to ask you about your life in the FBI. I've warned him not to pester you."

So the newspaper article mentioned that, too. What else had it put in there? His favorite color? Boxers or briefs? The reason he left the FBI?

Maida grabbed his mug from him to see if he needed a refill. Adding more of the brew, she said, "It seems odd for Mr. Rockingham to bequeath you the Opera House. Do all your clients do things like that?"

"The occasional golf course, villa, or yacht." Drayco took a sip and swallowed too fast, scalding his throat.

It was Maida's turn to look confused. "Golf course?"

"A lame attempt at humor."

"Poor Cape Unity will be a comedown from D.C."

"If you'll pardon the sailing term, it's more of a come-about." Maida's potent concoction was doing the trick. You should need a prescription for that stuff. *Take two cc's of Maida Tonic before bedtime and call me in the morning.*

A man poked his head around the doorway, enough for Drayco to see he was Maida's age. He had shocks of gray hair streaked in clumps through the black strands. Less salt-and-pepper, more akin to a skunk pelt. He sported a matching beard long enough to have a white rubber band dividing it in half.

Maida motioned for him to come in. "You won't have to wait for breakfast, after all. This is my husband, Major. And this is Scott Drayco, dear."

The Major pressed Drayco right away. "The paper called you a crime consultant. Tried for the police force, myself, but they didn't want people with bad backs. Old war injury. Still, a crime consultant—sounds detectivy. Might consider that. Catch bad guys, do you? Do you get to use handcuffs?"

When Drayco said it wasn't part of the job, the Major replied, "Where's the fun in that?" He folded his arms over his chest. "So, who's the bad guy you're after?"

Maida jumped in, "Remember, Scott's the new owner of the Opera House." She turned to Drayco. "I'm sure you're eager to see it. It was a beauty once."

Drayco noted the word "once" and had a sudden vision of his accountant laughing hysterically in the background. "I was there this morning."

No need to spring the news of the murder on them yet. He was accustomed to death, to corpses, to depravity. Drayco and his colleagues lived those nightmares by day, so others didn't have to dream them at night.

"You probably ran into Seth or Paddy Bakely at the Opera House." Maida chewed on her lip. "Seth's the caretaker and Paddy's his son, though neither is the warmest fuzzy on the planet. Paddy's a loose cannon, but Seth is a stable influence. Seth's the primary custodian, and Paddy helps out from time to time. When he's not walking on a slant."

A phone ringing in another room interrupted them, and Maida scurried off after excusing herself, leaving the Major and Drayco alone. The older man sighed. "No handcuffs. No guns, either?"

"I'm more cloak than dagger these days." He didn't mention the gun packed in his suitcase. But he hadn't read any rules against guns on the inn's website, and with any luck, he wouldn't need it.

"Used to be a fair shot myself, in my youth. Used to be good at a lot of things before the wrinkles and arthritis. Kinda like the area around here. Once shiny and new, full of promise." The Major held his hands next to the fireplace but twisted around to stare at Drayco. "Word of advice, young fellow, don't ever stand still or life will fossilize you on the spot."

When Maida walked back into the room, gone were the rosy cheeks and laughing eyes. Her shoulders were stooped forward and her arms wrapped over her stomach as if she were on the verge of losing her breakfast.

"What's wrong?" Drayco asked.

"That was a friend of mine. She says Oakley Keys was murdered. In your Opera House."

Reece's STS again. At least, there went all need for Drayco to hide the truth from them. "Unfortunately, your friend is right. I met with the sheriff earlier."

The Jepsons exchanged looks of disbelief, the only sounds in the room the hissing and moaning from the fireplace logs. In a way, those sounds would be better for a funeral than the plasticized music from those instruments of the devil, Hammond organs and Wurlitzer spinet pianos.

Maida dropped into a chair. "Damn it all. Oakley wasn't one of my flock, but I knew him all the same."

"Sorry, I don't follow. Your flock?"

"I'm a lay pastor at Unity Presbyterian. We're too out of the way to attract someone full time. We have lay pastors who alternate duties."

Drayco had a sudden mental image of the red-headed Reverend Maida hurtling through parking lots in a cassock and surplice on her red motor scooter. "Oakley's troubles with the condo project—are they intense enough to lead to murder?"

Maida rubbed her forehead. "Oh, I do hope Oakley's death isn't related to that mess."

"Why do you say that?"

"Oakley Keys and his neighbor Earl Yaegle own several acres of waterfront property side-by-side. Along comes a Washington developer with talk of a resort complex and money as big as a pirate's chest of gold. Next thing you know, Oakley and Earl aren't speaking to each other."

"Not enough cash? Or maybe they didn't agree on how to spend it."

Maida sighed. "There was plenty of money. Earl wants the cash to retire. Nanette Keys was agreeable to a sale, but Oakley appreciated the town the way it is. Didn't want to see it become a generic beach resort. It's getting hard to tell towns apart up and down Route 13 with all the billboards and strip malls popping up. Places like Cape Unity aren't in plentiful supply anymore."

The sign on the road to Cape Unity was more and more like a call to battle. "Sounds like you're on Oakley's side."

"Don't want to take sides, mind you. Tourism from development could generate jobs and bring traffic to our inn. What I hate to see is neighbor turned against neighbor. But to kill because of condos—for heaven's sake, what's the world coming to? And I fear it will only get worse."

Drayco wished he could reassure her, but experience taught him there were no boundaries in the field of motives. "People kill for less. But this could be an isolated incident."

The Major perked up. "You don't think we're suspects, do you? Never been a suspect."

Maida swatted him with the newspaper. "The day someone believes you're capable of murder, we're all doomed. Hell would freeze over and be carved into ice cubes for devilish martinis."

"This neighbor of Oakley's, Earl Yaegle," Drayco drained his mug, trying not to choke on the glob of spices and fruit pulp on the bottom. "Where would I find him?"

"He owns several businesses in the area. His favorite is the gun shop. I'll give you the address."

Maida grabbed a scrap of paper from underneath a crab paperweight to scribble on. "Technically, we're a bed and breakfast, but we'd love to have you join us for supper. Nothing fancy, but it'll stick to your ribs."

Unlike Councilman Squier's invitation, Drayco didn't hesitate to say yes. A night without fast-food mystery meat and rubber potatoes would be a nice change from his typical fare. And no sultry specters of former fiancées as a distraction.

He excused himself to call his answering service, which yielded a message from his accountant. Those were getting more frequent. He dialed another familiar number and waited for the steely baritone voice, which said, "Unloaded that damned Opera House yet?"

"Actually, Dad, something else came up."

"It'd have to be a killer reason, as hot as you were to dump that thing and head for Mexico. Unless it's a woman. It's a little soon after Elizabeth, isn't it? I liked that one. You should have married her while you had the chance."

Drayco didn't feel like arguing, again, that the flame-haired cellist with a temper to match was a disaster from the start. Still, it had been nice to have someone warming his bed every night. "I found a body in the Opera House. A local man, murdered. He was going to meet me there."

A heavy silence weighed on the other end. "And you're a suspect. I'm in the middle of this Princeton case, but I can send down Jeffrey if you need a good lawyer—"

"No Jeffrey. Not yet."

"Not the best way to get over that Cadden fiasco, right, son?"

"Thanks for reminding me, Dad. I'm sure I'd completely forgotten."

His father's gruff voice dialed down a notch. "I've said it before, and I'll say it again. What happened wasn't your fault. Take my advice and don't get involved. It's too soon."

"I'll keep that in mind." As Drayco hung up, a draft of air swooped up Maida's scrap of paper with Yaegle's address, and Drayco grabbed it before it landed in the fireplace. The sudden twisting caused a shooting pain up his right forearm, but it was a familiar pain he ignored.

Tracing the address on the paper with his good hand, he memorized the street name, Rumble Road. That was appropriate for Oakley's neighbor and nemesis, Earl Yaegle—the man with a lot of land and a shop full of guns, the all-American dream.

Maida's foreboding that neighbor-against-neighbor tensions could escalate bothered Drayco. And the axis in the center of that wheel of tension revolved around Yaegle. It wouldn't hurt to ask a few questions here and there, would it?

Then again, what was it Councilman Squier had said? "A symbolic lynching?" Maybe that mob would be lining up for Drayco, too, if feelings against him, the Opera House and their place in the whole development quagmire sucked them down along with it.

Drayco tucked the paper into a pocket. He headed out into the cold, dank wind that wrapped around him like a wet straitjacket. It was late in the afternoon, but if he hurried, he might just make it.

6

The sign on the door still said, "Open." As Drayco stepped over the threshold, he was assailed by the gun-shop bouquet of metal, plastic, and hints of Hoppe's gun solvent, an aromatic blend reminiscent of bananas and diesel. He counted the rifles and shotguns stacked neatly in racks, losing count at four dozen. For a town with a small population, its one gun shop was well stocked. Earl Yaegle's inventory filled cases holding everything from an antique Derringer to a left-handed Cooper rifle to the latest in laser sights. Drayco eyed a gun on sale and picked it up.

A vertically challenged man, sporting a blue vest with buttons that may have reached across once, hurried over to greet Drayco. "That's one of our newest Glocks. Came in only a few days ago. Sure is a beauty, isn't it? Looks comfortable in your hand there. Shoot much?"

How many thousands of rounds did he go through at the academy? Enough to open his own ammo shop. Not to mention the rounds in the gun currently hidden in his shoulder holster. He put the Glock down to shake the man's hand. "I'm Scott Drayco—"

"You're that crime consultant guy, aren't you?"

"And Opera House owner." By now, Drayco wasn't surprised his micro-fame had followed him again. But this clerk was the first to elevate the law enforcement role to the top.

"True. Though people don't need guns in Opera Houses." The clerk had an asymmetrical grin with one corner of his mouth at half-mast. "I'm Randy, by the bye. Manager here. What can we do ya for?"

"I thought I'd drop by to check out your inventory while I'm in town." Drayco already had a fair idea of what he'd find, but it wasn't the latest death tech he was interested in.

"Guess you don't get a chance to see these in the District. Now that guns aren't outlawed up there, our boss Earl should open a franchise."

Drayco noted the two of them were alone in the shop. "Not many customers today. I'm surprised."

"Because of the murder, you mean?"

Drayco was certain he missed a giant neon sign hanging over town flashing *Oakley Keys Murdered in the Opera House!* Reece's STS moniker was too tame. News around here spread like the plague.

Randy straightened a pyramid of cartridges where two boxes were poking out. "Give it time. These things mushroom. One person buys a gun, tells his neighbor, then the neighbor decides it's a good idea. And there you go."

"Did you know Oakley?"

"My girlfriend worked with his wife Nanette over at Social Services. Didn't know the man myself, but he was friendly toward Earl's two sons. Came by the store once while the boys were here. Guess it was before they went off to college. I remember him telling them how they should treasure the heritage their father was giving them. Ironic, that."

"Because of the infamous land dispute?"

"For sure. Oakley stood in the way of the property sale, preventing Earl from passing along that so-called heritage."

A nasal voice behind Drayco's back chimed in, "Oakley was like that, Randy, and you know it. A fuckin' nut case, if you ask me."

Drayco spun around to see a man with mullet hair and a blue vest similar to Randy's, but one that easily buttoned. "I'm Joel," he said to Drayco. "Not a manager. Yet." He shot a bitter glance at Randy. "That must be your blue Starfire out there with the D.C. tags. A real beaut. Don't see many of those."

"She's rare, all right." Drayco had never cared how rare the Starfire was, blasphemy to true car acolytes. It was partial payment for an early case of his after he went solo. Maida was right—he did get unusual gifts from clients.

Joel snorted, "Rare's a good word these days. As in we rarely have any peace and quiet around here anymore." He pointed out the window to a construction site, with cacophony from backhoes and jackhammers bleeding through the shop windows. "As in we rarely have murders. Until the new people started moving in. Goddamn spics."

Drayco had seen a couple of those "new people" coming out of the shop ahead of him. At least their money was welcome. "You don't think the murderer's lived here a while?"

Randy butted in, "Why didn't they strike sooner? Timing's too coincidental."

Joel keyed open the cash register and flipped through the twenties. "The development money, that's why. And our good boss Earl's up to his waist in that pile of paper shit."

Drayco said, "Yaegle's businesses provide several jobs around these parts—yours, for instance. Is he a good boss?"

Randy nodded with bobble-head vigor. "Earl's the best."

"He's okay." Joel slammed the register shut.

Drayco leaned against one of the cases. Workplace rivalries were goldmines for nuggets of truth if you mined down deep. Drayco was a patient prospector. "The land dispute must be stressful for Earl."

"Earl can be moody, but he's always been that way. He's a straight shooter." Randy's eyes grew wide at his choice of words. "I mean, he's opinionated but honest. Not violent."

Joel pounded his fist down on the counter. "Everyone can be violent. And Earl's been grumpier, missing more work. Not to mention what he said the other day—that he wished Oakley Keys would disappear."

Randy pointed his finger at Joel. "Be careful what you say, Joel."

Joel waved his hand dismissively. "I know what I heard."

Drayco positioned himself between the two, in case he needed to referee. "I hoped to bump into Earl in person."

Joel's laugh was more like a goat bleat. "Good luck. He's in hiding."

Randy hesitated. "He might be willing to come to the store if I called him."

Noting it was five-thirty, and the store closed at six, Drayco said, "That won't be necessary. I'll run into him eventually. There is something else you can help me with—I want to buy a knife for a friend. A small pocket knife, nothing fancy, but sharp. Do you sell those, too?"

Randy pointed to a small case. "We've got a few. Multi-tools, Remingtons, Spydercos, mainly the sportsman type."

Drayco asked, "You don't sell many knives?" The carving on Oakley's chest was likely made using a small but sharp blade like a surgeon's scalpel or a Kodi-Caper knife.

Randy replied, "Haven't sold any lately, not since the new megamart decided to carry knives. Cheaper, too. You might check there."

Once back outside, Drayco rolled up his car window to drown out the construction noise Joel mentioned. In the growing darkness, he barely made out the sign in front of the half-finished foundation for the new building: "Coming soon—another fine hardware store from the Luckett Corporation." Future customers could buy guns from Earl Yaegle and plowshares at the neighboring hardware store. Not quite biblical, but close enough.

He was disappointed to miss Yaegle. He consoled himself with the tidbit he gleaned from Joel about Yaegle wanting Oakley to "disappear." An angry neighbor who also happened to be a hot-headed gun shop owner was easier to bet on as a murder suspect than a saintly wife or vengeful historian. Too bad murders weren't solved by the numbers.

He drummed his fingers on the steering wheel, reminding himself to drop it. It's. Not. Your. Case. But there wasn't anything wrong with doing a little friendly checking to allay Maida's worries, was there? Especially if he stayed under the sheriff's radar.

Out of the corner of his eye, he caught sight of a figure silhouetted against a building across the street with *Going Out of Business* painted on the front. The figure who moved out of the shadows for a split second looked for all the world like Darcie Squier, staring at him. The woman stepped back into the cover of the shuttered building. By the time he pulled his car around in front of where she'd been standing, the woman had vanished. Vanished so quickly, in fact, he wondered if he imagined the whole thing.

7

He awoke gasping for air. This one felt more real than the others. It was the three of them, submerged so deeply they couldn't tell which way led to the surface. He reached his hand to the boy, but their fingers drifted farther apart. The boy's sister wasn't moving at all, arms out to her sides, floating like a piece of driftwood—eyes open, mouth and lungs filled with water. The details changed, but the gist was the same. The twins always died, and he was always unable to save them.

Drayco peered at the clock, then let his head flop back on the pillow. Five a.m. So much for sleeping late on his pseudo-vacation. He kicked off the covers, waiting for the violent images to fade and waiting for the cool air to hit his bare skin. This bed, with its toffee-colored down comforter was far too comfortable, too easy to melt into.

Drayco's first morning in Cape Unity dawned with an overcast sky out his bedroom window, the meteorological equivalent of elevator music. Weather, yes, interesting, no. He must be insane to leave that comfortable sanctuary for a run in the cold, but he didn't want to get out of the habit and have his muscles atrophy. The brain was like that, too—allow the frontal lobe to decondition, and before you knew it, senility crept in.

Pulling his favorite FBI sweatshirt over his chest, he inhaled two lungs full of frosty air and the scent of marsh mud, a combination of mud, fish, sea salt, and a bit of sulfur. He started along the sand-filled road away from the Lazy Crab, which the daylight revealed in its full glory. It was the sole English Tudor building in town, the reason Major Jepson bought it, in a nod to his roots.

Maida told him there weren't any homes left from the Revolutionary War, the "pinnacle days for Virginia," but a few dated from the Civil War. She'd added, "Unfortunately, that was a different story for the area, pitting fathers against sons, brothers against brothers. A little like the present."

Drayco expected he'd be the only one up, but he passed one man on his front porch, dressed in plaid pajama bottoms and a neon yellow raincoat with hood up, despite the lack of raindrops. His eyes followed Drayco all the way down the road. When Drayco jogged back a half hour later, the man was still there, this time standing by his roadside mailbox, waiting.

Drayco stopped. Time to show the neighbors he wasn't a stranger casing their homes. "Morning," Drayco offered. "I'm staying at the Lazy Crab down the road. Nice houses through here. Very picturesque."

The man thrust his hands into his pockets. Hopefully, he wasn't reaching for a Smith & Wesson. "We ain't Virginia Beach. Give us a year or two, the way things are going. People buying and selling property like it's crack cocaine. No thought of what it means to have land passed down through generations. As my granddaddy told me, trees without deep roots topple in the first bit of wind."

"You've lived here a long time?"

"Six generations. Nowadays, we got people and money pouring in here like a tidal wave. Most of 'em from D.C., like that new Opera House owner."

Drayco smiled. "That would be me."

The man tilted his head to one side. "Kinda coincidental, ain't it? That you buy the Opera House and Oakley Keys gets murdered there?"

That word again, 'coincidence.' First the sheriff, then Randy at the gun shop, now the Jepsons' neighbor. "Coincidence is a four-letter word in my line of work."

"So's d-e-a-d. The newspaper called you a crime consultant, didn't it? Well, why don't you consult on this—with tidal waves you also get rotten fish. We got people in this town who don't belong. Nothing but trouble. And all this construction will lure 'em like worms on a corpse."

Drayco tensed at the corpse remark. If this man wasn't the artist responsible for the sign at the edge of town, he might as well be. Was that why Oakley Keys wanted to hire Drayco? An investigation into the development company, anything to stave off the inevitable? Drayco wanted to ask the man about Oakley, but he turned his back on Drayco and strode toward his porch, the edges of his yellow raincoat flapping like the wings of a duck.

As Drayco returned to the Lazy Crab, he noticed the smoke from the chimney also struggling to get up this morning, blowing sideways and down. What did that old wives' tale say? If chimney smoke falls toward the ground, it's a portent of bad weather ahead. Sounded much sexier than "downdrafts" or "temperature inversions."

Inside, the Major was oblivious to much of anything other than his third cup of Darjeeling. He raised the cup in Drayco's direction, "Care for a sugar lump or two? They're maple."

Drayco declined. He perfected the art of surviving on buckets of black coffee back in his college and FBI days. Or when he got his hands on one, a bottle of Manhattan Special espresso soda. Someone should create an injectable form. Better yet, an implant.

The Major was in rare form, regaling Drayco with tales of previous Lazy Crab guests, like an alleged old salt of a sea captain with an eye patch, bushy beard, and pipe. He turned out to be an investment banker gone daft, traveling up and down the coast conning unsuspecting residents. "His family traced him here, and we got a visit from his brother who took him back to New York for therapy. Nice fellow. Had all the lingo down. Funny thing—he was allergic to fish."

Maida popped in the doorway, wagging her finger. "Not that story."

The Major flattened another maple cube with a spoon to add to his coffee. "It was a remarkable thing, really. Our sleepy hamlet isn't scandal central."

Maida flopped down into a chair. "That was before Oakley's murder and that god-awful development mess."

Major Jepson stirred his cup of tea until the liquid turned into a continuous whirlpool. "I dropped off some wood for Oakley Saturday. Didn't realize it was the last time I'd see him. Makes it hard to believe somebody's gone when you don't have a chance to say goodbye."

Drayco joined the Jepsons in silence, thinking back to the man in the yellow raincoat and his not-so-veiled accusation. What odds would a mathematician give that Oakley's murder and Oakley hiring Drayco were related—sixty-forty? Fifty-fifty? He closed his eyes for a moment but opened them again to stop the parade of red carnations marching across his eyelids.

He said, "The sheriff called Oakley an odd bird. Aside from being an endangered species, what did he mean?"

Maida sighed. "Nothing about Oakley seemed to fit. He didn't fit in town. His career didn't serve him. Sometimes I think he wore his personality like a too-tight suit."

The Major added without a trace of irony, "When they measure him for his coffin, that'll fit him."

Maida's eyes started to water. Was it grief or stifling a morbid laugh? Drayco bet on the latter. It was good to see her in better spirits, so when she popped up to answer a phone call, he hoped it wasn't more bad news.

The call took less than a minute. When she rejoined them, she cast a sheepish look in Drayco's direction. "I hate to spring this, but Nanette Keys wants to come by to talk to you. I didn't know how to turn her down."

Now that was a bit of welcome luck. With Mrs. Keys taking the initiative, it would save him butting heads with the sheriff. Drayco tried thinking of a sneaky way to arrange a meeting, and here one was dropped in his lap. "Did she say what it was about?"

Maida shook her head. "But she was persistent."

The Major said, "Probably thinks that developer did it. Wants you to dig up some dirt." He laughed at his double entendre. "Developer. Dig up some dirt. Ha!"

"Maida, the sheriff said Nanette Keys does a lot for this community. What's she like?"

To his surprise, the Major answered first. "Hell of a woman. Oakley was a friend, mind you, but had I been female, I wouldn't have married him. You'd have to have the patience of Job, the dedication of Saint Joan, and the tolerance of Buddha all wrapped up in one."

Drayco asked, "The drinking and the affairs?"

Maida replied, "And maybe more. Though Nanette didn't talk about Oakley much. She's always interested in how everyone else is doing. The type who's first to send flowers or a sympathy card. But when it comes to her own problems, nary a word."

With the Jepsons' description in mind, he formed a profile of Nanette. A meticulous appearance. Well-mannered, reserved, a perfectionist, trying to make up for all the things in her life she couldn't control—most of all Oakley—with a cauldron of emotions bubbling under the surface. The type of woman perfect for a starring role in a Greek tragedy. But women in Greek tragedies were often as much villain as victim.

Oakley's widow didn't waste time making her way to the Lazy Crab, arriving half an hour after her call. Maida led her into the den, where Drayco stood to shake her hand. Her grip was firm and not the gelatin flipper from D.C. lobbyists' wives, who didn't want to ruin their expensive manicures.

Nanette smiled and nodded at him, but her puffy red eyes belied her emotional state. Tall and slender, she wore the same hot-designer cowl neck dress he'd seen on his father's wannabe-model secretary, only this looked less expensive, possibly a knockoff. She sat in a wing chair but perched on the edge. Was she aware she was sitting on her hands?

Earlier, Maida showed Drayco a photo of Oakley when he was alive. Time seemed kinder to Nanette, at least on the surface, with her unwrinkled skin and that spark of intelligence in her eyes. Reece said Oakley was a researcher and writer. Did a shared intellectual bond hold Oakley and Nanette together?

Maida offered to leave Nanette and Drayco alone, but Nanette asked her to stay, her words coming out in a rush. "I had to get out of the house. The sheriff and his deputies were there late in the evening. And again early this morning, looking for—whatever it is they're looking for. They could have stayed all night because I didn't sleep. All I could think about was an image of Oakley dying on the floor, and knowing there was some mystery quest of his. .. it's tearing me apart."

She paused to catch her breath. "Why would he hire somebody like you?" Nanette clasped her hands together.

Out of the corner of his eye, Drayco saw Maida frown. He'd have to tell her later he was long past taking offense at such slights. "As I told Sheriff Sailor, Mrs. Keys, I had no prior calls or correspondence from Oakley. Other than to set up the meeting."

"I just—" Nanette wrinkled her forehead. "This is going to sound like paranoia. .."

She faltered, grasping for the right words. "For years, Oakley traveled on business and was gone two weeks at a time. He wouldn't leave an address. Only an emergency phone number. When I tried ringing it once, it was an answering service."

She blinked watery eyes at Maida, who gave her a nod of encouragement. "I don't want to believe ill of my husband. Not now. Even though he knew his drinking bothered me. And all those nasty rumors   "

Maida reached over to touch Nanette's arm lightly. "Just small-town talk, dear. No need to rehash old fiddle-faddle."

Nanette thanked her with her grateful eyes. "When we first moved here, I fell in love with the place—the sea air, the unspoiled fishing-village atmosphere. Oakley never came to love it as I did. A part of him resented it. I asked him many times if he wanted to move, but he was hell-bent on staying here. Wish I'd tried harder." Her eyes welled up again, and Maida patted her hand.

Drayco thought back to his FBI case books full of black-widow tales where a woman killed her husband, sometimes more than one, for financial gain. Maida mentioned a "pirate's chest full of money" at stake. Elaina Cadden, from his most recent case, looked like Nanette, with the appropriate tears and a slight tremor in her voice.

"The sheriff said nothing went missing from your house, Mrs. Keys, except for a mask of some kind. Can you describe it?"

"It was a wooden owl's face, intricate, with feathers and all. There was writing carved on the bottom, 'diable' I think. I don't know what it meant. Oakley spent a lot of time working on it, yet didn't want to discuss it."

"Oakley made the mask himself? I thought he was a writer."

"He was also a skilled wood craftsman. Someone once offered a thousand dollars for a console table he made, but he turned it down. It was one of my favorite pieces, so he kept it."

"When did he start working on this mask?"

"Recently. A few weeks."

A man carves a mask right before it's stolen, around the same time the man is carved up and murdered—it was the type of detail that slithered its way under Drayco's skin. It was also another "coincidence." He asked, "When did you notice the mask was missing?"

"It was at the house the day before he died. I didn't notice it was gone until after Oakley's death. I assumed Oakley took it with him."

"Could someone have broken into the house to steal it without your knowledge?"

"I've had a cold the past few days, so I was home the entire time. The mask was a nice piece of artwork, but I'm not sure why anyone would want it. It wasn't valuable."

"It may relate to his murder."

Nanette's eyes widened. "I hadn't thought of that. But a mask of an owl?" She laced and unlaced her fingers together, as if nervous, but she leaned toward him, not away. Mixed body language could mean a lot of things. Reading people was more effective than reading tea leaves when it came to predicting behavior. But like all forms of divination, scientific or not, it was flawed.

He smiled at her, encouragingly. "Mrs. Keys, I'm also curious about the red carnation Oakley wore."

"That's a puzzle to me, too. He's never done that before."

"He had on a thin seersucker coat, not much protection against the cold. Did he wear it all the time?"

"The opposite. I hated that mildewed old thing. He bought it right after our marriage and used it a lot at first. One day he stopped wearing it and hung it in the back of the closet. I tried throwing it out, but he wouldn't let me."

"Do you have any idea why he was at the Opera House? Did he play the piano, for instance?"

Nanette pinched her nose, looking like someone holding their breath underwater. "He hadn't expressed any interest in that Opera House lately. And he doesn't know how to play the piano."

Drayco hesitated before asking his next question. He didn't know what the sheriff had discussed with Nanette. "Did Sheriff Sailor tell you how the body was found?"

"That you found him. That he was. .. he was. .. yes, he told me. I can't fathom what any of it means."

"Can you think of anyone who hated him enough to kill him?"

For a fraction of a second, Nanette's eyes flitted almost imperceptibly toward the foyer, then back. "He wasn't well-liked. But no mortal enemies as they say in the movies. He was bitter over the development and angry with Councilman Squier for pushing for it. I'm glad he had a few friends who stood by him, Major Jepson, for one."

Nanette launched herself off the couch, knocked her handbag to the floor in her haste, spilling items all over the floor. As she and Maida picked them up, Nanette apologized. "Guess I'm still shaky."

Drayco and Maida both walked her to the door, as Drayco said, "I know this is difficult, Mrs. Keys. I'm sure the sheriff will do his best. And if I can help in any way—"

"I don't know how you can, but thanks." She stood less tall than before, more hunched.

Maida kept her waiting long enough to dash into the kitchen and grab some muffins she baked earlier. Apparently, Maida had an endless supply of food and sympathy hiding in her cupboard.

When Nanette was gone, Drayco asked Maida, "Does the letter 'G' have any special significance for you? A place, a name?"

She thought for a moment. "The development company behind those condos is Gallinger. But no high-profile places or founding family names beginning with 'G.' If that's what you mean."

The Major poked his head in. "What's that?"

Maida waved her hand. "Nothing, dear. Chewing the fat."

The Major stroked his beard. "That saying has a nautical origin. Sailors would complain about their staple food, hardened salt pork fat. Sounds dreadful."

"My better half," Maida saluted with amusement in the Major's direction, "Is a fount of trifles and minutiae. Don't play Trivial Pursuit with him. You won't stand a chance."

"I'll keep that in mind." And Drayco added his own salute to the Major. "There was nothing trivial about my run-in with Paddy Bakely yesterday. He didn't pay Oakley any compliments."

Maida said, "The townspeople don't know what to make of Paddy. Part town drunk, part poet—he had a book of poetry published locally, if you can believe it. Makes a hobby of being in and out of jail. You'd think Seth would have washed his hands of him long ago. Paddy's a middle-aged man and should know better."

"Between Paddy and Oakley, the town must have its share of colorful characters."

"Try crazy-quilt. Small towns bring out the best and the worst in folks."

Drayco was quickly learning that about small town life. Humanity thrown together in the equivalent of a Petri dish under a microscope bred malignant organisms as often as benign. "Why did Paddy hate Oakley?"

The Major, who was sitting so still, it was hard to tell if he'd nodded off, piped up. "Jealousy. Oakley had everything Paddy didn't. Talent, land worth a small fortune, a loving wife, and a few other lady attractions, to boot. Paddy, well. You've seen him. Oakley's opposite. Reminds me of a fiddler crab. Kind of spindly, scuttles along and waves his claws around. At least he doesn't molt."

Maida eyed Drayco with an impish grin. "So you're leaving us peasants tonight for the lure of lofty Cypress Manor?"

"Cypress Manor? Sounds like a retirement home."

"That's what Councilman Squier calls his house, though no one remembers the last time there were cypress trees. Most died of blight. The good councilman brags both sides of his family trace their roots back to the Mayflower. Guess he feels he's got to look the part."

"Mayflower roots, but no cypress roots. Got it. And it's for one dinner only, scout's honor."

"Were you a scout?"

"A scout dropout. Never could get the hang of sewing those badges."

"Don't you come back putting on airs," Maida said. "And dress frumpy. So Darcie Squier won't notice what a handsome stallion you are."

Drayco gave her a double-take. "You think I need a bodyguard?"

Maida held up her hand and replied, "I'd happily fill that role, but I'm allergic to shrews."

Drayco grinned, but his grin quickly faded when he recalled one particular item from the contents of Nanette's purse. Why would she need a passport? A brand-new one, at that. He rubbed a hand through his hair but stopped when he caught sight of a small wooden sailboat on a table in the hallway. Instead of sailing in with answers, Nanette's visit left more questions. Oakley's mysterious trips, those were definitely worth pursuing. That owl mask was another jarring note of dissonance. Owls usually signified wisdom, but Drayco found nothing wise about Oakley's behavior.

Owls were also nocturnal, swooping down silently, with the soft edges of their feathers muffling the sound of the wings, before pouncing and swallowing their prey whole. Death unseen, death unheard, death from above—the military drones of the animal kingdom.

But most prey had someone who cared about them, cared if they lived or died. Nanette seemed to love Oakley if her concerns were genuine. Possibly Darcie Squier, too, in a warped way. Despite Drayco's efforts to distance himself, he was starting to care about the failed writer and talented woodworker, the odd and enigmatic little man with a red flower in his lapel.

8

The Seafood Hut was as prosaic as its name, plain white concrete blocks on the outside and sea-foam paint within. The owners, churning out the same crab cakes and "little nick" clams for decades, traded stereotypical nets and plastic lobsters on the wall for pictures of customers in a continuous collage. Drayco didn't see a greasy spoon anywhere.

Sheriff Sailor picked a booth in the back, but they were the only customers. "Thanks for meeting me here for coffee, Drayco. A chance to escape the office."

"And catch the wild animals in their natural habitat?"

"Something like that. You should come back for lunch. Specialty of the house is crab cakes. Lots of lump crab, no glue-dust filler. If you're a seafood fan, make a trip to Wachapreague while you're on the Eastern Shore. One of those blink-and-you'll-miss-it places, but it's the flounder capital of the world. Their fried flounder is a revelation."

"I'll keep that in mind." Drayco reached for the carafe and refilled his cup, having gulped down the first in two minutes flat. It was a dark brew with a taste so bitter, it didn't need salt.

The sheriff ignored the sugar but dumped what must be half a shaker of powdered cream into his coffee. "I released the crime scene—your Opera House." Sailor blew into the cup before taking a sip. "Sold the place yet?"

"You're certainly dead set on me selling it. Got a thing against music?"

Sailor flung his hat upon a nearby wall hook, nailing it straight on. "Checked up on you. You're former FBI like your Dad. Got a fledgling investigative gig in the capital. High-profile clients, consulting work for law enforcement. Can't see such a fellow wanting a small-town millstone dragging him down. Especially a relative youngster. Although shouldn't I be calling you Dr. Drayco?"

Drayco could hear the guys at the Bureau as they teasingly called him Doc. The memory brought a small smile to his lips. "I don't get that much these days, except when I teach the occasional seminar. It's buried on the résumé somewhere."

"A Ph.D. in criminology's gotta be worth what—a few hundred more a year?"

A few hundred was about right. Drayco was lucky enough to buy his D.C. townhouse before the housing market skyrocketed, but freelancing was more expensive than he'd budgeted, and he'd gone into debt to hang out his shingle. The Opera House money sure wouldn't hurt. "Am I scratched off your suspect list, Sheriff?"

"I didn't say that." Sailor signaled the waitress for another carafe of coffee. He was matching Drayco cup for cup. Not many people could do that. "You're toward the bottom of the list. Although if you did switch to the dark side, I have a feeling you'd make a formidable criminal, Mr. Consultant."

After the waitress came and left, Sailor continued, "I met your Dad once."

"Brock? When?"

"He spoke at a conference I attended. Interesting presentation. Had him sign his book for me."

"One of those law enforcement conferences where the highlight is the bar in the hotel lobby. Oh joy."

The sheriff hesitated. "More of a literary conference. With a law enforcement component," he hastened to add. "My mother named me so I got tagged with the Hemingway part. She's a retired librarian."

"Hemingway?"

"My middle name." Sailor pulled his coffee cup closer to him. "Anyway, your father wasn't as imposing as I'd imagined."

"He can be intimidating. With large shoes to fill." Drayco shifted his feet in his size thirteens. Symbolically, his father's were double that.

"I understand the intimidating part. His book was brilliant although I have it on good authority you had a similar rep at the Bureau. Some even placing bets you might make Director some day. Hell, you made it into the NCAVC after only four years. Quite a hopscotch from concert pianist to FBI to freelancer, isn't it?"

So the sheriff had excavated deeper into his past. Drayco replied slowly, "An accident ended my piano career. My arm wasn't fit for the rigors of a pianist's life, but it was good enough for the FBI. As for the Bureau, I'm not much of a bureaucrat. Ten years was enough."

Sailor didn't press him for details, looking out the window at the shell-strewn driveway that separated the restaurant from a boarded-up building with crumbling pink siding. "Lousy view, isn't it? Same as a lot of the town, it's seen better days."

Better days, better years, better moods. "Seems like development would be welcome. And yet there's a lot of tension between people against and those in favor. Like Earl Yaegle and my dead client Oakley Keys."

The moment the word "client" came out of Drayco's mouth, he knew there was no turning back. He'd been sucked in, against his better judgment, allowing the counterpoint to win him over again. It was like walking out on stage in front of an audience and sitting down at the piano. Once your fingers hit the keys, you were committed.

Sailor kept rubbing the back of his neck. The man was as tense as their first meeting in the Opera House although at least his jaw was no longer clenched. One corner of the sheriff's mouth turned up briefly as he took a pause from guzzling coffee. "Your client?"

"Oakley said he wanted to hire me, he was murdered on my property, and I don't know the reason for either. I can't leave it at that."

"Sounds like you're going to be poking around."

Drayco kept his own face blank. "I have a detective poking stick I keep in my car. It's a divining rod. Point it toward the suspects and it's drawn to the killer."

"Better patent it, because if you're like me, you're not getting rich in this line of work."

The sheriff's creased forehead belied his joking manner as he stared at Drayco long and hard. "Don't often run into investigators representing dead clients. Guess I'll have to make doubly sure I keep my eye on you."

Someone in the kitchen dropped a glass, but the sound barely registered with either man. "Look, Sheriff, I have no intention of muscling into your territory. I'm looking for answers. Same as everybody else in town."

"At least they're not paying you to find those answers. Murder's rare around here. Makes people jittery. Since this is the first such case with me in charge, they're not sure what to expect. I don't aim to let them down."

Drayco caught a whiff of rotten fish followed shortly by the sight through the window of a kitchen worker emptying a trash can. Perhaps not everyone liked the crab cakes. "You said you were one deputy shy. In my new, albeit unwelcome, role of Opera House owner, I might get info from people you wouldn't."

"Not so sure about that. Folks around here close themselves off to strangers. What makes you think people will answer your questions?"

Drayco studied his coffee spoon. "It's not what you ask, it's how you listen."

The sheriff thought for a moment. "I can't keep you from conducting legitimate business regarding your own property. And you're a perceptive young pup. Just be sure and pass along any info you come across to the old dog who was on a beat in Richmond rounding up drug dealers when you were playing 'Twinkle Twinkle Little Star.'"

"I skipped that part. First time I sat at a piano, I picked out 'Take the A Train.'" Drayco understood what Sailor wasn't saying. A newly minted sheriff didn't need rumors he was incompetent and needed outside help.

Sailor motioned to the waitress for the check and waited until she got out of earshot. "Since we're on the same page and since you'd find out anyway, why don't I save you divining with that stick of yours. The Keys' attorney got back from the Caribbean. We know what was in Oakley's Will."

"The Caribbean? I could use some sunburn."

"You and me both. My wife keeps pestering me for a vacation. Nanette was the sole beneficiary. Between the money she'd get from the land sale and being unhappy with Oakley's extramarital affairs, plenty of motive. More than Yaegle. Then there's that problem of no alibi. Says she was at home by herself."

"The Keys lived alone?"

"Oakley and Nanette are virtually alone in this world. Nanette has one sister on the west coast, but that's it."

"Nanette came to see me earlier today. Not to confess. She was curious why Oakley wanted to hire me. And she did describe the missing mask."

"Yeah, there's that. A damned owl mask, just the clue I need."

With the passing thought the sheriff's middle name would be more appropriate as Ernest Sarcasm Sailor, Drayco asked, "Have you found the gun yet?"

Again, to his surprise, Sailor didn't hesitate to provide details. "We ran the bullet through the ATF database. No match. The firearms examiner from the state lab in Norfolk gave us preliminary ballistics—it's a .455 caliber, potentially from a vintage British Webley. And no, Oakley didn't own a gun. It's not the type that's easy to come by around here, anyway. Unless you're a veteran, a historian, or a gun dealer. .." his voice trailed off.

"Yaegle?"

"Has to be considered."

"That would be too obvious, wouldn't it?"

"Yaegle's a hothead but I pegged him more as the litigious type. Looking at the historian angle, Reece Wable has resources for antiques that might include guns. He and Keys had a dispute."

"So he told me, even made a point of it. He also said he had a run-in with a detective once. A 'misunderstanding.'"

Sailor stopped counting the change he'd pulled out of his pocket. "So you have been poking around. That incident must be before my time."

"Have you tied Wable or anyone other than the Gallinger company to the letter 'G'?"

"Oakley's middle name is John, no 'G' there. But Earl's middle name, on the other hand, is Gerik. Hell, it'd be handier if the letter were a la Hester Prynne—an 'A' for Oakley's adultery."

Drayco rubbed his finger along the smooth metal of the spoon. The handle was cold and had an unusual bird pattern etched into the curved handle. At least it wasn't an owl. "I hope Oakley wasn't alive when the carving was made on his chest."

"The M.E. may be able to tell, but it's possible."

Adding torture into the mix told Drayco more than the killer possessed a sadistic streak. Psychopaths often enjoyed making victims suffer and were partial to mutilation. But this would make a random killer less likely, despite the fears of the man he encountered at the mailbox and his "rotten fish," the new people in town. "What do you think of the theory the murderer was an immigrant looking for work?"

Sailor grunted. "'G' is for gringo, you mean? We've had a few minor scuffles, nothing violent. Workers around here have long included migrants, with the seafood industry hanging out a Help Wanted sign twice a year for crab pickers. This murder smells too homegrown."

"What is homegrown anymore, when you get apples in December from New Zealand or oranges in March from Mexico?"

Sailor paused for a moment. "Point taken."

"Okay, if 'G' doesn't stand for a proper name, it could represent what—Gold? God?"

"Gold would be appropriate, if you're talking about the property. 'G' for God—Oakley wasn't a religious fellow, but the murderer could be. Nanette certainly was. Guilt? Gotcha? How about 'G' for Great Britain, since Oakley's from there. Makes as much damn sense as everything else."

"Was the knife found?"

"A pocket knife was left inside a dumpster behind Earl Yaegle's gun shop, but no prints. If it's the same one the murderer used, he wore gloves or wiped the handle clean. We won't get DNA results back from the lab for a while due to backlogs. And the fact we're small potatoes."

"Any residue for blood typing?"

"Enough to tell it matches that from the crime scene. A-negative, same as Oakley's and not common. As you know, only seven percent of the population carries it."

"A possible plant to cast suspicion on Yaegle. You should check with Paddy Bakely. I bumped into him the other day. He seemed thrilled Oakley Keys was dead."

"Considering the state Paddy's in most of the time, he'd be a suspect in any crime around these parts. Motive or no."

"By state, you mean alcoholic stupor? Or other drugs?"

"Just booze. We've got a drug problem around here, nothing organized."

"And Seth? Like son, like father?"

"Seth is clean. Or at least, he's never been caught. Seth and Paddy are nicely providing alibis for each other, saying they were together at home all Sunday evening."

"Motive-wise you've got the development issue and greed, and there's jealousy and revenge from Oakley's affairs. Anything else?"

"You summed it up. I haven't gotten the opportunity to interview the good councilman and his wife although they're next on my list. I'm dreading that one. Such is the life of a lowly county mounty."

Drayco leaned back in the booth. "If you're referring to Councilman Squier, he's invited me to dinner at his house tonight."

Sailor put his cup down with a loud clink and gave Drayco a hard look through narrowed eyes. "I would have preferred you wait until I had a chance to talk to them."

The coffee had grown cold, so Drayco pushed it away. "I didn't know they were officially suspects when I accepted."

"Well, they are."

Drayco joined the sheriff in looking out the window. Strips of pink siding on the building next door had peeled away, like a giant had nibbled pink frosting off a gingerbread house. Sailor gave Drayco the briefest of smiles. "I guess you'll be around Darcie, then. Best of luck. Fresh meat."

"The rumors circling around Darcie and Oakley are true?"

"Certified. Which means both Randolph and Darcie Squier have a possible motive to kill Oakley, if you believe Darcie cared for him."

"Sounds like her husband believed it."

"Squier tried to cover it up in public. In private, he was trying to run Keys out of town on a rail. As for Darcie, that's another 'G' for you. Her maiden name was Gentner."

Drayco tried to ignore the increase in his pulse rate at the mention of Darcie. "Tell you what, Sheriff. I've been told I write up a mean field report. You want it in duplicate?"

"Indexed and typed." As Sailor rose to leave, he rescued his hat and pointed it at Drayco. "While you're there, take a look at Squier's extensive gun collection. He belongs to a local hunt club. I hear he's quite the shot."

Drayco checked his phone, noting some voice mail messages finally made it through. One from his accountant and one from a reporter doing a follow-up story on the Cadden family. Drayco's finger hovered over the delete button, but he thought better of it. A third message from his attorney sank Drayco's spirits even more. Due to questions over Rockingham's estate and IRS taxes, there'd been a federal tax lien placed on the Opera House. Bye-bye, quick sale.

He headed for the front cash register to order more coffee, extra nuclear. They made coffee here the way it should be, the color of gunpowder and about as hot when lit. Drayco grabbed some teriyaki marlin jerky and a bag of Skipjacks nuts, a local treat with honey and Chesapeake Bay seasoning. That would have to do until his date with Randolph and Darcie Squier later.

So, a knife with blood matching Oakley's rarish type was in a dumpster behind Earl Yaegle's gun shop. Maybe it was a plant. Maybe Earl wasn't bright, maybe he panicked, maybe he was crafty and knew they'd think it was too obvious. The last time Drayco was involved with a knife-in-the-dumpster case, they found the knife with a hand still attached—just the hand. Earl Yaegle had better be careful. The owner of that other knife was on Death Row at Sussex State Prison in Waverly.

9

Drayco was a minute too late again. He hoped to catch Earl at the gun shop this time, but when Randy the manager pointed to Yaegle's car pulling out of the parking lot, Drayco decided to do a little tailing. Not a tactic he'd ordinarily undertake in his out-of-the-ordinary Starfire.

Yaegle drove at a slow, steady pace at exactly twenty-five miles an hour the entire time and never once checked his mirror. It was as if the man was operating on autopilot. As they passed the small downtown area, Drayco recognized some landmarks, and sure enough, they were soon in sight of the Opera House. He couldn't escape it.

Yaegle pulled into the circular drive in front and parked his car, sitting and staring straight ahead. After five minutes of playing zombie-Earl, he turned his head to look at the building. Drayco pulled out a pair of binoculars and studied the other man's profile. No emotion whatsoever, only a riveted stare at the building.

They sat there for ten minutes before Earl awakened from his stupor and started the car moving again. Drayco followed a few more blocks until Yaegle parked his car and ducked into a bank. After another thirty minutes and no Yaegle, Drayco decided to try him another time.

He'd only traveled a few miles when he caught a glimpse of a neon-bright object. Seeing who was attached to it, he made a sharp turn over some railroad tracks and parked next to a laundromat with a cracked glass front. The biting smell of coal tar creosote from railroad ties hit him the moment he opened the door.

He walked over to a man working under the hood of a fuchsia-colored car. "Guess you're handy in more ways than one, Seth."

Bakely didn't look up. "Helping someone. As a favor."

Drayco was amazed the man could be elbow deep in oil and grease and not have a speck on his denim coveralls. "If you need a hand—"

"I don't. Simple valve cover gasket."

Drayco took advantage of the man's silent concentration to study him. The wet ashtray-smell from a few feet away served as a dead giveaway the man was a heavy smoker. But Drayco had to lean in to see a small brownish-red crusted patch near Seth's ear, partly hidden by his hair. Drayco was no dermatologist, but he'd seen pictures of skin cancer.

Without lifting his head, Seth spoke up, "Washing machines are a buck a load, and the dryers are buck and a half."

"I'm more interested in a dirty problem those machines can't fix. The problem of why Oakley Keys wanted to meet me at the Opera House. Especially when, as you say, he'd never been there before."

"Why do people usually hire you?"

"More dirty little problems. Sometimes big problems, when people are at the end of their rope."

"To hang themselves?"

"Or to get someone else hanged."

"Oakley Keys kept to himself. Me too. Can't blame a man for that."

"Yet here you are at the laundromat, so you do get around. Surely you've heard rumors about Oakley. A feud, an argument, something at least one person felt was a deadly offense."

"Don't take stock in idle talk. Talk from miserable people who ain't happy until they drag others into their shit." Seth twisted the screwdriver so hard that he almost fell off the engine.

The sound of a high-pitched laugh filtered down from above. Drayco spotted the source at the top of stairs leading to a room over the laundromat, a woman, arm in arm with Paddy Bakely. She had on more makeup than a stucco frieze, which must take a chisel to scrape off at night. Poured into a short skirt over a tight red leotard, she teetered in high-heeled boots decorated with a leopard print.

The woman clomped down the stairs and said to Seth, "He's all yours, sugar. You done with my car?" Devoted fathers weren't rare, but it was unusual to find one who'd go to such lengths for a son—servicing a prostitute's car while she serviced the son.

The woman caught sight of Drayco. Her fluorescent-red rimmed smile exposed a mouth with at least two gold caps. "You looking for a good time, stud?"

"I'm not sure I can afford your good time."

She walked up to him and rubbed her hand up and down his shirt. "I don't get types like you too often. Tell you what. Half-price special. And I might throw in a few extras because I love your eyes."

Paddy strode up to the woman and dragged her by the arm back toward the stairs as he yelled, "Fuck, Regina, you don't want his type. Stay far away from him He's trouble. You go back up there. I'll take care of this."

Seth was at Paddy's side in an instant, whispering in his ear. Paddy's face looked so much like an inflated balloon that Drayco thought it might pop if he pricked it with a pin. But Paddy dutifully dipped into the Bakely's car and slumped down in the seat.

Seth said to Drayco, "Paddy's already had a few. He gets this way. I'll take him home."

Seth didn't acknowledge Regina or explain her away. He now had a grease smudge on his face, covering up the reddish-brown patch. Seth was like a war veteran who'd lost too many alcohol-hazed battles fought over his lost-cause-of-a-son. Who to pity more, the enabled or the enabler?

Regina blew Drayco a kiss as he steered his Starfire in a direction away from the Bakely's car. She had long brunette hair, and if you squinted, she'd pass for a seedy biker-bar clone of Darcie Squier. Was Paddy one more victim ensnared in Darcie's man-trap? A bottle fly perched on the edge of a human pitcher-plant, drawn to its sweet smell. Only a couple more hours, and he'd get to see that trap up close and personal when he joined the good councilman and his wife at Cypress Manor.

Drayco ran a hand through his hair. The sheriff didn't want him to attend the dinner. He was pretty sure Squier himself was regretting his offer. Drayco had made his personal rule about not getting involved with married women for a good reason. Two reasons, Lindsay and Anika. But he'd been alone and lonely on a concert tour and much younger, too young to know a lot about regret. And he didn't need any new regrets about Darcie. He pushed that thought out of his mind because right now, he had a tryst with a much older, more faded girl.

10

The desolate Opera House looked even less inviting in the rain. So much for finding any footprints the sheriff overlooked though Drayco got the impression this particular sheriff was thorough. Drayco wasn't sure what he'd find inside, but at least this time, there were no bodies. It was relatively quiet, but even the ambient sounds of the furnace and creaking floorboards assaulted his senses with swirling and geometric shapes and morphing colors. Nothing was ever truly silent. Or black-and-white.

He stood in the back of the hall, taking in the Spanish Moor design, the grimy blue and gold domed frescoed ceiling, the crystal chandeliers, the side box seats with their faded maroon velvet curtains. All expensive and luxurious, at the time it was built. Not surprising since Prince of Wales County had the highest per capita income of any non-urban area in the United States in the 1910 Census—a tidbit he'd learned from the Historical Society documents. Times changed, people moved away. The area had traded tourism for fishing, farming, and chicken processing plants.

Drayco moved next to the stage, catching a whiff of chalk and sawdust he missed last time. Sawdust? He'd have to line up a termite inspector. The stage had a catwalk above, with one room on each side for rehearsals or scenery storage, accessible via a twisting iron staircase. The catwalk railing exhibited bits of rust and was missing sections. He added that to his estimate of burgeoning renovation costs.

Drayco scrutinized the rusted rails of the catwalk. It was the only way to access the two rooms at the top, so he'd have to risk it. He trod gingerly on the first couple of steps. Sturdy enough. Encouraged, he scaled the remaining steps, his feet clanging on each metal rung. At the top, he navigated the narrow walk to the two rooms. Both empty. There was a rug on the floor in the stage-right room, but when he lifted the edges and rolled it back, nothing but floorboards.

Disappointed, he returned to the stage, to the red stain on the floor behind the piano and the chalk outline left over from where Oakley's body fell. Apparently, Seth took the sheriff's instructions to heart and left blood and chalk alone.

Without doing the actual trig calculations, Drayco estimated the distance and location of the shooter from the blood spatter. Fifteen feet from the piano to under the wings. To be thorough, he searched every seat in the house. All he found were decades-old spots and the scratches on seatbacks, including one unimaginative "Kilroy was here," to which someone scratched on the adjacent seat, "So was Roosevelt." The Opera House was a hundred twenty years old—which Roosevelt? Teddy or FDR?

He made quick work of the doors, lighting boxes, wiring, ropes, and pulleys. It was, in a way, a space frozen in time with no upgrades or modifications made to it since the mid-20th century.

The piano was in the same place as before, so Drayco lay on his side and checked around the feet. Nothing. He hoisted himself off the floor and went over the rest of the piano. It wasn't until he searched the interior above the sounding board near the tuning pins that he found anything unusual. A flash of orange caught his eye, and he used a handkerchief to extract the small object.

"What'cha got there?" a booming amber-tipped voice sounded near Drayco's ear.

"Whoa, Sheriff. Can you ratchet it down a few decibels?" Drayco faced him. "And are you following me?"

"Sensitive ears?" The sheriff teased, evading Drayco's question. He accepted the handkerchief-covered item as Drayco handed it to him. "A capsule?"

"Looks like powder, but not much of an odor. Too orange for hallucinogens like Foxy, AMT or LSD. Or a drug like molly."

"A prescription?"

"I don't think so. No markings."

"I'll sic the lab techs on it. Any other surprises for me, Drayco?"

"No such luck. I did verify the door Seth mentioned in the back would be a perfect entryway for Oakley or the murderer, thanks to a faulty lock. And the exterior light has a cracked bulb. Looks like an old incandescent fixture from the '40s. Probably hasn't worked in a long time."

"We didn't find footprints on the grass near that door other than Oakley's. The downpour the night of the murder washed away footprint traces on the concrete."

"No interesting hits on fingerprints?"

"Seth's and Paddy's, as you'd expect. And yours and Oakley's on the door handles. Since the knife from the dumpster didn't have prints either, we're likely looking at gloves. I'm beginning to believe it was the Invisible Man. No forced entry, no fingerprints, no footprints, no witnesses."

Drayco knew that look on the sheriff's face, had seen it on Drayco's former FBI partner Mark Sargosian, when looking at a new case file with all the earmarks of being unsolvable. Drayco preferred to see tough cases as a catalyst—do you allow a Gordian Knot to be a kick in the pants or a kick in the teeth? An image of the Cadden twins came to mind, and he reined in his inner cheerleader. He could use a big kick in the pants right now, truth be told.

Drayco replied, "Our Invisible Man must be wearing the missing owl mask, thereby making it likewise invisible."

The sheriff wrinkled his nose. "I could understand if the damned thing was encrusted with rubies or diamonds. But it was wood and paint. What value can it have?"

"Not financial, anyway." Drayco couldn't resist running his hand over the glossy finish on the curved arms of the Steinway Hamburg-D. The white keys were spotless. "Why no fingerprint powder?"

"4NTech loaned us one of those portable green-laser print detectors to try. One of my CSI deputies, Nelia Tyler, hated to see the piano ruined. So your piano over there was the laser's guinea pig."

"Did it work?"

"Yep. But I guess that fossil of a piano hasn't been played in God knows how long. No prints."

Drayco wasn't surprised. Nanette had said her husband didn't know how to play the piano, and a killer would have other things on his mind. But a small, irrational part of Drayco hoped there might be traces of Konstantina Klucze's fingerprints, despite the passing of time.

Time. Timing was everything. So were coincidences, in crime solving. Drayco mused, "I saw a newspaper article about a manuscript stolen from the library. It happened the week before Oakley was murdered. Think it's connected?"

"Yes. No. Take your pick. One of the very minor British royals visited Cape Unity in the '40s. This was an essay she'd written, pointing out highlights of her trip."

"Did she visit the Opera House?"

Sailor thought for a moment. "Haven't read the document, since they didn't make a photocopy, believe it or not. But it's possible Her Royal Whatever toured the building."

Drayco sat on the piano bench and automatically adjusted it to suit his height. "This Gallinger company in the middle of the development squabble—were they interested in buying the Opera House?"

Sailor lifted an eyebrow. "Are you that desperate to dump the thing? Or are you looking for a tie-in with Oakley's murder?"

"As to the former, not yet. I have to line up building inspectors, property appraisers, who knows what else. Maybe a demolition crew? It would be the easy way out, and a 'Land for Sale' sign might lure more takers than a rundown building."

When the sheriff lifted the other eyebrow, Drayco added, "I'm not serious. I think. But as far as the murder is concerned, yes. The Gallinger angle is worth pursuing."

"We're checking it out. To my knowledge, Gallinger's only interested officially in the Keys and Yaegle properties." Sailor rescued his hat from the top of the piano where he parked it but didn't put it on, twirling it in his hands. "I'm not sure it's going to matter." Sailor's face was grim.

"What's up?"

"Nanette Keys bought a gun."

"When?"

"Few years ago. Said when Oakley left her by herself for long periods of time, she was scared and wanted to have some protection. A co-worker bought one first, a Kahr 9mm, and suggested Nanette get a gun."

"Does the co-worker's story check out?"

"Yep. She was the one who told us, Nanette didn't volunteer the information."

"What make and model?"

"Nanette said she doesn't know. That it was 'some old gun' she bought from a classified ad."

"Where is it now?"

"Gone, she says. Discovered she hated having it in the house. So she dumped it in the trash."

"You kidding me?"

"Welcome to my world. Means she has motive, opportunity, no alibi, and a possible weapon. It won't take much concrete evidence to arrest her on top of that."

The sheriff, never a smiling man, looked less happy than usual. A lot of circumstances drove good people to commit horrible acts, and Nanette certainly had her fair share. But the same man who said Nanette was a fine lady and did a lot for the community was clearly disappointed.

The two men left the Opera House at the same time, Drayco noting the sheriff wasn't following him this time. Drayco understood

Sailor's wariness, just like Drayco could sympathize with the pro-development forces. Here he was ready to sell property in town that held no personal attachment for him. Purely business, no more, no less.

He remembered the day developers tore down the abandoned Prayers Mill when he was a boy. He hadn't mourned it for its historical value, but for the loss of a place to play—swinging from ropes tied to the rafters, sliding down piles of old grist that filled his sinuses and made him sneeze. No one thought to restore the mill before it was bulldozed into oblivion.

Where there is property, there are developers, and where there are developers, there are winners and losers. But it wasn't always money at stake. Cultural sensitivities, ghosts from the past, they all played a role, too.

Drayco was surrounded by ghosts of his own—the Cadden twins, his deceased client Horatio Rockingham, the murdered pseudo-client Oakley Keys, all the Opera House performers from bygone days. Now he had a dinner date with a woman who was a specter of his former fiancée. Hopefully, Councilman Squier had a nicely stocked wine cellar.

11

The deputy handed over Paddy's few personal effects, a thin wallet, a small folding knife, and two keys, making sure the paperwork was properly signed. Seth hovered in the background, then walked in silence with Paddy to the car. Finally, he muttered, "It's a good thing they didn't set bail for you this time. I'm not made of money. You never get arrested when you're sober, Paddy. If you're going to be drinking, then do it at home and maybe I can keep an eye on you."

Paddy nodded but stayed silent.

Seth drove them home and flopped into a chair, staring at the bare walls. The room was chilly with the thermostat turned down to save money. Paddy picked up an empty glass from the shaky metal TV trays that served as their dining table and headed to the kitchen for water. Seth knew his son always felt more comfortable with a glass in his hand.

When Paddy returned, he waited nervously for Seth to speak. Seth wasn't sure if he preferred the silences or the shouting matches, but Seth was quiet this time and avoided looking at his son.

Paddy blurted out, "It wasn't my fault. The other fellow baited me. He knew I'd fall for it, he knew I'd hit him. They were all laughing about it. The sheriff has it in for me, anyway. I know you said I had to be good. I know you said it was too dangerous for me to get in trouble again, but it wasn't my fault."

Seth sank farther back into the chair and closed his eyes. "You're right, Paddy. It's not your fault. It's mine."

Paddy's red cheeks, frown, and watery eyes make him look like one of the sad-faced clowns at the circus. Seth hated those clowns. Hated the circus, except for the high-wire act. Perched up there, without a net, that took guts.

Paddy thrust his hands under his armpits. "I can do better, you'll see. Everything will be all right."

"Of course it'll be all right. Don't I always make everything all right?" Seth's voice softened, and he added, "Why don't you go take a nap, get some rest. It can't be easy to sleep inside a jail cell."

Paddy meekly complied, and Seth flipped on the lone television. Without cable, they were able to get all of three stations thanks to a homemade antenna Seth rigged up. Not much to see, but with the volume turned low, the murmuring hypnotized him into a quiet stupor where he didn't have to think. He'd been doing a lot of thinking lately, and he was tired. Look where it had gotten him after all.

He was glad he'd finished his rounds at the Opera House. Rockingham had demanded he use the barest minimum of electricity to do his job, and the place was a sauna in July and a freezer in December. And always filled with darkness, as he turned the lights on and then off again, moving from room to room. It remained to be seen what Drayco would do. This might be Seth's last chance at the place before new staff took over. And then what?

He reached over and picked up the one photograph in the room, staring at the young woman gazing dreamily at him from the frame. He didn't believe in angels, but he knew she was the closest thing to redemption he and Paddy ever had.

12

Drayco took his time arriving for dinner with the Squiers. Obligations wrapped *en croûte* were still obligations. Especially when the host was a jealous man and tight-lidded politician. And Darcie. .. what to make of her alleged affair with Oakley Keys? He doubted she'd confess to Oakley's murder over cheesecake.

Resigned to a torturous evening, he zigzagged through Highbrow Hill, as the locals called it, although the Eastern Shore was flatter than that *en croûte* dough. He pulled in front of his destination. Not very encouraging, at first glance. Maida was spot-on about Cypress Manor's aspirations, with its antebellum design and row of gleaming white columns. Even the three-car garage was built in the same vein. Isolated in location and style, the house would look ill-matched among the Victorian architecture in town.

The interior gave the impression of an uninhabited museum, antique candlesticks on antique sideboards next to antique busts on pedestals. Artwork hung around every corner, in gold filigreed frames. The thick carpeting stretched throughout the main floor, muffling sounds like acoustical foam.

Randolph Squier seemed to have forgotten Darcie's flirting the other day and was all too happy to show his guest around his collections—mounted animal heads, built-in shelves creaking under the weight of books on the American Civil War, a variety of Native American pottery, and a curious assembly of scrimshaw.

"And last but certainly not least. .." The councilman drew Drayco's attention to a floor-to-ceiling display case that served as the focal point of the large drawing room. It made the massive marble fireplace look puny. The case was filled with guns of all types, many with pearl or ebony grips, one with filigreed deer engraved in the barrels. Death at its most beautiful. There was nothing subtle in the tastes of Randolph Squier.

As if on cue, Darcie Squier made a grand entrance down the rosewood staircase, dressed in a red strapless dress and a dazzling ruby necklace. With her ancient-Greek nose, long and thin, and her wide-set eyes, she was a modern Aphrodite. It was obvious from the way he beamed at her that the councilman was proud of this particular acquisition.

She gave the air of proper decorum, greeting Drayco with a casual handshake. But a second later, she put her hand on his shoulder and guided him into the dining room toward an elegantly set table, with taper candles that smelled of vanilla mingling with the scent from a platter of fresh-baked croissants.

"My gracious," she apologized. "Our chairs may be too short for you. I don't remember you being so tall." Her eyes slowly assessed his body from head to toe. "Well over six feet."

"Six-four. But this is fine. I'm used to molding myself into small spaces." He changed the subject, mindful of the warnings from Maida and Sheriff Sailor. "This table and chairs are unusual."

Squier was the one who answered. "It's a walnut dining table from the nineteenth century. Observe the detailed scroll work." He added happily, "My wife picked out the china. It's Dauphin Spode. Darcie knows blue is my favorite color."

Drayco was hating the color of Squier's voice even more. Worm-shaped blobs joined the burnt-caramel color, alongside the texture of razor tips. It was an unusual and unpleasant combination.

Squier grabbed his wife's hand. Darcie's strained smile couldn't hide a wince, but she quickly recovered, batting her charcoal-lined eyelashes and trilling out, "You flatter me, my darling."

The councilman bobbed his head, a repetitive mannerism of his. "I must apologize again for the other day, Mr. Drayco. Everyone hoped Seth Bakely would send Paddy off to an institution. Poor Seth.

He's devoted to the Opera House. Aside from Paddy, it's all Seth has, which explains his obsessive work ethic. He spends a great deal of time there. Not much of a social life."

Drayco fingered his silver wine goblet. "I told him there wouldn't be any personnel changes yet and he should plan on staying. I'm not sure he believed me."

Squier laughed like a terrier baying at a snake. "Seth has never impressed me as the brightest bulb. After the Opera House is restored, I assume there will be need for more skilled labor?"

Drayco was going to answer when a high-heeled foot brushed up against his leg. Subtle, but. .. there it went again. He put the goblet down and reached for his water glass instead, so he could casually adjust his seat back an inch or two. Doing so meant it was harder to reach his plate of venison medallions, but he wasn't hungry, anyway. Shouldn't have eaten those Skipjacks nuts earlier.

"Those documents you sent along, Councilman—interesting reading. There were break-ins decades ago, though nothing was taken from the Opera House."

"You must mean those thefts in the seventies? Every historic building in the area was targeted. A few things were taken here and there, but it was haphazard, and valuable items were left behind. The police had no suspects. After a few years, it magically stopped."

Drayco asked, "Only historic buildings?"

Squier took a loud slurp from his glass. "Perhaps they were looking for proverbial buried treasure. Or someone reading too many *National Enquirers*. I am pleased to say," he added in a self-congratulatory tone, "Nothing was taken from Cypress Manor. Of course, that's long before you arrived on the scene, my dear."

Squier's hand that clutched Darcie's pulled her closer to him. "I'd have been upset knowing you were in jeopardy."

Darcie slipped her hand out of his grasp like one practiced in the maneuver and reached over to give Squier a micro-peck on the cheek. "You're always keeping an eye on me, aren't you?"

She didn't look at her husband often. Whenever she did, as now, her hand reached up to touch her necklace. Nervous habit or a reminder to herself of why she married him? If it was gold and silver pheromones that attracted her, it made the appeal of a dirt-poor Oakley all the more inexplicable.

Her eyes flitted to Drayco as he watched her fiddle with the necklace, and her hand dropped to her lap. "I was thrilled to hear you're a detective. We don't get a lot of excitement. Until the murder." She leaned forward, far enough for her foot to reach his leg under the table again. "Give us your expert opinion on who-done-it."

Squier interrupted, "A transient, dear, an illegal. I doubt one of our good citizens was responsible."

Darcie tugged on a lock of hair. "A lot of people think Earl Yaegle lost it. Flipped his lid." Her eyes grew meditative, closed off. "Oakley was freakish to some. And stubborn. But something could be worked out over that land sale. He didn't deserve murder."

A flash of annoyance crossed her husband's face. "Now, Darcie, we mustn't repeat unfounded hearsay. There are too many rumormongers in this small town. Earl Yaegle does a lot of good around here. We need him."

"Of course, love." She nodded to her husband while giving Drayco a meaningful glance. "I'm sure you and I are the subjects of many rumors."

Drayco waited for an explosion from Squier. The saccharine smile plastered on the man's didn't waver, but a vein on his neck stood out in a purple ridge. It was a well-used vein, tapping into a ready supply of suppressed anger.

Drayco asked, "Has the town council taken an official stance on the development?"

Squier pushed his chair back. "Why don't we move over to the drawing room for coffee."

Darcie jumped up to link arms with Drayco and made certain he was seated next to her on the small, tight settee. The councilman chose a gold high-back chair that bore a passing resemblance to a throne. He continued, "The bottom line is that Cape Unity's tax base is in need of a boost. The Yaegle and Keys properties are the ideal locations. It's a most generous offer from the developers."

"Not everyone in town agrees."

"Is there an issue where they do?" The councilman crossed his arms over his substantial barrel chest. "The major sticking point was Oakley Keys. I have never seen a man more determined to stay put. You'd think the damn fool didn't appreciate the value of money. I hope the sheriff solves this case soon as there's too much gossip going around. Gossip can be death in a small town."

Darcie chimed in, "But there's often truth in gossip, isn't there? I heard the other day from your secretary, Adah Karbowski, that Nanette Keys was having an affair with Earl Yaegle." Darcie batted her eyelashes.

Neither Drayco nor the councilman said anything for a few moments. Randolph Squier cleared his throat, then chided his wife again. "Remember what I said about rumors, Darcie. I'm sure Mr. Drayco didn't come tonight to hear idle talk. Beware lest he get the impression you're a common busybody."

Unfazed, Darcie winked at Drayco. "I hope he has a far better impression of me than that." She reached over him toward the carafe, making it difficult for him not to notice how low-cut her dress was.

It was safer for Drayco to study the large oil painting on the wall. "A local artist, Councilman?"

"A reproduction of a Frank Stick hunting illustration from the Brandywine school right up the Delmarva. I liked the scene but needed something more grandiose, so I had the fellow recreate it."

Grandiose was an apt word. The table-sized frame alone must have cost hundreds, enough to make the National Gallery jealous. Drayco asked, "So you're a hunter."

"A small band of us formed a local hunt club. Earl Yaegle's a member. The sunrise on the marsh, the flapping wings of the waterfowl, you can't beat it. You should come with us. I imagine you know your way around guns."

"I prefer hunting for information."

Darcie reached over Drayco again for the carafe. She put only a tiny bit of coffee in her cup each time, which gave her excuses to reach for more. This time, she put a warm hand on his thigh as she sat back down as if to steady herself. It was hard to believe her husband wasn't noticing his wife's flirtatious behavior. Drayco hazarded a quick peek at Squier. The purple vein had reappeared.

The awkward situation hovered in the air like a flock of water balloons over Drayco's head, but at the same, Darcie's touch was—not entirely unpleasant. Was this how it started for Oakley?

Using the Jepsons as an excuse, he bowed out as quickly as possible, happy to extricate himself from the suffocating grasp of Cypress Manor. He headed out into the cold night air and breathed in a lungful. He was greeted not by the stillness he expected, but by purple-tinged, high-pitched quavers from the American toads Maida mentioned in passing. It was the breeding season.

Nanette Keys and Earl Yaegle having an affair? Perhaps Darcie fabricated the whole thing, but why? And there was Randolph Squier himself, with so much jealousy twisted into his DNA, murdering Oakley would have felt compulsory. Drayco tried to catalog all the details of the Squier home, particularly the guns, but his mental inventory got interrupted with visions of white teeth and ruby lips smiling back at him.

13

The next morning, the day of Oakley's memorial service dawned with patchy gray clouds and a surprising call from Nanette, who wanted to see Drayco again, this time at her house. He got directions and made his way past the historic district, into an area north of the small picturesque harbor.

The Starfire nosed down a sandy road turnoff, and the further he went, the more deserted the landscape became. Not being far from the shoreline, he wasn't surprised when a stilt-legged heron flew above the road. He tried to envision the tousled Virginia pines and broomsedge grass replaced by future particleboard condos.

He also tried to tell where the Keys property ended and the Yaegle border began.

Nanette met him at the door, casting a quick look around the yard behind, before inviting him in. Drayco was grateful for the shelter, the wind beginning to cut through his thin slacks. The house was a small two-bedroom cottage, ringed by a wraparound porch with views to the water's edge. The furniture pieces included a mismatched poinsettia-red sofa and goldenrod-yellow chair—which gave him the fleeting impression of being inside a McDonald's—with throw pillows strategically trying to hide worn spots.

A handcrafted console table took up the better part of one wall. It must be the Oakley Keys original Nanette had told him about, but even it was bare. Taking a look at the humble furnishings, few people would have blamed Nanette for wanting to milk the developer cash cow for all it was worth.

The landscaping around the house consisted of a few trees and not much else, although a look out the casement window showed a small, but more elaborate, planting area in the back. Surrounded by a bed of seashells, it stood out against the khaki winter grasses. He pointed it out to Nanette and asked, "Are you the gardener?"

"That was Oakley's creation. When we moved here, he found an unusual heart-shaped rock. He added the benches and arbor around it and planted the weeping willow and passion flower vines. He called it his shrine to life, spending many a morning there watching the sun rise."

"He took good care of it. Like you have with your home. It's immaculate."

"After the sheriff and deputies were here the other day, I gave the place the cleaning of its life, top to bottom."

She slumped onto the red sofa and wrapped her arms around her as if to hold in her grief, keep it from spilling out. "I have to be honest—when Oakley told me he wanted to hire you, I was furious."

She bit her lip, drawing a speck of blood, which she wiped away. "We had our ups and downs. But lately, Oakley seemed more comfortable with his lot in life."

She started to smile, but the corners of her lips drooped as if too tired for the effort. "He'd gotten his drinking under control. And signed a new contract for a book."

"What was the topic of the book?"

"America's vanishing landmarks, a pet theme of his. I couldn't understand why he'd hire you and risk stirring up more animosity with Earl Yaegle."

Drayco studied her swollen eyes, quivering chin, nails bitten down to the quick. Despite being one of the chief suspects in her husband's murder, and the recent revelation of her possible affair, this wasn't another Elaina Cadden. This woman's grief was genuine. "He wanted me to find something incriminating on your neighbor?"

"That was my first thought." Nanette paused, eyes darting to the ceiling.

"Any reason he might do that, other than the property sale?" Drayco was fishing for an admission of her alleged affair with Earl, but if she was guilty, she wasn't ready to admit it. Or Darcie really dreamed up the whole thing.

She said, "Those business trips of his, when he was unreachable for a week or two at a time. It might have to do with that."

"How frequently?"

"Three or four times a year, often around Christmas. The trips stopped a decade ago. I guess I was afraid there was another family— you read about men with a double life. It sounds silly, and I didn't ask you here to burden you with my conspiracy theories."

Nanette sighed. "Although it's ironic, since Oakley himself always loved puzzles." She gazed outside, past the marshy channels circling lazily out to sea. The blue heron perched on one leg in the shallow water, waiting for a tidbit to come along, some unlucky frog. Drayco waited, too, sensing his companion was debating how much she was willing to tell him.

She brushed a hand across her face. "I hesitate to mention it. .. but it's been bothering me all these years. Now Oakley's gone, I find myself craving resolution."

She kept trying to smile but failing miserably. "Oakley and I moved here after we got married. I was a child bride, only sixteen. I never understood why he chose this area to live. Especially since he planned to write books, and we could have lived anywhere. He was originally from London, and I harbored a faint hope we might settle there. But Cape Unity is where Oakley wanted to come. Said he enjoyed the peace and quiet, the lack of interruptions. For the first several months, it was pleasant. Then I had a miscarriage and discovered I couldn't have any more children, which threw Oakley into a funk. Long story short, with the new book contract, things were looking up for the first time in, well, decades."

"How long ago did he start working on this book?"

"Five years or so."

"Did he send off the manuscript yet?" When she shook her head, Drayco asked, "Could I see it?"

"Take it with you. I haven't been able to bring myself to read it."
She darted into a back room, returning with a thick stack of papers
she handed to him.

She didn't sit down again, looking at Drayco shyly as she reached
over and pulled out a photograph. "This is Bendek. The name means
'blessed' in Polish. He's six years old. I haven't told anyone except a
couple of friends at work, but Oakley and I were working toward
adopting a child. We've been saving our pennies, long before this
whole development issue. It was Oakley's idea we adopt a Polish child
because he had a college friend from Poland who died his senior year.
His way of honoring the roommate's memory."

A boy with a gap-toothed grin stared back from the photograph.
He had coal-black hair and brown eyes with flecks of black like
pecan shells, resembling one of Drayco's childhood friends he lost
track of, one of many who took second place to the piano. "Are you
going through with the adoption?"

"If they'll agree to it. Our application was already approved, but
it was based on us as a couple, not me as a single mother. Although I
guess I'm old enough to be a single grandmother." She sported the
first real smile since he met her. But it soon faded. "Getting arrested
for murdering my husband might change their minds. I know I'm the
sheriff's chief suspect."

She fell back into the role of hostess. "Would you care for a
drink? I'm forgetting my manners. I should have offered first thing."

He declined, and she added, "Do you mind if I open the
window? The radiator knob in this room is broken, and I can't turn it
down. Only on and off. It gets a bit stuffy."

He offered to help, but she made quick work of opening the
casement window before heading into the kitchen. With the window
open, Drayco heard the low-pitched, lime-colored cry of the heron,
as well as ripplets lapping up on the beachless shore.

He took the opportunity of Nanette's absence to study the
room. Spying a shelf with LPs and 78s, he bounded over to examine
the contents. Mostly classical, the greatest-hits variety, but a few

oddities. He stopped at one of the latter, his hands sweating with excitement as he pulled it out.

Nanette returned and noticed the record in his hand. "Something of interest?"

"This is a recording of pianist Konstantina Klucze. Her last performance was here in town at the Opera House. This is rare."

Nanette sat down again and waved a hand in his direction. "By all means, you must keep it. It doesn't have any significance for me. Oakley would want it to have a good home."

Drayco stifled the urge to ask if he could listen to the recording on the spot. "Over the phone, you mentioned something you wanted to show me. I'm guessing it's something other than the photograph?"

"It was a letter. The letter that prompted Oakley's downward spiral."

"An old-fashioned letter via the post office?"

"One page, in a plain white envelope. Oakley was reading it when I came home from work one afternoon. He was quiet at first. And then his face convulsed with anger before he threw the letter into the fireplace and ran outside. He didn't come back for hours."

She rested a hand on her chest. "Here is where I have to admit a sin. I tried to grab the remains of the letter from the fire before it was consumed. All I rescued was a small fragment, and I couldn't tell anything from it. I hid it away and never told Oakley what I'd done."

"Any other suspicious letters or e-mail you intercepted?"

"No other letters. And Oakley was terrified of technology. He never got near a computer."

Drayco hazarded a guess, "After he received this letter, he began drinking?"

"With a vengeance. It was as if someone traded personalities with him. The difference was night-and-day."

"Do you remember the date?"

"As if I could forget. The six-month anniversary of us moving here." She got up and opened a buffet table drawer, handing Drayco a blackened scrap of paper that she kept in a plastic bag. "This is what I rescued."

Drayco peered at the fragile paper through the plastic, afraid to pull it out and have it disintegrate. The charred smell reminded him of the burned newspaper that greeted him at the Lazy Crab. A few legible words remained, penned in neat block letters. "Can't make out much detail. A closer examination with a microscope or a fancier instrument might help."

"But that's what I want you to do." She put her hand on his arm, pleading. "You must think I'm hysterical, the grieving widow grasping at straws. I don't care if nothing comes of it, I want to hire you. No matter what it is—another woman, debts, family feuds. I want to discover the part of my husband he kept from me."

With Oakley's memorial service at noon, Drayco didn't feel like adding to Nanette's anxiety. But he didn't have much hope the decades-old burned fragment would cough up useful information. He played the diplomat and told her he'd at least take a look.

"Mrs. Keys, I hate to bring up a difficult subject, but do you have any further thoughts on what the carving on Oakley's chest, the 'G,' might symbolize?"

Nanette deserved an Academy Award if the look of horror and revulsion on her face weren't authentic. It was hard to see her pulling the trigger of a gun that splattered her husband's brains on the floor. She touched the corner of her lip that started to bleed again, looking at the blood on her finger, transfixed. "That image keeps lunging at me, making me relive it over and over again. It's hard enough to imagine someone evil enough to kill Oakley in the first place, but to cut him in that way? It was so vindictive, so hateful."

She paused to wipe away a few tears. "I have no idea what the 'G' means. Unless it stands for that dreadful developer, Gallinger. But as emotional as the pro-development people are, I can't believe it would lead to this."

There was something noble about Nanette. A dignity formed through years of wondering where her husband was, or with whom, and learning to hold her head up, regardless. An innate strength, a will to persevere, no matter how brambled the journey.

"What will you do now, Mrs. Keys?"

"To be honest, I haven't made up my mind, regarding my future or the house."

"Oakley's Will left you the burden of dealing with both the property and the developers?"

"That's what the attorney told me. Frankly, I wouldn't care if Oakley left the property to Peter Pan."

She rose to walk him to the door, her eyes shining with hope. Her grateful parting words to Drayco left him feeling like the proverbial knight in shining armor. "I'll always be grateful for how you took my concerns seriously. I'm not sure anyone else would."

As Drayco climbed back into his car, he admitted that plenty of investigators would agree with the hysterical grieving-widow part. They'd also be as curious as he was why Nanette hadn't looked him in the eye when she denied knowing what the "G" stood for. He picked up the bag with the letter fragment from the passenger seat. Were the two related? It was such an insignificant fragment. Then again, the Rosetta Stone hadn't looked like much, either.

On his way back into town, Drayco drove through the east side of town where the grander buildings gave way to the "have not" homes. None of these were listed on the National Register of Historic Places. This cheerless real estate lacked much in the way of color, none of the vivid hues of Victorians restored by wealthier D.C. expatriates, nor the green of cold hard cash.

A billboard caught his eye, and he parked beneath it. It was a typical rectangle on wooden poles, featuring what some marketing genius must have thought was a happy scene of a family frolicking on a small beach in front of shiny new condos. The name Gallinger, with a large initial-letter "G," occupied one corner of the sign. What the marketing genius couldn't foresee was a personal touch by a local artist—the letter "G" had been slathered with red paint that made it look like it was dripping with blood.

Either the murderer copycatted his idea from the sign or took his symbolic gesture to literal new heights. The billboard and the plywood sign at the edge of town, both marred with red paint, were signs of anger dotting Cape Unity's landscape like giant measles. Or maybe like the peeling-paint pox on the Opera House door. If the Opera House survived, someone should stage *Romeo and Juliet* there. A plague on both your houses, indeed.

After Drayco's car pulled away from the house, Nanette felt a pang of regret. Should she have told him? He seemed like a nice young man after all. Oakley was handsome once, filled with ambition and confidence. That image of him was burned in her memory, long after the weathering of time and Oakley's self-destructive behavior cooled him into a virtual stranger. She walked again to the window to look out on Oakley's strange little shrine. There were so many things about him she never understood, so many questions unanswered. He had closed off a part of himself from her, something she fought valiantly for the first part of their marriage. But after a while, she gave up trying.

She'd spent hours on the eulogy for Oakley, tearing up draft after draft. It was a task she wished someone else would fill for her, but who was left? Friends of Oakley were few and far between.

It wasn't the eulogy she held in her hand right now. It was an odd letter she'd found earlier and didn't know what to make of. More bizarre, drunken ramblings from one of Oakley's benders? His reputation in town was already one of a lunatic, a nut, and she didn't want to add to that after his death. If only he could be remembered as the man she had married so long ago.

Or was this letter important, something that might explain everything she'd wondered about her husband and his behavior? Should she have shown Scott Drayco? The burned letter she'd given him was what had precipitated Oakley's fall from grace, after all, wasn't it? This other letter she'd sleep on and think about tomorrow. Perhaps she'd show it to Drayco then. For now, it was all she could do to muster enough strength to get through the memorial service.

She looked out the window again, at the howling winds forming whitecaps on the water. The weather was so ugly lately. It would serve as a fitting backdrop for the end to a wretched life.

14

The tire-busting cracks in unrepaired streets made Cape Unity's delicate two-step around budget woes clear. It also made it hard for Drayco to avoid all the potholes in the gathering darkness of a clouded twilight sky. Not that streetlights would help since several at the end of Main Street were broken.

It felt good to be outside after spending the last four hours following his visit to Nanette culling through more records at the Historical Society. Neither he nor Reece had attended the Memorial for Oakley. Neither of them felt welcome, or at least Reece hadn't. Drayco feared his presence would be a distraction.

He pulled in front of the Novel Café. Not only did it serve decent coffee with free refills, in addition to selling books, but he'd also learned it was another of Earl Yaegle's businesses. Drayco hoped to have the place to himself, but an elderly woman in a black-and-yellow crocheted sweater pressed against the counter like an overripe banana. She waved her hands at the salesclerk, whose face and neck sported a mottled red flush.

"He's a traitor, that's what." The elderly woman's voice pitched as high as an aging tremolo would allow, and she banged her cane down on the counter. "He has no business selling out to those big-city sharks. They slam through town like a hurricane, put up some hideous monstrosity and slink away with their ill-gotten gain."

Drayco walked to the counter. "Good afternoon, ma'am. I don't believe I've had the honor of making your acquaintance. I'm Scott Drayco."

She stopped her tirade for a moment. Gradually, the muscles of her face relaxed. "You're that new Opera House owner. It's a pleasure to meet one who appreciates historic buildings for a change, instead of tearing them down willy-nilly."

"I'm sure most people have the town's best interests at heart, don't you?"

She said, "You'd think so, wouldn't you?" and marched outside.

The salesclerk waited until the other woman left. "Thanks for coming to my rescue, Mr. Drayco."

"My pleasure," he read her name tag, "Zelda."

"We haven't had many customers like that. Guess it was a matter of time. Business has been down since—" Zelda gripped the edges of the counter.

"You think people don't want to buy books from a murder suspect?"

She paused, then moved her hands to straighten a rack of crossword paperbacks on top of the counter. "It's only been a few days. I hope it will pick back up because I need this job. Earl's a generous man. Without him, I couldn't pay for my son's asthma meds."

"How long have you worked here?"

"It'll be my tenth anniversary next month."

Since the elephant in the room was already out and marching around, asking about Oakley appeared to be a safe topic. "Did Oakley Keys come here often? He was a writer and historian, so he must have bought his share of books."

Zelda pointed to a section in the corner. "He practically lived over there for a while. That's the history and reference section."

"For a while? But not lately?"

"He stopped coming. .. I think it was last year sometime. I asked Earl why."

She hesitated, and Drayco prompted her, "What did Earl say?"

"He didn't want to talk about it. Seemed angry. So I never brought the subject up again."

"What were your impressions of Oakley? Other than as a customer."

"He was sweet. And great with kids. Always seemed to be here when we had children's story hour. He volunteered to read to them a couple times."

"After he stopped coming by the store, did you see Oakley around town?"

"On occasion. He was friendly enough. Waved, asked about business, the kids, my son. Things like that." Zelda's hands no longer gripped the counter. Good. One little victory.

He said, "I can help a little with business. Some books on the area's history. And the Opera House if you have them."

To his surprise, the store had an extensive and varied collection. Drayco cast a wistful eye at the travel section before purchasing a few books and ordering the biography Reece mentioned about Konstantina Klucze. Reece said the pianist was killed after she returned from Cape Unity to Britain. From the meager research Drayco could do via his smartphone—when he got a connection for more than a few minutes—he discovered Konstantina was murdered, the culprit unknown. Maybe the book would suggest some potential suspects.

As he threaded his way through narrow aisles toward the exit, he flipped through one of his new books, a title on brewing the perfect cup of coffee. Grinders, gold filters, a French press? Who knew?

Someone in front of him blocked his path, forcing him to look up. Darcie Squier was planted between him and the door. With a quick two-step, she moved in closer, pinning him to the shelves behind. "Fancy meeting you here," she purred. "After our dinner party the other night, Randolph and I were discussing how interesting it is you show up in our tame little town—and all of a sudden, we have a murder."

Her tone was fogged with rebuke, but her eyes sparkled like a sundog prism. "You must be intimate with crimes and all the passions they arouse." She drew out the word passions to three syllables.

Darcie smoothed the outlines of her form-fitting sweater dress. She had the form such a dress could love, accentuating every curve. She moistened her lips, looking at him the way Drayco's neighbor Abyssinian did when it was ready to pounce. "With a dangerous killer on the loose, it's comforting to know you're on the trail, Scott. And the sheriff, of course."

Drayco recalled Maida's offer to be his bodyguard and looked around for possible avenues of escape. "I'm sure the sheriff's grateful for your confidence in his abilities."

Darcie examined him from head to toe like she had at Cypress Manor as if sizing up his abilities on a more personal level. "It's Earl Yaegle who did it. I mean, if I got offered millions of dollars for land and someone stood in my way, I'd do something about it."

The way she said "about" set off light bulbs in his brain. She had a regional accent hard to find anywhere else, not so much Tidewater as Tangier. "Are you from this area, Mrs. Squier?"

"It's Darcie, remember? And I grew up on Tangier Island although we left when I was a young girl. You've heard of it?"

"I flew a small plane there once. Quite a history, that island. Captain John Smith, pirates, the British using it during the Revolutionary War. Some residents have a more Elizabethan accent than you although you sound a little like Seth Bakely. Is he from Tangier?"

"I believe so. Several people in Cape Unity are from there."

He'd picked up on the hints of an accent earlier, but her years spent away from the island had watered down the tells. No "noyce" instead of "nice," or "ye" instead of "you." That was the problem with melting pots; all flavors started tasting the same.

Darcie positioned herself closer to Drayco as the almost-forgotten book dangled from his hand. Her lips were tantalizingly close, her breath warm on his face and smelling of cinnamon and alcohol—not booze but the distinct odor of fresh mouthwash. She'd come prepared for this?

He let go of the coffee-brewing book, where it fell with a thud. Stooping to pick it up, he backed away from Darcie, half-knocking

over a display of books in a rack. "Oops. I'm so clumsy. It was great
to bump into you," he lied. Maybe only a half-lie. Okay. Not a lie at
all. He wasn't running from her because he didn't want to see her, but
because of the part of him that stirred at the prospect of being close
to her.

"I'm sure we'll meet again." Darcie's expression was now the
Abyssinian licking its lips over catnip. "Sooner rather than later."

Drayco climbed into the Starfire, refusing to acknowledge his
growing attraction to Darcie. Besides, if the figure across the street
from Earl's gun shop was Darcie, it appeared she was stalking him.
And what of her flirtations? Was he "fresh meat" as the sheriff
suggested, or was this a misdirection, to cover up the fact she'd cared
for Oakley? She projected the air of someone on a hunting
expedition—whether for him or for information, it was hard to say.

It got dark early in the Mid-Atlantic this time of year, but
looking back, he caught a glimpse of Darcie leaving. In his haste to
put distance between them, he gave only a passing glance toward the
black sedan parked on the curb behind him, a car that was vaguely
familiar. He might go days or weeks in D.C. without bumping into a
soul he knew. Every car around here was beginning to look like an
old friend.

He caught a quick glimpse of the stars through his windshield.
In such a dark-sky site as this, it was easy to see some of the Milky
Way and constellations. Should have brought his telescope. He pulled
the car over and got out long enough to take a better look. There was
Cancer, appropriately—the crab. Leo, the lion, was there. That would
be Squier, king of his jungle. And Darcie? What constellation would
best suit her? Hydra, the water serpent. Or better yet Orion, the
Great Hunter, chasing after hapless males. Oakley would be Ursa
Minor, the lesser bear.

Back on the road, he passed through town and spotted a group
standing around in a parking lot. The group of teenage boys on the
left wore the same type of jeans and famous-athlete-du-jour sneakers
as in private schools like Georgetown Day or Sidwell. On the right, a
group of young men with dark hair and olive complexions sported

extra-large hoodies and defiance. No gang emblems anywhere, just some cuts and bruises.

A car with flashing lights and Sheriff's Department lettering on the side sat in the middle, with a deputy talking to a boy in the back of the patrol car. This same scene played out in southern border states or a host of larger cities, except it was only now coming to Cape Unity. And it was also likely why many people in town found it more palatable to pin Oakley's murder on an outsider.

But it wasn't an outsider who was the main murder suspect, and if Drayco stayed around much longer, he'd likely see the sheriff arrest Nanette Keys. Another husband-wife dispute turned deadly. Remembering his conversation earlier with Nanette, and her heartfelt pleading, he didn't feel much like a white knight at the moment.

He headed back to the Lazy Crab, met at the door by Maida who gestured him wordlessly into the kitchen. Her pale face had traces of tears leaving red streaks. Piles of dirty dishes lay untouched in the sink, and the reek of food baked to a blackened crisp in the oven hung over the room. "I have horrible news, Scott."

Somehow, he didn't think it was related to the brawl aftermath. A skein of foreboding crawled up his spine. "What is it, Maida?"

"The sheriff called. It's Nanette Keys. She was murdered earlier today. Sometime after the memorial service."

Part Two

All that I long for is faded and gone.
I wander here in anguish, lonely and sad.
The sun has gone from my heaven.
And I must languish here in this loveless place.

—From the song "I want what I have not," poem by Bohdan Zaleski,
music by Frédéric Chopin

15

The small windows surrounded him in a circle of unblinking glass eyes. The pressure continued to increase; he could tell by his ears and skull. Not like flying at altitude, more like scuba diving. He was falling fast, with flotsam from shipwrecks floating by. Callie Cadden's terrified face was plastered against a window as if adhered by a suction cup. Calvin Cadden soon followed at another window, his small hands scratching at the glass. A sound Drayco heard behind him added to the eerie symphony, and he turned to see Oakley Keys at a third window, a dripping red "G" on his chest, rapping insistently with his knuckles as Nanette joined him, her skin pale and blue.

With the reproachful faces around him, the knocking grew louder and more intense, until he awoke in a sweat. But the knocking continued and soon morphed into Maida's concerned voice. "Scott? Are you all right? You said you'd be down at seven, and it's eight."

He was grateful she'd interrupted his latest nightmare, but he was sorely tempted to doze off until noon. He didn't like taking pills and declined Maida's offer last night of melatonin, hoping her alternate plan of warm milk and a turkey sandwich would do the trick. He couldn't stomach any Maida Tonic right now.

Where was a bottle of Manhattan Special when you needed it? If he'd been home in D.C., he would have gotten up at four, called it quits on getting any more sleep and dug his fingers into a Prokofiev piano sonata, grateful he had an end unit, and his only neighbor was hard of hearing.

He rushed to get dressed, not wanting to miss the appointment he made after Maida gave him the news about Nanette. But first, he made a phone call to cancel his reservations for the Mexico trip.

Sheriff Sailor's office was tucked inside a former fish processing plant bought by the town a decade ago and renovated for his staff and occupants of the jail cells. Drayco sat across from the sheriff's desk with its color-coded trays stacked so straight Sailor must have used a plumb line. On the walls hung artifacts from the building's previous incarnation—a mounted fish and a vintage scaler in a piscine shape.

The sheriff noticed Drayco's scrutiny of the objects. "A few mementos from a bygone era. Took us months to get the smell out of the place. Took me a year to want to eat fish again. It was the Seafood Hut's crab cakes that brought me back from the abyss."

Sailor yawned three times in succession. "We were up late at the Keys' house. I believe you said you had something to discuss. Please tell me you've solved everything and I can take a nap."

Drayco sank back into the bucket seat of the swivel chair, grateful for the extra leg room. "Nanette Keys invited me to her house yesterday morning before the service. She wanted to hire me, too."

The sheriff sat up straight. "Another dead client? Forgive me for being blunt, but wanting to hire you is the kiss of death. It'd explain the set of tire tracks in the driveway that didn't match Nanette's car or the car of the friend who found the body. We'll take an impression from your tires. And I guess we'll find your paw prints in the house."

Drayco's head filled with images of Nanette at her house yesterday, so hopeful, placing her trust in him. He welcomed the sheriff's recriminations. He'd missed seeing something, and now she was dead.

He scanned mental maps of the layout of her house and thought back to every word Nanette had said, hoping to figure out why she'd been targeted only a few hours after he left. Was the killer hiding in the house all the time? Nanette did open a window, and if someone were lurking outside, that provided an opportunity to listen in. But was there anything they discussed that would lead to murder?

He grumbled, "Take all the casts you want. And no, potential clients don't usually drop dead the minute they hire me."

Sailor rubbed his eyes. "Any self-respecting lawman, including your former FBI buddies, would find this hard to ignore. Two clients, both murdered right after you set up a meeting with them?"

"You want me to back off." That wasn't a surprise. Drayco had seen it coming.

"Would make things easier in some ways. This is turning into one giant clusterfuck." The sheriff picked up a pencil and rolled it around in his hand.

Neither man spoke for several moments. The closed door muffled any hallway noise, and humming from inside the guts of the computer and the coffee maker were like thunder in the stillness. Machine noises to Drayco were like nails on a blackboard to most people. Waves of mildew-green, or if he were lucky, sealskin-and-pewter bumps.

Sailor laid the pencil back on the desk. "Why did Nanette need your help?"

"Nanette said she wanted closure." Drayco gingerly pulled the plastic bag from his briefcase and placed it on the desk. "This is the crux of it."

The sheriff scrutinized the fragment, the size of a large index card. "Looks like a document. Charred around the edges. A letter? A bill?"

"A letter sent to Oakley Keys not long after he and Nanette moved here. According to Nanette, it made Oakley so angry, he threw it in the fire. His behavioral changes started afterward."

"What changes? Dr. Jekyll or Mr. Hyde?"

"Oakley began drinking heavily and became withdrawn. Nanette was afraid the letter and his secretive business trips meant he was hiding a double life."

"In light of Oakley's other affairs, I see why."

"Yet I don't think she believed it deep down."

"She wanted you to investigate his double life?"

"Not directly. Just this." Drayco pointed to the letter fragment. "That's where all their troubles began. She hoped if I solved the letter mystery, it would explain both his character one-eighty and why he wanted to hire me."

Sheriff Sailor squinted at the fragment on the desk. "Not much to go on."

"That's what I told her. Since it might be evidence, I don't think I should keep it."

"Glad you brought it by." The sheriff scanned Drayco's face. With a knowing look, he added, "I guess you want a copy?"

Sailor had managed to surprise him a third time. And Drayco nodded his thanks. "I don't know if it will be possible, fragile as it is."

"We're a small department. Prince of Wales County only has ten thousand residents after all. We don't have one of those elaborate movie crime labs. Our new CI, the only other one besides Jake, has some training in document forensics. I'll have her take a look at it first. If need be, we'll send it off to a state lab. But between the blood, ballistics, and corpses I've sent them this week, I think they're tired of hearing from me."

The sheriff peered out the wired-glass window on his office door and immediately popped up out of his seat. After motioning in a woman from the hallway, he said, "This is the investigator I was telling you about, Nelia Tyler. Tyler, this is Scott Drayco, a D.C. consultant."

Nelia shook Drayco's hand. "I saw you at the crime scene. You're the infamous new owner of the Opera House."

"Guilty as charged."

Nelia grinned. "Better not use that word around here. You might find yourself in the lockup quicker than you can say Paddy Bakely."

"I understand I have you to thank for keeping the Opera House piano out of harm's way."

"It's a handsome instrument. I'd love to hear it played." She was 30ish, five-ten, the same height as the sheriff, with her blond hair tied back in a braid. Not what you'd call drop-dead gorgeous, but not plain, either. And her mocha brown eyes were clear and bright with a hint of mischief. She was the only female deputy he'd seen around Cape Unity, but there must be others. Sailor didn't seem the sexist type.

The sheriff handed her Nanette's letter fragment. "Think you can make something out of this?"

She took the bag by the corners and peered inside. "I've seen worse. Is this related to Nanette Keys' murder?"

Drayco spoke up. "It's a long shot. But I like long shots."

She poked a stray hair behind her ear. "And I love a challenge."

Drayco pulled a thick envelope out of the briefcase at his feet and placed it on the sheriff's desk. "Here's more reading material, Oakley's manuscript for his new book. He had an entire chapter on Cape Unity, blaming Randolph Squier for destroying local architecture. He also wrote that Squier was going to buy the Opera House and tear it down for restaurants and shops to provide more revenue for his secret embezzlement habit. I have a feeling Oakley's editor would have removed those incendiary bombs to keep from getting sued."

Sailor idly riffled the corners of a stack of papers on his desk. "I remember reading that some city clerk leveled embezzlement charges years ago. Didn't name any names. Later recanted his story."

Nelia chimed in. "How old is this manuscript?"

Drayco smiled—he'd asked Nanette the same thing. "Oakley started it five years ago."

Nelia added, "That would coincide with Oakley's affair with Darcie Squier. Oakley could have written the chapter to discredit Squier. Or to frame him and get him out of the way. If it's true and Squier knew about the document, might be another reason for Squier to want Oakley dead."

Sailor said, "Could be. Doesn't explain Nanette's murder."

Drayco handed over the envelope. "And if Oakley was murdered because he didn't want to sell the land, why would she be murdered because she did? Unless she figured out who killed her husband."

"If she did, wish she'd let us in on the secret." Sailor looked over at his deputy. "Since I'm handing out reading assignments today, I'll give you custody of the manuscript, Tyler. Check out that embezzlement angle, too. Get Jake Giles to help you."

The sheriff waited until she was out of earshot. "Damned fine credentials. And before you make any wisecracks, I mean that literally. We're lucky to have her since we almost lost her to law school. Plus, the job forces her to have a commuter marriage."

"She's married? I didn't see a ring."

"Tyler's husband is an attorney up in Baltimore. He's got MS, the primary progressive kind. He's able to get around on crutches for now. Tyler doesn't discuss it, but I can tell it's hard on her."

Sailor reached around and pulled out a photograph. "Found this on a table at the Keys' house."

Drayco gave it a look. "That's Bendek."

"Bendek?"

"A child from Poland the Keys were going to adopt. Which makes him another victim, in a way. Guess he's going to stay an orphan."

Sailor stared at the child's chubby-cheeked face in the photo. "The wife and I considered adopting once." He looked at the photo again and laid it carefully back on the desk.

"Did you find anything else at Nanette's house, sheriff?"

"Nothing's changed since Oakley's murder, with one exception." The sheriff looked like he'd taken a gulp of milk a month after its expiration date.

Drayco said. "I'm not going to like this, am I?"

"There was a cardboard file box, yay big," the sheriff indicated the size with his hands, similar to a shoe box. "It was there last time, and now it's not. Considering how it was labeled, we checked through it after Oakley's murder. But it was only historical documents."

"How it was labeled" could only mean one thing. "It was about the Opera House."

"Yep. Big black letters in magic marker. You didn't see it there?"

Drayco shook his head. "Nanette was unaware of it?"

"It lay on top of a file cabinet for years, but she never looked inside. Assumed it was a writing project he was working on."

"A valuable or incriminating item in that box could be a motive for her murder. Either because the murderer believed she knew something, or she was an innocent bystander who got in the way of theft."

Sailor said, "*Possible* innocent bystander."

"Either way, all roads lead back to the Opera House." Drayco stood up and went to examine the mounted spotted flounder on the wall. With its mouth hanging open, it was ready to bite down on a hook. Drayco gingerly fingered the piranha-like teeth. "Have you completely ruled out a random killer, Sheriff? I drove by a brawl your deputies were working last night. Townies-versus-foreigners, with a pinch of juvenile testosterone."

"A transient wouldn't make sense. One murder, Oakley or Nanette, but not both, and not a few days apart. Plus, their house is off the beaten path and hard to find. The murderer or murderers knew how to avoid being seen or leave tracks."

Drayco said, "Someone who knows his way around the out-of-doors, like a hunter?"

"Squier? Yeah, I thought of that."

Drayco tried not to match Sailor's continuous yawns. But he did feel obligated to pass along one more tidbit. "My dinner with the Squier duo Tuesday night was enlightening."

Sailor tilted his head. "I'm impressed as hell you escaped unscathed from Cypress Manor. Although the good councilman keeps a tight leash on Darcie these days."

"Not enough to keep her from spitting out gossip. She says Nanette Keys and Earl Yaegle were having an affair."

Sailor's wide eyes matched those of the mounted fish on the wall. "Huh." He scratched his head. "In a place where secrets are scarce, I'm embarrassed to admit I hadn't heard that."

"Even Squier looked surprised."

"Would add to Yaegle's motives, but since the M.O.s aren't the same, it's possible we're talking two motives, two killers."

"Different gun?"

"No gun at all. Nanette was strangled."

"Manual or ligature?"

"Mugging, we think."

"I assume you mean as in holding her neck in the bend of the elbow?"

"Yeah, but again, no forced entry, no signs of struggle, no prints. And more importantly, no mutilation this time. No 'G' or anything else. Oh, and the M.E. is fairly sure Oakley was alive when his chest was carved up. Maybe not conscious, but then again, maybe so."

Drayco had truly hoped Oakley was dead at that point. But since he wasn't, this meant the killer not only wanted to mark his victim but inflict pain and terror before he died. The psychopath angle again. He tried not to think of Nanette's own moment of terror as she was strangled, struggling for every last breath. But he did, and his own chest tightened for a moment.

He slid back into the chair and stared at dirt on the floor that must have shaken loose from the soles of his shoes. "There's a billboard on the west side of town, an ad for Gallinger."

"With the red circle and slash over the 'G'?"

"Has it been there long?"

"The billboard, yep. The circle, we're not sure. One of my deputies spotted it after Oakley was killed, not before. Might be the work of the same guy."

"Or Oakley's 'G' may be the work of a copycat or accomplice."

"I thought of that. No one claims responsibility for the billboard, big surprise."

"In D.C., graffiti artists sign their work, often a symbol or nickname."

"Nothing here." The dark circles under Sailor's eyes were far too deep to have accumulated from one night's missed sleep. Next time, Drayco would bring some espresso with extra shots.

Drayco realized he was drumming his fingers on the sheriff's desk when Sailor pointed. "You do that a lot. Old habits die hard?"

"I guess. Music plays in my head constantly. An earworm parade."

"So what's playing now?"

"*Dies Irae*. It translates as day of wrath." Drayco tried to remember the last time he had an upbeat piece as mental background music. Nothing came to mind unless he counted the seduction aria from *Carmen* when he first laid eyes on Darcie Squier. And he really didn't want to count that.

Drayco asked, "Besides Earl Yaegle, any other suspects top your list for both murders?"

"Depending upon which murder and which motive, we've got a few for each. Possibly Seth or Paddy Bakely. Nanette was a social worker and one of her co-workers—that same one who encouraged her to buy the gun—brought over a box of personal effects this morning from Nanette's desk. There were a couple of items Seth gave her after she helped him out with Paddy. The co-worker said clients often get crushes on staff and wondered if Seth or Paddy had one on Nanette. Seth and Paddy have provided alibis for each other. Again."

"Anything else helpful in that box of effects?"

"There's a book of Paddy Bakely's poetry."

"Can I see it?"

The sheriff reached around behind him and lifted the cover off a box. "Take a look, but I'll have to keep it."

Drayco opened the small chapbook and read through the poems. They were rambling, as you might expect from Paddy, with violent and disturbing imagery. He stopped on one page and reread a few lines aloud. "Black Angels strangle the innocents and leave their babies homeless in the cold. We all cry, we all die, to know what could have been."

Sailor said, "Nice, huh? Gimme Robert Frost."

"Black Angels? Like the Velvet Underground song?"

The sheriff pursed his lips. "Never would have guessed you're a closet rock-and-roller."

"I have my moments. Although I draw the line at body piercings." Drayco flipped through a few more pages. Paddy's poems were fodder for a psychologist's wet dreams.

Down the hallway, someone blew on a police whistle, followed by sounds of laughter. Drayco looked up, with a frown and shake of his head.

"So," Sailor nodded toward the door. "What's it like? That chromesthesia thing you got going on. It must be—"

"Overwhelming?"

"I Googled it and only one percent of the population has it. It's gotta be weird."

"Several composers had it. Liszt, Rimsky-Korsakov, Scriabin, Amy Beach. It's not weird if it's the only existence you've ever known. Doesn't make me some kind of super detective. In fact, I have to work hard to keep from being prejudiced for or against someone because of the colors and textures of their voice."

Drayco handed the booklet back to the sheriff who asked, "You don't want to take notes?"

"I'll remember."

"What, you've got a photographic memory, too?"

"Technically, eidetic. From learning all those long piano scores. Have you checked all of Nanette's other clients? Some of those social worker cases get ugly."

The sheriff tapped a list of names on the desk. "We're working on it. Halfway down the list, things don't look promising. Nanette was good at what she did. Not an enemy in the world that we can find."

Drayco had yet to meet a person without enemies. Maybe not the murderous kind, but the type to take one word or one oversight, no matter how small, and sharpen it into a blade of ill will. "So you're not ready to arrest someone."

"If I were a betting man, I'd put my money on Earl killing both of his neighbors. There's the gun shop, the knife in the dumpster, his middle name Gerik—which Oakley made fun of, I found out—the development money, threats he made, and now the affair with

Nanette. He was alone at his house yesterday when Nanette was murdered. Said he was taking a nap and didn't hear a thing."

"That's a nice laundry list of motives you have there for Earl."

Sailor frowned and said in clipped tones, "You're not convinced."

"Laundry lists are too tidy."

"Nothing tidy about this shitty business. What exactly do you expect to come out of this dirty laundry, anyway?"

What had Drayco told Seth, about the dirty little problems people at the end of their ropes use to hang themselves? "My instincts tell me it's like those Russian *matryoshka* figures stacked inside each other. Secrets within secrets." Drayco pulled himself up out of the chair. "I think I'd like to poke around some more."

Sailor dropped the poetry booklet in the box next to his desk. "Just try to keep your nose clean, if not your shirts."

"And I promise when I find all your missing socks along the way, I'll page you."

Sailor snorted. "Nobody's that good a detective. Where you off to next?"

He didn't blame the sheriff for wanting to keep tabs on him, but Drayco wasn't the type who liked working under a magnifying glass. He'd left those days behind at the Bureau. Drayco flashed his best cryptic smile. "Me? I'm off to see some ghosts."

16

Drayco picked up a handful of the grainy white soil that choked out plants in the flower beds and formed small dunes like the backs of buried camels. The sand also had an unpleasant way of propagating itself inside shoes and on the floor of his car. Lies were a lot like that—surrounding you, clinging to you, and if you got in deep enough, making it impossible to dig yourself out.

The forecast called for a possible nor'easter early next week, yet the winds were already gusting to twenty knots. Drayco turned up the collar of his jacket and stood under a stand of pine trees for shelter. He surveyed the small beach that wound its way around the front of the Keys' lot toward the north. The house itself was dark and silent, a dispirited castaway.

Drayco looked for anything to shed light on the importance of "G." It was a long shot. Nothing else had turned up in Oakley's background, but gum trees and greenbriers weren't viable candidates.

He walked to the beach over a carpet of pine needles, perfect stealth-material for a murderer. This was put to the test when Drayco felt, more than heard, a presence behind him. He swirled around to see a man in his fifties wearing an orange hunter's vest over camouflage overalls. A man he now knew was Earl Yaegle after following him from the gun shop. Of average height and build, the most arresting thing about Yaegle was the rifle he was pointing at Drayco.

"Who are you and what are you doing on my property?" he bellowed.

Drayco countered him in a calm voice. "Scott Drayco."

Yaegle's face registered his recognition of the name, but the gun held steady. "That answers the who. Now the why."

Drayco took a gamble. "Nanette Keys wanted to hire me before her death. I feel obligated to follow through."

Yaegle's shoulders drooped at the mention of Nanette. "Hire you? Now why in the world would a classy lady like her want to hire some sleazy operator who snoops through people's garbage cans?"

Large blobs of rain pelted them both and Yaegle hesitated, then dropped the rifle to his side. "Don't want to stand out here getting soaked. Why don't you come inside my house? It's a short ways up this beach path."

Drayco marveled at how close the two houses were. You couldn't see one from the other, but only because the curvature of the shoreline and dense trees blocked sight lines. The Yaegle house was slightly bigger than the Keys', although more expensively furnished, with signs of Yaegle-the-successful-businessman everywhere—satellite dish, a large LCD TV, and state-of-the-art entertainment system.

Yaegle motioned Drayco toward a leather chair as he sat on the sofa opposite, his eyes like cat-slits assessing a snake in the grass. He remained silent for a minute, before grumbling, "The boys at the shop told me you stopped by asking questions. You think I killed them both, Nanette and Oakley. Everyone else does."

"I never assume anything."

"Only a matter of time before the law comes knocking on my door and marches me away in handcuffs."

He paused, but Drayco didn't say anything. "So you're not going to ask me why I murdered my neighbors? Or why I want to sell out to a big-city developer? Or alibi this or alibi that?"

Drayco looked around the room before he turned his focus on Yaegle. "Is it true you had an affair with Nanette Keys?"

Stunned at first, the man deflated into a lump of misery and put his head in his hands. He said in a soft voice Drayco strained to hear,

"You must believe me when I say I loved my wife Tabitha. She was everything to me, and when she died of ovarian cancer. .."

His fingers tightened around his temples. "I made some bad investments. Tabitha understood. But I didn't want her to understand, I wanted her to hate me and tell me I was a miserable failure. It was a moment of weakness, on both our parts, mine and Nanette's. It didn't last long. A few months."

He straightened up and raked his fingers through his thick silver mane. "To this day I don't know if Tabitha guessed. She was such a hard worker, my wife. Often clocked seven days a week at the bookstore. It was her favorite of my businesses. Not too strange since she had dreams of being a writer. Then we got married, and the kids came along. She gave up her dreams for me and that's how I thanked her."

Earl paused, looking down at his damp camouflage-colored shoes, which he took off and turned upside down. "Does the sheriff know?"

Drayco nodded. "But it's hardly proof you murdered anyone. Some might say you have less of a reason to murder Nanette. Were you in love with her?"

"I cared for Nanette, admired her, but I wasn't in love with her. And I certainly didn't kill her."

"If your wife Tabitha did have knowledge of the affair, you think she would have retaliated? An affair with Oakley?"

Yaegle didn't hesitate. "Odds are far greater I'd win the lottery—twice—than Tabitha having an affair. Especially with Oakley. She was old-fashioned that way. Besides, between all the hours she worked at the store, raising the kids, taking care of the home, she barely had time to breathe."

"Did Oakley know of your affair with his wife?"

Yaegle shook his head slowly. "Our dispute didn't start until well after. But I guess it would explain his determination not to sell his land. To get back at me."

"And he never said why he didn't want to sell?"

"Which is strange, don't you think? Any ordinary person would try to change my mind, argue with me, to see his side. But when the developers approached him, he refused to sell. And when he learned I wanted to take their offer, he stopped talking to me."

A sizzling sound from the kitchen caught Yaegle's ear. He hurried off to catch the pot of clam chowder he was heating on the stovetop, now boiling over and leaving a gooey mess dripping down the stove. Some of it had dripped on a burner, filling the room with the smell of scalded milk.

His absence left Drayco to study the carved black cherry table in front of the sofa, with a marquetry pattern and intertwined ivy branches. He traced the scrollwork on one of the legs as Yaegle returned with apologies for the interruption.

Yaegle pointed to the table. "Oakley made that. See the ivy leaves? The symbol for friendship on British family crests. His initials OK are hidden underneath. He signed his pieces that way. A private joke."

"Oakley made this? It's a stunning piece."

Yaegle sat down again with his legs stretched out. "And then you've got someone like Paddy Bakely who's always fancied himself an expert carpenter, although his pieces can't hold a candle to Oakley's. I think it made Paddy jealous."

"That's like the blind leading the blind, isn't it? One unsuccessful person envying another unsuccessful person?"

"When Oakley's writing career sagged, he could have made a fortune selling his wood handiwork. He wasn't practical. Might be why he didn't want to sell his land. It's as good an explanation as any."

Drayco didn't for a minute believe Oakley was immune to the value of money and what it could mean for himself and Nanette, especially with a pending adoption. Oakley had some compelling reason that overrode his capitalistic sense, a reason forceful enough to end a friendship.

"Have you lived on this property all your life?"

Earl pointed to a framed photo on the wall of a European-looking city—cobblestone streets and neat rows of buildings with flower boxes and terracotta-tiled roofs. "I was born in Weimar. My father beat me and my stepmother hated me. When I turned eighteen, I stowed away aboard a freighter headed for Canada. I was discovered, fled across the border and wound up in Maryland, where I met Tabitha. Long story short, we got married, I got my green card and was naturalized. Sounds like I married her because I didn't have legal status, but I did fall head over heels. If the citizenship thing hadn't worked out, I was going to ask her to move back to Germany."

"Did you start the gun shop right after you settled in Cape Unity?"

"It wasn't my first business. I worked as a fisherman, saved up to buy my own boat, then another boat, then I got a few employees of my own. It kept branching out from there. People like to hunt around here, so guns made good business sense."

"Did Oakley go fishing with you?"

"He loathed everything fish. Wasn't a big fan of the water, either. I tried to get him to give the Anglers Club a try, but he wouldn't budge. We argued over that."

"Did any of your disputes with Oakley come to blows? Especially over the development?"

Instead of taking offense, Yaegle grinned. "You mean was I angry enough to blow his brains out? Nah. And I never hit him."

Yaegle apparently wanted to set the record straight, even if it was to an outsider. "You might not believe this, but I'm sorry he's dead. We were friends and neighbors for many years. Certainly more good times than bad. He and Nanette were godparents to my kids."

Yaegle pointed to a family photo. "I remember birthday parties, fishing trips, the days at the beach when Oakley and Nanette joined Tabitha and me and the boys. It's for my children I want to sell. I was born into a family with no spoons, let alone silver ones. I want to leave my kids enough money to buy fancy platinum spoons if they want."

He was on his way to doing just that, with the land sale. A couple million greenbacks, to be precise. "G" again. The letter popped up everywhere. Drayco asked, "Your middle name is Gerik, isn't it?"

"How the hell you know that? My wife researched it. It's Polish. Means 'spear ruler.' Appropriate for someone in my line of business. Oakley kidded me all the time."

The burned-soup smell now permeated the room, making Drayco want to sneeze. "Did Oakley mention a city embezzlement scandal?"

"Embezzlement?" Earl paused. "Not a word."

So Oakley didn't mention the ranting accusations in his literary opus to his neighbor. More fuel for Nelia's hypothesis that Oakley hoped to discredit Squier, keeping the manuscript a secret until he got it published. Nelia and he were on the same wavelength, it seemed.

Drayco asked, "Did the letter 'G' have any special meaning for Oakley?"

Yaegle didn't register any emotion at the question. "I can't think of anything." Then he sighed. "'G' for ghost, as in Oakley was a ghost of his former self. I used to have Oakley over for drinks. When it became apparent he was turning into an alcoholic, I stopped. I didn't want to be a pusher."

"It wasn't your fault. Alcoholics are their own pushers." And worse, when their morals got swallowed along with the gin. "Since we're being honest about affairs, were you aware of Oakley's extramarital pursuits?"

"Hard not to know. Nanette tried to ignore it. They got worse after he started drinking, but I recall a few before. Not long after the Keys moved here. Some fellows can't be faithful to one woman. Myself included."

Yaegle rubbed his hand over his eyes. "You act like a cop. You sure you aren't a cop?"

"Former FBI."

Yaegle's jaw dropped, and he jumped up. "Good God, I don't want to get tangled up with the FBI. The sheriff's bad enough. Knew I shouldn't talk to you. Before I say anything else, I want my lawyer present."

"I'm not here on a witch hunt, Earl. I only want the truth."

Yaegle snorted. "Whose truth? Tends to vary, depending upon your point of view, doesn't it? Truth is worse than a moving target because it changes shapes." Yaegle pointed toward the door. "I think you should leave now."

Drayco let himself out and retraced his steps through the trees to the Starfire. He looked back long enough to see Yaegle staring out his window in the direction of the Keys' house. Earl stood there for a full minute, as if hypnotized, before drawing the curtains and vanishing into his cottage of exile.

17

An empty concert hall was eerily like a tomb. Drayco had certainly been inside plenty of both. There was an air about this place, this Opera House—a sense of tragedy going beyond Oakley's death, which settled around the stage like a twisted curtain. After his conversation with Earl and the man's parting tirade, Drayco felt compelled to come here. He wasn't sure why.

He wandered from room to room, noting wires dangling from holes, patches of missing wallpaper and warped floorboards. At the end of a long hallway, he discovered what likely served as the main office, complete with a massive partners desk made of oak, leather, and brass, and some floor-to-ceiling mahogany cabinets.

A ladder partially hidden between one cabinet and wall beckoned to him. Drayco pulled it out and put his full weight on the first step. It groaned, but he judged it sturdy enough. He started on the top cabinets and worked his way down, checking for anything left behind. Just when he thought it was a waste of time, he discovered a section filled with yellowed programs and receipts.

The programs confirmed the roster of artists the Opera House lined up when well-heeled gentry still made the pilgrimage to Cape Unity. That was long before winds and storm surge from the 1933 hurricane caused many of the resorts to close down.

Big-name headliners tapered off after that time, and Drayco only found a few, including one program from Konstantina Klucze's concert in 1955. An item even Reece Wable didn't have.

Drayco flipped to the biographical page. It included the same photo of a young woman with upswept golden hair and fierce eyes from one of Reece's articles. The accompanying blurb detailed Konstantina's promising career, curtailed in her twenties due to the Nazi invasion of her native country. Drayco had a growing connection to the exiled pianist whose music dreams were cut short by violence.

Chafing at how long it was taking for the book he'd ordered on Konstantina to arrive, he'd made a call to a musicologist friend who filled him in on Konstantina's early career and acclaim. Despite the post-war chaos, her unsolved murder sent shockwaves rippling through the music world at the time. Several names were bandied around as suspects. The musicologist would probably ignore his calls in the future after the way Drayco grilled him about each possible culprit.

He left the documents on the desk and continued his tour through the bowels of the building, stopping by the main greenroom for performers. The vanity area, a counter lined with makeup mirrors and drawers, waited forlornly for artists who never came any more. Indentations on the floor hinted at heavy sofas that once stood there. Gold anaglyptic wallpaper would have seemed regal contrasting against the burgundy carpeting, now faded to the familiar salmon.

He tried opening one of the vanity's drawers, but it stuck. After maneuvering it back and forth, and using the knife from his Leatherman tool, he was able to pry it open. As if on cue, an object rolled nonchalantly toward him. Drayco held it up to the light. The detailed etching on the ivory-colored article looked for all the world like one of Randolph Squier's scrimshaw artifacts. Except this was larger and more detailed, with a fleet of tiny ships on one side and various marine creatures on the other—a humpback whale, a pod of dolphins.

It was hard to believe the scrimshaw piece went overlooked for fifty years. And what was it doing here in the first place? A forgotten gift left behind, or a performer's good luck charm? He carried the scrimshaw and programs back to the stage, where he set them down next to the piano.

The Steinway dated from the early to mid-twentieth century, a product of the company's Hamburg factory in Germany. A rare find in these parts. If you want to start a fistfight among pianists, ask which is better, the New York Steinway with its mellow timbre and growling bass? Or the Hamburg Steinway, with a wider range of dynamics and sweeter treble? Either way, you were looking at over twelve thousand parts in one of these babies. Each instrument took a year to craft, and that didn't count the long seasoning process for the wood before the first parts were assembled.

Despite not having been used in a while, the instrument wasn't in horrible shape, certainly nothing some refurbishing couldn't fix. He hadn't been able to practice his daily half hour as of late and missed the cathartic surrender from the chance to sit down and play.

He returned to the greenroom long enough to see if the hot water worked. Once it heated up to a sub-scalding temperature, he filled the basin and soaked his right hand and forearm for four minutes. Satisfied with his efforts, he headed to the piano and reeled off a few scales and arpeggios. Not too badly out of tune. He put the piano through its paces with Chopin's "Minute Waltz."

Following on his morbid thoughts earlier, Drayco started the "Funeral March" from Chopin's second sonata. He fingered the opening B-flat minor chords gingerly, but soon got lost in the music's dark meditation, the slightly out-of-tune keyboard all but forgotten.

When he came to the end of the piece, he kept his hands on the keyboard, soaking up the last fading overtones and inhaling deeply, as if breathing them in. The only trouble with starting a piece is that he never wanted to stop.

The sound of slow, heavy steps echoed down the hallway, steps he recognized as Seth Bakely's. Seth also had an apricot, conical-shaped wheeze from his years of smoking that preceded his appearance. He looked from Drayco down to the pile of programs and scrimshaw, but his impassive features didn't change, nor did he ask about the artifact.

He said, "You play the piano."

Master of the obvious, eh, Seth? Drayco bit back an acerbic retort. "In my spare time."

"I never liked the piano."

So Seth didn't like the piano in general or this particular pianist? "There's a lot of music that doesn't involve the piano. There must be something to suit your taste."

"Don't like music much. Too showy. I guess guitar's okay. I work with my hands, and I fix things. Don't need anything else."

Seth's hands were rough and callused, his fingernails dark and cracked from neglect. But no signs of palsy. Overall, he appeared to be in decent health except for the wheeze and the possible skin cancer. Seth was the type who would likely go on working until he dropped dead.

"You said you only met Horatio Rockingham on a couple of occasions. Yet he continued to keep you on the payroll as caretaker. He must have had a good opinion of you."

"Doubt it. He was happy he didn't have to deal with this place."

Drayco shared a brief empathetic moment with the late Mr. Rockingham. "You've been the Opera House caretaker for decades. Don't you get tired of it? Want to retire or take some time off?"

As if reading Drayco's mind, Seth replied, "Don't have a pension. And I have to work to take care of my son—. My bills."

Drayco had a good picture of what a drain Seth's son must be, emotionally and financially. "I ran into Paddy the other day at the courthouse. He seemed to think Horatio Rockingham should have left the Opera House to the two of you."

Seth coughed and wheezed at the same time. "People around here have learned to ignore Paddy. Got a temper he can't control. I'll speak to him." Seth didn't address the legacy issue, ignoring the subject altogether.

"You were acquainted with Nanette Keys, I understand?"

"Saw Mrs. Keys at the agency. While trying to get help for Paddy." Seth wheezed a few decibels louder. "There's a rumor going around they'll arrest Earl Yaegle soon."

"The sheriff will arrest someone when he has the right culprit."

Drayco hopped off the piano bench to gather the documents he'd found. He glanced up as he heard what sounded more like a gasp than a wheeze. Seth was staring at the cover of the top program in the pile, the one with the picture of Konstantina, and a look of dismay appeared fleetingly across his face.

Drayco picked up the program and showed it toward Seth. "Someone you recognize?"

"Don't know any musicians." He paused, still looking at the program. "But she reminds me of my wife, Angel. Looks a lot like her. She died when Paddy was born."

"I heard that, and I'm sorry."

"It was a long time ago." Seth straightened up. "Nanette Keys was a good woman. She shouldn't have gone like that. You looking into her murder?"

"I'm going to try."

"As I said, don't get around much but I'm happy to help. Say the word."

"Thanks, Seth. I appreciate that."

"I got rounds to make. If you need me," Seth jerked his head toward the back of the building, "My house is back there. Drop by any time."

Drayco watched him move as he always did, like a lumbering bear out the door. What to make of a man like Seth? Arousing pity yet tolerating none. Hardworking, but unable or unwilling to do what it took to hammer out a more productive existence. A man who tried to get help for his son from Social Services, at the same time he's paying for the services of a prostitute for the son. A conundrum dressed in denim coveralls and tan chukka boots.

Although Sheriff Sailor released the crime scene three days ago, Drayco wasn't at the point where he could hire a cleanup crew to remove the bloodstains from the stage floor. Not that he was inclined to do so until the case was solved. Hell, it wasn't as if anyone was going use the place.

The crimson liquid had soaked into the unvarnished wood floor in macabre artistic patterns. Not the type of artwork Randolph Squier would hang on his wall. Darcie on the other hand—she might go for a wilder print, Jackson Pollock or Chagall. He'd gotten the distinct impression at Cypress Manor she'd been bored out of her skull with her husband's hobbies. Perhaps her affair with Oakley was nothing more than a way to banish that boredom.

He toyed with the idea of calling her. For professional purposes, of course, more questioning. He wasn't at all thinking about that tight dress, no sir. He forced himself to concentrate on the bloodstains. Oakley Keys was lured here, murdered here. And the only thing missing after Nanette's murder was a file box concerning this very place—an empty building, save for one mysterious piece of scrimshaw.

18

The early afternoon light should be streaming through the window if it had a chance. But mountains of books were piled throughout Reece Wable's office, where he sat buried up to his black-and-white checkered bowtie reminiscent of a NASCAR souvenir. The panorama of dust-covered spines saturated the air with a musty stench. He wore reading glasses, or glass to be more specific, a reading monocle. Drayco poked his head in the doorway.

Reece groaned in exasperation. "I've been overrun by history. Or at least, a little old lady's collection thereof. You're a detective, find me a way out of here."

Drayco picked up the top book on one pile. Daily Bible meditations. A quick scan of other titles showed more of the same. Well-thumbed religious books, except for one title on garden pests. The only thing that wasn't a dusty book on Reece's desk was a carousel music box peeking out from behind one pile.

Drayco picked up a newspaper from a table near the door and fanned it up and down. "Got a window you can open?"

"I did. Once. It's buried behind the stack of Virginia church history tomes somewhere over there."

"The Historical Society received a gift?"

Reece snorted. "When the late Grace Waterworth's husband said he had a few books of hers he wanted to donate, I said no problem. One of my volunteers let them in while I ran an errand, and I come back to find Mrs. Waterworth apparently saved every book she ever bought. Since childhood. Or before. But hopefully there's a gem or two, and I can sell the rest. All this dust will wreak havoc with my rheumatiz."

He looked hopefully at Drayco. "Tell me you have something interesting to discuss. I need a break from my hardcover hell."

"I have to confess I brought more documents. Should I back out the door and dodge the brickbats?"

Reece stood up and picked his way through the maze. "If it doesn't smell like my granny's old hope chest, it's welcome."

He led Drayco through the hallway toward the reading room where Drayco opened his briefcase and took a whiff. "Aged, but infused with an earthy bouquet. Like a red Bordeaux."

"Ah, a wine aficionado. Were you aware Thomas Jefferson was a wine advisor to several other presidents?"

Drayco laid the briefcase on Reece's work room table and pulled out the contents. "I uncovered these while inspecting the Opera House." He pointed out Konstantina's program. "Here's one I don't think you have."

Reece picked it up, and his eyes widened. "Where did you say you got this?"

"Buried in a cabinet. Why?"

Reece quickly opened the program and leafed through it. "Konstantina Klucze's last concert. My mother attended that event, did I tell you? She went backstage to meet the artist who was gracious despite all she'd been through—and the fact a pipe burst in the Opera House greenroom making it unusable. My mother did say Konstantina was on edge. She wasn't enamored of Konstantina's manager. Had a weird name, musical, like Harmony. Hovered over the artist like a guard dog. Konstantina was complimentary of the people she'd met in the U.S., though. Even said she was going to immigrate to the States."

Reece was close—it wasn't Harmony, but Harmon Ainscough, as Drayco learned from his musicologist friend. Ainscough was one of the possible murderer suspects. There was a falling out, and Konstantina dumped the manager after her American tour.

Looking at all the files and papers around, it occurred to Drayco that if Reece were the one who stole Oakley's Opera House file box, no one would know, its contents lost among the many in Reece's collection.

Drayco pulled out the inscribed tusk. "Do you have any idea where this might have come from originally? It was all cold and lonely in a drawer."

Reece rolled the tusk over and inspected the engravings. "Scrimshaw. Councilman Squier collects these."

"I saw his collection when I had dinner there, but he didn't mention anything missing. It would be interesting to hear him explain how one of his pieces wound up in an empty Opera House."

Reece snapped his fingers. "It must be those burglaries years ago. The authorities never uncovered a who or a why, but the thief didn't take much. Now that you mention it, I think there was something like this tusk thingie. Wait here." He ducked around the corner.

Drayco took the opportunity to say "Hi" to Andrew Jackson, who mumbled, "I'm afraid of banks." More historian inside jokes via Reece's coaching. When Drayco got closer, the bird said, "Drayco sorry." *Is* sorry? *Will* be sorry? He'd never been threatened by a bird before.

Reece bounded back with a newspaper in hand. "The break-ins took place thirty years ago. I checked my index and found this."

Drayco read the article Reece pointed to. A home owned by banker Maxwell Chambliss was burglarized, with two pieces stolen—a gold necklace and a scrimshaw walrus tusk dating from the nineteenth century. The banker's name was one of the hosts who feted Konstantina Klucze in their home after her concert.

"I hate to say it, Reece, but if this tusk is one and the same, it's stolen goods. I should hand it over to the sheriff."

Reece sighed. "If you must. These things sell for thousands of dollars. Chambliss is deceased, meaning his estate that will get it. Who knows? There might be a rare stamp in one of Mrs. Waterworth's books. A consolation prize."

"That could fall under the finders, keepers law." Drayco studied the details of the work table where they were sitting. "This looks handmade." He ran his hand over the elaborate carving of a Scales of Justice. "This wouldn't be one of Oakley's pieces would it?"

Reece tapped his finger under the tabletop. Drayco bent down on one knee and examined the spot Reece pointed out where OK was carved into the wood.

"When Oakley worked here and we were still friends, he made this piece for the society. Took the design from my name, an old German word meaning bailiff. Talented fellow, don't you think? At least at woodworking."

"Did you see any other of Oakley's projects—specifically a wooden mask?"

"A mask? Oakley did adopt some Native American beliefs. I think Nanette hoped it would help Oakley find some peace. Guess it didn't take."

Reece leaned against the table. "I learned of Nanette's death this morning from one of my volunteers. Made me want to go out and get falling-down drunk."

Drayco had passed through the "getting drunk" stage last night after Maida gave him the news. Following the initial shock, Drayco, Maida, and Major shared some of Maida's concoctions that tasted even more potent than usual. "I didn't think you knew her that well, Reece."

"She was beautiful, kind, and loyal. And yes, I'll admit I had a strong crush. She may not have had money like that pretentious alley cat Darcie Squier, but she more than made up for it in class."

Crush indeed. Every time Reece mentioned her name, especially in conjunction with Oakley's, he looked the part of a school geek whose dream prom date whirled off with a dull-witted jock.

Drayco said, "I met with her before her death. She tried to hire me."

"Hire you? I hope she wasn't in any trouble."

"A personal matter. Did Oakley or Nanette mention an unusual letter they received not long after they moved here?"

"We didn't discuss the post office. Except bills. We were both getting more than enough of those. But other than that, nope."

"So Nanette never volunteered here?"

"She was partial to children's charities. I didn't have many opportunities to spend time with her. But we toured the Opera House together once."

"Did Rockingham take you?"

"Councilman Squier played tour guide. We asked Oakley if he wanted to go, but he didn't. Wouldn't say why."

Drayco didn't know which part of that surprised him more. That Squier was familiar enough with the Opera House to play tour guide, that Nanette and Reece were there together, or that Oakley, a man obsessed with the place, turned down an opportunity to explore it. And yet he died there.

Reece touched the edge of Oakley's work table. "I wish I could feel sorry about Oakley's death. But I don't. Between his treatment of Nanette and the clock—"

"Reece, are you certain no one else had an opportunity to steal that clock? I see a pattern of theft here."

"It must have been Oakley. And I'll bet he got a pretty penny for it, too. Guess I'll have to make an exhibit on him now. I'll file it under 'G' for greedy."

Reece's face always held a remarkable sameness of expression, as if injected with a permanent dose of Botox. It was impossible to tell from his features if he'd uttered a startling coincidence or it was a secret jab at Drayco's expense.

Andrew Jackson banged on his cage, and Reece pulled some pellets out his pocket that resembled the bran cereal Drayco loathed and poured them into the bird's feeder. "Everybody thinks Earl Yaegle killed the Keys, but I don't. We get a few tourists and looky-loos stopping on their way from Virginia Beach to Ocean City. Cape Unity's too stagnant to harbor murderous wildlife. I'd bet my money on an outsider."

"That makes for a good story, but it's unlikely, Reece."

Reece countered, "Then I'll bet on Paddy Bakely, the town sot. That's where I'll put my money."

Drayco crossed his arms. "Is there really a betting pool on this?"

Reece smiled inscrutably and tapped his nose with one finger.

Drayco paused to look at the Historical Society's neighbors on his way out of the building. As Maida indicated, they were primarily Victorians in various stages of renovation. One sign marked a weaver's shop, not hard to guess with the colorful assortment of rugs and alpaca-yarn blankets hanging on the porch. Another, a ceramics artist. From watermen to weavers to writers, Cape Unity and the rest of the Eastern Shore were stuck in mid-evolution.

Drayco fingered the Leatherman multi-tool in his pocket. The knife it contained wasn't too different from what sailors once used to make scrimshaw on whaling ships. Why all the interest in scrimshaw? First Squier, now Rockingham's father. Valuable, yes, but Drayco preferred his ivory on top of piano keys. At least, pianos made before the 1950s like the Opera House instrument, before ivory was wisely banned.

"G" is for greedy, Reece? Drayco liked the historian, liked almost everyone he met in town, but maybe that was the trouble. His reasons for coming into town had already crashed and burned around him, and his objectivity was in danger of getting burned in the wreckage.

A flock of Squier's waterfowl flew overhead, but Drayco wasn't listening to their musical honking calls, synchronized with the downbeat of their wings. All he heard were the dark sable-hued timbres of the dissonances.

19

The gazebo needed paint and patching on the Swiss-cheese platform, but it afforded a decent view of the beach. A towheaded family of four braved the cold on bicycles along a path winding through Cape Unity's Powhatan Park. Drayco noted that the father of the cycling foursome detoured his family around a couple of men speaking in Spanish.

Maida pointed toward the area off to their left. "You can't see it from here, but that's in the direction of the Yaegle and Keys properties. There are channels and inlets and a maze of trees nestled in between. You could walk from here to there, but you might get lost if you didn't know your way around. If you were familiar with the area, I'll bet you could do it in fifteen minutes."

This gave the Yaegles, the Keys—and future condo owners— privacy, preventing riffraff from wandering onto their private land. Unless said riffraff were determined, like a murderer with an agenda. Drayco eyed the undergrowth, calculating the potential hazards.

Maida sounded wistful. "It's nice to have more families moving into the area." She pointed to her hair. "Most of our residents have some snow on top. The young blood should invigorate the town."

Drayco had yet to hear the Jepsons mention any family. And no pictures of youngsters at the house. Most likely, Maida wanted to keep the place depersonalized for guests, but it might also mean the Jepsons weren't able to have children, a potentially painful subject. Should he ask?

"You and the Major don't have children?"

Maida gripped the railing of the gazebo. "We had a son. It's a long story and a long time ago, but we're lucky to have terrific nieces and nephews to dote on." She peered at Drayco. "Our son would be near your age."

"At least you didn't have to attend all those kiddy piano recitals."

"Oh, I doubt your recitals were boring, you child prodigy, you."

Drayco gaped at her. "How in the world did you know that?"

"I have a friend who thought your name sounded familiar, so she looked you up. She was impressed. Carnegie Hall at age twelve, soloing with the New York Philharmonic at fourteen."

His father Brock certainly wasn't impressed. Not that Drayco was impressed, himself. It was never about the applause, it was always the music, the need, the craving like a drug to immerse himself in the notes. At times, he wasn't sure in which city he was playing. He showed up, they pointed him toward the piano, and he happily fed his habit.

"I wrote down part of a review my friend found." Maida patted her coat. "Now where is it?" There was a crinkling sound in one pocket, and she triumphantly pulled out a piece of paper. "He plays Beethoven's Appassionata in a more maniacal, furious, and apocalyptic manner than Sviatoslav Richter—I think that's the name, the pianist's name, right?—and yet pulled it off like a seasoned pro."

Drayco remembered that review. He hadn't paid much attention to reviews, but a friend cut that one out and read it to him. He was all of fifteen at the time. And here Maida was, reading it to him again two decades later.

Maida said, "How did you change gears from Mozart to murder?"

A fair question. And Sheriff Sailor and Maida weren't the only ones to ask it. He rubbed his finger along the gazebo railing until the pain from a splinter stopped him. He pulled the splinter out, hoping none was left buried below the top layers of skin. Things buried too deep can fester.

"Musicians are a conduit for the composer. We try to get into the composer's mind, revealing what he was trying to say through the music. In the same way, investigators try to find clues into the mind of a criminal."

"The output of composer versus criminal is sure different."

"True. Yet some criminals are also inordinately proud of their handiwork, almost like their children."

Drayco monitored the cyclists as the older man stopped to tie one child's uncooperative shoe. "Did Oakley have family other than Nanette? The sheriff didn't think so."

"He once told Major he was orphaned and alone. Might be why he was so antisocial." She pulled a pipe and pouch out of another coat pocket and tamped tobacco down in the horn of the pipe before lighting it.

"I didn't know you smoked. I didn't smell it at the Lazy Crab."

"I don't smoke there. Might cause problems for guests with allergies. Only when I'm outside like this."

Drayco watched her take a few puffs, and the aroma of bergamot and citrus wafted in his direction. He said, "My great-aunt told tales of her friend who smoked a corn-cob pipe. Maybe you should try it."

"I think I'll keep roasted corn on the menu where it belongs." She took another puff. "I always loved the way my father smelled when he smoked his pipe. It was a treat to pick out new tobacco for his Christmas present. Tobacco used to be king in Virginia. I heard tell it's only five percent of the crops now."

Maida pointed out two large birds flying overhead with iridescent purple and green feathers, smaller than the geese from earlier. "Grackles. They may be nuisance birds at times, but they're pretty. Sure hate the noisy Fourth of July fireworks. Earl Yaegle's businesses sponsor the annual celebration here at the park. I guess if he's arrested and his businesses go under, they'll have to find money from somebody else. If they can."

Maida ran her gloved hand across the gazebo's lattice work. No splinters for her. "He helped pay for this, too. It makes me fit to be tied thinking he'd have anything to do with Oakley's or Nanette's deaths."

Drayco suggested they walk along the path to warm up in the frosty air, and Maida readily agreed. He wished he'd packed warmer socks, his feet blocks of ice. She was right, though. The park was scenic, despite the chill. Not like his typical concrete-and-asphalt D.C. haunts. Did Oakley and Nanette Keys ever come here? Maybe have a picnic? Oakley didn't seem the type, at least not the later-life Oakley.

He mused aloud, "Oakley, the enigma."

Maida paused to keep from tripping over two black squirrels chasing each other pell-mell across the pathway. "When Oakley and Nanette first moved here, it was exotic to have this young British-accented writer in town. Doesn't seem that long ago, but he would have turned fifty-five in August."

Maida sat in silence for a moment. "Don't think Oakley had the sense God gave a goose, to tell the truth. The curse of the artistic spirit. After all, how many artist-types live miserable lives only to turn out masterpieces?"

"I guess Oakley forgot that last part. Or pickled it in booze along the way."

"And always by his side stood Nanette. I swear she made the Rock of Gibraltar look like a pebble."

Drayco had also pegged her as a graduate of the stand-by-your-man school. Unwilling to leave a bad relationship, tied emotionally to the husband even in the face of assault. He'd stood in morgues beside body bags of women who made that same mistake. "Do you think Oakley hurt her?"

"Nanette never had any bruises I could see. If anything, Oakley went the other way. Neglect."

"Did she travel much? Have friends in other towns, near or far?"

"She was a homebody. I never heard her mention many friends other than co-workers, but I don't think they were close."

They stopped at a small boardwalk area designed to offer a glimpse of an egret or brown pelican. They watched for a few moments in silence, enjoying the panoramic view. Maida craned her neck looking around, telling him to look for pelican nests common in March and April. Not seeing any, she sighed with disappointment.

"With all the new development, you have to wonder if wildlife will adapt."

Maida parted company to head back to the Lazy Crab, leaving Drayco alone. The park was surrounded by thick vegetation, and she said it would be hard to walk from here to the Keys property unless you knew what you were doing. He didn't, but wanted to gauge how hard it would be for a potential murderer. The hiking boots he brought came in handy, with tree stumps, fallen limbs and slick pine needles creating a muddy obstacle course.

True to Maida's word, it wasn't long before he reached an impasse due to a marshy inlet intruding into the forest. With persistence, he was able to navigate around it. After a few more twists and turns, he ended up at the edge of a naked clearing where he came upon the Keys' property. He checked the time. Maida was good. It took him twenty-five minutes, and with practice, he could do it in fifteen, as she'd estimated.

He looked at the ground after he'd walked on it, but no prints among the thick carpet of pine needles, no signs he'd been there. Like the murderer? Since twilight was less than an hour away, he didn't stay long.

Feeling more confident about his path on the return trip, he starting paying attention to the undergrowth. Halfway back he spied a disturbed patch of leaves near a persimmon tree, twisted in a pattern that a skidding shoe might leave behind. He examined the tree and found sections of bark recently shorn off. Someone bracing against a fall?

Drayco bent down and poked his fingers into the wet slime of the decaying organic goo at the base of the tree, avoiding the potential shoe print. His hand brushed against a round, smooth object, and he stopped and pulled a handkerchief from his pocket. The object, protected by a mini-hut of twigs and leaves, turned out to be a pill capsule filled with an orange-red powder. Identical to the one he discovered at the Opera House.

Not far from the spot where he found the capsule, a white triangle peeked out from under a leaf. He grabbed the tip between two fingernails and pulled out a yellowed newspaper clipping, damp and smeared, but legible. It detailed a rumor about Horatio Rockingham selling the Opera House, and in the margins, someone had doodled "b-b" and the words "phonic" and "diabel." This must have dropped from the missing file box. He gingerly tucked both capsule and clipping into the left pocket of his coat.

And then he froze. With a skin-tingling sixth sense, he knew he wasn't alone.

He heard a low, snarling growl, right before something launched itself at him and tore into his right leg. The animal was spotted like a coyote but larger, like a wolf. At this point, he didn't care what the hell it was. He just wanted it off him, so he kicked as hard as he could with his left foot at the animal's head. It worked for a moment, as the beast fell to one side, slightly dazed. Then it roused itself, snarling louder. It was coming back for seconds.

Instinctively, he pulled the Glock out of his shoulder holster and with his first shot, he knew he hit his target. The animal fell still and didn't move again.

Drayco wasn't sure he could get up again easily if he sat down, so he propped his injured leg up on a rock to see how bad it was. Most of the bite chomped down on Drayco's thick boot, but a few teeth broke the skin, the warm blood flowing down into his sock, the ripped pant leg exposing puncture wounds.

Canid attacks on humans were rare, but there was a report of a rabid coyote spotted near Pungoteague last week. He was not looking forward to getting rabies shots. Limping, he headed back to the overlook as seagulls picked their way around the waves in the gathering darkness.

He made it back near the overlook when a rustling in the woods off to his right got his attention. The wax myrtle branches were grouped in dense thickets that blended into a forest of American holly, providing a perfect hiding place. Mindful of the coyote, he pulled out his gun, maneuvering painfully around the brush where he heard the sounds. He stopped to listen. Silence at first, then the unmistakable crunch of a footstep. Heavy-sounding for a coyote. A hunter? Drayco sincerely hoped he wasn't the prey again.

The adrenaline pumped as he prepared for another battle. Instead, the ringing of his cell phone punched an immediate hole in the tense stillness around him. It was Maida, checking on his plans for dinner. When he told her of the attack, she said she'd phone the sheriff's office straight away so animal control could find and test the carcass for rabies.

Gritting his teeth the entire way, Drayco made it safely to the Starfire but continued his watchful eye on the perimeter. The only movements came from the flapping of reproachful birds settling back into their roost in the trees. Using his left leg on the accelerator, the Starfire soon lumbered out of the parking area. At least he could be grateful his sock and boot would keep blood from pooling on the Starfire's floorboard.

The road into town was empty, save for one lone black sedan. It had a tinted windshield which meant either the driver had a medical exemption for tinting or was doing it illegally. Seeing as how it didn't have a required front license plate, Drayco was betting on the latter.

But if someone was following him, he didn't have time to deal with it right now.

20

"You sure you don't want to go to the hospital?"

"No doctors, unless the rabies test on the animal is positive. Besides, Maida did a fine job with her magic poultice." Drayco moved his leg slightly where he had propped it up on a chair. If he took deep breaths, he could ignore the throbbing.

"Suit yourself." Sheriff Sailor's eyes, parked at half-mast above dark circles, were carbon copies from the other day. Add in a toiletry bag in one corner and the smell of a charred coffee pot, and you'd think Sailor lived at the office.

As if two murders weren't enough, a migrant worker looking for a landscaping job wandered onto someone else's private property by mistake and got beaten for trespassing. Since the Keys' deaths, there'd been an increase in people spouting off threats, some motivated by race, others by the developer mess. It was primarily the bar crowd and primarily gun-free. So far.

Sailor examined the scrimshaw tusk now lying on his desk while Drayco placed a photocopy in front of him of the newspaper article Reece dug up. Sailor scanned it. "If this turns out to be the same item stolen in the early '70s, it could have been in that drawer all this time. Any other Easter eggs hiding in your basket?"

"Possibly." Drayco reached into his briefcase and pulled a plastic bag where he'd placed the capsule and clipping from his trek in the woods. "I also found these near a tree where someone took a fall. On the trail between Powhatan Park and the Keys' house where the coyote attacked."

The sheriff sat up straight. "You see anyone?"

"I got the impression a human animal was watching me. A phone call from Maida intervened."

The sheriff picked up the plastic bag and pointed at the newspaper clipping. "Look familiar to you?"

"The handwriting on it resembles Oakley's. I'd hazard a guess it's from the stolen file box. The murderer must have dropped it during his dive."

"Don't suppose you could show Giles that spot you stumbled on?"

"I may not be Daniel Boone, but I think so. Near the tree, there's also the potential for a footprint."

The sheriff rubbed his hands together. "No more Invisible Man. I'll have Giles take a cast. And that's all your Easter eggs, now?"

"Unless you count some old Opera House receipts and concert programs."

"Did any of those receipts have a line item for murder, assassins, weapons?" When Drayco indicated no, the sheriff said, "Damn. I could use a few cut-and-dried clues."

"Hardly any clue is cut-and-dried. Ask any defense attorney. So what's up?"

"Can't trace the bullet or Webley used on Oakley. We tried to match them to guns at Earl's house and shop as well as those in Councilman Squier's collection. That last one was fun. Actually, Squier was cooperative since he and Darcie are vouching for each other's whereabouts during both murders. Like Paddy and Seth. I doubt Yaegle or Squier would have left the murder weapon in plain sight, anyway. Hell, both bullets and gun could have been hiding in a drawer for decades, like that scrimshaw."

"And the red carnation?"

"A garden-variety flower, if you'll pardon the pun. We traced it to the one and only local flower shop. Oakley bought just one the day he was killed. Paid for it in cash. First time he'd set foot in the store."

So Oakley wasn't the flowers-and-candy type of guy. Had he never given Nanette any gifts or remembered her birthday or their anniversary? "Any luck tracking down Oakley's family?"

"Nope. Maybe he was an alien—not the illegal kind, the flying saucer kind."

Drayco picked up a pad of paper and drew a Roswell alien head with large black eyes. He added a caption for his wanted poster, "Have you seen this man?" and pushed it over to the sheriff.

Sailor glared at him. "I got a subpoena for credit card and phone records. No interesting calls, but Oakley charged a few trips to London Heathrow. Only airfare, no lodging. Must have stayed with someone he knew. Those trips ended ten years ago."

"Have you been able to determine if Nanette had a Will, too?"

"It's straightforward. Oakley's the beneficiary unless he preceded her in death. Which of course he did, leaving Nanette's sister in California as next in line. There's considerable optimism among the Gallinger ranks she'll be favorable to the right deal."

Sailor picked up a pencil with a broken lead. "It's been less than a week, but the town council and a few other notable citizens are antsy. Councilman Squier is eager for me to move away from Earl as prime suspect."

The sheriff pushed the tusk around on his desk with the pencil. "Oh, and Deputy Tyler tracked down that city clerk. The one who made the embezzlement accusations ten years ago."

He pushed a button on his intercom. "Nelia, you there?" When there was no answer, he said to Drayco, "Forgot to ask Jake this morning if we'd heard from Norfolk about the DNA. Be right back. If I see Tyler, I'll send her in."

"Before you go, a woman named Grace Waterworth died recently. Did she and her husband have a difficult relationship?"

"Didn't see them together much. But they acted normal enough. Why?"

"I'd be interested to know if there was any weed killer or rat poison in her system."

Sailor scratched his head. "Without probable cause, we can't get an exhumation order."

"I understand. Thought it was worth an ask."

With a last, hard look at Drayco, Sailor withdrew down the hall. He'd only been gone for a minute when Nelia's blonde head popped in the open door. "Hi, there," she said. "Come to check on that fragment?"

"Among other things. I appreciate your help, especially since it may not have anything to do with the murders."

"Over fifty percent of the leg work we do is wasted effort. But you have to cull through the chaff to get to the wheat. Or should I say wheatberry."

"Wheatberry?"

"My mother's on a health food kick. If she hands you one of her green smoothies—run."

Drayco readjusted his leg on the chair, and Nelia went to a file cabinet and pulled out a doughnut-shaped cushion that she propped under his leg. "Sheriff Sailor used this for a while. I don't think he needs it anymore."

"He had a bum leg?"

Nelia coughed, trying to hide a laugh. "'Bum' is the operative word. We don't call him anal-retentive for nothing."

Drayco wrinkled his nose at the cushion. "From his ass to my leg. I don't know whether to feel honored or disgusted." He adjusted his leg a few inches. Much better. "The sheriff said you'd tracked down the clerk with the embezzlement claims?"

"I got the clerk to admit it was Squier who did the embezzling, to the tune of a hundred grand. Unfortunately, the clerk's alleged proof burned along with his house five years ago. We'll see what the city attorney can dig up."

"Five years ago? The same time Oakley wrote that manuscript."

"Uh huh. Curiouser and curiouser."

He missed it the first time they met, but Nelia had a small S-shaped scar at the base of her neck, with the hallmark pink of a newer mark. She hadn't been on duty long enough in Cape Unity to get it there, surely? Not that it detracted from her appearance. "The sheriff told me about your husband and the multiple sclerosis. I was sorry to hear it."

Nelia leaned against a wall, and the light in her eyes dimmed before she looked away. Being a primary caregiver was a soul-sucking task. The physical and emotional demands chipped away at your sanity as slowly as melting ice on a glacier. Perhaps she didn't mind her commuter marriage as much as the sheriff thought?

She replied, "It's a hideous disease. Enough to make anyone bitter and irritable."

She must have realized how that sounded because she quickly backpedaled. "Not that Tim is difficult to live with. He's just—"

"Bitter and irritable." A slow smile worked its way across Drayco's face.

After tilting her head at him, trying to gauge his meaning, Nelia matched Drayco's smile. "Are you an expert on the subject, Mr. Drayco?"

"Irritable, yes. Bitter—depends on what I'm drinking."

Her face broke into a full-fledged grin. "If we need an expert irritability witness for a court case, we'll know where to come."

The sheriff bounded back into the room. "You found her."

"My first real catch of the day."

Sailor glanced from the beaming Nelia to Drayco and back, and he didn't join in the joking. In fact, he didn't look happy at all. "No DNA results back yet. Hopefully, in this lifetime."

Drayco said, "Tyler's having more luck. She filled me in on the clerk and his embezzlement story."

Sailor said, "Tyler pulled several of his teeth to get it out of him. But if we can prove it, it'll put Squier on the barbecue grill."

Nelia laughed. "Now there's an image for you. Grilled pork barrel." She turned to Drayco, "So you've decided to hang around in town a little longer slumming with the locals."

"If I have to slum with the likes of you two, I guess I'll survive."

The sparkle had definitely returned to her eyes, and she was oddly out of breath as she made a beeline for the door. "So nice to have a big-city boy to keep us in line."

Drayco watched her leave. "Have I been insulted?"

"Don't underestimate Tyler, Drayco. She graduated summa at UMD. She's nobody's fool."

Drayco snapped his attention from Nelia's retreating figure back to the sheriff when Sailor added in a low but intense tone. "She's also vulnerable right now, at least where her marriage is concerned. Try not to forget that."

The sheriff added, a little louder, "Speaking of fools, while you were at the Opera House earlier—did you have any more run-ins with our charming Paddy?"

"Not lately. I think I'm beginning to feel slighted."

"Don't be. We released him from jail again Monday. Which is, of course, two days before Nanette Keys was murdered. Puts him squarely on the suspect list for her murder. And it's a paltry list after pinning down alibis for the rest. Even annoyingly convenient ones like the Squiers and the Bakelys."

Drayco shared the sheriff's frustration. After Earl Yaegle, most directly affected by the affair with Nanette and the land sale, they had few other clear-cut candidates. "Reece Wable mentioned Paddy as a potential suspect since he's out of it half the time. But it's a weak motive. Didn't you say Paddy's record only includes minor assaults, the barroom brawl type?"

"Some of those brawls included knives."

"It would be easy for him to gain access to the Opera House. Think he could stay sober long enough to shoot straight?"

"If he got in a lucky shot, maybe. And he's strong enough to strangle Nanette. But where's his motive for that? Nanette was the one person who was kind to him."

They were also running out of motives, except for increasingly less pleasant ones. "Was there evidence of rape in Nanette's case?"

"The M.E. didn't find any telltale signs. She wasn't able to put up much of a fight. But she wasn't a muscular woman. No signs of blood or skin under her nails to indicate she tried to scratch the murderer."

"Any signs she was drugged first? That would make it easier for a small-framed person to strangle her."

"Like a woman, you mean. Darcie Squier, the woman scorned."

"Drugging would make it easier for a smaller man to strangle her, too."

"The basic tox screen was negative. Since cause of death was ruled suffocation, the M.E.'s office didn't see the need for a confirmatory test. They've got other corpses lined up, anyway, so we're lucky we got that much."

"Out of curiosity, what was Paddy in for this time?"

"Drunkenness, another fight. Seth keeps bailing him out every time. Should let Paddy rot in there a while."

Yeah, some tough love might not hurt. Or better yet, an enforced vacation to a rehab center. "After chatting with Reece Wable, I'm getting the impression Nanette was Paddy's opposite. Close to sainthood if you overlook her one brief indiscretion with Earl. Loyal through Oakley's many affairs. No disagreements with anyone. Except her husband."

The sheriff pointed to a stack of interview transcripts. "Maybe she murdered Oakley after she'd had enough of his behavior. Shot him in a fit of passion. Of course, she couldn't have strangled herself."

"A secret lover other than Earl? One who killed Nanette when she learned he was behind Oakley's death? Or when she refused his further advances." Reece would be at the head of the line for that, Drayco had to admit. His not-so-secret obsession with her, the missing file box, the same intellectual curiosity she'd once shared with Oakley.

Sailor said, "Again, we've uncovered no such evidence. You don't believe either of those possibilities, do you?"

"I didn't spend much time with Nanette the day she died, but I'd bet a large sum of money against the secret-lover scenario. Guess I'll have to join Reece's pool."

The sheriff blinked three times. "Pool?"

"An office betting pool, or town pool, I suspect, on the murderer. Or it may be Reece's little joke. Regardless, I think most townsfolk have their money on Earl Yaegle. Earl himself thinks you're going to arrest him at any moment."

"You saw Earl?"

"I wanted to take a look at the Keys' property and wandered across the Yaegle border."

"Did he threaten you?"

"It started to rain, and he invited me into his house." Drayco didn't mention the rifle incident as he couldn't blame Yaegle for being on edge and wanting to defend himself. And it wasn't the same make of weapon as the one that killed Oakley.

Sheriff Sailor pushed the stack of papers aside. "Huh. You must have a sympathetic face."

"He did mention his affair with Nanette."

"So you do have a sympathetic face. Spill."

"He said it was a decade ago when he was having financial troubles and Nanette was depressed over Oakley's drinking, but it only lasted a few months. It's possible Earl's wife Tabitha suspected, although Earl wasn't sure. It was never discussed between the Yaegles or Keys."

"Or so Yaegle says."

"Unlike everyone else, I'm not ready to pin Nanette's murder on Yaegle."

"Another gut feeling?"

The sheriff's mocking tone barely contained the acerbic layer underneath. He and Drayco had done well so far, but Drayco was one clash away from causing an ulcer in Sailor's patience. He'd adapted to working alone, wandering the investigative wilderness, going off trail with his wild theories. But Sailor, like his namesake, imbibed the Hemingway Code like a man thirsting for a cold martini on a hot day. Drayco kept his voice light. "Not so much gut feeling as crunches. Keeps the gut in working order."

"So that's the secret. Here I thought you have ESP."

Drayco tapped his briefcase. "I keep a crystal ball in here. It says Sheriff Ernest Hemingway Sailor murdered both Oakley and Nanette Keys. Having read all the books in the local library, he was thoroughly bored and needed a diversion."

The sheriff picked up a small rubber fish he used as a paperweight and threw it in Drayco's direction, barely missing his head. "Reece Wable's rubbing off on you. Get out of here, you interloper."

Drayco got the impression Sailor was only half-joking.

21

Drayco spent the evening resting at the Jepson's but got only three hours of sleep, thanks to the painful leg. After popping four ibuprofen, he headed down to the pier for Maida's much-touted sunrise extravaganza, but the skies were cloudy. Again. How did people in the Arctic Circle—the Inuit, northern Finns and Swedes—manage to keep their sanity through months of darkness? He'd take the hot sun on a Bermuda beach any day.

The air always felt different along the coast. Humidity, or the S-trio of salt, sand, and sea. The light appeared different, too. Although there wasn't enough sunshine lately to illuminate town treasures like the Aquia sandstone building in front of him where he'd headed after the pier. Inscribed in green marble above the entrance were the Latin words *In Spiritu et Veritate*. He ducked through the large wooden doors with stained-glass panels and sought out the office with the name Randolph Squier in large gold script.

The secretary and source of Darcie's gossip, Adah Karbowski, picked at the eyeglasses on a chain around her neck. But as soon as she spied Drayco, her eyes darted around the office before she popped the glasses back on. She pasted on a smile and seemed to go out of her way to be friendly and accommodating as she chirped, "You're early. Down the hall, first door on the right."

Drayco limped in the direction she'd indicated and reached his hand out to open the door, but the sound of agitated voices made him step back. Squier wasn't alone. Spying a tall bookshelf at the end of the hall, he hid on the other side and waited. Moments later, Paddy Bakely stormed out of the office and left down a different corridor. Another way into the building, which could explain why Adah hadn't known Paddy was here. Unless she did know and wanted Drayco to walk in on them. But why? Drayco needed to come back another time and interview the secretary when the councilman was out.

Drayco waited two minutes before heading into the office. No paintings lined the stark white walls above minimal furniture although the pricey filing cabinets and executive desk would be at home on Madison Avenue. Even the oxblood leather chairs smelled expensive. Squier apparently wanted to give the air of tax money stewardship but wasn't able to resist trappings of the same luxury pervading Cypress Manor. Drayco assessed the leather chairs. Did the townspeople know how much of their tax money those cost?

Squier was dressed in his usual tailored suit, but more rumpled, less starched. Gone was the accommodating host from Cypress Manor, replaced by an unsmiling man as rigid as a statue. But not as welcoming. He still had the drawl, but it was less caramel and more Campari bitters. "You weren't specific why you wanted to see me, Mr. Drayco."

"Councilman, Reece Wable told me you gave him and Nanette Keys a tour of the Opera House once."

"Mr. Rockingham loaned me a key. He thought it might be prudent for someone else to have one in case of an emergency."

"Do you still have it?"

Squier's posture grew so rigid, if he were a bridge beam, he might snap in two. "Are you inferring I might have used that key recently? That I was complicit in Oakley's murder?"

"Inferring? No. Not implying, either, although you have to admit, it looks suspicious you haven't told the sheriff about the key."

"I simply forgot the damned key, as I haven't used it in a long time. When I find it, I'll have my secretary courier it over to the sheriff. You can pick it up from him."

Was it only a few short days ago Squier bent over backward to send documents to Drayco? "You must be familiar with the Opera House, Councilman, to feel comfortable giving tours."

"I did my best, poor though it was." Squier approached his chair twice as if to sit, but backed off each time. Maps and aerial photographs lay sprawled on Squier's desk, and Drayco moved to take a closer look. They covered the Cape Unity area and most of Prince of Wales County.

Drayco pointed to the spot he believed the Keys and Yaegle properties were located. "Is that where the future condos are planned?"

"The Keys boundary line is here." Squier jabbed his finger at a yellow divider. "And the Yaegle property goes to this point."

"These surrounding parcels—like this undeveloped land to the north. I'm surprised it wasn't included in Gallinger's plans. Surely other neighboring landowners are affected?"

Squier coughed, making a theatrical production out of grabbing a wad of tissues from his pocket. For now, Drayco allowed him his stalling tactic, beginning to suspect why the man was nervous.

The councilman finally replied, "The Yaegle and Keys properties are all Gallinger is interested in." He gestured behind Drayco. "You can see an artist's rendering of what the finished product will look like, right there."

As Drayco moved toward the framed blueprints on the wall, Squier added, "Compare the two aerial photographs to your left. One is from Cape Unity forty years ago, and the other is more recent. Not much different, are they?"

In fact, they weren't. If not for shoreline erosion and the addition of a few structures, they could be identical. Drayco turned around and noticed Squier had picked up a box from the floor and placed it over the maps and photos on his desk, covering them. Covering up more than photos?

"That is why we need this project, Mr. Drayco. Without an increased tax base, the town will die. Roads don't pave themselves. There are more students in need of school buildings, the illegals eat us alive in social services costs. We may have to cut the sheriff's budget."

Squier didn't answer Drayco's question about the land ownership. Squier was also sweating, even as his chirpy secretary thought it cold enough to wear a heavy jacket over her wool pantsuit in the outer office. Drayco prodded him again, "And once the condo project is built, it's only natural more construction will follow. Perhaps on the virgin plot of land to the north?"

Squier glowered at the now-hidden papers. "Gallinger hasn't discussed anything else yet."

Drayco put on his best gauntlet smile. "Cape Unity can dig itself out of the hole. I read about one small town in Maryland where an official embezzled thousands from city accounts. Yet that same town bounced back with a budget surplus after they lured a new resort to the area. Pity about that employee. He was sentenced to ten years."

Squier's jaw hung open, and he snapped it back with an audible click. As he sank into his chair, he was like a trawler setting down anchor as a refuge from a storm, and his face clouded with dark tempests. "You're new in town, Mr. Drayco, and don't have a feel for how we do things around here. I think you'll find we're not the small town emasculated hicks you believe us to be. There has been talk on the council of taking the Opera House forcibly through eminent domain."

"Has there, now?" Such an action would save Drayco the worry of having to deal with the building, and he could walk away as he'd yearned to do when he first learned of Rockingham's bizarre bequest. Yet there wasn't a chance in hell he'd let Squier get his hands on the Opera House without a fight. More and more, Drayco was seeing how quickly Squier lost his gentlemanly charm and speech patterns once the Southern dandy gloves came off.

The corners of Squier's lips curled upward forming a half-moon, and he tented his fingers together. "We don't take kindly to interference with our plans for progress. As I'm sure you wouldn't want me interfering in your little consulting business."

Sheriff Sailor mentioned Squier's network of influential contacts throughout the Mid-Atlantic via those "Mayflower roots" Squier bragged about. A few ethics complaints, unfounded or not, and Drayco's client list might dry up. The law enforcement agencies he often worked with might think twice about hiring him. It was a threat that had some teeth.

The intercom on Squier's desk buzzed, followed by Adah's disembodied and distorted voice, "I hate to interrupt Councilman, but your wife Darcie called to tell you she's on her way."

At the mention of Darcie's name, Squier jumped up and strode toward the door. "We can discuss these matters another time." But the evil eye he directed toward Drayco indicated he'd prefer Drayco vanished. Permanently.

Drayco obliged with the vanishing part and headed toward the door, adding right before he left, "*In Spiritu et Veritate.*"

Squier sputtered, "What the devil do you mean?"

"In spirit and truth. It's on the front of your building."

22

This was one building likely to dodge the wrecking ball. Officially called the Fiddler's Green Tavern, Maida referred to it as the Ole Trunk and Drunk. Patrons filled up their cars with cases of brown ale and amber pilsner before carting them home, presumably to drown their sorrows. If you wanted immediate intemperance, you could sit inside on one of the barstools. Or the handy tables near the john.

Drayco liked the smell of places like this, the aromatic cocktail of wood, dust, and whiskey serving up an unapologetic embrace of life's indulgences. A photo on the wall taken years ago showed the original sign boasting *House of Spirits*. The building dated back to 1880, the only commercial structure in town older than the Opera House. A few flirtations with fire and hurricanes necessitated changes, but it stood mostly as it had since the first thirsty customers staggered weak-kneed through its doors. The wide-plank flooring and ship figureheads carved in mermaid shapes were all rescued from local shore wrecks.

Maida had asked Drayco if he'd mind picking up some red wine for another of her famous after-dinner toddies. Drayco paid for his purchase and headed toward the door when a familiar marmalade voice called his name. He circled to the back and found himself in the presence of none other than Paddy Bakely, looking forlorn in a tattered coat and grease-stained shirt. Halfway between sober and soused, Paddy observed Drayco with watery eyes moderately engaged in reality.

"You're the Opera House guy." This was an about-face from Paddy's actions at the courthouse. So far. Drayco waited for a new tirade, but Paddy took another sip of his beer. "Oakley broke in there once. Into the Opera House."

A revelation from a drunk was hardly a solid-gold tip you could take to the bank. And Paddy was probably a fair liar when he drank, but this was too intriguing to let go. "Why did he break in?" Drayco asked.

"It's all about birthright," Paddy said, in an unsteady voice. "Birthright and lust." He grabbed Drayco's collar, pulling Drayco closer to Paddy's face where he was blasted with a strong odor of malt. Paddy added in a whisper, "Beware the sins of the father shall be visited upon the sons." He laughed hoarsely. "Or is it the mothers?"

He released Drayco's coat and sat staring vacantly into his beer mug. Drayco looked over at the proprietor who shrugged and said, "Paddy's here a lot, but you can never be sure where he really is if you know what I mean."

"Hello again, Mr. Drayco. Back to see if we have any new guns?" Like last time, Randy the gun shop manager was red-faced and out of breath.

Joel, sweeping the floor, scowled in Drayco's direction. "Doubt a guy like him is here to window shop."

Drayco picked up a pistol, weighed it in his hand and wrapped his fingers around the grip. Lightweight, but capable of pumping several rounds into the heart. The smoothness of the gun was similar to the satiny feel of the piano keys beneath his fingers. He remarked as such to his former fiancée, who was horrified the same fingers that created beautiful music were capable of squeezing the trigger on an instrument of death.

Drayco said. "Following up on a few things. For instance, I'm guessing you don't carry any Webleys?"

Randy cocked his head. "Sheriff Sailor asked that. We have a few antiques, nothing like that. Mostly American, not British."

"Any other stores in the area that might?"

Randy stroked his chin as he thought. "Can't say for sure, but I don't think so. There was one in Accomack County that sold antiques, same WWII vintage—Lugers, Glisentis, Enfields, Tokarevs, Nambus—but it went out of business. The closest ones now are up in Maryland or down in Norfolk."

He perked up. "You helping the sheriff find out who killed the Keys?"

"I have an interest in the case since they were clients of mine."

Joel narrowed his eyes. "Clients of yours? I thought your arrival in town was too coincidental. That's when everything went tits-up. It's got something to do with Earl, don't it?"

Randy didn't look convinced. "It's not Earl, Joel. Somebody new to town. Or two somebodies." He leaned toward Drayco conspiratorially. "I heard from one of the ambulance drivers that Nanette wasn't shot. Strangled. Now why in the world would the same guy kill two different people two different ways?"

"Okay," Joel said. "So there were two strangers involved. Working together."

Randy offered a derisive laugh. "I thought you were blaming Earl for the murders."

Joel propped himself against the case next to Drayco. "I did see him and Nanette Keys in a non-neighborly embrace once when I dropped off some parts at Earl's house."

Randy picked up a gun from a case and pointed it at Earl and pulled the trigger. He said, "Bang bang," and laid the unloaded gun back down. "Things aren't always what they seem, Joel."

Joel's wide eyes again shuttered into slits. "Day after Oakley's murder, deputies were all over this gun shop, snooping around, digging in the trash. They carried off something, too. What do you think about that?"

Randy coughed once, loudly. "I think if you want to be a manager some day, you'd better be more careful when talking about your boss."

"Guess I'm more interested in truth than you are."

If the sheriff hadn't told Drayco that Joel had an airtight alibi for the night of Oakley's murder, he'd have entertained the notion Joel killed Oakley to frame his boss. Everywhere he went in Cape Unity, Drayco encountered divisions with tension spreading out like aftershocks of an earthquake. Perhaps the negative energy was simmering for a long time and the murders brought it to the fore. Maybe it was time the town changed its name because unified it most certainly was not.

There was a heavy silence until Randy broke the impasse. "We should all go to that town meeting tonight. They're going to discuss the new development. Joel and I need to put our two cents in before more new stores come in and run us out of business."

This must be the same meeting the sheriff mentioned. Might be a good chance to take the town's temperature. Drayco said, "I'll see you there. Is Earl here somewhere?"

Joel surprised Drayco when he pointed out the door to the adjacent shooting range. Drayco could catch Earl in his natural business habitat for a change. Maybe Joel was the original source of gossip about Earl and Nanette's affair, maybe not, but the news had spread far and wide now. Reason enough for Earl to hide away inside his house. But here Earl was, wearing ear protectors, and pointing a Smith and Wesson at a human-silhouette target. He looked over at Drayco, then back at the target, and shot a neat hole right in the center of the target's forehead.

The local newspaper article on Oakley's murder said he was shot—but not where in the body he was hit. "You always aim for the head?" Drayco asked.

Yaegle took off the protectors. "An easy kill, if done right. A nice shot to have in your repertory." He handed the gun over to Drayco. "Three rounds left. You game?"

Drayco grabbed a set of ear protectors and took the gun from Yaegle. He peeled off all three rounds in rapid succession, crack, crack, crack. Yaegle stared at the target where the holes from all three rounds were clustered over the X in the center, a new respect in his eyes. "Left over from your G-man days?"

"I try to stay in shape." Drayco handed the gear back to Yaegle. "But targets aren't the same as real life."

"Look, you're welcome to practice all you want, but I told you I'm not answering any questions without a lawyer."

Drayco squinted at the target. He'd done better. "I've decided I might like to join that hunting club of yours. Squier belongs to it, doesn't he?"

Yaegle nodded. "And other faithful members, none you'd know. Major Jepson, from time to time."

"I had dinner with Squier the other day. Amazing gun collection. Obsessive-compulsive in scope."

"Obsessive?" Yaegle placed his hands on his hips. "As a boy, he watched his father get beaten during a robbery at his family's drugstore. The punks weren't caught, people didn't shop there anymore, and it went bankrupt. If Randolph's father had a gun, things might have turned out different."

Bankrupt? That was a long climb back uphill to Cypress Manor. And how much of that climb was legal? "Looks like Squier has made up for it. Money, success, property. Does he own a lot of real estate?"

"After he rebuilt his father's old business years later, he was able to sell it for a huge profit. He's a wiser investor than I am. Said something not long ago about a big property purchase. Joked it was for another house to hold all of Darcie's clothes."

"When you sell your land, the condo project might raise property values all around. His, too."

Yaegle still had the gun in hand, and his index finger slid up and down the barrel. It paused on the trigger, making Drayco glad Yaegle had emptied the thing. "I don't like where this is headed. You enjoy going after an innocent man, do you? No wonder Squier told me to stay away from you."

"Are you that certain Squier isn't guilty?"

Earl didn't answer, but he didn't repeat his Squier-is-innocent claim, either.

"Truthfully, Earl, I'd rather not catch the bad guy at all than put someone innocent behind bars."

Yaegle's index finger stilled. "Can't think of any more ways to say I'm innocent. I should hire you to prove it."

By the bear-trap clamp of Earl's jaw, Drayco could tell he was serious. "I'm already representing two innocent people who happen to be dead. Not sure you'd like those odds. Besides, hiring me wouldn't change the way I investigate the truth."

Yaegle regarded him for a moment. "Guess I'll have to hope you're good at what you do."

Randy poked his head inside the range and shouted, "Hey, Earl, hate to bother you, but our supplier for the Winchester 12-gauges still can't find out where our shipment went. Squier is getting antsier by the hour."

Yaegle fiddled with the empty gun. "I'll deal with it."

"Thank you, oh fearless leader." Randy stopped to glance at the target, his eyes wide, before heading back to the shop.

Yaegle stowed the gun in a drawer and fixed Drayco with a stare. "Next time, we'll see how you do on the expert course."

Drayco watched him follow Randy, then stood there, musing. Oakley's shooter was expert enough to take out Oakley with a shot to the head at the same distance Earl stood from the target. But why a Webley when Earl had access to newer guns? Squier, too, for that matter. Was the gun choice a calculated redirection or symbolic? One of the many conundrum entrées piling up on Drayco's plate. He looked at the target again, with the bullet hole in its head, and had the oddest feeling it was laughing at him.

23

As darkness fell, so did the rain, with the deluge transforming Cape Unity's streets into rivers and its parking lots into lakes. Drayco picked his way from one parking-lot island to another, but his foot slipped, and he stepped in water up to his ankles. He paused to let the wave of pain from his injured leg pass. At least the pain was more *mezzo-forte* than *fortissimo* now.

He was glad to reach the shelter of the courthouse which looked less drab at night. The interior's fluorescent tube lighting turned the gray into sapphire, although it made the clothing on hundreds of people packed into the courtroom for the town meeting look like a sea of blueberries.

A woman he didn't know, but who recognized him, marched up and pumped his hand. "I want to tell you how thrilled we are about the Opera House. I have six kids, and it's all Nintendo and Spiderman. We need culture. And jobs. My oldest is sixteen and where's he going to work, the Seafood Hut? That's why I came. To make sure it's not the anti-everything mob."

Drayco thanked her and extricated himself as politely as he could. He arrived late, hoping to sneak in and keep a low profile. Waiting a few more minutes wouldn't hurt, so he ducked into a dark, empty alcove near a *Staff Only* door, which gave him a hidden vantage point to watch the people as they poured in. It was also, as it turned out, the door where Randolph Squier made his entrance, his voice dialed down to a low rumble.

Squier turned to a companion Drayco recognized as another town councilman, Calvin Grully, and said, "This will be such a horrid, pointless affair. Townsfolk venting their same petty little grievances like they always do and expecting us to care. It makes one so. ... what's the word? So vacuous. Yes, I'm sure that's it, vacuous."

The other councilman paused a beat or two, then replied, "I, uh, yes. I imagine you're right."

From his shadowed alcove, Drayco saw the two men in profile— Squier with his monolithic jutting chin, the other councilman with his head down, fiddling with his coat buttons. Squier was a lot more "vacuous" than he thought. And what happened to all those "good citizens" Squier had bragged about? Now they were just vassals with "petty little grievances?"

The second councilman said, "You don't think they'll drag that murder business in?"

"They will drag it in with flags and a marching band." Squier huffed. "Those murders are a warning, Cal, signs of a community plague out of control. The transients, the day laborers, those Mexicans multiplying like rabbits. A filthy plague, that's what it is."

"What about Yaegle? A lot of people are blaming Yaegle."

"The murderer is most certainly not Earl Yaegle, as that unimaginative sheriff thinks. Sailor will be up for reelection in two years. I think we should consider running our own candidate against him."

Cal Grully tugged one of his coat buttons too hard, and it popped off. "That investigator fellow from D.C.'s been asking a lot of questions. Making people nervous."

"You leave him to me, Cal. I'll make quite sure he doesn't interfere with our plans."

Squier's voice trailed off as they walked away, and Drayco waited until the pair entered the courtroom before he peeked inside. It wasn't a huge room and barely big enough to hold the SRO crowd. The object of Squier's scorn, the tired-looking sheriff, stood in one corner with his arms folded over his chest. In the opposite corner, he spied Nelia Tyler, who waved at him.

As he made his way inside, he passed a few other familiar faces including Joel from the gun shop, with bloodshot eyes and smelling of turpentine. He'd either been painting or drinking some bathtub gin.

A hand gesturing in Drayco's left field of view got his attention. Tracing the hand to Reece Wable, who was leaning against a back wall, he walked over to join him. "Hello, Reece. Here to document this bit of local history?"

"Oh, there'll be a write-up in the paper tomorrow that I'll add to the files. And I can get a transcript of the speakers from Inez over there. I'm here for the entertainment value. It's better than SmackDown wrestling. And free."

Drayco took in Reece's dapper-as-usual getup, a neon green shirt and brown velveteen blazer. "I don't see your flak jacket."

"An oversight. We'll all need armor before the night's over. Oh, and I heard about your fun little incident. Have you had your rabies shots yet? In case you bite."

"I promise I'll bark out a warning beforehand."

Drayco trolled the sea of angry faces, many people already lining up in front of microphones. Sleepy beach town or crime-ridden city, it was the same—the desire to protect their culture, their way of life from change, from the unknown.

Not too long ago, the audience would be all white-bread. More ethnic variety was sprinkled in now, more than Squier wanted to acknowledge—Indian naan, Arabic pita, and Mexican tortilla. Drayco recalled his "melting pot" thought about Darcie and Tangier. What was up with the food metaphors? He must be hungry.

Up at the podium, Councilman Squier handled ringmaster duties that were ordinarily the realm of the mayor, recuperating from bypass surgery. Squier was a man accustomed to being in control of his little sphere. Despite his arrogant comments to the other councilman, his hands were sweating as he gripped the stand, his words a robotic monotone. He'd opted for a more casual getup, slacks minus the suit coat. If it was to show solidarity with the common folk, it was unfortunate his bow tie was crooked.

Reece whispered to Drayco. "Oakley made a fool out of Squier in a meeting like this. Pointed out errors in an article Squier wrote for a state publication. Most people can't tell it, but Squier has serious self-esteem issues. Especially when it comes to his intelligence. I don't think he forgave Oakley."

Drayco wished he had a magazine to fan himself, the cumulative heat from all those ninety-eight-point-sixes and the dry, heated building air beginning to get to him. The attendees were split between anti- and pro-camps, and both bandied around the name Gallinger as a rallying cry. If this microcosm couldn't agree, how could the entire town?

It wasn't long before any initial attempt at polite discourse degenerated into shouting, both factions blaming all the town's problems and the murders on each other. And a few blamed Drayco. If he'd hoped to hear anything helpful from the crowd about the Keys or the murders, he might as well have gone to the local kindergarten and asked the kids—he'd have learned more from them.

The Jepsons wisely decided not to join Drayco tonight. Thoughts of a peaceful evening at the Lazy Crab sounded good right now, along with some dry socks. Since Sheriff Sailor and Nelia had this circus in hand and Drayco found himself again a potential distraction, he excused himself to Reece. Hurrying back to the car didn't keep him from getting drenched in the nonstop rain.

He climbed into the Starfire and pulled out his keys. The rain cascaded in sheets so dense that he couldn't see out any of the windows, like being inside a tin drum. But the sound of loud tapping on the passenger window got his attention. It was like his most recent nightmare; only this was real. He reached over and thrust open the door, and a woman hopped in, slamming the door behind her. Darcie Squier combed her hair back with her fingers and kicked off her shoes. As if thumbing her nose at the chilly weather, her insubstantial sandals accompanied a miniskirt that set off her shapely legs.

"I followed you," she said. "Good idea to get out of there early. Who knows how long that hatefest will go on."

"You've been keeping track of the development issue?" It was hard to believe Darcie was civics-minded, more tabloid journalist than a Rachel Carson.

"Oh, I'm all for it. This place is too provincial. It may never be New York, but at least I won't have to drive hours for a decent dress." She grinned at him. "Or bra."

Not so much a social conscience, then, as a fashion ethic. Drayco wasn't a fashion expert, but he could tell when clothes were expensive, and hers were. How many days must it have taken Squier to work off that diamond necklace Darcie wore? Maybe she cared for him deep down, or perhaps men were all a game to her. Or the money simply mattered more.

"You shouldn't be seen palling around with a detective. You being a suspect and all."

She stuck out her tongue at him. "Here I am flirting with you and you have to bring that up."

"And what about your husband, Darcie? Think he'd be happy to know where you are right now?"

As she slowly combed her fingers through her hair, she cast a furtive glance at the courthouse. "He's too busy playing the big man to see what I do. Besides, I'm just having a nice chat with a new friend. All very innocent. Even if the new friend happens to be sexy as hell."

She was trying to bait him, and her efforts at distracting him were working a little too well. "Let's talk about Oakley Keys. He was a friend of yours, too. His name came up several times tonight."

Darcie picked at a loose thread on the leather trim. "It was horrible how they kept dragging his name through the dirt. Like road kill. I don't appreciate my friends being treated that way. Or murdered."

"You're not ready to turn yourself in as his murderer?"

"Only to you. But they should be arresting Earl Yaegle any minute. Haven't you pinned it on him yet?"

"You mean that he's the love child of Lizzie Borden and Jack the Ripper?"

She ignored his sarcasm and persisted. "I hoped you'd have more details on how Earl did it."

"You're the one who's tuned in to all the gossip. I have a feeling when an arrest is made, you'll be the first to know."

Any disappointment Darcie felt was hidden as she used the rearview mirror to check her makeup. "Oakley called me an incorrigible gossip. I had to ask him what incorrigible meant."

Incorrigible—hopeless, incurable, unreformed. That pretty much covered it. "Did Oakley talk about himself, Darcie? His past, his family?"

"One Mother's Day, he mentioned his mother, that she'd been good to him. He did say her name was O'something. Something Irish. O'Hannon, I think that's it. But that was as personal as he got. At least, with details of his life."

This time, she gave him that Abyssinian when-you-least-expect-it-I'm-going-to-pounce look. Drayco shifted in his seat, focusing instead on what Darcie had said. Oakley had a mother as recently as a few years ago? Major Jepson said he was an orphan.

Drayco asked, "Was Oakley enough of a friend to consider putting you in his Will?"

"You kidding? He was flat-broke. That whole thing with the development money came after we'd parted company." She uncrossed her legs, and the seductive smile on her face and roving eyes made him feel like he'd already been stripped naked.

She added, "You can put me in your Will. Maybe I'll be Mrs. Darcie Drayco by then. Doesn't that have a nice ring?"

Each time Drayco was with Darcie, his defenses slipped a degree further. The way her honey-hazel eyes let fly with stings of passion was like looking directly at a photo of his former fiancée, whose Russian temperament matched those passionate eyes. She even used a similar perfume, with a hint of jasmine.

Drayco massaged his right arm out of habit, and Darcie noticed. She said, "Let me see what a pianist's hands look like," and scooted closer, placing her palms under his wrists. She pulled his hands down until they were resting in his lap and traced the outlines. "Strong hands. And long fingers."

"How did you find out I play the piano?"

"I have my sources. I want to learn everything about you."

He didn't pull his hands away. He should, but he didn't. She wasn't making it easy for him to abide by his cardinal rule of staying away from married women. He also understood what the sheriff meant by saying Darcie wasn't secretive abou her relationship with Oakley, sitting as she was in Drayco's car behind a public town meeting.

He sensed she was on a fishing expedition. But for what? He had hints of that same feeling from his meeting with Nanette the day she was killed. "Were you friends with Oakley's wife, Nanette?"

She didn't take her eyes off his hands. "Hardly. Doesn't mean I murdered her. What would be the point with Oakley dead?"

"The point? If your husband had a financial stake in the condos, he'd lose it all if the development didn't go through. With Nanette out of the way, the project's a done deal. Gallinger can wait patiently, a vulture hovering over that road kill of yours."

For a split second, he caught a glimpse of worry passing across her face before she said, "You do like to spoil a mood, don't you? I honestly don't keep up with how my husband gets his money. I just spend it."

The rain died down enough to part the curtain of water off the windshield. A few people exited the courthouse, and Darcie tensed. "I have to leave now. I should try to keep up appearances." She squeezed his hands one last time and reluctantly let go.

She opened the door and as she left, adding, "If you want to do some in-depth exploring, I'll give you a long, detailed tour. I'm sure you'd find it stimulating."

He rubbed his arm again, the soft touch of her hands lingering on his skin. For the first time since Darcie entered, he was aware of his cold, wet feet. Dry socks now and a treatise on the wiles and treachery of married women, or at least this married woman, tomorrow.

24

A typical morning in D.C. might find Drayco out for a run along the Tidal Basin. They didn't call the area Foggy Bottom for nothing—every now and then a fog would settle in thick enough to cloak the Jefferson Memorial. This morning had that same air, white vapor settling on Cape Unity pines like angel hair swirled around a Christmas tree, partially obscuring the Yaegle house from Drayco's view.

"Both Squier and my lawyer told me not to talk to you anymore." Yaegle thrust his hands into the pockets of his fraying wool plaid jacket. The forecast for temps ten degrees below normal were spot-on, and trees behind Yaegle's house did little to brace against the chilly, damp air.

"And yet here I am, at your behest, not mine."

Yaegle rubbed his forehead. "I thought over some of the things you said last time. Besides, don't think I want to cross someone who shoots like you do."

Drayco walked with Yaegle along a sandy walk imbedded with thousands of tiny seashell fragments down to a small dock. Earl stooped to pick up an intact shell he rolled around in his hand. "The money'll be welcome, but I'll miss the place. It may not be as grand as Cypress Manor, but it's been a good home."

Drayco inspected the shell in Yaegle's hand. It was a knobbed whelk, shaped like the carousel on Reece's desk. Or a circus tent. Either was appropriate for Earl's situation. Drayco asked, "Will you stay in Cape Unity?"

Earl rested his arms on the dock railing with his shoulders sagging, making him look more seventy than fifty. "If I'm arrested, I'll have no choice."

"And if you're not?"

"Depends on my businesses. Hell, I should buy one of those new condos myself." Yaegle laughed briefly. "If they get built."

Despite what Drayco overheard at the courthouse, he had a feeling it was all but a done deal, barring a tsunami or a meltdown at the Calvert Cliffs Nuclear Power Plant across the Bay. "You weren't at the town meeting. At least, in person. Your name was mentioned quite a bit."

Yaegle snorted. "Didn't think they needed a lightning rod in their midst. But I hear tell they set off some fireworks without me." He looked at the rhinestone beads of water forming on Drayco's coat. "Why don't we go inside? I'll try to burn some more soup like the last time you were here."

Maybe not soup, but he did offer Drayco a steaming cup of black coffee he gratefully accepted, salt or no salt, and took a seat near the fireplace. The eastern red cedar kindling from Earl's property was pungent, but the loud popping made Drayco jumpy. It sounded too much like gunfire.

Earl threw a couple more logs into the fire and grabbed a loose-leaf stack of papers. At first, Drayco thought he was going to throw them in the fire, too, but instead, he thrust the papers into Drayco's hands. "I want you to have this."

The author's name on the title page was Oakley Keys. Like Nanette said, Oakley was a true Luddite—no CDs, no computers, and this undated manuscript was typed on an old manual typewriter. Sheriff Sailor had said they found a vintage Royal Quiet De Luxe in the Keys' home.

"Was this published?" Drayco asked.

"It's out of print now. Take a look at the index page."

Drayco flipped over to the spot. Oakley's handwriting leaned to the left and was small and geometric, like on the clipping from the woods. Oakley wrote cryptically, "May we find the valuable things that lie hidden from us and discover what is rightfully ours."

Drayco asked, "He never said what this meant?"

"Since it's a book on the war, I guessed it had to do with that."

Earl got up to stoke the fireplace logs. "Your question the other day—why Oakley didn't want to sell his land? He said something to me once, probably his war research. It was along the lines of not appreciating land until someone tries to take it away and wipe all traces of you off the face of the Earth."

"Did he mean you, Earl? You emigrated from Germany."

Earl's hands folded in his lap, although his thumbs kept crossing over and under. "You'll find out, anyway. My father belonged to Hitler's youth organization and believed in the Nazi cause, lock, stock, and barrel. I didn't and so cut ties with my family when I moved here. But I never mentioned it before now, so I doubt I was the subject for that inscription."

Despite the seriousness of the subject, Drayco caught the irony of Earl's use of a gun-based phrase. "When did he give you this?"

"Back during the time he came over for a beer on a regular basis. Or should I say beers. The more he drank, the more depressed he got. Even quoted depressing poetry."

"Such as?"

"One of his favorite poets was a British soldier. Omen, Odon, something like that."

"Wilfred Owen?"

"That sounds right. Man, were those poems depressing."

"Owen was only in his twenties when he was killed in the First World War."

"That figures. Oakley had one favorite poem—death was absurd and life absurder."

Drayco thought about Paddy Bakely's own depressing poetry, his "black angels." Maybe they weren't bosom buddies, but Paddy and Oakley shared much in common. Poetry, woodworking, alcoholism. Could be why they didn't get along—they were two magnetic poles repelling each other.

The morning fog lifted enough for Drayco to see outlines of the dock silhouetted against the pale green sheet of water beyond. Light contrasted against dark, like a chiaroscuro photograph. "Going back to when Oakley's personality changed, did anything unusual precede it, any odd, even subtle, signs?"

A series of loud pops from the fireplace even got Yaegle's attention. He hopped up to shove the fireplace screen in closer. "It was the same time he built that garden shrine. Not long after, he came over and got falling-down drunk. Kept mumbling over and over about a destiny that makes us brothers. I thought he was referring to me. But Oakley and I certainly didn't end up like brothers."

Earl focused on the fire, the yellow and orange light reflecting off his wide pupils. Only an occasional hiss from the complaining logs broke the silence in the room. Fireplaces were an enigma in many ways. Noise, fire, smoke, ash—it was like a controlled volcano people willingly put in their homes.

They sat in silence for a while, and the firewood was a good two minutes further charred into nonexistence when Earl spoke again. "Guess I'm still the main suspect. Every knock on the door, every phone call. .." He paused, straightening up in his seat. "Any day now I expect to find myself behind bars."

He might be right, but if Randolph Squier had his way, Earl was safe. A lot rode on Earl's innocence—jobs, taxes the new development would cough up, the fate of a few charities thrown in for good measure. And Squier's prospects for a future property sale.

Drayco read the inscription on Oakley's manuscript again. Something valuable, something hidden, something he felt to be rightfully his. The Opera House scrimshaw? Reece's clock, or a different piece Oakley stole? Even more worrying, had Nanette been involved? *In Spiritu et Veritate.*

25

Drayco pulled up in front of a weathered clapboard-box of a house. Squier's secretary Adah Karbowski waved him inside but kept casting her eyes from him to the sofa, as if hoping he wouldn't stay long. He heard coughing from a back room, and Adah briefly turned her head to listen. "That's my sister, Emily. They once called it ague, now it's flu. Ague, flu, they rhyme, don't know why I never thought of that," she babbled. She licked her lips, then stood up straighter and pointed at the sofa. "Won't you sit down?"

He sat on the low-pitched sofa, which pretzeled his long legs into odd angles. She needn't worry, no chance he'd get too comfortable. He caught a strong scent of Vick's VapoRub, and he also noted a box of chamomile tea on a side table next to a box of Mackenzies Smelling Salts. "I'm sorry your sister isn't well. Is there someone who can help?"

Adah settled into a chair opposite. "The Haberlands next door. She said she ran into you at the town hall. They struggle to make ends meet, what with six kids, but they're fine neighbors. Cape Unity is full of good folks. We're not all louts and murderers."

The muscles around Drayco's lips twitched, threatening to smile. "I doubt the whole town is involved in a conspiracy. People blame the murders on new arrivals, it seems."

"Can't stomach such nonsense. Those unfortunates have a hard life and want the same things as everyone else. A little work, a little chance at happiness. Let 'em alone, I say. Half the town is immigrants—the Spencers, the Coles, Reece Wable's family, even Ari Johnsson, the photographer, he's from Iceland. We're all mutts."

After a quick scan of the decor, some might label the decor of Emily and Adah's house as shabby-without-the-chic, but it was spotless with knitted pastel seashell designs on pillows, throws, and a wall hanging. The exception was a blood-red woven rug on the floor. Compared to the palatial accommodations of Cypress Manor, it was like a dollhouse furnished by the Salvation Army.

Drayco leaned forward to examine a hand-lettered book of family recipes lying on the coffee table, bound together with brown jute thread between the pumpkin-orange covers. "Maida says you're the chef who created the fine meal I enjoyed at the Squiers' home."

Adah picked up the book and opened it to a page with a recipe for braised venison with oyster dressing. "That's the one I made, right there. From my grandmother Maribel to you."

"I hope the Squiers appreciate your culinary talents as much as I did."

"They're not much to notice. Guess they've come to expect it."

He read the ingredient list for the venison dish. Red wine, rosemary, shitake mushrooms. So that's what those were. "You've been employed by Mr. Squier for some time?"

"Fifteen years. Doesn't seem that long."

"You were a live-in housekeeper. Your duties changed when the councilman married?"

"Mrs. Squier didn't want a live-in. I still clean for them, but only once a week. He kept me on as his secretary."

"Was it a smooth transition after the marriage?"

Adah swallowed hard. "There were issues at first. I'm not sure Mrs. Squier wanted to have me around. That's to be expected, of course, her being a new bride and all. But it hasn't got much better."

Drayco found himself wanting to defend Darcie but bit his tongue. "The night I was there, Mrs. Squier mentioned a rumor about Nanette Keys and Earl Yaegle. And that you were the source."

Adah twisted a lace doily in her lap until the cloth was in a tight roll. "I guess I am guilty of repeating gossip from time to time. It's a bad habit."

Adah and Darcie had more in common than either thought. Drayco said, "We all have bad habits. But in this case, any bit of information could make a difference."

As he'd observed at Squier's office, Adah's eyes darted around the room. She might be an inveterate gossip, but she was also as nervous as a child on a balance beam, not knowing when she might fall off.

Drayco leaned forward, like a conspirator discussing a shared secret. "There's an outbreak of affairs going around. Is it something in the water?"

Adah released the doily, allowing it to unroll into wrinkled lace. "I've wondered that myself. I'd say we're on par with the rest of the world. Nanette and Earl—that was a shock."

"And you heard this recently?"

"It's been a while. But I mentioned it to a friend on the phone after Oakley was killed. I guess Darcie overheard."

"Ironic, don't you think? That Darcie would repeat such gossip, considering it's common knowledge she was linked with Oakley. Was the gossip line active about them?"

Adah licked her lips again. "No one heard it from me. Didn't have to—they weren't discreet. I wasn't surprised, mind you, that Darcie might stray. Wouldn't have picked Oakley as her choice."

"Did the affair last long?"

"Don't think it lasted a year. Hard to tell when Darcie cares for anyone if you ask me." Adah looked directly into his eyes, unconcerned to be maligning Darcie in front of him.

"No signs she and Oakley had rekindled that relationship recently?"

"Darcie's been good about reining in her flirting." She tilted her head at Drayco. "But I think she's getting restless again."

Drayco let that pass and carefully phrased his next question. "The councilman was understandably angry about the affair. But did that anger translate to violence or abuse?"

She hesitated. "He gets fits of temper. Never saw him hit anyone if that's what you're asking. Not even his wife. But I've seen him throw things so hard they broke into a million pieces."

"Apparently the townspeople don't mind electing a councilman with a temper."

Adah frowned. "For two terms, so far. Don't know he'll make a third. Some of the folk against development think he killed Mr. and Mrs. Keys so his pet project could go through."

"Do you believe that?"

Adah shifted in her seat. "I don't know, in all honesty. But people aren't talking to me as much as they once did. Me working for Squier and all."

Drayco felt sorrier for Adah by the minute. Why couldn't she have found employment with an accountant in town or Earl Yaegle, for that matter? At least Earl was a decent boss if you believed Randy and not Joel.

Drayco asked, "Was that why you were afraid the day I visited the office? That Squier and Paddy Bakely might come to blows?"

She squirmed in her seat. "I was more afraid of Paddy. He's been arrested so many times. I shouldn't have sent you into the office, knowing Paddy was there. But Mr. Squier didn't tell me he had company coming through the back door. It wasn't my fault if you walked in on them, was it?" Still squirming, she opted for staring at the floor.

"It might be fun to put Squier in one corner of the ring and Paddy in the other and watch them duke it out."

He was rewarded as she lifted her head with her eyes lit up. "Like those wrestlers on TV? Emily and I watch them on Friday nights. I like the one called Prince Dynamite."

In light of Reece Wable's reference to SmackDown wrestling, Drayco decided Reece should be introduced to Adah and Emily. The trio could have wrestling night, complete with a Virginia Merlot and some of Maida's muffins made with black huckleberries from her garden.

"Did Squier threaten Oakley?"

She paused. "He was critical of Oakley's decision not to sell his land. He talked about all the money to be lost if they couldn't convince Oakley to sell."

"Tax revenue, or personal funds?"

"Tax? He didn't use that word. He was agitated, asked what could be done." She caught herself as if realizing how her words might sound. "I don't think. .. He couldn't mean murder."

"Who was he talking to?"

"I couldn't hear the other end of the conversation on the phone." She blushed again. "Not that I'm a snooper."

It was difficult for Drayco to imagine Adah's lonely life. Maida had told him townspeople called the Karbowski women the Westminster Spinsters, after the street on which their house stood. Emily had been on disability for years, and a good portion of Adah's paycheck went to helping take care of her sister. Gossip was Adah's lifeline to the outside world, and he didn't begrudge her the indulgence. Besides, it had already come in handy.

"According to the sheriff, both Mr. and Mrs. Squier are providing alibis for each other for the times of the murders. Were you here with Emily?"

"I was here Sunday night, when Mr. Keys was—" She stopped, her lip trembling. "When Mr. Keys died. And I was at Cypress Manor on Wednesday the afternoon of Mrs. Keys' death, preparing for the dinner you attended. The Mister and Missus were running an errand at the time. Not sure when they returned, though. I was in the kitchen in the back of the house, you see."

Drayco asked gently, noting Adah's increased distress, "Any unusual behavior from either of them recently?"

"The Missus was the same as always. Mr. Squier, on the other hand, has been out of sorts. He had me call Doc Vrooman to get a prescription for sleeping pills."

Drayco heard Emily coughing again, from the back bedroom. "You need to attend to your sister, so I won't overstay my welcome. One more thing. How did the councilman find out about Darcie and Oakley?"

"Near as I recall, it was Earl. Earl Yaegle."

26

Each Cape Unity dollhouse got more claustrophobic. Drayco hadn't known what to expect inside Seth's apartment-sized home, tinier than Adah Karbowski's. But it would take about two minutes tops to survey the space, just one combination living and dining area, a galley kitchen, one small bedroom and one bath. That the Bakelys were able to afford this on the meager salary Rockingham paid Seth was a tribute to Seth's money-management skills.

The living room was devoid of personality, the one couch and a lone chair covered in faded stripes once psychedelic, likely refugees from the sixties. Furniture on acid. It was almost a pity Drayco wasn't wearing that tie-dyed shirt his former partner gave him as a gag present.

A spring poked him in the back of his chair, and he sat forward to get away from it. Seth looked ready to spring, too, the fibers of his being wadded into tight coils. This wasn't a man accustomed to dealing with people.

"I think you and I are in the same boat, in a way, Seth." The muscles around Seth's ears twitched, but he remained silent.

Drayco continued, "Neither of us saw this bequest of Rockingham coming. Neither of us wanted it. But we're both stuck with his decision, so we should discuss how to make the best of it."

Seth sat back so hard against his chair that it squeaked out a complaint. "You asking my opinion on what to do with the thing?"

"Some townspeople want it reopened. Do you agree?"

Seth moved his jaw from side to side as if chewing on the thought. "Should be used or torn down. Empty, it's insect bait. Makes no business sense. Always wondered why he let it rot."

The words came out of Drayco's mouth without him thinking. "I'm sorry he didn't pay you more. We can do better than that." Where exactly Drayco would get the money was a mystery. And it also presupposed him not selling the building, didn't it?

"Don't need charity."

"It wouldn't be charity. Regardless of whether the Opera House is sold or restored, it'll generate money for such purposes."

"Why would you do that?"

Why, indeed. Drayco conceded he didn't owe Seth anything. He only inherited the messes Rockingham left behind. Some might argue it would be kinder to the Bakelys if he cut them loose, forcing them to find a better situation. Drayco had learned Seth got a tiny social security check, but he doubted it was enough to live on. Seth wasn't young and didn't have employable skills, other than manual labor. Labor that any number of younger folk, including some of those "illegals" the locals were worried about, would be able and willing to provide more cheaply. What was to become of Seth?

Drayco replied, "Because it's the right thing to do."

Seth stared at Drayco with a curiosity Drayco related to a zoologist trying to figure out how to classify an anomalous specimen. Drayco added, "I had another reason for coming. Something Paddy said the other day."

Seth almost smiled, although since Drayco had never seen what a Seth smile looked like, it was hard to tell. "Was he drunk or sober?"

"A bit of both. But he told me Oakley Keys once broke into the Opera House."

Seth definitely wasn't smiling now. "He spoke out of turn."

"Was it true?"

Seth bowed his head. The fingernails of one hand raked across the armrest. "It's true. Saw him myself, as he was headed out."

"When I first asked you at the Opera House, you said you'd never seen him there."

"Was many years ago. Didn't think it mattered."

Or perhaps, Seth didn't want to give Rockingham or Drayco more reasons for him to be fired. "Do you have any idea why Oakley snuck in?"

"Valuables. Lots of places broken into around the same time. Might be him, might not. I didn't want to get involved in all of that. Hard enough keeping Paddy out of trouble."

"Did you see Oakley and Randolph Squier there together?"

"Not together. Squier came a couple times by himself. Had his own key. He'd try to come early, before my rounds. Don't think he wanted me watching him. But I saw him."

"It's possible Squier was looking for valuables, too?"

Seth's eyes widened a fraction. "A posh guy like him?"

"Maybe that's how he got rich."

Drayco spotted a small wobbly homemade wooden table against a wall. If that was Paddy's handiwork, Yaegle was right—Oakley's woodworking skills left Paddy swimming in the wood dust. "Oakley and Paddy had a lot in common, Seth. Too bad they didn't get along."

Seth leaned forward. The acrid smell of cheap cigarettes enveloped him like a cocoon, making it all too obvious where some of his paycheck went. "Keys was a drinker, like Paddy." Seth's voice had grown raspy. "Those thefts I told you about. It was the late sixties or early seventies. Everything was upside down. Vietnam. Course, you weren't born yet. You don't know war."

Drayco might not have lived through Vietnam, but it wasn't like he was born on another planet. There were no family photos around the room, certainly no photos of soldiers in uniform. Perhaps Paddy's troubles had a military basis. Post-traumatic stress disorder would explain a lot.

"Did Paddy serve in Vietnam? He'd be the right age."

"He was called up. Rejected 4F. Epilepsy. Might be better if he made it. Might have sobered him up."

Or made things worse. If Paddy had problems with reality as it was, the horrors of war wouldn't have helped. "Does he still suffer from epilepsy?"

"Seizures stopped in his twenties. Good thing, without insurance." Seth stopped himself. "Paddy don't drink because of that. It's who he is. Makes him a target. He's easy to blame for everybody else's evils."

Drayco scanned the room again for photographs, yearbooks, albums. Nada. "Is there no family who can help keep an eye on him?"

Seth stiffened again although his fingernails continued raking over the chair. Was he being defensive, that Drayco implied he couldn't handle Paddy by himself?

Seth said, "A few in-laws. We don't see 'em much. Don't live around here."

"And your own kin?"

"Don't get along." Seth's dark tone of voice and his flashing eyes indicated that line of questioning would go no further. It might be a hundred different reasons, most of which Drayco had encountered at one point or another. A hundred different ways for families to grow apart.

Drayco asked, "I thought Paddy's mother was born in this area, but you said her family lives far away."

"They moved after Angel died. Not much to keep 'em here."

"Not even a grandson?" Seth didn't reply. "I'm sure your wife's death was hard on all of you. Again, I'm sorry."

"It hurt Paddy more since Paddy lost his mother young."

"So did I," Drayco said, although "lost" hardly described the reality. He wasn't trying to force an empathetic bond with Seth, but Seth did nod. His almost-smile was soon eclipsed by a grimace, as he twisted in his seat.

"Are you all right?"

"Upset stomach. Probably those." Seth waved his hand at a half-eaten pack of barbecue pork rinds. "You staying in town long?" he asked.

"I'm not sure. I have to make some decisions on the Opera House, but I also have two clients who deserve justice."

By now, Seth had raked the armrest so deeply Drayco expected threads to start coming loose. "You said Nanette helped Paddy at the Social Services Agency. Can you tell me more about her?"

"She was kind to me. And Paddy. Not because she was paid to. That's the way she was." Seth looked up briefly then down again, not adding any details.

"Are we talking about counseling—"

"Don't want to talk about Paddy anymore." The intensity in Seth's eyes underlined his warning, the message clear. Paddy's mental state was off-limits, period.

"When you were at the agency, did you see or hear anything that would indicate a motive for Nanette's murder?"

"Don't think anyone would want to murder Nanette. Must be a thief who thought they had money. A lot of new people in town. But old-timers know better."

On Seth's stoic face, ruddy from working in the sun on the Opera House grounds, lines formed like dried-up rivulets of sand in a desert. Small lines, from efforts to form themselves into smiles or frowns, or into something Drayco couldn't identify. Regret? Seth didn't move as Drayco rose to leave.

"Thanks for your time, Seth." He closed the door behind him, with Seth molded in the same position, staring off into the distance.

In what condition Paddy would come home? Drunk, sober, bruised, staggering? Paternal love or not, this was one enduring family tie that withstood the hundred reasons families go their separate ways.

27

Drayco stopped at the local art gallery shop to see if anyone had tried to sell a wooden owl mask like Oakley's stolen handiwork. It was a wasted trip. The clerk, whose spiky purple hair rounded off on top made him look like a human thistle, said nothing like that was brought in.

Saturdays in March didn't draw crowds in the downtown, only a few vehicles braving the dismal weather. One, a black sedan parked down the street from the gallery, pulled out right after Drayco did. It looked like the same car that followed him after the animal attack in the park.

He took a meandering route through town, the sedan maintaining a discreet distance. Looking for a way to confront his shadower, Drayco got caught off-guard when the sedan zoomed off at a ninety-degree angle. It sailed through one of the town's few red lights and was a hair's breadth away from broadsiding two cars.

The other cars swerved to avoid the sedan but hit each other instead, with a sickening crunch of metal-on-metal. Drayco stopped long enough to make sure everyone was all right. He jumped back in his car and headed in the direction his quarry had taken. But it had too much of a head start.

Lucky break for the sedan. Small towns weren't conducive to tricks of the surveillance trade, making it hard to follow someone without being seen. Sheriff Sailor remarked it would be easier to find a gray E.T. than it was to keep investigations on the Q.T. Drayco needed to ask the sheriff about his obsession with alien life forms.

The more Drayco witnessed the sheriff in action, the more he admired him. Drayco was accustomed to a law enforcement scene mired in territorial quicksand, but Sailor didn't have an egotistical bone in his professional body.

Drayco called the sheriff's office to report the accident location and a description of his car-stalker, then continued on to the Opera House, pulling in front. He walked around the perimeter looking for cracks or anything that would send a contractor's adding machine into overdrive. He got halfway around when a silver Jaguar pulled up on the street, and the passenger door swung open.

"Get in," Darcie demanded.

"Why?"

"Because I'm kidnapping you."

His inspection of the Opera House exterior could wait. The second after he closed the door, Darcie sped off, arriving ten minutes later at an area of town he hadn't seen before. They parked in front of a small graveyard next to a foundation slab where a few dogfennel weeds poked through cracks in the concrete. Many of the graveyard's headstones were leaning and no sight of flowers on the graves. Not even dried-up stems.

"Where's the church?" he asked.

"Burned down long ago. That's not what I want to show you." She took his hand and led him between headstones through a grove of shrubs until they reached a clearing. A small drop-off in front led straight to the water. A view of the Bay greeted him, more unobstructed, more breathtaking, than any other he'd seen from Cape Unity's shores.

"Leave it to the dead to have the best view in town." She had an impish grin. "Oakley and I used to meet here."

"For the view, of course."

"That depends on what view you mean."

She had the good sense not to wear high heels this time, and her shoes weren't sinking into the damp soil, but now her head barely reached his shoulder. "Where else did you and Oakley meet, view or no?"

"Other than this spot and his home? We met one other time at a place near and dear to your heart. The Opera House."

"You mean you broke in together?"

"Only a little bit. We snuck in while Seth was there and the door unlocked. We hid until he left. Oakley knew exactly where to hide."

"Did he, now?" So Seth and Paddy were right. Oakley had broken into the place, and from the sound of it, more than once. "And you had sex with Oakley there in the Opera House in front of all those ghosts?"

Darcie wrapped both arms around one of his. "Now you're pulling my chain."

"Deservedly so. Did he tell you he'd been inside the Opera House before?"

"He was a music fan. I wasn't surprised. He loved piano music, even though he couldn't play."

She moved toward an oak tree and pulled him along until they were beside it. He moved in closer to inspect a section with a carving in the wood.

"Oakley made that," she said.

"Looks like a key."

"It is. Because of his name, of course. An oak. A key. A joke."

Drayco fingered the center of the key. "What are these? Lowercase letters?"

She punched him lightly in the arm. "You're good. I never guessed what they were. It says b-b. I asked him what it stood for. If he had a BB gun as a kid, or a pet named BB. But he laughed at me."

B-b again. Same as in the margins of the newspaper clipping he found in the woods. The sheriff would be thrilled with this added enigma. But Nanette did say her husband was fond of games.

"Oakley sure knew his way around a knife."

"That's why he taught Randolph. Because he was so good at it."

Drayco had to process that for a second. "Oakley taught Randolph carving? I didn't think they could stand each other."

"Randolph loves those ivory tusks. The scrimshaw. He collected them for a long time and wanted to make his own. So he asked

Oakley to teach him how to carve. They weren't best buds, but friendly back then. Before my time."

"Was your husband talented enough to make an intricate carving?"

"Can't imagine he would be. And I haven't seen him pull out the knives in a long time."

She grabbed onto his arm again, allowing her fingers to trail down to his hand. "You're wondering if I'm the reason they became enemies, aren't you?" She traced the outlines of each of his fingers with her thumb.

"It did cross my mind."

"Men have always fought over me."

"Pistols at twenty paces?"

"You know what I mean."

"I'd think that would make it awfully hard for a man to trust you."

"Oakley did."

"Enough to give you anything to keep for him—files, documents, records?"

"I'm the last person anyone would trust with important things. Ask my husband." She turned her head to the Bay, her eyes reflecting the whitecaps on the water.

She shivered and clung tighter to Drayco's arm. Her sweater was hardly enough to provide a hedge against winds skipping off those white-capped waves, but he wasn't sure that was the real problem. "Are you afraid, Darcie?"

She deflected his question. "Everybody's afraid of something, aren't they? Randolph's afraid of his own shadow these days." She reached up to brush aside a lock of Drayco's hair from his forehead, and despite her cold hands, her touch felt warm on his skin.

He didn't want to admit it, but he'd been glad to see her. In this secluded spot with her beside him, he was more at peace than in days. Perhaps it was the cameo she made in one of his dreams last night. Not one of his nightmares. Decidedly more pleasant.

"That's a lovely blue shirt you have on," she said. "You should wear it more often. It matches the color of your eyes."

"Did you bring me here to compliment me?"

"Just being neighborly. Thought you'd enjoy the view."

Drayco stepped back. "If you meant for this to be that detailed tour you mentioned, I'm not sure that's such a good idea."

"I make a good tour guide."

"I'm sure you do. So why is Randolph afraid of his own shadow?"

"It's that development battle. And the murders. Not that he's next in line. It's always about his image. His standing in the community."

"How far do you think he'd go to preserve that image? Especially if someone had proof of his involvement in embezzlement or fraud?"

Darcie twisted strands of her hair around her finger. "He can be—he's been known to throw things. He has a loud voice when he yells like those drill sergeants in the movies. I guess I could see him throwing a tantrum, but beyond that. .." She shook her head, not looking at him.

"Did Oakley seem afraid?"

"I hadn't seen him for months. I can't tell you if he knew he was going to die if that's what you mean. When we were together, I never saw fear. Anger, yes, like a geyser ready to blow. Or maybe I should say, blow job." She smirked at him.

"Were there other women, other affairs?"

She reached up again to stroke his hair and the sly grin returned to her face. "Lovers never talk about other lovers when they're making love. You can call it Darcie's Law."

Seeing the hunger in her eyes and the succubus pout, he fought the urge to recreate Oakley's tryst with her right there against the oak tree. Drayco took her hand this time and pulled her back in the direction of the car. "Come on. I think that's enough viewing for one day."

It was a peaceful place, with the wind rustling dead leaves clinging to the trees. The castaway tombstones must have witnessed a spectacle during Darcie and Oakley's "meetings." Drayco noted the date of death on one, June 6, 1944. D-Day. Had Oakley, the World War II buff, chosen this place by design? It would be a fitting location for his final resting place. Yet his Will left instructions for his body to be cremated and the ashes scattered over his backyard shrine. It wouldn't happen now, with condos slated to occupy that very spot.

28

As soon as he headed through the door, Maida handed him a cup of coffee "double black," as she called it, having learned his tastes quickly. He ran the cup of warm liquid up and down against his aching right arm as he headed upstairs to his room.

He froze in place outside the doorway.

His suitcase lay open on the floor, items half-in and half-out. The books he bought at the Novel Café were lying on the end of the bed in disarray. Drawers in the chest were pulled out, and the closet was wide open. He took a quick inventory and headed back downstairs.

Intent on fried catfish and pumpkin fritters, Maida jumped at his quick return. "What's the matter?"

"Either you've turned into a sloppy housekeeper, which I doubt, or someone's been rifling through my room."

Maida gasped. "Was anything taken?"

"Not that I can tell. My guess—they were hunting for a specific item."

"The only one here was Major, working in the garden during gaps in the deluge. Major?" she called.

The Major appeared on cue, sniffing the air. "Time for dinner already? It's not six-thirty."

"Major, dear, were you here all afternoon?"

"I spent time tidying up papers in the library. Then I checked on the progress of the crocuses, hyacinths, and bluebells. Oh, and the checkered lilies. Can't forget them."

"The entire afternoon?"

"Except for a walk I took down the road. It was still raining a tad. You know I love walks in the rain."

"But what time, dear?"

"I think it was three-ish. I was gone for a half hour, I think."

"Did you notice anything unusual when you returned?"

"Unusual? Not a thing except for the cream gone south. Tea's not the same without it."

Maida sighed in exasperation. "Someone broke into the house and rummaged through Scott's room. Probably while you were taking your walk."

"A burglary, you say? How extraordinary."

Drayco interrupted, "Technically not a burglary if nothing was stolen. At least in my room. You two should verify your belongings are intact."

After a search, the Jepsons were relieved to find nothing missing. Maida said, "Our burglar must think you're as rich as Croesus now you own the Opera House."

"A real estate magnate, I'm not." Drayco didn't bring any valuables with him, nor had he picked up anything while he was here, except Nanette's letter fragment. "I should mention this to our town gendarme if you don't mind."

A call to the sheriff's office found Sailor working late and willing to stop on his way home. "Besides," the sheriff said as he stepped inside the hallway, "Maida knows I'll do anything for a slice of her sweet potato pie. But don't tell my wife. She'll be furious if I don't have room for the meal she's been slaving over. Liver and onions." Sailor wrinkled his nose.

They made a detailed search of Drayco's room. He said, "They must have been in a hurry. Or didn't care if I knew they were here."

The sheriff removed the books on Drayco's bed, using a pencil slipped between the pages. He flipped down the covers at the head of the bed and picked up a letter-sized piece of white cardboard. "Are you in the habit of leaving yourself threatening notes?"

The pair studied the letters in blood-red paint forming the words "Leave it alone."

"That's original. And how specific," the sheriff muttered.

"Leave what alone? The murder investigation? The Opera House? The town? The piano? My playing is rusty, but it can't be that bad."

"This could be a prank. Until I know for sure, I'm treating it as a bona fide threat, Drayco." Sailor added, "Be back in a sec," and returned moments later with a paper bag into which he carefully slid the cardboard note. "Why don't we meet at the Hut tomorrow? I'll put someone on this first thing tomorrow, and we might have more around noonish. If I light a fire under her feet. And by her feet, I mean Tyler."

He pulled out another paper from his pocket and handed it over. "While we're on the subject of threatening notes, here's the copy of words Tyler recovered from Nanette's letter fragment. You can make out phrases—'I'm capable of. Your wife. Silence is golden. Consequences.' Tyler put it under a microscope, and she detected a few additional words around the burned bits, such as 'schedule' after wife and also 'in the past.'"

"Multi-spectral imaging can detect black ink on burned paper."

"That's what Nelia said. But as I told her, our department doesn't have that kind of money."

Drayco smiled grimly. "Sure sounds like blackmail."

"That's the way it came across to me. One of Oakley's early conquests."

"But there's a hint of a threat against Nanette. A little extreme to get someone to end an affair with your wife."

The sheriff considered that for a moment. "Can't see it has a connection to the murders. Still feel the development angle is the ticket. We tracked down who owns the plot of land north of the proposed condos."

"Let me guess—Randolph Squier. He's been a dog with a bone defending Earl, who he'll need free and clear for the sale to go through. When I was in his office, he also tried to deflect questions about other property owners who'd benefit."

"Squier is the owner all right, in a roundabout way. It's in his mother-in-law's name. She's ninety and has Alzheimer's. I doubt she understood what she was signing."

"Darcie's mother? Didn't you tell me their family name was Gentner?"

"Yeah, but we haven't been able to connect Gentner with Gallinger."

"We can't rule it out, can we?" Drayco didn't like pointing that out, still finding himself trying to protect Darcie. But from what, he wasn't exactly sure.

"Gotta wonder if Darcie knew her hubby used her mother's name on that deed. If so, that makes her complicit. If she didn't, maybe Squier hoped Darcie would take the fall if the deed came to light."

"It sounds like you're moving Squier up a notch on the suspect list."

"Got a tip from Gallinger. After the condos go up, the north property is next in line. A hotel, shops. Tons of money for Squier. Ironic, isn't it? He's been piling on pressure for me to exonerate Earl, but in so doing, he gets to take his place. Add in Oakley's affair with Darcie, the alleged embezzlement angle, Squier's woodsman ability, the fact he's a gun collector, and he's a burly guy big enough to strangle Nanette. .. he's dueling Earl for the top spot."

"And he's handy with knives."

"What?"

"Used them to carve his own scrimshaw. Carving up flesh would be easy next to ivory or bone."

"Didn't see any knives in that gun case of his. Wonder where he hides them?"

"In that palatial manor of his, there'd be plenty of places."

"So you're liking Squier as our killer, I take it?"

"Might even be willing to bet some money on it." The sheriff was right—Squier had the most motive, the most opportunity, and all the right skills and tools to kill both Oakley and Nanette. And Drayco hadn't run across anyone with a voice as grotesquely colored as Squier's who wasn't guilty of something. If Darcie were a synesthete, she wouldn't have lasted more than few days with that voice, surely.

He said, "If we could finagle a sample of Squier's block printing, we might be able to match it with the block letters on Nanette's letter fragment."

Sailor whipped out a notepad from his pocket to jot something down. It was a standard white Rite in the Rain flip-top pad, four bucks each. Not like the pricier personalized leather-bound pads some officers used or a high-tech handheld PDA.

"Your department budget keeping you stuck in the 20th century, Sheriff?"

"What budget?" He stuffed the notepad back in his pocket. "I don't mind these pads. They never break down, don't need batteries and they impress a jury. Harder to forge an officer's handwriting than with a digital file."

"Going digital would save you a lot of time."

"Next century. We just got laptops in the patrol cars two years ago."

Tourism, taxes, some of Squier's buried treasure. Cape Unity needed some of each if it were to survive, let alone thrive. The threads of the past, when wealth rode into town on rails from tourists with deep pockets, lingered like gossamer strands of hope scattered in the breezes of time. And Drayco's Opera House was the patron saint of that past.

Drayco said, "Did you find out if Gallinger wanted to buy the Opera House?"

"They said no way. That's the polite version. They phrased it more colorfully."

Drayco fingered the copy of the letter fragment. It brought to mind Nanette's face, sorrowful yet determined, unable to stop picking at old emotional scars. "And Nanette's murder, any progress on that front?"

"Can't find anyone with a bad word about her. Let alone a reason to kill her. But we haven't forgotten her." The sheriff picked up his hat. "Don't you be a stranger. That love note of yours could indicate you're next in line for an early demise. And I don't need a third murder."

Sailor slapped on his hat with more force than usual. "Or should I say fourth. I had somebody check into that woman's death. Grace Waterworth. I think we'll be able to get that exhumation order now. Turns out her husband had a secret life. Gambling, drinking, women, lots of trips to Vegas. Fortunately, he's also your typical crook with the IQ of an orangutan. And a guilty conscience. He practically confessed to putting rat poison in his wife's stew, from the moment we walked through the door. How'd you know?"

"He donated her collection of books right after her death."

"They were religious books, right? So what? So he didn't share his wife's devotional habits."

"Widowers tend to hold on to reminders of their wives for sentimental value, at least for a while. He couldn't get the books out of the house fast enough. Also, the only new book in the lot was one on how to kill garden pests with poisons. Complete with the sticker from a bookstore in Nevada."

Sailor smiled slightly, before heading out with the threatening note from Drayco's room and one pie box, compliments of Maida.

Since he was a guest of the Jepsons, Drayco decided to tell them about the threat. "If you'd prefer I stay somewhere else, in case," he offered.

"Oh, Lord no," Maida was adamant, and the Major headed to the library, bringing back a black fabric case he unzipped to reveal an Enfield pistol. "Don't you worry, my boy. I've got Bertille here, handed down from my father, a veteran of the WWII RAF." He stroked the gun, cradling it in one arm. "Besides, you aren't going to find a finer place around these parts than the Lazy Crab."

Maida scolded him, "I doubt you'll be needing that any time soon, dear. You know how I feel about guns. Scott's a big boy and can take care of himself. So you go put that away." She turned to

Drayco to explain, "Bertille's the name of a former French heartthrob of Major's."

"Aha. Another reason to put the old girl back in mothballs."

"At least he didn't name it Angelina, after his first wife."

The Major clucked his tongue. "I doubt our bandit will show his face again, now he's discovered we're not the Ming vase type. Hardly worth his time, I'd say."

Satisfied the Jepson household was safe, Drayco headed into the den but didn't sit down. He stood looking out the window at the unaccustomed sight of a nighttime view with no man-made lights, leaving only the phantom shapes of trees.

He settled beside a vintage wood cabinet the Jepsons owned, with an AM radio above a fan-shaped speaker grid. Opening the lid, he placed the 78-rpm record Nanette gave him on the turntable inside. He'd never heard any recordings of Konstantina Klucze playing the piano, and he wasn't sure what to expect.

From the first few notes of the Brahms Capriccio, he was entranced. The age of the well-played recording and its scratchiness aside, it was clear Konstantina was a masterful and soulful pianist. He was sorry the 78 gave him a mere three minutes on each side, and this was all he had. He sat back and listened to the Brahms and the flip side Chopin waltz several times each.

It was easy to picture Konstantina on the Opera House stage, lights focused on her as she lifted her hands and prepared to play. It was if she were in the room with him, enjoying his reaction to the music. She'd been so young, yet her playing was as mature as Van Cliburn in his forties. Who knows where her career would have taken her had she not been brutally murdered? If she'd lived, she would be around 90.

Watching the record as it sped around, he compared it to the circle of truncated careers. Konstantina's. Oakley's. His. It wasn't yet ten o'clock, but he was unusually tired and called it a night. Lying enveloped in his bed's oversized goose down comforter, images of Oakley and Nanette kept flashing through his mind. Eccentric Oakley, looking like an anachronistic throwback to, what? The 1950s?

The 1850s? And Nanette? Oakley's opposite. Stylish, composed, outgoing.

Now both husband and wife lay in a morgue, any hopes and dreams within them forever extinguished. Nanette's parting words to him the day she died haunted him, as they went around and around in his head like the turntable. "I'll always be grateful you took my humble concerns seriously. I'm not sure anyone else would."

What had he given her in exchange for that trust? So far, zilch. But if the murderer had indeed set his sights on Drayco, then he believed Drayco was on his trail. Meaning Drayco might be closer to keeping his promise to Nanette than he knew.

Part Three

Oh, could I love again I'd sing with gladness.
Here, far from home, I long to dream.
I want what I have not - to love;
And there is no one to love, nor to sing to.

—From the song "I want what I have not," poem by Bohdan Zaleski,
music by Frédéric Chopin

29

Sunday 21 March

True to his word from the previous night, Sheriff Sailor arranged to meet Drayco at noon. On his previous trip to the Seafood Hut, Drayco hadn't paid much attention to the decor. As he waited for the sheriff to arrive, he inspected a wall behind the register with signed photographs. They were the Seafood Hut's version of celebrity patrons, including a TV news anchor from the D.C. area, a former Washington Senators baseball player, and a few other notables.

Drayco was surprised to see Oakley Keys on the wall, with the title "Author" beneath his signature. Drayco barely recognized him in the photo. This version of Oakley was smiling, with no signs of the male-pattern baldness that later plagued him, a Kirk Douglas cleft chin and a confident gaze. It was dated prior to the letter incident.

Sheriff Sailor piped up behind Drayco's back, "They should put your picture up there. World-famous pianist, Opera House impresario, crime consultant to the rich and powerful." He ignored Drayco's glare. "I've got a digital camera in the car."

"That's one gallery I'll stay away from. Most of them are deceased, some violently. That anchorman died in a plane crash, the Senators baseball player was killed in Vietnam, and of course, there's Oakley."

"Good point."

They headed for the same booth as last time, and the waitress, who couldn't be much over sixteen, poured two cups of coffee in a rapid-fire succession that would impress Earl Yaegle. Sailor eyeballed

Drayco over the coffee cup he held in front of his face. "You seem faraway. Am I keeping you from a hot date?"

Drayco sat back in the booth and ran his finger across the table's decoupaged pictures of beach scenes, tracing a "G" pattern. "Sorry. I didn't sleep much."

Sailor pushed the salt shaker over to him. "You having bad dreams or does our fine sea air disagree with you?"

"It's not the sea air." Drayco closed his eyes briefly, remembering. As if he could forget when the images were burned into his nightmares. "Two months ago, a high-ranking diplomat and friend of Brock's put pressure on me to find his grandkids. They were kidnapped by his son-in-law, their father. I never sensed the mother in the custody case, the diplomat's daughter, would do what she did."

He stopped to take a few sips of coffee. The Hut's dark roast had that same smoky, charred aftertaste, but seemed darker, more bitter. "After I tracked down her children, twins, a boy and girl only five, she drowned them. Not just drowned them, but in a ritualized way—lily blossoms strewn across the pool, candles around the perimeter, the hands of the children tied behind them, their feet weighted. She invited me over to the house to show me what she'd done. I jumped in after them and tried CPR—"

"But they were already dead."

The EMTs told Drayco there was nothing he could have done. He'd agonized not only over the deaths of the twins but how for a brief moment, he felt he was playing God by choosing which twin to resuscitate first.

During the graveside service, he parked across the street and watched from afar, not wanting to be a negative presence. Some family members were none too happy with him, though the twins' grandfather, Drayco's client, didn't blame him. Drayco hadn't been able to bring himself to visit the two small graves on his own.

Sailor's voice shook him from his reverie. "Surely you don't blame yourself?"

Drayco looked at his hands, which for once, were still. "I shouldn't. Elaina Cadden developed schizophrenia. Her own family didn't realize it, not even the twins' father who absconded with the kids for selfish reasons."

He shifted his gaze to Sailor, who had his elbows propped on the table, looking at Drayco calmly over the coffee cup he grasped in both hands. Drayco said, "You're not surprised by any of this."

Sailor leaned back. "Remember that research I said I'd done on you? I read the news articles and police report on the Cadden case. The doctors concluded the Cadden woman had Type I schizophrenia. Comes on suddenly. She was apparently high-strung, so it'd be hard to notice the signs. But you know all that, don't you?"

"Maybe I'm not to blame for her behavior, but—"

"Look, you're not a screw-up. The police knew it, you know it, I know it. Hell, if I'd thought that from the beginning, I'd have found a way to kick you out of town."

Drayco reached for the salt shaker and rolled it around in his hand. Someone had added little grains of rice to the shaker. To draw out the moisture? He dropped the shaker on the table, the salt spilling into crystal spirals. "Nonetheless, I was a conduit for the loss of two innocent lives."

"You think it's happening again, with the Keys."

"If neither Oakley nor Nanette tried to hire me, they might be alive today. The timing of their deaths is too coincidental. And personal."

"We don't have suspect number one in jail, let alone a motive. You're jumping the clichéd gun. Or Webley."

The bags under the sheriff's eyes weren't any lighter, and Drayco suspected he knew why. "The town council giving you grief again?"

The sheriff took his hint to change the subject. "Squier at least backed off after I asked about his property. And there's talk of a recall vote."

"Against Squier?"

"No, me."

"Is Squier behind that?"

"Don't know. Don't care. One bit of good news—a deputy tracked down the widow of Maxwell Chambliss, owner of the stolen scrimshaw, to Ocean City. Her son drove her here to claim the piece you found, picture in hand to prove it was her late husband's. It was one of a pair. They sold the remaining one in the early '90s for ten grand."

Drayco let out a whistle. "A decent haul. Makes me wonder why the thief never sold it."

"Could have feared selling it would provide a traceback."

"Or our thief was looking for something else and picked this up on a whim, not knowing its worth. When I ran into a besotted Paddy, he accused Oakley of playing Opera House cat burglar. And another source confirmed Oakley was familiar with the place."

Sailor said, "Hmm," through crimped lips. "That source wouldn't be Mrs. Squier, would it? One of my deputies thought he saw Darcie getting out of your car after the town meeting."

"We've run into each other a few times. She's been helpful." Drayco didn't mention Darcie's account of having sex with Oakley at the Opera House. It didn't feel necessary. For now.

Drayco turned the subject back to the thefts. "Hard to believe Seth wouldn't have run across the scrimshaw piece before."

"We questioned the Bakelys and Squiers. They denied knowledge. And the only fingerprints on it were yours. Hell, maybe Squier-the-scrimshaw-fanatic planted it as a joke."

The waitress brought their plates, and the sheriff attacked his food with gusto, pausing long enough to wash it down with a few loud gulps of Orange Crush. Drayco was amazed. "You weren't kidding when you said you liked those crab thingamabobs. Don't forget to breathe."

He gazed out the window to the crumbling pink shack the sheriff pointed out last time. Only now, it had a big *For Sale* sign plastered across it. Like everything else in town. "Thanks for bringing by a copy of Nanette's letter fragment last night. It referenced 'the past,' but Oakley was in his mid-twenties at the time. Not much of a past at that age."

The sheriff used bread to mop up the last traces of crab. The plate was so clean, it could have come straight from the dishwasher. "Might go back to his collegiate days. I'll have Tyler contact the college. Can't say I'm convinced it's relevant."

"You're fixated on the condo project and Oakley's refusal to sell his land as the murder motive?"

"And you aren't. We'll have to agree to disagree."

Drayco said slowly, "I think the fragment is connected and something older is at work. For several reasons."

"Such as?"

"Such as Nanette being murdered shortly after she gave it to me. Such as, why would Oakley wear a jacket he hadn't worn in decades the night he's killed?"

"You tell me, Ellery. If you want to pursue it further, knock yourself out."

Sailor's situation wasn't helped by losing not one, but two deputies now to the mumps, out for weeks. Drayco was none too happy to spend a week in bed when he was eight with his neck swollen and a fever high enough for ice packs, but now, he was grateful. He said, "I'll save you one hassle, checking Oakley's immigration records. I have a friend at the National Archives."

The sheriff accepted the offer with a grateful nod. "Deal. FYI, we found no prints on the note left in your room."

"I didn't expect any."

"Nor did I. But I also didn't expect something else we found." Sailor called the waitress for the check, then studied it as if trying to divine some deep secret. "You should be careful."

"Any reason in particular?"

"Tyler took a closer look at the red paint on that note of yours. It was paint, all right. With flecks of dried blood."

"Human?"

"Type A-negative. Like Oakley's and what was on the knife from the dumpster. The author of the note wants his message heard loud and clear. Must have collected some blood in a vial before he left the murder scene or from gloves he used."

Drayco smiled. "Guess there goes my dream of a cottage in town with a white picket fence."

"You don't seem the picket fence type."

"And you're no poster boy for the Stereotypical Sheriffs Association. What hooked you into this racket?"

Sailor was quiet for a moment. "An unsolved murder. My younger brother's. I'd gone off to college when it happened during his night shift at a convenience store. I wasn't there for him and vowed I'd make it up to him."

Russian roulette again. The two men exchanged a wordless glance of understanding before the sheriff cleared his throat and added, "Of course, if I hadn't picked this illustrious career, I'd be a penniless poet drowning my sorrows in a bar somewhere. Like Paddy."

"Or Oakley."

"Too much type A personality to be depressive."

"Type A personality to go with type A blood."

Sailor frowned. "Yeah, there is that. Maybe you should leave it alone like the warning said. Go sell your Opera House, take the money and run. Be a lot healthier for you all around."

Drayco appreciated the concern but didn't feel in imminent danger. The real threat was out there in a town not accustomed to urban woes of murder and rapid demographic changes. And the blame-gaming. With fingers pointed in every direction, the murderer would find it easy to blend in, one target among many.

"I almost forgot, Sheriff, did you track down the car with the tinted front windshield?"

"Have to wait until tomorrow at the earliest, since it's Sunday." Sailor got in one last passing shot before they got up to leave. "I'd be careful around Darcie. She can be dangerous when she wants something. And Squier filed a complaint against you with both me and the Virginia Department of Criminal Justice. I've already gotten a call from some suit named Zeickert."

That helped explain why Drayco had seen a few townspeople turning away from him as he approached them this morning. Such a move on Squier's part could do more than make Drayco a pariah in town. A few days ago, he wasn't sure he'd care about having to go before a review board or losing his license. But now. .. "On what grounds, Sheriff?"

"Threatening bodily harm. Harassment. And stalking."

"He must use a different dictionary than I do."

"Like I said, might be a good idea to avoid Mrs. Squier. Not just to make her husband back off. All that thorny ethical stuff."

Drayco deflected the other man's scowl with a small nod. "No worries, there." But as the words left his mouth, he had the sudden sensation of smelling jasmine perfume.

30

Zelda at the Novel Café placed the book triumphantly in Drayco's hands. "I have a contact who specializes in hard-to-find books."

Drayco thumbed through the pages, inhaling the new-book smell. "What do I owe you?"

"This is a gift. The Opera House is a community treasure after all."

"At least let me buy you a drink from your café by way of thanks. And in honor of your anniversary at the store."

She grinned but nodded at a stack of boxes next to the counter. "That's kind of you, but I'll have to take a rain check. We got in two big shipments, and I'm swamped."

Drayco toted the book into a corner of the café where he settled into an overstuffed purple chair near the window, the view filled with wood-and-metal scaffolding across the street. Why did he feel drawn to the life of this one pianist? Certainly the fact Konstantina's last concert was in the Opera House was enticing. Maybe his mind was fixated on murder, in this case, an unusual one—it was rare for classical pianists to suffer such a fate.

As he read, he learned Konstantina's rise to fame was meteoric. Which is why everyone was shocked when she got married at the peak of her talents to the rich businessman Edmund Gozdowski, a Polish Jew twenty years her senior and a widower with a son. Although Edmund and Konstantina's relationship read like a fairy tale, there was family grumbling, and she became estranged from the stepson.

For a wedding present, Edmund gave his wife a rare Chopin manuscript of the Piano Sonata in B Minor, one of the few items saved in their flight from persecution. It wasn't seen since. That made Drayco sit up straight. It was the same composition he played at the Opera House the other day.

After reaching the back pages of the book, he was surprised to find he'd been reading for three hours. The clicking of heels on the parquet floor got his attention. Darcie Squier approached him, two cups in hand. "Mind if I join you?"

Drayco made room on the small table next to him. "We'll be the talk of the town grapevine tomorrow."

"As if I care."

"At least you're one of the few people in town who doesn't mind being seen talking to me. Ironic, since it's your husband who is responsible. Thinks I'm either unethical or dangerous. Or both."

"Oh, I hope you're dangerous." She picked up his book. "What's this about?"

"A concert pianist, her career, and her love affair that ended badly."

"What happened?"

"She was murdered."

Darcie could match Reece Wable in their ability to hide emotions behind a mask of indifference. But at times small openings popped up before she caught herself, like the fleeting ray of worry he observed at the graveyard, and again just now.

"A mystery novel?"

"True crime. The couple escaped to England from Poland in 1944, but the pianist's husband ended up joining the Polish resistance during the war. He was never the same and died of a heart attack a decade later."

"That's a sad story, all right. But why does it matter to you?"

"The pianist's last concert was in the Cape Unity Opera House. Before his death, her husband encouraged his wife to go on a concert tour in the States."

A tour on which she was accompanied by her agent, Harmon Ainscough, one of the main suspects in her murder. The others included Konstantina's stepson and her brother-in-law, now deceased. In fact, many of the suspects had long since died, throwing roadblocks into Drayco's unofficial investigation. Like Oakley, Drayco was becoming obsessed with the unsolved murder. The two cases were some fifty years apart, but both tied to the Opera House.

Darcie's voice interrupted his digression. "Was she killed here?"

"She was strangled in London. She'd only recently had a baby."

"Why don't you find her kid for more information?"

"Apparently the child died." Drayco put the book down on the table. "The pianist and her husband were very much in love. Like I think Oakley and Nanette were, deep down."

Darcie picked her nails. "Perhaps."

"Were you merely bored and toying with Oakley? What was it that attracted you, pity?" Time to force a few more cracks to open.

"You think I'm shallow, don't you?" She seemed genuinely hurt. "Bet you don't know I have a degree in social work."

Darcie was definitely the "sociable" type, no doubt about it. "Was Oakley your thesis?"

"He was warm and kind. A friend. He gave me gifts."

An elderly woman carrying a PBS tote bag walked in, heading in their direction. When she spied Darcie and then Drayco, she tutted and turned around. Yep. On the news grapevine soon.

"What type of gifts did Oakley give you? He didn't have much money."

She smiled. "A book of love letters between Elizabeth Barrett and that Browning guy. I don't read much, but it was sweet."

"Were you in love with him?"

Darcie put her cup down on the table. "He was a diversion. I was an ego boost."

"Have you boosted the egos of other men, Earl Yaegle, Reece Wable?"

"Reece? Now there's a fun thought." She crossed her legs, showing off her fishnet stockings. "I'm picky who I have affairs with." The sly grin returned. "Why, I think you're jealous. That's why you're asking me these questions."

"I call jealousy the dandelion emotion. Innocent-looking, until it morphs from sunny yellow to a gossamer skeleton. And impossible to stop from destroying your yard once it spreads." He picked up the cup of coffee she'd brought and tried not to recoil when he tasted sugar and cream. "Were you jealous of Nanette?"

"Of course not. I didn't want a permanent relationship with Oakley."

"You said he gave you gifts, plural. What else besides the book? Some of his wood carvings like a mask?"

Darcie twirled her hair around her fingers. "Nothing interesting. And what would I do with a wooden mask? It's not like we have masquerade parties."

Darcie jumped up and moved to the front of Drayco's chair where she stood between his legs and traced a finger slowly down his cheek and across his jaw. She placed her lips next to his ear and whispered, "Oakley loved my kind of parties. I'll bet you would, too."

With a carefree wave of her hand, she left him sitting alone, lost in his thoughts. A few minutes later his cell phone rang, and he was surprised to hear Darcie. How had she gotten his number? "I almost forgot, darling. Meet me tomorrow evening at six at Cypress Manor. I won't take no for an answer." Then she hung up.

31

Still mulling over Darcie's phone call, Drayco collided with someone outside the Historical Society's entrance. Randolph Squier pushed past him without saying a word and hurried around the corner street. Drayco opened the door to the Historical Society half-expecting to trip over more of Grace Waterworth's books, but the hardcover mountains were nowhere in sight. The thick, musty smell was gone, and even Andrew Jackson seemed to be breathing easier.

Drayco was impressed. "You must be a conjurer, my friend, because there's no way you cataloged all those books in such a short time."

Reece snapped his fingers. "I did that three times, and voilà, they vanished."

"Allow me to translate. You dumped them somewhere else."

"The library," Reece crowed.

"Why am I not surprised? Libraries are the dumping ground for every unwanted moldy book."

Reece replied defensively, "I think the library staff, all one and a half of them, were grateful. Seeing as how the council slashed their budget. Old Squier led the way on that one. He's rich enough to afford all the books he wants."

"You didn't keep any of them?"

Reece sniffed. "The sheriff snagged that garden poison book. But there were a couple of other gems for our archives."

"Speaking of the pompous councilman, is that why he was here? To add to your archives on a weekend when you're not ordinarily open?"

Reece took his time replying. "We're both collectors. We keep each other informed of interesting pieces we come across. Animals desperate for fodder need access to all available fields. Even toxic ones."

Was that really all it was? Drayco didn't like where a Reece-plus-Squiers collaboration might take him. Down into a dank crypt of conspiracy built on top of the duo's shared hatred of Oakley Keys. Was there room in that crypt for Darcie and Nanette, too?

Reece motioned for Drayco to follow him into a back room filled with vertical files. Pointing to a large black metal cabinet, he said, "Now for why I called you here. See that?"

The cabinet looked like a standard office-supply item. The most unusual thing about it was the compact hygrothermograph sitting on top. It showed the humidity was forty-seven percent, which should make Reece—and the archive materials—happy.

Drayco looked askance at Reece. "It's a nice cabinet."

"I've been burgled."

"You mean someone broke in and stole something?"

"Broke in, but I can't say anything was stolen."

"Back up a minute. What made you think someone broke in, to begin with?"

"Whoever it was bumped into the table by the back door where I keep figurines. When I came in this morning, they weren't in their usual places. Like someone knocked them over and tried to put them back."

It was hard not to feel skeptical. But nothing was taken from Drayco's room, either.

Reece continued, "Also, file cabinet drawers weren't closed all the way. I always shut them tight to keep dust and moisture out."

"Were there signs of forced entry? Footprints?"

"No and no. I admit this fellow must be clever. With all the wet weather, there should be some dirt tracked in. Of course, it could be a woman, since they're neater creatures. But I swear there was someone here."

"Are you the only one with a key?"

Reece started to answer, then stopped himself. "The only living person. Oakley had a key he never gave back."

Squier had done the same thing with the key to the Opera House. "Whoever murdered Oakley could have stolen his key and waltzed right in, Reece."

Reece wrinkled his forehead in alarm. "I planned on having the locks changed, but I kept putting it off."

"You say certain file cabinet drawers weren't closed completely. Which ones?"

"That's what I wanted you to see. Only cabinets containing Opera House memorabilia."

Drayco peered at the labels on the front of the cabinet in the corner and read *Cape Unity Opera House* in large black letters on the inserts. "How can you tell nothing was taken?"

"I'm a meticulous record keeper. I have indices for each drawer." Reece peered at Drayco out of the corner of his eye. "You're the one person who would be interested. Did you sneak in?"

Drayco shot him a withering look. It wasn't out of the question this was a ruse on Reece's part to throw Drayco off. Reece was one of the suspects who didn't have an alibi but plenty of motive for Oakley's murder. Yet visualizing Reece Wable as a cold-blooded murderer was like imagining the face of the puppet Charlie McCarthy—with whom Reece shared more than a passing resemblance—as a serial killer.

"You didn't contact the sheriff's office?"

"Since this is your bailiwick, both in profession and ownership, you were the logical person."

"I could wrangle some fingerprinting gear."

"Too much trouble. Besides, I have something more remarkable to tell you."

They moved into Reece's newly uncluttered office, where Reece made a big production out of being able to put his feet on his desk again. "You remember that stolen clock? After Oakley's murder, I had to know the truth. To absolve Oakley if he didn't do it and forgive him if he did. I uncovered an auction house that listed a similar clock sold at the same time. As it turns out, my father and the owner of that auction house were old friends. I thought you might be interested to know who sold the clock."

Reece tipped his chair back, pausing for effect. "It was Oakley Keys. He didn't bother to use an alias. He said he might have another piece to sell, even more valuable. Sounds like he planned more thefts."

Drayco pondered that for a moment. More thefts. Scrimshaw, perhaps? On an impulse, he reached over to turn on the miniature carousel on Reece's desk and watched it go round and round in circles as it played the tune "The Windmills of Your Mind." *Like a clock whose hands are sweeping. .. keys that jingle in your pocket. ..words that jangle in your head.*

"That doesn't prove Oakley stole your clock, only that he was the seller."

"Oh, I'm past being angry. I mean, the man was murdered, for God's sake. I guess we'll never know why Oakley did it. But if you apply Occam's Razor, it was to fund his drinking habit. You tell me, you're the crime consultant."

"Do you have the name of the buyer?"

"Unless it's absolutely necessary, I want to keep that private. It's a respectable woman who comes from a long line of philanthropists. She has children, grandchildren, great-grandchildren and is a paragon of virtue."

"It doesn't sound like she'd have any involvement in Oakley's murder. But if there comes a time when talking to this woman might be necessary—"

"Then I'll be happy to tell you. I can be a cooperative citizen."

Andrew Jackson squawked on his perch and repeated his familiar refrain, "Oakley's a madman, Oakley's a madman."

Drayco rubbed his temple. He'd been working on a headache since he woke up from another nightmare this morning. It was amazing how rhythmic the throbbing was, like the drum beats at the beginning of Brahms's first symphony. "One more thing about the break-in, Reece. You said only drawers with Opera House records were opened. Can you tell which folders the burglar was interested in?"

"As I said, I'm a meticulous sort. One, and only one, folder was rifled."

Drayco was growing tired of Reece's melodrama, although the headache wasn't helping. "Which folder, Reece?"

"The file with old drawings of the Opera House layout. They're not the same as detailed blueprints, mind you."

"Too bad they weren't. I would love to see some blueprints."

"Must be some dusty old archives that has them. Did your benefactor, Mr. Rockingham, leave any?"

"He left little. Definitely no blueprints. The courthouse didn't have them, either."

"Pity. I'll do some digging."

Drayco was beginning to feel that all the "coincidences" were merely variations on a theme. Historic buildings broken into. Historical documents stolen—from Oakley, the Opera House and. .. "Reece, any theories why that manuscript was stolen from the library recently? There could be a connection."

Reece tapped his finger against his nose and grinned. "How can you be sure I didn't steal it? It's a pain waiting for people to donate items to the society. Mrs. Waterworth's moth-eaten donation, notwithstanding."

"Did you?"

"The head librarian and I get along well enough. The old I-scratch-her-book, she scratches-my-book thing."

As usual, Drayco ignored Reece's bad jokes. "I'm surprised the document wasn't here in the society to begin with."

"I can't keep all the best stuff for myself. Although I don't see what anyone would want with a letter from a long-dead member of the British royalty waxing poetic about Cape Extremity. Might get fifty dollars for it on eBay."

"Keep me posted if you have more mysterious break-ins. And since the crime rate seems to be skyrocketing in town, you should change that lock."

Reece used his hands to mimic a noose that he held over Drayco's head. "I should set a trap. I can give as good as I get when my corner of the universe is threatened."

32

Sheriff Sailor and Deputy Tyler stood next to the body positioned parallel to the coffee table. Arms and legs lay straight and close to the man's torso as if already laid out neatly on a slab in the morgue. Blood from his head seeped into the blue and green shag carpet, turning it a rusty brown mini-forest.

The victim's son, Nicholas, was the sheriff's age, although you couldn't tell it from the unnaturally black thatch of curly hair. Sailor hadn't seen Nicholas in several years, but he remembered him as having more wrinkles, too. But that was before the man's divorce, and near as Sailor could recall, his ex-wife ran off with one of her twenty-one-year-old students from a class she taught at Eastern Shore Community College.

"I called you right away when I found him," Nicholas said. "The first thing that came to my mind was Oakley and Nanette Keys."

That same thought was the main reason Sailor was here. Was this a sign of the serial killer link he'd been dreading? "When did you last see your father?"

"Yesterday I brought him supper and visited for a while, and then we returned home. He seemed fine at the time."

"You say you called as soon as you found him. When was that exactly?"

"About forty-five minutes ago. He knew I was going to drop off a new emergency weather radio I bought him. So when I knocked on the door and got no answer, I feared the worst."

All three turned toward the front of the house as the sounds of a siren drew closer and then quickly shut off. The sheriff turned to Nicholas, "Did you call anyone else besides me?" Sailor himself had called for a fire and rescue ambulance, but the closest team was already tied up with a near-drowning at the park. The best estimate dispatch could give him was fifteen minutes.

Nicholas shook his head and moved to open the door as two emergency medical technicians rushed in and surveyed the scene. "We got a call from this location and came as fast as we could," one of them said, quickly spying the man on the floor and setting to work.

Sailor knew they were checking for life signs out of professional duty, but it was clear to him it was way too late for that. The sheriff queried the first EMT as the other bent over the body. "You mean someone dialed 9-1-1 about this?"

"'Bout ten minutes ago." The EMT looked apologetic.

"What was the nature of the 9-1-1 call?"

"A man, obviously with trouble breathing, told us he was having chest pains radiating out to his arm and that he was dizzy. We suspected a heart attack."

"And the blood on his head?"

The EMT gently lifted up the man's head before lowering it again. Then he pointed to the corner of a coffee table. It was a dark wood, but if you looked closely, you could see traces of blood.

Sailor said, "He hit his head on the way down."

"That'd be my guess."

The sheriff observed the obese form of the man on the floor, a known two-pack-a-day smoker, and gave Nelia a sideways look of relief. They waited for verification the man was officially deceased, then left the body in the experienced hands of the EMTs. The sheriff consoled Nicholas and promised he would share the autopsy results with him to make certain the father had died from the suspected natural causes. The M.E. was certainly earning his pay lately.

Back in the patrol car, Nelia said, "A waste of your time to tag along. I was surprised you wanted to come in the first place."

Sailor ran his hands along the steering wheel. "The deceased is Darion Stanz."

"Stanz, as in Stanz Marts?"

"He and his cousin own the chain."

"Isn't that the same chain where your brother—"

"Yes. It is."

Nelia rubbed the small pink scar on her face. "Sorry. Sometimes I speak without thinking first."

Sailor had relived the moment he heard the news about Zeke so many times that the edge was gone. But for a brief second, when the call came in about Stanz, the psychic nerve shot pangs through his soul. Now that it was cauterized again, Nelia's comment washed over it more like a mild sting. "The Stanz clan was good to my family after Zeke's death."

Nelia surveyed the ambulance with her forehead creased in thought. Sailor sensed she'd been thinking along the same lines as he, which was verified when she said, "Well, Stanz's death looks straightforward. But it would almost be easier if we were dealing with a serial killer, you know? We'd have a better idea the same person killed Oakley and Nanette. One murderer and not two."

The death of Stanz was straightforward, all right, though people like Nicholas were understandably jumpy. Sailor hoped there wouldn't be a spate of additional false alarms from over-imaginative relatives. Or worse, nervous new gun owners causing tragic accidents. Business at Earl Yaegle's gun shop was brisk lately. As it was, focusing on the Keys' investigation was stretching the limits of manpower available to his small office. In truth, he was grateful Drayco got involved, if by default. He'd never tell him that.

The sheriff radioed the office to indicate they'd be returning sooner than first thought and pointed the car down Route 13. "Our friend Scott Drayco believes it's one murderer, not two, but I'm not entirely sure I agree. A killer doesn't usually go to the trouble to mutilate one corpse and then leave the other one fairly pristine. Still, we can't pin down two separate motives. At least ones we can verify."

Nelia nodded. "I suppose a love affair gone awry would be a logical jump for the two-murders, one-perpetrator scenario. Although I interviewed three women who admit being linked romantically with Oakley decades ago. They all remember him fondly. That makes Darcie Squier the wild card. Why her? Or I guess I should say why him? And why so long after the other affairs ended?"

"Darcie maintains it was platonic. That she was just bored. She talked to me as if Oakley were a trifling plaything, a temporary novelty. Hard to refute when the other person involved can't speak for himself."

Sailor hadn't enjoyed talking to the disagreeable Squier duo. He'd come away frustrated with the Squier's convenient alibis for each other, a tactic that bordered on stonewalling. If the councilman knew his wife was involved in the murders, he was definitely the type who would think nothing about covering up her culpability to save his own reputation. On the other hand, Darcie wouldn't risk being arrested as an accomplice if her husband were involved. Unless she was motivated by maintaining a stake in her husband's fortune.

Nelia said, "Drayco didn't seem to take the warning note from his room seriously. But it has to be related to the Keys' deaths in some way."

"Nothing he's come across seems incriminating enough to inspire a threat. But it does appear he's hit a nerve with someone."

Nelia turned to look out the window as they passed by a dirty white building with broken windows and a rusting *Mexican Store* sign out front. "Do you really trust him?"

"I checked on him. He's known to be intense, focused. He's got good instincts. And a sharp mind, making connections between bits of information and tying them together. In one of his first private gigs after leaving the Bureau, he solved a case mired in law enforcement purgatory for a decade. Takes after his father, I suppose. Brock Drayco developed a well-regarded international reputation during his own career. But to answer your question, yeah, I'd say I trust him."

Nelia's shoulders relaxed, and she smiled to herself. Sailor was still getting to know his newest deputy, and he was a little worried by that smile. Tyler apparently found Drayco appealing, but the sheriff also knew Nelia prided herself on her objectivity. She once turned in a boyfriend for stealing cases of beer to sell at top dollar to minors.

Objectivity was one of the tougher parts of the job. Sailor had lived in Cape Unity longer than Nelia, but they were both acquainted with many of its residents. Thefts, drugs, fights—those were the pebbles at the bottom of the criminal rock heap. The town certainly had its share. It was far more troubling to believe one or more of the townspeople committed a double murder. But he and his deputies had a job to do and were determined to see this case through, no matter what the consequences. The town's sense of security depended on it.

33

Monday 22 March

Maida let Drayco sleep late on Monday, but a late-morning call from Sheriff Sailor lured Drayco to the downtown docks. Sailor had filled him in about a local man's death the Sheriff and Nelia were involved with earlier, but Sailor didn't think it was related to the Keys' murders. It made Drayco feel a little guilty Sailor had been up and on the job early.

Drayco watched a man in a neoprene wetsuit slide down the tie rope into foamy water, dodging piles of driftwood, plastic bottles and Styrofoam containers washed against the pier's stanchions. As the diver's head sunk beneath the waves, Sailor said, "That's his third time down and his last. Water's above freezing, but not much. You a diver?"

"I'm supposed to be diving in Cancun right now. I think I'll let your deputy handle this one. I don't fancy being turned into an ice cube."

"Could suit you up, anyway. Be good for that gimpy leg. Get the circulation flowing."

"If I drink antifreeze first, perhaps. You say a witness swears they saw someone dump a gun down there?"

"A reliable fellow. It was dark, so I'm not holding out much hope." The sheriff clenched his jaw constantly now. Drayco hoped he had a good dental plan.

"I don't think you've taken a day off since the day Oakley was killed, Sheriff."

"Thanks to TV dramas, the public thinks I should've solved this thing in an hour."

"More like forty minutes, if you don't count the commercials." Drayco concentrated on the spot where the diver descended, but no head emerged. A flash of a brown uniform caught his attention as it moved toward them from the side. "Tyler's being given a trial by fire her first month on the job."

"I told her not to get used to working a murder case. It'll be back to bar fights and domestic disputes in no time."

Nelia caught up to them and smiled at Drayco, "Hello again. I was hoping to see you."

"Then I guess it's a good thing I missed my vacation to Cancun, after all." He pointed at a small notebook in her hand, identical to the type Sailor used. "What have you got there?"

She opened it up to show it was filled with her scribbled notations. "Per your suggestion, I located Oakley's advisor from college. He said Oakley was hardworking and ambitious, with a double major in English and History."

The sheriff butted in, "And here I expected geography or geology so we might have a 'G' to go on."

Nelia continued, "Oakley did a massive senior thesis on genealogy—there's a 'G' for you—focusing on Europeans after World War II. I also scanned a few of Oakley's books at his house. Books on the war, some tour guides. Decent writing, but they're out of print. He didn't have anything published beyond 2005, except a monthly column for a British expat magazine, à la Alistair Cooke. I haven't gone through them since there are a hundred or so."

The sheriff added, "If you'd like some torture, Drayco, they're all yours."

"This professor couldn't add anything else? Nothing unusual?"

Nelia consulted her notes. "No scandals, no skeletons, no controversy. Oakley wasn't a sociable kid, bright but otherwise ordinary."

Drayco asked, "You said Oakley's senior thesis was on genealogy? Yet he never wrote a book on that subject. Wonder why?"

Nelia replied, "Perhaps he didn't think it would be profitable. Or he couldn't interest a publisher."

"Was there a copy of that thesis?"

"The school doesn't keep copies of undergrad works. The university also has no records of roommates."

"Sorry to have wasted your time with a dead end, Tyler."

"Ya never know."

"As penance, I'll check Oakley's columns for clues."

She raised an eyebrow. "It's a big box."

"I'll be sure and drop it on my foot. I can sue the county government for pain and suffering and use the money to restore the Opera House."

The sheriff grumbled, "Wish you better luck coaxing money out of the Board. They make Scrooge look like Andrew Carnegie."

Drayco pulled a thick envelope out of the briefcase lying at his feet and pulled out a rubber-banded sheaf of papers. "Here's a copy of another Oakley manuscript, one Earl gave me. Note the unusual inscription."

Sailor perused it. "Odd indeed."

Nelia peered over the sheriff's shoulder and read aloud, "'May we find those valuable things that lie hidden from us and discover what is rightfully ours.' Did he think there's buried treasure on his property? And that's why he didn't want to sell?"

The sheriff replied, "If so, why isn't there evidence of digging? Oakley's lawn was more immaculate than Cypress Manor's. Since he was murdered at the Opera House, maybe he thought something was buried there."

Drayco sighed. "Ask me how excited I am about hiring an excavation crew. Yet Oakley didn't have any tools on him and was hardly dressed for archaeology. Not so much as a pith helmet."

Nelia grinned, "You do realize that's an outdated stereotype."

"Is it?" He put a hand over his heart. "There goes another one of my cherished romantic notions." He was glad to see her impish grin and relaxed stance. He'd found out she was one of only two women on the force, and her body language was a sign she was holding her own with her new boss and testosterone-heavy co-workers.

Sailor gave the manuscript back to Drayco, who crammed it in the envelope and asked, "Who gets reading honors this time?"

Sailor pointed at Nelia. "Since she's becoming Oakley's librarian, I'll have to go with Tyler."

Drayco handed the envelope to Nelia, who asked, "I've been wanting to ask you something. Sheriff Sailor said your father was a former FBI agent? Did he retire or. ..?"

"He decided to go into private practice. Got tired of paperwork."

"Like you?"

"Me? I headed for the fabulous riches of self-employment."

She sighted Drayco's ancient car with its dents and dings. "And the riches the Opera House will bring."

Drayco grinned. "After several million dollars spent restoring the place first. But don't worry, I'm sure I'll make that amount on my next case."

"The case of the client who bequeaths you something practical?"

"A Van Gogh painting or the Hope Diamond? Hope so. Leonora needs bodywork, and in D.C. nothing comes cheap."

She stifled a laugh. "Leonora?"

"My car. She's seen me through several murders, kidnappings, thefts, forgeries and other fun times. She's a trouper."

"Leonora—the Beethoven heroine?"

Drayco was momentarily speechless. "A literary sheriff and a musical deputy?"

Nelia rolled her eyes in mock indignation. "Not all small town constabulary are uncultured savages, although I'm more of a blues girl, myself. But isn't a Starfire too, well, eye-catching for surveillance?"

"I've got the GSC for that."

"GSC?"

"My generic silver Camry. I keep it parked in the garage at my office. Although if I want to blend in around D.C. these days, I should get a Prius or a Jaguar, depending upon which end of the political spectrum you're on."

Nelia laughed. "I guess that leaves my Chevy Malibu square in the middle. I always did feel like an independent." Nelia hesitated briefly, as if she was going to add something, but waved at them and headed over to the pier where the diver stayed submerged.

As the sheriff looked from Drayco to the departing Nelia, he didn't utter any warnings this time, but his voice was rough. "The techs got back to me on that newspaper clipping and the two orange powder capsules. The handwriting on the clipping matches Oakley's so it could be from his stolen files. The capsules turned out to be cayenne pepper."

"Ordinary cayenne?"

"You can find the pills in health food stores and the corner Safeway. And we did get a partial cast on that shoe print. Haven't matched it up yet. But we'll need a suspect first. Then a warrant."

Sailor grabbed his own pocket notebook and flipped it open. "Per your other tip, we tracked down a woman named O'Hannon who lived near London, first name Arlene."

Drayco said, "Oakley's adopted mother. She's dead, isn't she?"

"Ten years ago. How'd you know?"

"You and Nanette both said Oakley's mysterious business trips ended around that time. I'd guessed they were visits to his mother. And he no longer needed to travel there after her death."

Sailor slipped the notepad back into his pocket. "That's a pretty big guess."

"The adopted part was a hunch. Bendek started me thinking along those lines. And, although Oakley told Darcie he had a mother, he indicated to Major Jepson he was an orphan. Being adopted fits both. The fact the mystery trips involved his mother and not a mistress or shady business dealings—Oakley didn't leave a paper trail, hard to believe from someone who didn't own a computer. The missing file box was too small to store years of incriminating documents. He had no friends to cover for him. Except Darcie, who said he never gave her any papers to keep."

The sheriff stayed silent for a moment. "Did Mrs. Squier tell you how her family, the Gentners, lost their land in a tax dispute? Be worth a small fortune now. I always wondered why Squier would marry a penniless woman, even a looker like Darcie. The Gentners may have a few secret money stashes. Darcie remains a suspect in my book." Sailor rubbed the back of his neck. "Looks like you didn't heed my warning about the councilman's wife."

"Whatever it takes to investigate."

Sailor didn't comment further. "But why all the secrecy on Oakley's part over his heritage? Why the different last name, Keys and not O'Hannon?"

Drayco shook his head. "I've got a theory or two. Nothing concrete."

The sheriff clenched his jaw. Their detente only stretched so far, and Drayco hated to withhold anything. But if he were wrong, having the sheriff follow his own line of investigation was best. If Drayco had trusted his instincts more on the Cadden case, two children might still be alive.

Sailor took off his hat and inspected the brim which had picked up some debris from the wind, before putting it back on. "I'll trade you wild theories. I'm bringing Reece Wable in for questioning."

Reece was high on Drayco's list at first. But now he realized how far down Reece had dropped, clinging to the page by a chad despite the possible Reece-Squier link. "This is the first you've mentioned it. What's changed?"

"An anonymous tip. Checked out the trunk of Reece's car and lo and behold, we found a bloodied knife wrapped in cloth. Dried blood, not fresh, no prints on the knife—"

"You can't arrest him for that."

"We'll have to match that knife to the cuts on Oakley and get a blood type. The knife from the dumpster behind Earl's gun shop might be the wrong one."

"Even though the first knife was the right blood type? An anonymous tip, Sheriff? And a second knife with blood on it?"

"I admit it feels hinky. But I also checked up on that story Wable mentioned, the run-in with a private eye. Wable was driving a car involved in an accident that killed his passenger, an antiques dealer. The doctors said it was a pre-existing aneurysm. The deceased's relatives claimed Wable had it in for the guy because he stole some document Wable wanted. They were pushing for manslaughter."

"Any evidence for the charge?"

"The detective didn't find anything. Neither did our department at the time."

"You must have more than that to bring Reece in."

"A witness heard Oakley and Reece arguing the day before he was murdered. Apparently, Oakley accused Reece of having an affair with Nanette."

Drayco wanted to cheer at the thought of Nanette getting back at Oakley for all those years of one affair after another, but he had a hard time imagining Reece and Nanette together, despite her indiscretions with Earl Yaegle. Perhaps there really was something in the water, an escaped mutagenic bug from Fort Detrick's biomedical labs that altered pheromones. He'd listened to far too many of his former FBI partner's summaries of his favorite sci-fi movies.

"Is this witness solid, Sheriff?"

"Well," Sailor hemmed. "She's one of these overly eager lonely widows who's always calling our office with tips. I think she's too partial to peach schnapps, frankly. But Reece Wable has motive, opportunity, and there's the knife."

Drayco wanted to point out that several others, including Earl Yaegle and especially Randolph Squier, had equally good cases against them, but he didn't. "Maida said you'd called about the coyote autopsy but didn't give specifics."

"Your arms are safe, no needles for you. The coyote—not an ordinary coyote, but a coyote-wolf hybrid—wasn't rabid."

"Then why did it attack?"

"She apparently gave birth not too long ago."

Drayco's spirits sank even more at that. A mother defending her brood. "Any way to find the litter?"

"I asked a wildlife rescue friend to check, but it's been a couple days. Not much hope."

One dead coyote mother, never to return to the hungry cubs. Was there anything he could have done differently during the attack? It was like being in the Bureau, second-guessing your actions. Wondering if only you'd chosen another course of action, the bad guy wouldn't have gotten away. Or your partner wouldn't be lying in the hospital. Or the Cadden twins would be alive to see their next birthday. Second-guessing broke more cops and agents than anything else.

A shout from the pier drew their attention toward Nelia as the diver handed her an object, and she dropped it into a plastic bag. The sheriff and Drayco walked over for a closer inspection. It was a gun all right, waterlogged with some seaweed clinging to it.

"Looks like a Webley to me," the sheriff grinned.

Drayco studied the gun. "It's the right vintage. Think the state lab will be able to run a quick comparison with the.455 bullet from the Opera House?"

"Wouldn't count on it. Right now, I should get my depu-sicle back to drier quarters."

Drayco waited until Nelia and the deputy diver took off in one car and the sheriff followed in the other, then surveyed the pier and dock. Not the best time of year to show them off, with only a couple of covered boats and lots of empty slips. It was a shame he couldn't arrange a trip to the Atlantic-side barrier islands, closed for all but a few months to protect nesting birds.

With one last eyeballing of the pier, he headed to the Starfire. He didn't get far because Paddy Bakely was blocking the door. It wasn't noon, yet Paddy's speech was already slurred, his eyes and nose beet-red. "Why did you have to come here?" he shouted. "You've messed everything up."

"What do you mean?" Drayco hoped engaging Paddy in conversation would calm him down.

"You're in love with her. And the way she looks at you."

"Who?"

"Worse than Rockingham, you are. You'll tear the place down, and my Daddy'll be out of a job. But it'll give all those wetbacks jobs, won't it? Jobs that shoulda gone to law-abiding taxpayers, that's what."

Taxpayers? It was hard to believe Paddy paid any taxes in his life since he'd never held a steady job. And Drayco doubted anyone would place Paddy and "law-abiding" in the same sentence.

He didn't think Paddy's voice could get much louder, but it did. "All we want is what's rightfully ours." Paddy moved closer to Drayco and grabbed an arm with both of his hands. He was surprisingly strong. "Why don't you go back to D.C. with those slimy maggots, goddamn you."

Drayco heard a car pull up behind them, but Paddy's eyes didn't move toward it until a hand clapped Paddy on the shoulder, causing Paddy to spin around. The sheriff asked, "Is there a problem?"

Drayco replied, "We were having. .. a conversation."

"Paddy's had enough conversation for a while. Why don't you go over and get in the back of my car, Paddy. I'll take you home." Paddy's defiant façade crumbled, and he started blubbering, tears streaming down his face. The sheriff nudged him toward the squad car. "Go on now."

Drayco watched him lurch across the street. "Not a happy man."

"He's not going to find his answers inside a bottle."

"If there are any answers to be had. Did you forget something, Sheriff? Thought you were long gone."

"Saw Paddy out the back of my rearview as I was leaving and had one of your famous hunches."

"I like your hunches better."

Sailor smiled grimly, "Just don't go rogue on me, Drayco."

Paddy's face peered out the squad car window as the sheriff drove off a second time, resembling an abandoned puppy being hauled off to the pound. Who was the "she" he was afraid Drayco was stealing? Darcie? Paddy was a soul lost in a haze not entirely of his making. Drayco looked out over at the water of the Bay, a sight that usually made him feel at peace. Not this time. Only an empty horizon as far as the eyes could see.

34

Drayco was alone at Cape Unity's Powhatan Park this time. Both the sheriff and Maida would throw a fit if they knew he was here, but he wasn't afraid of another animal attack. A human one, perhaps.

He headed toward the area where he discovered the Opera House clipping and orange capsule, but it was clear the sheriff's team had been here, so he left well enough alone. That wasn't the real reason he'd come, anyway.

Heading back toward the overlook, he stopped at the place where the coyote hybrid attacked him. The tree stump where he'd propped his leg sported a streak of his dried blood smeared against the side.

Drayco parked the mostly empty box he was carrying onto the top of the rock, and using his compass, started a sweep to the north and then the west. A few steps forward, then listening, then a few more steps. It was a fool's errand after three days, but he had to try.

He recalled a night long ago, when his father, in a rare moment of that hated sentimentality of his, took his son to the shore to watch the spawning of tiny horseshoe crabs. Brock patiently explained how they weren't crabs at all, but closer to spiders, and it was the copper in their blood that made them blue. The hatchlings, descendants of ancestor crabs 450 million years old, were endangered by overfishing from humans and birds and loss of habitat. Yet they found a way to survive.

A small sound carried on the wind caught his attention. Another bird? No, this was more of a faint mewling. He triangulated the sound, using the trees like mirrors to localize the source, and crept toward the large, dark hole carved out under the roots of a dying tree. He whipped out his flashlight and trained it into the opening.

The mewling of the two infant cubs crescendoed as the light hit them. They were likely so desperate for food that their hunger overpowered their fear. Both coyote and wolf fathers often helped out with their young, but since only one animal attacked Drayco, he was fairly certain these little guys belonged to a single-parent household.

He reached into another pocket and pulled out some soft gloves and carefully slid his hand into the den to pull out first one cub and then the other. They were blind, meaning only days old. But his flashlight had also revealed the mother chose her den well—a trickle of water via an underground water source kept the twins alive.

Bundling the cubs inside his jacket, next to his shirt, he carried them back to the box and set them down onto the blanket inside, speaking to them soothingly. Once the box was safely parked onto the passenger floor of Drayco's car, he headed toward a wildlife center Maida had told him about. The woman who greeted him was thrilled to see the cubs and said they would raise them until they were old enough to release.

After he returned to the car, he noticed in the rearview mirror how deep the dark circles under his eyes were, worse than the sheriff's He was happy to have helped out those two orphans, but he had a much larger problem looming down the road.

Unlike *Phantom of the Opera*, the Cape Unity Opera House had no subterranean chamber where a villain could lurk. Neither did Drayco agree with some locals the building was haunted. He ran one finger over the piano keys, often likened to bones. On this damp evening, the only vibe was akin to an archaeological dig, the structural skeleton a mute witness to a forgotten past.

Drayco and the piano, alone on an empty stage under a spotlight. A scene he knew well. He had a strong sense of *déjà vu* similar to the first time he stepped inside the Opera House, the same funk he experienced then. Why such a sense of loss now?

Sitting on the bench, he wondered what would become of the piano if he sold the building and its contents. It had a warm tone he liked, and when tuned, would sound quite good. This must be the same instrument Konstantina Klucze played. She would have sat in this same spot, focused on her concert, unaware of the cruel fate ahead.

He tried a few scales before launching into Bach's "Goldberg Variations." Bach was a lifeline whenever Drayco had something to puzzle through. The musical counterpoint was like a reverse prism, taking scattered colors of light and focusing them into a cohesive whole. It helped him to concentrate on abstract thoughts.

He made it through the opening aria, but after a few measures of the first variation, his hand started cramping. He tried again, but it only took a few notes for the pain to shoot up his arm like an electric shock. Frustrated, he banged his hands down on the keyboard. Should have performed the water bath first.

He rubbed the arm until the cramps subsided, and started in gingerly this time, with a silent apology to the piano. Time always stood still when he played. He had no idea how long he'd been at it when he heard a familiar wheeze above the sound of his playing.

He stopped, irritated.

Seth walked over. "Thought I'd let you know I was here."

"Just checking out the piano, Seth. Needs tuning, but otherwise, you've kept it in good shape. For someone who hates pianos."

Seth coughed and ran the back of his hand across his mouth. "Shouldn't have said that. It was rude. And the instrument's a beauty all right." He stared at Drayco, "You should do that for money. You've got your own place to play now."

"I'm happy doing what I am, for the most part."

"The detective stuff?"

"Helping people. Solving puzzles. Right now one of the biggest puzzles to me is why Oakley Keys was so obsessed with this place."

Seth shrugged. "Ask Major Jepson."

"Why is that?"

"Oakley was a hermit. Didn't have a lot of friends. But Major was his closest, them being ex-Brits and all."

Drayco tried not to laugh at Seth's description of Oakley as a hermit since it took one to know one. He no longer felt like smiling when Seth continued. "Oakley gave gifts to his friends. Once saw Major with a wooden mask Oakley made him."

"When was this?"

"Been a while." Seth coughed again. "If you don't mind, I've got mops back there that'll stink to high heaven if I allow them to sour."

Drayco waited for Seth to leave, then dug into the Bach with a renewed intensity. Major Jepson never mentioned a mask. Not even when Drayco discussed Oakley's creation with him. He only played a few more measures before something drew him out of his concentration, and again he stopped. He peered into the back of the hall where a figure headed into the light. He waved her forward. "I see you made it on this lovely afternoon."

"Of course." Maida laughed. "I've always wondered what the inside looked like. I must say it's nicer than I imagined."

Drayco gestured around the hall. "Virtually the same as it was half a century ago, with faded makeup and a few wrinkles. You were expecting cobwebs?"

"Worse. Spooky sheets, a few mice and dust everywhere. You didn't have to stop playing. Was that Bach?"

"The Goldberg Variations."

"You're good, you know."

He grinned. "You sound surprised."

She whisked the Nationals baseball cap off her head and ran a hand through her hair. "I didn't mean it that way. I thought with your injury, you couldn't play much."

"Not enough to have a piano career. Too many hours of practice. But I can play in small bursts."

Maida circled the bottom of the stage to sit in the front row. "How much would a seat like this cost nowadays?"

"Here, it's free. At a place like the Kennedy Center, anywhere from eighty to a hundred dollars a ticket."

"Too rich for my blood. I'll stay right here and take the free ticket, thank you very much."

"Some rock concerts will set you back three or four times that."

"Tell you what—next time you have a concert, we'll get a group of ladies together and throw some underwear at you. Make you feel like a rock star."

"I think you might be hard-pressed to come up with such a group."

"Not from what I've seen. I'm sure Darcie Squier would pay double for the opportunity."

Drayco winced. "I think I'll stick to investigative work."

Having one woman at a time throw herself at him was enough. Especially since she was married. And a suspect. And like the Saproshin vodka Tatiana's father smuggled from Moscow—a toxin you know you should avoid, but once indulged becomes a guilty pleasure. Darcie in a nutshell.

He stood up and offered a hand to Maida as she climbed the stairs to the stage. "I promised the five-cent tour."

Maida pointed to the circular stairs and catwalk. "That looks like fun."

Drayco considered the creaky rails with reservation. "I've tried it once, but I need to get it inspected. If it passes, I'll take you up there."

Maida caught sight of the fading red stain on the wooden floor, and she shivered. "Is that—"

Drayco nodded. "Afraid so." He focused on her expression. "Are you all right?" Blood, viscera, decaying corpses—he'd been around them often enough to disassociate life from the mangled flesh of death. But he kicked himself mentally for not thinking about the stains when Maida asked for a tour.

"Brings the murder closer to home. Makes it more real."

Then, she startled him. Straightening up to her full five feet one inches, she put her hands on her hips. Then she said in as loud as voice as he'd heard from the lay-pastor Maida, "I hope you catch whoever did this, no matter who it is, and stuff their worthless carcass into a cell so dark they'll never see the light of day. Beneath the roguish exterior, Oakley was a sensitive man who wouldn't hurt a soul. And there's Nanette—"

She stopped in mid-sentence, her eyes growing wider. "I've been assuming it was one person who killed both. You don't think there are two of these animals running around?"

"We're not sure. But if it makes you feel any safer, I believe the murders are related. And I don't think we're looking at random killing."

"Don't want you to get the idea I'm another hysterical old bat, Scott."

"Old, hysterical, and bat are not terms I'd use to refer to you, Maida, trust me."

She squinted at the rows of empty seats. "Nanette told me something odd over a year ago. She had a premonition about Oakley's death."

"Did she say how she saw him dying? Or why?"

Maida shook her head and looked up toward the ceiling although Drayco doubted it was in supplication. "You don't believe it was a premonition, do you?"

"Some people believe the subconscious creates images. Images that provide insights into problems the conscious mind suppresses. Perhaps Nanette picked up on signals from Oakley, but wasn't aware of it."

"A dream message in a bottle?"

"In a way." He thought of his own reproachful nightmares. Signposts from the Freudian Id.

Maida nibbled on her nails.

He said, "That's not the only thing bothering you."

"The same time as the premonition, another strange thing happened."

"With Nanette?"

"She stopped going to church." Maida swung her feet forward so they could touch the floor. "Nanette used to volunteer for everything and sang in the choir."

"Her absence must have raised eyebrows."

"It did. She said she was ailing and needed a break. The rumor mill had Oakley drinking again. But I'm not sure either was true. I tried to talk to her, both as pastor and friend, but she kept waving me off, using the health excuse."

He heard the sheriff's voice in his head, *"Well, now—was the affair between Earl and Nanette not as brief, or as long ago as Earl led us to believe?"*

"I'm sure you tried your best, Maida. Even if you aren't the hellfire and brimstone type."

"My sermons nudge people in the right direction instead of beating them upside the head with be-saved-or-else boxing gloves. Though that might be more effective."

"And you could charge for ringside pews."

"We sure could use the money." She excused herself to run an errand, leaving Drayco alone, at last. He switched from the Goldbergs to Bach's "Art of the Fugue."

As Drayco's fingers flew over the keys, he thought of Oakley and his inscription in Yaegle's book. And what of the cryptic letter fragment? His left hand highlighted inner voices in one passage, up the scale then down. That word "phonic" on Oakley's newspaper clipping. Phonic as in acoustics or speech? And the b-b on the clipping and tree? He forced his fingers over the keyboard ever faster. The questions lit up the parietal lobe in his brain, even as the musical notes brought forth a rainbow of colors to his senses.

Oakley sprouted from nowhere, sans family or friends. Or that's the impression he wanted to give. Then there was the sheriff's brother and his murder, left unresolved. Was it better sometimes not to have family if all it meant was sorrow and loss?

Frustrated with his inability to fit all the pieces of the puzzle together, Drayco's fingers dug forcefully into a section where Bach introduced a new counter-theme before bringing back the original melody, now inverted. Inverted—turned on its head.

He stopped cold, as an idea occurred to him, something wilder than the theory he hinted to the sheriff, part allegory and part tragedy of operatic proportions. It fit together so beautifully, like Bach's counterpoint, it was a possible solution to the murders. Trouble was, it could be nearly impossible to prove.

35

Reece Wable stood looking at the Fairmont Hotel. Now, it was the crown jewel of downtown Cape Unity, but not too long ago, it symbolized the collapse of the tourist trade. It took a chunk of grant money, but the building now stood proudly on Atlantic Avenue as if it had always looked this elegant and unblemished. The movie star coyly denying knowledge of any plastic surgery.

Although a few blocks down the street from the Historical Society, Reece always parked his car in front of the Hotel and walked to work. Partly because he liked the grandeur of the place and partly because he needed the exercise. He was terrified of middle-age spread.

Reece was a few steps from the car when another vehicle screeched into the space behind his and came to an abrupt halt. Reece was relieved to note the driver barely avoided a fender bender, but annoyed all the same. His annoyance turned quickly to alarm when Paddy Bakely pulled himself out of the driver's seat and headed in a rush toward Reece.

"I've got this for you," Paddy had a long slender object in his hand that vaguely resembled a weapon. Was he drunk or was he sober? Reece steeled himself against a possible assault and looked around for potential witnesses. Paddy held out the object at arm's length and indicated Reece should take it. It was a walking cane, with a maple shaft tipped in silver and a silver animal figure for the handle. Reece wasn't sure how to react. Better stick with the basics. "Thank you," he said.

Paddy pointed to the cane, "It's been lying around the house gathering dust. I think it's old. More your thing than mine. I reckon you can add it to your museum." He rocked up and down on the balls of his feet, his face scrunched like he was in pain, although Reece doubted it was from ill-fitting shoes. Paddy was holding something else behind his back, which he pulled around. "Thought you might want this, too."

Reece accepted both offerings with a stiff nod. "I'll take them back to the Historical Society with me."

As quickly as he had come, Paddy sped away, leaving a mystified historian in his wake. Just as Reece collected his thoughts enough to head once again toward his car, a dark blue coupe pulled into the slot vacated by Paddy and another man rolled down the window. He called to Reece, who wondered, how did I get in the middle of Grand Central Station all of a sudden?

He fumbled for his cellphone in case he needed to call for help, but relaxed when he recognized the new arrival as the man hopped out of the car.

Scott Drayco strolled over and considered the two articles Reece was holding tightly in his arms as Reece beamed at him. For once, someone seemed glad to see him. "New toys?"

"Souvenirs from Paddy. Guess I'll have to put him on my Christmas card list."

"Gifts from Paddy? I guess that explains why you looked distressed. You were standing so still, I had to stop. I was worried you were having a seizure."

"Seized with stupefaction, is more like it." He handed the cane to Drayco. "Paddy said he had this goodie lying around all cold and lonely and thought it might find a better home at the society. Too bad it's not solid gold. I could sell that."

"If it were solid gold, I doubt Paddy would part with it. Looks like sterling silver, at least the accents." Drayco fingered the handle. "Is this a foxhound?"

"Beats me. Guess I need to watch those dog shows on TV."

Drayco pointed out three letters engraved on the silver band at the tip. "H-A-H."

Reece twitched his nose. "Hah, indeed. Maybe Paddy thought he was getting the last laugh. I suppose that's the manufacturer. I'll have to look it up. Might be some value there after all."

Drayco handed it back and eyed the angel clutched in Reece's arm. "What's the story behind that?"

Reece laid the angel in the back seat of his car. "With Paddy, who knows? Maybe he gave me the cane out of fear Seth would use it on him."

"Somebody needs to knock some sense into Paddy, cane or no cane."

Reece scrunched up his face muscles. "You think it's stolen and Paddy's trying to get rid of it?"

"I don't think so, Reece. He'd be more likely to sell it. Or throw it away."

"You can tell your friend the sheriff since you're in the habit of giving him all my valuable goodies. Hell, I should tell him in person since we're bosom buddies now. Thanks to me being a person of interest."

So, Sheriff Sailor wasted no time on his threat to bring Reece in for questioning. Even if it was a waste of time as Drayco suspected. "You and the sheriff had a nice talk?"

"Oh, lovely. Someone plants a knife in my car, some busybody biddy gets in the act, and ta-da, I'm infamous. Guess I'll have to go on all the chat shows. Or write a memoir."

"You weren't arguing with Oakley before his death as the witness described?"

Reece squinted his good eye at Drayco. "Witness? You knew about this beforehand?"

"The sheriff told me earlier today about it, but that was the first I'd heard. What about that argument, Reece?"

Reece hesitated. "We might have had a word or two. But I didn't start it, he did, and I think he'd been drinking again."

"Drinking? Nanette said he was sober."

"That's what he wanted her to think. Alcoholism is a disease with no cure. Only remission. Or relapses."

"And Oakley's charge about your affair with Nanette?"

Reece slammed the cane down on the sidewalk. "You don't pull any punches, do you? Maybe you're the one who ratted me out to the sheriff. Look, I've told you I had a crush. That's it. I doubt she would have been interested in a cranky historian. I'm one of those wussy males who's afraid of blood. Which makes that whole knife thing ludicrous."

"You told me you hadn't spoken with Oakley in a while, Reece. You lied."

Reece shuffled his feet. "You may be one of those macho types who looks death in the face and laughs, but I'm a coward. Genetic. A man once besmirched my sainted mother's honor at a bar, and Poppy crawled away with his tail between his legs. Wable spines are notoriously spindly."

"You were afraid you'd be a suspect early on? Because of that manslaughter charge?"

Reece sighed. "STS. Just takes a rumor to convict someone these days."

"About that manslaughter thing, Reece. The family of the passenger in your car said you killed him intentionally over a manuscript."

"We both coveted it. Me for my archives. He wanted to sell it for a profit. But he's the one who forced his way into my car that night."

Drayco stared into Reece's good eye. "So what is it you're not telling me?"

Reece swallowed several times. When he replied, his voice was a monotone. "I wanted to teach him a lesson. Scare him. I drove him home, very fast, pretending I was going to run into things. He was scared all right. Begged me to stop."

Drayco prompted, "And then you hit something for real."

"A deer ran across the road. I swerved to avoid it, and we ended up wrapped around a tree. It was my fault he died, I admit that, and I've had to live with that knowledge every day since. But his family was wrong. I didn't mean to do it. Afterward, I didn't even pursue the damned manuscript. I have no idea where it wound up."

Drayco let that pass. It should be easy to prove or disprove. Instead, he pointed at the book in Reece's hand. "Paddy's great American novel?"

"A book of his poetry. You read any of his work?"

"From the looks of it, that same volume."

"What did you think?"

"His writing is everything you'd expect from Paddy, except darker and more incoherent."

"Since he's a local writer—of sorts—I'll find a place in the archives for it."

"I can understand him giving it to you, a touch of ego, but why the cane? It doesn't fit his behavior pattern. Unless the cane's purpose is to sweeten the deal so you'll take the book."

Reece shrugged and looked at his watch. "Five bells. It's so-called happy hour at the Fiddler's Green Tavern. Been to that illustrious establishment yet?"

"The other day, to pick up some wine for Chef Maida. Ran into Paddy as a matter of fact."

"Oh, now there's a surprise. Anyway, they have several regional microbrews half-price at this time of day. Care to join me? Or are you afraid of being seen in the company of a degenerate?"

"A degenerate with a reading monocle? What's up with the whole monocle thing, anyway, Reece?"

"I only need one lens, so why pay for another I don't need?"

"Because of the glass eye?"

Reece tipped the cane in salute. "Most people don't notice. Guess you are a detective after all." He pointed to his left eye. "This one's glass. Got it after a bout with cancer as a tot. One eye, one lens. You want to come along and get plastered?"

"Why not?" The tavern had a unique charm, the kind that didn't come out of corporate test markets. Pulling into the parking lot, Drayco saw several more cars than on his other trip. Reece explained that for Cape Unity, this was a crowd.

Fortunately, Reece snagged an open table, and they studied the daily specials written in pastel colors on a small chalkboard. Reece said, "The Beach Lite Beer is malty but good. It's from the Tidewater area."

"Is beer good for your rheumatiz?"

"I don't care. Although I should get my doctor to prescribe it. It's easier to swallow than glucosamine horse pills."

Drayco chose the Cacao Espresso Stout. "Coffee, dark chocolate, and beer. Three vices in one. Could it be I've found a new addiction to replace Manhattan Special?"

Reece rolled the golden liquid of his Beach Lite Beer around on his tongue with a happy gurgle. "I would say this helps me unwind at the end of a stressful day. But I toiled solo in my private cave of history without a single visitor. Can't blame them, since I'm now persona non grata."

"Is attendance better in summer?"

"Somewhat. Much as I hate to think of those dreadful rows of shanties Gallinger has planned, it might mean more patrons for ye olde Historical Society. We barely break even. I'd hoped one of Earl Yaegle's charities could come through for us, but if he winds up in jail. .."

Drayco said, "I wonder if two murders will affect sales of those shanties?"

"Good point. Wonder if Gallinger considered that. Hell, it might increase sales. People are fascinated with notoriety and scandal after all. As long as it doesn't affect them personally, then they're all for it."

Drayco sensed his companion wanted a break from conversation. The three B's, his father always called it. Beer, bumming, and brooding. Drayco surveyed the tavern, cataloging the faces of his fellow imbibers. In its long history, the Fiddler's Green must have seen its share of notorious customers. One local tale told of a sailor in the early 1900s who wandered into town. He killed a matronly fishwife, chopped her body into pieces and packed them in a steamer trunk to dump at sea. Reece was right about scandal. The mad sailor story was one of the town's most cherished legends.

He studied Reece across the table. "Notoriety can hit close to home. Take you, for instance. The Keys' murders affected you personally."

Reece grabbed some of the pretzels in a bowl on the table, rolled them around in his hand, then threw all but one back. "You ever think about Kismet?"

Drayco relaxed into his chair, enjoying the tang of the stout. "Are you getting fatalistic on me?"

Reece started chewing on the pretzel, then coughed up a piece of it, with an apologetic look. "Bear with me. I mean, here we are, strangers until a few days ago, sitting in this particular bar connected by the deaths of two people who were friends of mine. I ask myself—is it possible you've been sent here by some twist of Kismet to solve their murders? That you're the only one who can? Then you have the Keys themselves. If they hadn't moved here, they never would have bought that land and wouldn't have died because of it. And Nanette—if she married me, she'd be alive today. Instead, she married a man who didn't appreciate her."

"Not to be rude, Reece, but are you sure that's your first beer today?"

"Putting on my armchair philosopher's hat."

"Your historian hat fits you better. Makes you less depressed."

Reece's eyes were bright and direct. "If you want to make me a happy human, you'll find who killed Nanette. If there is eternal fire and damnation for the wicked, he'll head straight there. Do not pass Go."

If-only scenarios made for good research papers, but in real life they were diseases nibbling away at emotional cells, leaving only skeletons of grief and guilt behind. Still, Drayco couldn't blame

Reece. Nanette was a woman with a great capacity for love and devotion.

That set him thinking about Konstantina Klucze. If he'd been her peer, he'd be captivated the way Reece was with Nanette. Following Reece's line of thought, would Konstantina also be alive today if she married someone else? He was bemused by his own fixation with a woman long dead. Must be something they put in the beer. Depressing thoughts make people want to drink more, hence more profits.

Reece seemed happy to be depressed, at least until he drained his mug. He asked, "What brought you to this place?"

"You did, not more than thirty minutes ago."

"I mean, how did you get started in the biz? Maida filled me in on your prodigy youth. Someone steal your piano?"

"My car." He'd stopped at a station to gas up his Mustang on that frosty night fifteen years ago. Such a simple thing, to stop at a station, fill up your car, pay the attendant.

Reece pointed at Drayco's exposed right forearm where his sleeve had slipped when Drayco raised his glass. "I'm guessing that's a souvenir?"

Drayco glanced at the line of pink scars branching off into a tree as they faded into his palm. "A carjacking. The gunman slammed the door on my arm. Dragged me several feet."

Reece said, "Got mangled nicely. Good plastic surgeon."

"Although I swear the physical therapist had a sadistic streak."

"That makes two pianist careers silenced by assault. It was luck of the draw your life didn't end that night like Konstantina's. Or else I'm right about our friend Kismet. Kismet, the universe's dick."

Drayco took another sip of the beer. If there was a silver lining from the whole carjacking mess, it was when he realized he could help more people directly via a law enforcement career. Provide a little justice, maybe help prevent tragedies like the carjacker—only seventeen when sentenced, he died not long afterward in a prison riot. *Ars longa, vita brevis.*

Reece signaled for a second mug. "You asked me to look up Angel Quillen. Her entire life can be summed up in a paragraph. Nothing on her childhood. Married Seth when she was eighteen. He was ten years older, by the way. Had Paddy when she was twenty. Her parents originally moved here to work in the crab industry, and up and left after her death."

Reece pulled some papers out of his jacket pocket and thrust them across the table. "I've got a newspaper clipping that mentions her. And since you asked about Oakley's early life, I included an article on him."

Drayco examined the photo on the first clipping. "That's Paddy's mother, Angel Quillen?"

"She was a beauty, wasn't she? Pale skin, red hair. Striking."

"Are you positive that's Paddy's mother?"

"Look at the caption, if you don't believe me."

"Her appearance doesn't match what I had in mind."

"If you're thinking Paddy doesn't resemble her and is adopted, think again. She died in childbirth after all—his. Must be a genetic mutation somewhere. She was apparently as much a saint as her name suggests, and Seth has kept his nose clean. Makes you wonder why Paddy couldn't be more of a chip off the old blocks."

Drayco flipped to the next piece of paper, the article about Oakley. Drayco took a closer look at Oakley's photo. He sported a dead ringer for the seersucker jacket he had on the night he was murdered. "Reece, you remember this jacket?"

Reece grabbed the clipping. "Seersucker. Not a fan. Looks too cheap, like those polyester leisure suits popular then. I don't remember him wearing it, but when I showed this photo to Oakley once, he was not amused."

"Did he say why?"

"He mumbled that picture was taken on the worst day of his life. And how the righteous shall rejoice when they see vengeance. Or something Bible-ish."

The worst day of his life? Drayco had his suspicions about that day. The same date Nanette told Drayco that Oakley came home, read the life-altering letter, and threw it into the fireplace.

Reece pointed to the last document in the pile. "Go ahead, look at that one."

Drayco unfolded it. "Blueprints?"

"Am I a good historian or what? A copy of the original Opera House drawings from the Library of Virginia archives."

"This is above and beyond the call, Reece. Did you keep a copy for the burgled drawer?"

"It's in my wall safe. Don't want to take any chances with Senor Sticky Fingers."

"Thanks, Reece. This is better than I'd hoped for."

Drayco stood up, signaling to Reece he was ready to leave. "And Kismet notwithstanding, someone made a conscious decision to kill Oakley and Nanette. A decision the murderer will live to regret once locked away. You can bet on it."

Reece said, "Those are shaky odds. How can you be so sure?"

Drayco gathered up the blueprints and other documents and folded some money on the table for a tip. "Because I never give up."

36

Cypress Manor looked even more the drama queen, framed against an evening mist that hovered around it like a theatrical scrim. Drayco noticed a brocade drapery pulled aside a few inches. Someone was following his progress up the long driveway.

Darcie greeted him like a picture of sultry bewitchery in a tight black dress as she beckoned him into the drawing room toward the settee. She placed her hand on his shoulder, pressing him down into the seat, then positioned herself mere inches away.

Drayco coughed. "Is the councilman going to join us?"

Her hand pressed down harder. "He's been called away on business."

"That's a shame. He was a fine host." At least, a fine actor. In retrospect, it was clear the dinner party was more an excuse to feel Drayco out rather than any welcoming gesture on Squier's part.

Darcie scooted close, their thighs touching. Drayco allowed himself a brief moment to enjoy the contact before he forced himself to refocus on the conversation. "Do you entertain often? The layout of this house is tailor-made for it."

"Not as much as I'd like. Other than you, the last people we had to dinner were some of those boring councilmen. And the Yaegles before his wife passed away. If it were up to me, we'd have parties every week. There are times I think I'll be the first case of death-by-boredom. But I doubt you have that problem."

"Oh, my life is more boring than you think."

He extracted himself from her grasp and got up to inspect one of the cases he noted on his first visit, the one with the Native American crafts, which had a new addition. "This collection of your husband's is most definitely not boring."

Lying on a far right shelf toward the back was a rounded wooden object, half-hidden under a folded Navajo crystal rug. Drayco had cast a wide surveillance net around the room as soon as he entered, looking for an item like this. The right shape and size for what he envisioned Oakley's mask would be. He picked up the object with the sides of his hands, studying the intricately carved feathers of an owl's face. At the bottom was inscribed *Diabel.* He flipped it over and saw the initials OK.

"This is unusual. One of a kind."

She twirled her hair with her fingers as she avoided looking at him. "We got that from a local artist. I don't know who."

Drayco lay the mask on the coffee table, then cupped his hand around Darcie's chin to force her to look at him. "Nanette Keys said Oakley crafted a similar mask. A mask that went missing at the time he was murdered. The same mask I asked you about at the Novel Café when you denied knowing anything."

Darcie froze, and her artfully rouged cheeks paled. "I didn't know it was linked to Oakley's murder, honest I didn't. You believe me, don't you?"

"Surely you've seen the initials where it's signed OK?"

Drayco released his grip, and Darcie resumed twirling her hair around her fingers. "When Randolph brought it home, I saw the initials and guessed it was Oakley's. It was after the murder, and I was surprised Randolph bought it Thought he'd forget about it, and I could sell it myself. Art goes up in value when the artist dies, doesn't it?"

Drayco didn't say anything, so Darcie continued, with a nervous laugh. "My dear husband gives me an allowance. I have to beg him for money. So I hoped to make some on my own. After all, what does he spend his fortune on?"

She pointed toward the collections. "Those nasty old tusks and ridiculous guns. For what? We could be traveling, or meeting interesting people in Washington, or catching designer fashion shows in New York. What good are a bunch of old relics? They don't help you live in the present, do they?"

She must not show this side of herself to her husband. Perhaps she did, and he wasn't the understanding sort. Perhaps she was afraid to—that he might turn violent. Or that she'd lose Mr. Moneybags. But seeing her sitting there, holding back tears, that characterization didn't seem fair. For the first time since he met her, she looked lost in uncharted waters. He fought the urge to close the distance between them.

She kicked the table hard enough to make the mask slide a few inches. "You keep that nasty thing. I don't want it in the house."

"Did your husband say where he bought it?"

Darcie shook her head so violently, Drayco thought it might snap off. "I've learned not to ask Randolph where he gets things. It's better that way. As if he'd tell me."

She turned away from him. "I wish you'd stop looking at me like that."

"Like what?"

"Accusing. Your eyes are so intense sometimes. Look into them too long, and you'll get sucked in."

She jumped up and walked over to the massive fireplace and rested an arm on the mantle, holding out the other hand to feel the warmth from the glowing coals. "Have you made friends here?" she asked unexpectedly.

"Why?"

"My husband doesn't want me to have friends. He wants his property all to himself. Sometimes I feel I'm going to suffocate."

"Does he get physical, violent?"

"Has he hit me? Of course not. Too much a gentleman for that." She spat out the word gentleman as if it were a bitter pill.

"Not violent toward you, perhaps."

She looked away. "If my husband did decide to hurt someone, I'm sure it would be neat and efficient like he does everything else. Believe me, he's not the physical type. I won't pretend our relationship hasn't had rocky moments. Whose hasn't? Oakley's wife had an affair with Earl Yaegle. Yet Earl and Tabitha Yaegle stayed together until she died."

Darcie reached up to twist her hair again, then caught herself and stopped. "How's the investigation? Why hasn't the sheriff arrested Earl?"

"Because the murderer may not be Earl."

"Of course it's Earl Yaegle. He and Oakley were enemies. You think it's him, don't you?"

Drayco joined her in front of the fireplace. He was again amazed at its size, large enough to park a Cooper Mini inside. The marble was a dark gray with streaks of black forming patterns like Rorschach inkblot tests. One pattern resembled two devils dancing.

He said, "I'm not ready to pin the murders on Earl."

Darcie tilted her head. "Why not?"

"You're eager to brand him. Any reason?"

"I'm not smart, but I can't imagine why anyone else would want to do it. Oakley was too much like a child."

She glared at the framed hunt scene on the wall. "I've always hated that painting. Guns, guns, always guns."

She was silent for a moment, her hands clasped in front of her. "I wasn't honest when I said I couldn't imagine anyone else wanting to kill Oakley."

"Your husband?"

She nodded. "I thought you already knew about that mask. And was goading me into pinning the murders on Randolph."

"You hid it well."

"My husband was furious when he found out about Oakley and me. Threatened to kill him. But when I allow myself to believe he went through with it. .. I get terrified. It's already unbearable around this dark cave as it is. Lonely, cold and soulless."

She reached out to take Drayco's arm and led him toward a corner where she pointed up at an elaborate tapestry. "That's called 'Love at the Old Mill.' It looked so romantic, I had Randolph buy it."

In her stiletto-heeled shoes once again, she was closer to Drayco's height and easily reached her hand around his shoulder to maneuver him so his back was against the wall in the corner. "Aren't the details exquisite? The couple is so full of life."

She drew closer until her face was inches from his. "The young man is kinda sexy. Like you, only you're far more appealing."

If he succumbed to Darcie, who spun a web like a black widow spider around Oakley, would Drayco be consumed as the other man had? To his chagrin, at this particular moment, he wasn't sure he cared. On some level, deep down, they were both vulnerable like Earl and Nanette, when they instigated their affair.

Drayco was keenly aware of the smooth skin on Darcie's hand as her fingers wrapped behind his neck, and of her rapid heartbeat as she pressed her chest against his. Her eyes sparkled with an emerald glint, and her full red lips were warm and soft as they teasingly brushed across his cheek and mouth. He envisioned Oakley, weak from his faded dreams and vanishing self-esteem, helpless before this tempting siren. His rule about married women was in imminent danger of being revoked.

She asked, "You do find me attractive, don't you?"

"I think it would be difficult for any man not to."

She pressed her lips to his, kissing him gently at first. Her left hand slipped under his sweater, her fingers caressing his chest, slowly moving downward. As in the car behind the courthouse, he didn't stop her, didn't push her away, but returned the kiss, and wrapped one arm behind her shoulders, the other around her waist.

He could argue with himself all day on the morals of having sex with a married woman, but he was afraid his arguments would ring hollow. He was tired, lonelier than he cared to admit, and his pulse picked up speed every time he was around her.

The wails of mental sirens tried to drown out his desire. *Ethics, Oakley's murder, don't surrender.* Yet the thought of lying in Darcie's arms was far more pleasant than dealing with the Opera House or fighting a convoluted case that might not be provable. He pulled her tighter against him, and Darcie deepened the kiss as her fingers moved again, farther south, sliding under his waistband.

An image of Oakley in his bloodied pince-nez glasses and red carnation popped unbidden into Drayco's mind. Reluctantly, he pulled his arms free and stopped Darcie from going any further. He held her left hand in his outstretched palm. She wasn't wearing her rings.

"Darcie, I can't."

"Of course you can. There's no one here except us. Who's to know? If you're worried about that fire-and-damnation thing, it'd be a sin to let a body like yours go to waste. Besides, I always get what I want."

It wasn't easy to push her away. But he did.

"I'll let myself out," Drayco said, picking up the mask and heading toward the door. He paused before turning the knob, looking back at her.

No defiance, no artifice to be seen now. Her lower lip was trembling, and tears trickled down her face. She said softly, "But I think I'm falling in love with you."

It took everything he had not to run over and fold her into his arms, so he hurried out the door, picking his way across the granite cobblestone driveway to the Starfire. He started to slide into the driver's seat, but a flash of white that wasn't there before caught his eye.

He grasped one corner of the piece of cardboard to study this latest note though it didn't take long. A simple design—one large red "G," circled with a slash. He whipped around but didn't see anyone. Cypress Manor was isolated in its own mini-forest, providing an abundance of hiding places. And the only sound was the wind whistling through the evergreens.

He examined the note again. The sheriff would agree Drayco's stalker was more specific this time. What would the murderer carve on Drayco's chest—another "G"? Maybe "D"? Or a simple "X."

37

Drayco drove downtown and parked. He needed to walk, to think. About the case and especially about Darcie. Had he done the right thing? Even if he knew the answer deep down, he was surprised at how close he'd come to throwing aside his scruples. What did that say about his judgment these days?

Despite the darkness of the cloudy, moonless evening, he could see the architecture on Main Street dated back to the town's early days. No steel or mirrored glass anywhere. Reece said it wasn't a spirit of preservation so much as a lack of developers wanting to build in a "blighted area."

The sidewalks rolled up at six, but he wasn't alone on his tour. A Hispanic woman holding the hand of a small child singing the nursery rhyme "Baa Baa Black Sheep" passed him. Mother and daughter hadn't gone much farther when a car driving alongside slowed to a crawl, and someone yelled out a window, "Go back to El Salvador! You don't belong here."

The woman and child hurried off down an alley, and Drayco watched them until they vanished safely into a building in back. Wasn't that what Paddy yelled at him, that Drayco didn't belong here?

He walked on, hands in pockets, as he nodded absently at the elderly owner of an antiques store, who was closing up shop. Lost in thought on the conflicting pleasures and puzzles of small town Americana, he headed back to the Starfire, preparing to cross a side street that was dark, thanks to a burned-out street light.

Out of the corner of his eye, he glimpsed a low flash and heard the unmistakable roar of an accelerating car engine. Just in time, he twisted his body away from the car as it passed within mere inches. Losing his balance, he fell hard onto the asphalt, gritting his teeth at the pain shooting through the same leg the wolf-coyote had bitten.

The car, its lights off, continued to speed down the street into an empty lot where it paused with the engine gunning. Then it peeled around and hurtled back down the street with the screaming engine at full throttle, straight toward Drayco.

The antiques store owner rushed over to help, but on the rain-slicked streets, he slipped and fell. Drayco realized with horror that if the car hit Drayco, the old man would be mowed down, too. Drayco rolled onto the curb, managing to grab the older man by the arms and hoist him up, using Drayco's body to shield his, his back to the car. The car passed so close, the edge of the side mirror brushed against the hem of his coat, almost dragging him along with it. The tires emitted one last high-pitched squeal as the car vanished into the night.

"Damn fool driver," the store owner grumbled. "One of the local high school boys. They don't have enough to keep them busy, so they go hot-rodding. Thanks for the help. Thought I was a goner. You okay, young man?"

Drayco brushed some of the wet grit off his coat. "Still in one piece. You?"

"As right as rain. Sorry I didn't get any details from the hotrod. You get a plate?"

"None, other than the car was a dark color." Drayco gave the man a visual check, then shook his hand. "You should get some place warm and dry. The forecast calls for mid-thirties tonight, weather not fit for man nor beast."

"I think we had a little of both." The man waved and headed off into the night.

Drayco slowly folded his long-legged frame into the car to avoid hitting his various new bruises, and made his way back to the Lazy Crab, keeping an eye out for other "hot-rodders." The brush with death-by-car dredged up more emotional pain than physical, thrusting him back in time in a way his conversation with Reece hadn't.

His return to the Lazy Crab was a welcoming beacon drawing him back to its cottage utopia. He must really be tired. Fatigue invariably brought on Beethoven references, this time from the Ode to Joy, *Himmlische, dein Heiligtum.* Heavenly sanctuary, yes sir.

Maida greeted him as he came in, her welcoming smile changing to alarm. "What happened to you? Your hair is wet, you've got dirt all over you, and there's a cut near your temple."

"I was an inch shy of getting run over by a car."

"Did the driver stop?"

"I think he hoped I'd be the one to stop—or more precisely, drop—dead."

Maida nudged him back toward the kitchen. "A hot toddy first. Then details." She rummaged around in the kitchen and brought him a cup.

He took a sip of her latest concoction and coughed several times. "What's in this?"

"Tea, honey, cloves and several shots of dark rum and cognac. Better than aspirin."

"Another family recipe?"

"My grandmother's favorite. Although as a child I never understood why." After she sat him down near the kitchen hearth with his hands cupped around the tea, she joined him in one of the high-backed cane chairs. "I'll give you a first aid kit for that cut." She turned his face to one side and examined it closer. "Nothing scar-worthy. Anything bruised or sprained?"

"Nothing serious, Nurse Maida."

Maida gripped his shoulder. "An accident or intentional?"

"The car had its lights out and waited to accelerate until I stepped onto the street. An older gentleman, who almost got hit himself, said it could be a local teen on a joy ride."

"The kids around here do their racing on Old Harbor Road, where there's a long straight stretch." Maida chewed on her lip. "I was afraid the note in your room might lead to nastiness."

She left long enough to get some more cognac to top off his cup. "Let's assume for a moment this demon car incident is related to the murders. Who did you talk to today? Was anybody particularly upset?"

"I don't think any of my conversations today was inspiration for an automotive rampage." Drayco paused to drink more of the peculiar grog. An acquired taste.

"We should call the sheriff." She dialed the first few numbers when Drayco stopped her.

"Let's wait until tomorrow. I doubt there's much the sheriff could do tonight, anyway. The man's exhausted and needs his sleep."

Maida tsk-tsk'ed a few times, but acquiesced. She looked at him like a bloodhound with a bone being dangled in front of it. "But it must be tied to the investigation. Who are the chief suspects? Maybe we can track down the driver that way."

Drayco grinned at the "we." She took his Deputy Maida comment to heart. "The sheriff has a nice list of suspects in Oakley's murder. The Squiers, Bakelys, Yaegle, Reece and a few other exotic animals in the suspect zoo."

Maida patted him on the shoulder. "Having run a B&B, I know about being a zookeeper. Does the sheriff have a chief animal in mind?"

Drayco leaned back in his chair and closed his eyes. "Reece mentioned Occam's Razor."

"You mean to think horses, not zebras?"

"Ordinarily, but in this case, I've thrown Appaloosas out the window and started looking at zebras because of Nanette's letter fragment."

He observed the wooden beams in the ceiling and their support structure. Simple linear posts running parallel to one another and not touching. But nature hated straight lines. If the beams were off by the slightest degree from true, they'd eventually intersect. Same with humans. Divergent paths connecting people in ways they didn't expect.

He yawned. Maida's brew was doing the trick again. "To be honest, right now my brain is as foggy as the air outside. A hot shower and sleep are all I need."

Maida whirled into action. "Only if you let me send you up with a bite to eat first."

Drayco agreed, surprised at how ravenous he was, as he made short work of Maida's stew. "This is an unusual recipe. One of your creations?"

"It's from a Cape Unity cookbook from the forties. I checked it out from the library and copied a few interesting recipes. This is one of our favorites—Polish borscht. Of course, it helps to like beets."

She reached for a ring binder and opened it to the page. "The part with the contributor is cut off. At least you can rest assured it's a local creation."

"Knowing you, it's better than the original." He caught a glimpse through the window of the rain gauge Major emptied this morning. It was half-full.

"Maida, do you know of anyone who uses capsules of cayenne pepper for cooking or anything else?"

"Cayenne is one of my favorites. But you wouldn't use capsules for cooking. The cooking kind comes powdered in bottles. The capsule kind is used in folk medicine for inflammation and digestive problems. A few years ago, Major took some for his arthritis."

"I guess microbes don't stand a chance against that firepower. Are red carnations used like that?"

"I don't think so, though you can make a tea out of dandelions. And red carnations? Folks in the South wear them to church on Mother's Day as a sign your mother is living. You wear a white carnation if she's deceased. Morbid, but that's tradition for you."

She picked up some papers from a sideboard near the table that she handed over. "I almost forgot. These were faxed today."

Drayco read the cover sheet. "The immigration records I wanted from the National Archives. My good friend in D.C. is efficient."

"You got records for Oakley, then?"

"For several people." He flipped through the pages, getting the highlights. He stopped on one page, reading the dates more closely. "Huh. January 1955."

Maida regarded him with curiosity. "Something helpful?"

"Possibly. Or a huge coincidence." He rubbed his eyes and yawned.

Maida ushered him off to his room for some rest. "You know what the Bible says. God makes the sun rise on the evil and the good and sends rain on the just and the unjust. And tomorrow you can continue your pursuit of the unjust."

Part Four

Sometimes I look to heaven, imploring,
And the howling storm hears my grief.
The rain is cold, and its roar is loud.
"Sing," cries my heart, "for we shall soon be leaving."

—From the song "I want what I have not," poem by Bohdan Zaleski,
music by Frédéric Chopin

38

Following another night of only a few hours' sleep, Drayco was relieved to get a call from the sheriff to meet him at the office for a stakeout. Might be dangerous, he'd said. But adrenaline sure beat a keg of caffeine, anytime. After a brief consultation, they headed off in a squad car toward the southern end of town that gave way to a sparsely populated stretch, dotted with an endless quilt of switchgrass and the pervasive pale, sandy soil.

They parked and headed toward a skeleton-of-a-shack hidden among a thicket of wax myrtles. Drayco kept a wary eye on the dead trees around as a few of the rotted husks swayed and threatened to fall. The sheriff had to hold onto his hat with both hands to keep it from becoming airborne.

As they got closer, Sailor gave up on the hat and drew his gun, ready to flip open the crumbling door of the one-room shanty with his foot. Drayco headed around to the back door, and they converged on the interior at the same time. Empty, save for an orb-weaver spider in a corner.

"You sure he'll show up?" Drayco asked.

"If he takes the bait. My informant gave me the code they use to set up meetings."

They didn't have to wait long. The crunch of approaching footsteps in the gravel outside alerted them to the man's approach. A figure in familiar camouflage overalls flung open the door with a confidence denoting his regular visits to the site, as he bellowed, "Paddy, I thought I said—"

He'd barely set his foot in the room before he spun around and took off, running toward the woods. Drayco was closer and gave chase, dodging pools of mud as thick as wet cement. Clearing first one fallen tree trunk and then another, he was like a track-meet hurdler, just grateful the incident with the car hadn't reinjured his leg.

He grabbed a fistful of coveralls then pulled his prey against a tree into a modified carotid restraint. "Earl, what the hell do you think you're doing?"

The other man, breathing hard, managed to say, "I figured you were Gus Revell."

The sheriff caught up to them. "Paddy's so-called friend and cohort?"

"I was supposed to meet one or both as usual. But when I saw a gun, I thought they'd turned on me."

Drayco looked over at Sailor, who holstered his weapon. Catching a nod from the sheriff, Drayco released Earl. The trio walked back to the shack in silence and headed inside.

Earl collapsed into the lone chair which looked to be on its proverbial last legs. "You know why I'm here, then?"

The sheriff leaned against the wall before a loud creaking changed his mind. "We learned you come here to feed your ice cream habit. We just don't know which flavor."

"None of the hard shit. I'm not sure Paddy has that junk to offer."

"Why do you do it, Earl?"

Earl jumped up to pace. "I hurt my back when I fell off a ladder. I hoped the pain would go away in time, but it didn't. Kept getting worse. I went to several doctors, but after surgery and painkillers, more nonstop misery."

As if to prove his point, Earl carefully eased back down into the chair. "I hired Paddy Bakely for a few odd jobs, and he noticed my discomfort. He told me he could get medicine to help. So I said, what the hell, and he brought me what I thought was a hand-rolled cigarette, but figured out was giggle weed."

Drayco hadn't heard it called that in decades. Took him back to grade school and Barry Looney, the unfortunate-named kid who'd try anything once, which was why he spent so much time in the doctor's office. "You mean marijuana," Drayco said.

Earl turned up his chin in defiance. "And by God, it helped. It's the only thing that makes the pain bearable. I never touched the other drugs. Nothing like heroin or coke."

Drayco asked, "How long has this been going on?"

"A couple of years. I didn't want to let the community down. Not much of a role model for an employer to be a drug user, is it?"

The sheriff piped up again, "How often did you get your supply?"

"Whenever it ran out. Once a month, give or take a day."

"Was it only Paddy and Revell?"

"Just the two."

"When was the last time?"

"Over a week ago. We meet on Sunday evenings." Earl winced, but whether it was from back pain or his conscience, it was hard to tell.

Drayco perked up at the timeline. "You and Paddy and Revell were making a deal Sunday a week ago? The same night Oakley was killed?"

The sheriff narrowed his eyes. "Do you have an exact time, Earl? It would mean you and Paddy have alibis for Oakley's murder."

Earl was close to hyperventilating. "You can't ask them. Why would they tell the truth? They'd be arrested."

Sailor said, "Don't you worry about Revell. He's a two-bit lowlife from up in Salisbury. And Paddy will do what he can to avoid another sabbatical in my jail. We might arrange probation for the drug charges."

Drayco asked, "Earl, did Oakley learn of your habit?" He knew what the sheriff was thinking. Two drug dealers and a drug buyer vouching for one another weren't all that unusual. Honor among thieves. If Oakley discovered them, it could be a case of blackmail. And murder put a tidy end to it.

Earl's eyes shifted away toward the wall where he studied the spider web, fragile and easily destroyed. "I never told him."

Sheriff Sailor and Drayco headed back to Sailor's office where Drayco had left his car. They rode in thoughtful silence at first, broken only by occasional bursts from the dispatch radio. Sailor turned down the volume. "The wildlife rescue folks say those two orphaned cubs you brought in are doing fine. How did you find them?"

"A little persistence, a little luck. Though I nearly gave up after a couple of hours."

"Talk about not giving up—I had Giles check other names from Reece Wable's newspaper clipping regarding those old thefts in the 70s. One of the victims stumbled on a pawn shop in Delaware with a couple of his missing items. The victim never bothered alerting our department. Was shocked when we contacted him after all these years."

"Is the pawn shop owner still around?"

"Retired. He remembers those pieces because they were a higher quality than his usual fare. Gave us a description of the man who brought them in."

"Paddy?"

Sailor snorted. "Don't know why I bother telling you these things. The owner mentioned a jagged white scar over the man's left eyebrow. Like the one Paddy's had since he was a boy. He ID'd a photo."

"Paddy and Squier should go into business together."

"Funny you should say that. The city attorney dug up some irregularities in ledgers confirming that former clerk's story about embezzlement. The man in charge of those accounts was none other than Randolph Squier."

Drayco had visions of Darcie going to that same pawn shop in the future carrying her jewelry, with Squier in jail and her money source dried up. He ran a hand across his forehead, remembering the warm touch of Darcie's skin on his.

Sailor frowned. "Do contain your excitement over all of this. Or is it the knock on the head from that car incident last night?"

He hadn't mentioned that to Sailor yet. Maybe the man was psychic after all.

Sailor added, "Maida called to report it because she didn't think you would. You're popular—Tyler checked the G-warning-note from your car. Same as the first, red paint mixed with A-negative blood."

"It's nice to be loved. Any results on that Webley from the pier?"

"Not a match."

"You're kidding, right? How many Webleys can there be in one small town?"

"You got me. I'll have them re-test to make sure but looks like the wrong gun. Guess how thrilled I am."

"Did you ask the pawn shop owner about the missing library manuscript?"

"You think it's connected?"

"The document would be too hot to fence, but I don't think Paddy's behind it, anyway."

"So who is?"

Drayco didn't answer, and Sailor pulled the squad car into the parking lot next to Drayco's Starfire before turning off the engine. The air between them was like a loaded weapon, heavy with reproach.

"I've cut you a lot of slack, Drayco, more than I should. Holding out on me isn't the thanks I'd expect for that. This trust thing works both ways."

Drayco opened the door and stretched his cramped legs. "I've sent you and your mumps-afflicted department on too many wild goose chases. Spot me twenty-four hours and see if I can get that proof. I do have your best interests at heart."

"I hope so, Drayco. I bloody well hope so."

39

It was the most demurely he'd seen Darcie dressed. Sensible hiking boots, jeans and a thick wool coat. It suited her in a way the Barbie-doll look didn't. She immediately took his hand in hers, which he didn't resist. She didn't mention the "L" word again, and he didn't bring it up.

They walked over to the cheerless little shrine, destined to be bulldozed in the name of progress. Drayco circled around, viewing it from all angles. When he stepped back, he could see that the outlines of the shrine—with the rock, plantings, and benches—formed a large K.

Darcie said, "Oakley didn't want anyone out here but him, but I followed him once. Thought he might be meditating, but he was crying. I asked him why. He said because this was the best he could do for her."

"The best for whom?"

"I tried to get him to explain the shrine, but no dice. Said I wouldn't understand anyway since I had everything I always wanted, and he'd had everything taken away. What did he mean?"

"That sometimes life is unfair, and there's not a whole hell of a lot you can do about it."

She linked her arm through his, looking at him with curiosity. "Has life been that way for you?"

He meant Oakley's life, not his own, but he was uncomfortable with her question.

She pulled him down until they were near the ground, and she pointed at the base of one side of the heart. "There's a figure here. This is what I wanted you to see. I think Oakley made it. It's hidden by the plants that grew up since I last saw it."

He moved the plants aside. The stone had something etched into it, something that didn't come from nature. He traced it with his finger and said, "That's a G-clef."

"A what?"

"A G-clef. It's used in musical notation."

"I know Oakley liked music, but that's odd, don't you think?"

Drayco checked the other side of the rock and found a similar etching. But this second design wasn't a clef at all, just a plain recognizable "G."

Darcie asked, "Why would he put them where they're hard to see? And why not something more romantic? It is a heart-shaped rock, after all."

She clasped his hand and guided him to one of the benches Oakley made. "Do you think Nanette wasn't his first love, then? Some star-crossed love in his past?"

"Not lovers. But definitely star-crossed."

"Like you and me?"

He squinted at the tiny dagger of sunlight piercing a hole in the hide-and-seek clouds. Somewhere up there were millions of stars with names like Regulus and Aldebaran, totally oblivious to human lives and foibles. Like one of his favorite Bertrand Russell quotations, "Human life, its growth, its hopes, fears, and loves are the result of accidents."

He briefly and gently touched the back of his hand to Darcie's cheek and said, "I foresee a long and happy marriage for you and Randolph."

"I guess your prediction depends on whether my husband's a murderer, doesn't it?"

For the first time since he met her, she wasn't wearing any expensive jewelry except for the wedding rings, which were back on her hand. "Why did you marry him?"

She put her arm around his shoulders. "Because I hadn't met you yet."

"No, seriously."

"But I am serious. Oh, I suppose I was bored. He can be charming when he's not trying to prove himself."

Drayco eyed the heart rock. "Not to climb up on a moral high horse, but when you were seeing Oakley, did you stop to consider Nanette?"

"I didn't want her to find out. She wasn't a bitch or anything. But Oakley was unhappy, or he wouldn't have come to me, would he? And who am I to question someone's motives? I went along for the ride."

Life was a series of rides for Darcie. No real journey, no destination. This was both her greatest asset—an ability to live in the moment and drain every drop out of it—and her greatest liability. A beautiful bird hovering in the air, never touching down.

"What do you want from life?" he asked.

"No one's asked me that before." She sat quietly for a moment, her arm still wrapped around his shoulder. "I guess I'd say freedom."

"Freedom from what?"

"To be who I am instead of somebody else's idea of who I should be. My whole life I've felt like a portrait. Something people hang on their walls but don't expect to be a living breathing person."

"You should tell your husband that."

"Maybe I will." She kissed him again, but briefer this time, smoothing away a smudge from where her lipstick left a mark. "What does the 'G' stand for?"

He helped her up, nodding in the direction of their cars that it was time to go. "That's an easy one," he said. "'G' is for gullible."

40

Sheriff Sailor ushered Drayco into a room the size of two walk-in closets put together. One stark, hundred-watt bulb dangled overhead, illuminating the concrete-block walls painted basic eggshell. The sheriff pointed to a small wooden table with two folding chairs. "You can sit there. I'll spot you a few minutes, but we won't be keeping him long. You'd think these guys would have better things to eat for breakfast than eighty-proof Jim Beam."

"And the marijuana charges?" Drayco asked.

"Not enough evidence. I'm working on immunity for Earl, but Paddy's being cagey. And the statute of limitations ran out long ago on that stolen scrimshaw."

"Paddy's been in jail enough times to pay for both offenses, anyway. Did he start the fight?"

"Not this time, but the other guy wanted to press charges. Same song, different verse. At least it gives him a few hours to dry out. His episodes are getting more frequent."

Drayco had a good idea why that was the case. And he was pretty certain he knew the answer to his next question but asked anyway. "Were Paddy's prints on that mask?"

"Nope. Just the Squiers'. If he had it in his possession, he wiped it clean."

Paddy was led into the room and sat across from Drayco, eyeing him warily. Paddy's straggly mane was in desperate need of a trim, although it was a suitable frame for the broken capillaries in his puffy face. Alcoholism caused nutritional deficiencies, and under Paddy's thin shirt, the outlines of his ribs were poking through his skin.

Paddy's hands also had a slight tremor, but more daylight peeked through his bloodshot eyes than before. Drayco hoped to catch Paddy while he was sober for a change, and Paddy agreed to see him, something of a surprise.

It was Paddy who spoke first. "The sheriff said you wanted to talk to me. So talk." When his speech wasn't slurred, Paddy had a pleasant tenor voice. Not operatic, but the kind most church choirs would covet, if he could sing.

"You told me Oakley Keys once tried to break into the Opera House. Do you have any idea why he would do that?"

Paddy rocked back and forth in his chair as it squeaked in rhythm. "I didn't ask. He didn't say."

"Do you know why Oakley was murdered?"

Paddy didn't answer for a moment with his face flushed like he'd been burned. "That dumbshit had no common sense. Shoulda stuck to his writing. Paid more attention to that lovely wife of his instead of chasing after ghosts. And now she's dead, too."

Drayco continued to lean against the wall, watching Paddy, waiting as the seconds ticked by loudly on the black-and-white wall clock. Paddy swallowed several times and added, "He was killed because he couldn't let things go."

"Couldn't let who or what go?"

Paddy hesitated, then his rocking grew even faster. "The past. Could be no one I know, could be anybody I know. It's the way he was."

Drayco sat down across from Paddy on the other squeaky metal folding chair. "I saw a picture of your mother the other day. She was a lovely woman."

"She died because of me."

"You didn't intend to cause her death, Paddy. I'm sure if you could have prevented a death, you would have."

It was Paddy's turn to stay silent, so Drayco pressed further. "It must get lonely, just you and Seth. Surely there are other family members, grandparents, aunts, uncles?"

"They're all gone. Never knew them neither." Paddy's hands were shaking so hard now he thrust them under the table. To brace them or to hide them? "I guess you want to ask about that mask. I told the sheriff I don't know nothing."

Paddy's psyche hung by a thread. The small lifeline of reality Seth provided was the only thing keeping Paddy from being homeless or suicidal. Or a permanent resident of the jail. Any information from him would be useless, torn apart by lawyers in court who'd argue Paddy didn't know what he was saying half the time.

But Drayco hoped for at least a crumb of insight into one particular relationship. "Why did you hate Oakley Keys?"

"He was no good. Cheating on his wife. With married women, no less. But you wouldn't know about that, would you? You shoulda left her alone."

Drayco didn't have to ask who the "her" was anymore. Darcie had a stable of admirers, with a charter member right in front of him. "Come on, Paddy. That's not the real reason you hated Oakley, is it?"

Paddy jerked his rocking body to a halt and for the first time looked directly into Drayco's eyes. "You know why. And that's all I'm going to say."

Paddy wasn't defiant, angry, or sad. It was as if Drayco were staring into an unoccupied building where the human life within had slipped slowly and quietly away. True to his word, Paddy got out of his chair and walked to the door, rapping on it several times. Before he was led away, he turned back toward Drayco as if he changed his mind. But he stopped himself, then left for good.

Sheriff Sailor poked his head back inside the room. "So you and Paddy are best buds now. Did you get what you were after?"

"A fleeting glimpse of what Paddy could have been."

"Ready to spill the beans about that theory of yours? I have some bad institutional coffee in my office so thick you can smear it on bread. And if that doesn't tempt you, I don't know what would."

Drayco smiled. "How could I refuse? Lead the way."

41

Sheriff Sailor wasn't as ready to throw Drayco into a straitjacket as he'd thought, saying the coffee was harder to swallow than Drayco's theory—but it was like having all the pieces of a jigsaw puzzle in place and the lights out so you couldn't see the picture.

Drayco offered to read through Oakley's writings for some tangible clues, and now the boxes with Oakley's magazine columns filled the passenger seat and floor of Drayco's car. Even so, the last two decades of Oakley's creative life took up less space than a waste bin.

As he drove through town, Drayco caught a glimpse of a familiar object in his mirror. The mystery black sedan with the tinted windshield was behind him again. Sailor had given Drayco a list of cars in the area with medical exemptions for tinted windshields, so Drayco wasn't surprised to see the identity of the driver.

Time to set the record straight. He headed into the downtown's lone covered parking garage and waited. When the sedan followed, Drayco whipped the Starfire around and blocked the exit.

He called out to the other driver, "You've been following me."

Randolph Squier was out of his car in a flash, pounding his fists on the hood of the Starfire. "You're having an affair with my wife." He sported an uncharacteristic stubble matching an uncharacteristic stain on his collar.

Drayco climbed out and positioned himself diagonal to Squier with the hood in between. No need to resort to force, yet. "You're wrong." He pushed aside thoughts of how close to being true Squier's accusation was.

Squier resembled a caged boar breathing hard after the chase with the hunter. His words came out in puffed fragments. "I've followed you. I've seen you with her. You're no better than Oakley Keys. You know that?"

"Funny you should say that. Your wife has been snooping. She's afraid you killed Oakley Keys out of jealousy."

Squier removed his hands from the car, and Drayco was surprised there weren't any dents where his fists made contact. Judging from the way Squier was rubbing his hands, it had hurt. Squier stumbled back against the building behind him, his shoulders drooping into the concrete. "I did feel like killing Oakley when he was making a fool out of me and embarrassing me in front of the entire town."

He'd slowed his breathing, but his voice still held even more of an edge than usual. "Maybe you think if I can hit a duck with a single round at forty yards, I could kill a man. But you'd be wrong."

"You have a temper, at least where Darcie is concerned."

Squier kept rubbing his hands. His knuckles were bright red. "I get crazy when I think about Darcie and other men. I—look at you. And look at me. I'm more of a father figure with gout. But I have enough ego to believe Darcie married me for love."

"She told me you can be charming if you aren't out to prove yourself—"

"Success never lasts. You have to prove yourself, over and over."

"Is that why you ran for town council?"

"I'm beginning to regret it. This whole development mess has mushroomed into one political nightmare. I'm in danger of losing what little respect I have left in this town."

Drayco shot a quick glance into Squier's car. On the passenger seat lay a round scrimshaw box with an elaborate etched sailing ship and whale on the cover. The date on front said 1793. Beside it was a white catalog envelope, like the one containing the latest threatening note, but this one had Gallinger as the return address. Spoils of the Gallinger money? Or the embezzlement?

"Change is inevitable, Councilman. The development will come, one way or another."

"It's not only the development. It's the rumors about Darcie and the murders. If they're not solved soon, I'll be lynched, along with the rest of the council. And that sheriff friend of yours."

"You're worried about more violence?"

"We've been flooded with complaints about day laborers and foreigners." He snarled at Drayco with a caged boar's primal hatred. "Certainly you agree with me that immigrants are behind the murders? You must agree."

"It may play a part. Just not the way people think."

"My career is over one way or another. When word gets out about the land I purchased north of the Yaegles. .. it will be my head on a platter."

"If the new development brings in jobs and taxes, people will sing your praises." Unless the embezzlement charges were proven, in which case Squier losing his job might not be the worst thing to happen to him.

The vein on Squier's neck throbbed like a purple spaghetti eel thrashing in a net. "Easy for you to say. You can sell that Opera House and be done with Cape Unity. Come to think of it that might be for the best. The sooner you are gone, the sooner Darcie will forget about you. You're bad luck. These murders didn't start until you showed up."

The conduit theme again. At least Squier was right about that. Since they were engaging in some nice parking-garage *glasnost*, it was Drayco's turn. "Oakley's wooden mask. Darcie said you bought it from someone in town."

"I'm not the one who bought it. Darcie is. She saw the mask with Paddy and knew it was Oakley's. I was furious." Like an afterthought, he added, "Because of the murder, I was naturally worried how such an action might reflect upon her."

So Squier and Darcie were both pointing the finger of blame about who bought the mask at each other. That wasn't going to go well in the marriage-counseling sessions. "The day I was at your office, you and Paddy had a shouting match. Were you buying his silence about that mask?"

"Are you implying I would resort to blackmail, Drayco?"

"Not implying. Asking. I subscribe to the presumption of innocence, so if you're not guilty, you have no worries. Be it embezzlement or blackmail. On the other hand, a dark sedan tried to run me over the other night, one that looked a lot like yours. I don't suppose you'd know anything about that incident, would you?"

Squier's face was the color of framboise, but there was nothing sweet about the look in his eyes as he moved around the Starfire, his hands now balled tightly at his sides. He lost any remaining traces of his Southern dandy charm as he morphed from trapped boar into a fair imitation of the snarling wolf-coyote from the woods and launched himself at Drayco.

Squier threw the first punch, but Drayco sidestepped around him, forced him into a headlock, and manhandled him into the driver's seat of his Lexus. Drayco shut the door, quietly but firmly, and was surprised when Squier stayed put, a dazed expression on his face. Randolph Squier, manipulator, bully, and fallen master of his incredibly small universe.

Drayco headed back to the Starfire but paused to turn around. "And Squier—why don't you take Darcie up to New York, see the sights, schedule a romantic dinner at Tavern on the Green. It might do wonders to rekindle that flame."

Darcie said she'd never give up on Drayco, that she always got what she wanted. But he wasn't convinced she knew what that was. Hopefully, she wouldn't strangle her happiness with vague strands of discontentment only to find too late there's no turning back. Of course, if Squier wound up in jail, all that property and money would be hers alone. Drayco wasn't sure he or anyone else could compete with that.

Maybe it was too late for Tavern on the Green and flowers. Too late for a lot of things.

42

The nor'easter threatening all week gathered its forces together, taking aim at Cape Unity and other cities northward into Philadelphia, New York, Boston. Drayco awoke early Friday to the howling of wind under the eaves, rattling the storm windows. He peered outside in time to see an empty trash can launch across the street. Rain pelted the holly bushes where one lone cardinal hunkered down among the branches, fluffing itself into a ball.

The wind gusts awakened him several times from fragments of disturbing dreams. In one, Nanette Keys and the Cadden twins were begging for mercy as a laughing demon chased them into a pool where they sank lifeless beneath a layer of blood. Paddy filled another nightmare, methodically strangling each citizen of Cape Unity until no one was left. And in a third, Konstantina was at his side as the carjacker threw them both out of Drayco's car, only she pushed him away, leaving his arm intact, and it was she who was caught in the door instead, dragged to her death.

He sat on the edge of the bed for several minutes, waiting for the violent images to fade.

Undaunted by the storm, the Major was in his usual place, cutting his scone into four equal sections and placing one pat of butter on each. "Morning, Scott. You enjoying the gorgeous weather we arranged for you?"

Drayco plopped down into a chair, eyeing the pile of scones warily. He'd watched the wind churn the inlet waters into small whitecaps in the distance from an upstairs window, and his stomach was doing a remarkably similar impression. Something went clunk on the roof.

"This is a sturdy old house you have. Must have endured a lot of nasty weather in its history."

The Major cracked his knuckles. "It'll reach the century mark next year. The fact it's still standing is testimony to its craftsmanship. If this were one of those new-fangled homes they cobble together in a week, a storm like this would knock it all cattywampus."

Maida handed Drayco a steaming mug, and he asked, "No cognac?" His nighttime thrashing left him with another headache, and the cognac didn't sound like such a bad idea.

"No cognac. I can add some."

"A couple shots of caffeine straight up will do." He took a sip of coffee, his mouth only getting scalded a little. "Major, I've been meaning to ask about a piece Oakley made for you once. A wooden mask of some sort? When I asked you about it earlier, you couldn't recall."

The Major took his time finishing his buttered masterpiece. "I don't remember it, to be honest. But with senile geezers like me, memory's the first thing to go. My memory started leaking the minute I left the service. Self-preservation, I guess. Or that concussion I had that knocked me flat for weeks. They said I might have brain damage. Better that than dwell on some of the things you've seen and done."

Drayco might have agreed, having witnessed several cases of veteran PTSD, but this from a man who could nail a Trivial Pursuit tournament?

The Major washed down a piece of scone and smacked his lips. "You should ask Maida about that mask. If I leave anything lying around long enough, she'll cart it off to the Salvation Army."

A loud rattle announced the mail had arrived through the front door. Drayco was impressed. "I guess they mean it when they say neither rain, nor sleet, nor gloom of night will stop the postal service."

"Not Ed Alshire, anyway. He's been our mailman for as long as we've lived here."

When the Major left to get the mail, Maida went to a book and pulled out a photocopy, waving it at Drayco. "The Polish borscht recipe. I got the complete page from the library, including the contributor. It was Angel Quillen, Paddy's mother, of all people."

Drayco was grateful for Maida's efforts, but not surprised at the results. Another piece of the circumstantial puzzle that was fitting everything together.

"I have another question for you since you undoubtedly know the Bible better than I do. Is there a verse along the lines of 'the righteous shall rejoice when he sees vengeance'?"

Maida thought for a moment. "The Bible talks of vengeance a lot. But that particular phrase sounds like one of the Psalms—'the righteous shall rejoice when he sees vengeance and shall wash his feet in the blood of the wicked.'"

The Major returned and sorted the mail on the table. "Bills, bills, and more bills. Except—here's one for you." He handed Drayco a plain white catalog envelope. It had Scott Drayco and the Lazy Crab address. No return address, but the postmark was local.

He opened it and took out a note smaller than the two previous ones, but with similar red lettering. This was messier and uneven and said, "If you value your life leave now."

When Maida saw what it was, she craned her neck over to read it. "That's less friendly than the other. Perhaps you should call Sheriff Sailor."

Drayco held the note up to the light. No unusual watermarks. And while the lettering was indeed red, it didn't look the same. Maybe the note-sender ran out of Oakley's blood?

He dialed the sheriff who pulled the mouthpiece away while he coughed, apologizing between sniffles. "Exactly what I don't need right now, a cold. At least I was vaccinated against mumps so it could be worse. Drop off that letter, and we'll add it to the pile of your fan mail. But take a tip from Hollywood slasher movies and don't make trips along lonely stretches of roads or hikes out in the backcountry."

"Don't worry. I've got all those columns of Oakley's you gave me. Should make for fun reading on a day like this."

"Day like this is right. We've got our hands full of incidents already. And it's going to get worse. The weather gods sure aren't happy. Make me wish I could stay home myself and catch up on some reading."

"I'll toast some marshmallows in your honor."

"You do that. And tell everyone there to stay put. We don't want anyone outside today who doesn't have to be."

When Drayco returned to the kitchen, Maida handed him a book. "You asked if the local library had a Polish dictionary. Here it is."

"Thanks, Maida. We should get the Lazy Crab hooked up with the Internet and bring you into the twenty-first century. Next time I can bring my laptop."

She grinned. "Cape Unity's only now getting caught up with the twentieth. We just got semi-reliable Internet service on the Eastern Shore a year ago."

He'd already looked up a Polish dictionary on his smartphone, although with the spotty, painfully slow coverage on the shore, it was an ordeal. But he wanted to verify what he'd found via a more reliable source. Drayco flipped first to *D* in the book and found the entry for *diabel*. Devil. Then he flipped ahead to the *K*'s, and there it was. Oakley's joke or homage, it was hard to say.

Drayco commandeered the Jepsons' study, where they'd been gracious enough to allow him free rein. It was one of his favorite rooms there, a masculine room with dark oak paneling and the largest fireplace in the house, flanked with cast-iron lions. Drayco imagined they were glaring at him, asking why he hadn't kept his promise to Nanette.

He skimmed through several Oakley columns for "Brits Abroad," fascinated by the man's surprising sense of humor. But darkness and hints of rancor also peppered his writing. Drayco's former FBI colleagues would sink their teeth into Oakley's profile, recreating Oakley's character from nuances of his words like a forensic artist modeling a face from a skull.

Oakley ended up a hermit, but an intelligent one. As Earl said, "I figured we'd be reading about him in the papers one day, a Pulitzer. I guess it wasn't in the cards." Oakley was a gifted writer, but his real passion, and it was hardly a gift, was his inability to let things go, as Paddy said.

Every column contained at least one diatribe against some perceived injustice. The mind of Oakley Keys was like a mental prison forged from an all-consuming bitterness. In that sense, Oakley and the murderer shared everything in common.

Drayco wanted to trade places with Sheriff Sailor by the time he picked up column number eighteen and saw the pile of magazines still in the box. He waded through two more, surprised to see a reference to Konstantina and musicians silenced by Hitler's "final solution."

It was telling and poignant that Oakley singled out Konstantina. The same column rambled on with an odd reference to Orestes in Greek mythology and a snide comment that Americans knew more about the Osmonds than Orestes. The Osmonds? What was the date of the magazine? Ah, 1990.

He recalled seeing some reference books in the Keys' home. Including one on mythology. Well, the sheriff had given Drayco a key to Oakley and Nanette's house, hadn't he? Drayco looked at the key now, sparkling in the light from the fire as he rolled it around in his hand. Puny, compared to the Opera House key.

He didn't doubt Sailor and his deputies were meticulous in their search, but the sheriff was thinking horses, not zebras. Drayco briefly toyed with the idea of calling Sailor first, but the overworked man was swamped. He could do this alone.

A peek out the window revealed the rain was slacking up. The marshmallows for the sheriff would have to wait.

43

The house looked the same as when Drayco said goodbye to Nanette a week ago, except for a fine coating of dust lying on the furniture like a shroud. The place was beginning to smell abandoned, save for the dust mites and mold. Tidy Nanette would be horrified at this lapse in housekeeping.

From the sheriff's report, he approximated the location where Nanette's body was found and started his search there, in the kitchen. With no evidence of forced entry, Drayco agreed with the sheriff that Nanette let her killer inside. Someone she knew.

A gallery of framed photographs hung on a wall, including beatific wedding pictures of Oakley and Nanette. The youthful Oakley exhibited darker hair and fewer crow's feet than the older version lying on the Opera House floor. But Oakley's young eyes in the photo, clear and penetrating instead of cloudy with incipient cataracts, were eyes that now looked familiar on someone else.

He scanned the books on the shelves until he pulled out the one on mythology, with a citation for "Orestes" that Oakley highlighted in yellow. Drayco knew the play by Euripides but wanted to verify the plot. And there it was. Orestes killed his mother, Clytemnestra, in order to avenge the murder of his father.

Another book, on European folklore, caught his eye. Out of curiosity, Drayco leafed through the index and jumped to the section on owls, again highlighted in yellow. The article referenced the owl's symbolism throughout Polish history as an evil omen. Oakley wanted to make certain the message of his owl mask wouldn't be lost on the intended recipient, the "devil."

Furniture Oakley crafted was scattered around the house. But the granddaddy of all was the long console table, Nanette's favorite among Oakley's creations. This was the piece someone offered Oakley a thousand dollars for, but he wouldn't sell.

The smooth top resting on the legs was thick, for a table without drawers. The carvings were the most elaborate on any of Oakley's works, with passion vines like those in Oakley's outdoor shrine circling the legs. Two doves flew across the front panel, beaks pointing toward the central figure of the piece, a heart in the shape of Oakley's rock.

Drayco knelt to take a better look and ran his hand underneath the tabletop at the point behind the heart. Feeling a rough section, he ducked his head under the table. Seeing an area with slight seams, he tugged at it and slid open a small hidden drawer.

He retrieved an envelope wadded inside, with the familiar sideways lettering. It read, "To be opened upon my death." But it was opened already, steamed, not slit. He took a whiff of it, smelling traces of a sweet perfume, a woman's scent, but not like Darcie's jasmine. Inside the envelope was a one-page handwritten testament.

He read it several times. Had Nanette found it before or after Oakley's murder? And why didn't she tell Drayco when he was at her house? The murderer obviously hadn't discovered it. But if Nanette confronted the murderer over the contents, she sealed her fate.

Drayco felt a pang of intense loss. The narrative in Oakley's testament wasn't a surprise. But it touched upon so many tragedies, was so symbolic of the consequences of war—and the jealousy, greed, and hatred upon which war was based—it was hard to separate these two deaths from the many.

A disputable and rambling testament of a dead man, a burned letter fragment, the dates on an immigration record, a bloody "G" carved into a victim's chest, the b-b carving in a tree—he could find more tangible evidence in a supermarket tabloid. Darkness, distance, and the passing of time were what the killer counted on, and so far the formula was working well.

The only thing not counted on was the arrival of Drayco himself, new owner of a strategic Opera House—the wild card.

44

Sheriff Sailor read the testament Drayco discovered. His narrowed eyes focused like a laser on the paper, and Drayco waited to see if it would burst into flames. The sheriff growled, "Son of a bitch. Not sure how we missed this." He pushed the paper back to Drayco. "Leaves a few questions unanswered. But it explains in better detail that other letter, the burned fragment."

"It does, and it doesn't. Nanette likely read this testament before she met with me the day of her death. I've been puzzling over why she didn't tell me—it might have saved her life."

"She might have been killed anyway, but at least we'd have collared the murderer sooner. Why do you think she held back?"

"Fear, possibly, since she knew the identity of Oakley's killer. In giving me the letter fragment as a form of bait, maybe she believed I'd track down the murderer, and she wouldn't have to get involved. She couldn't have dreamed the killer was outside the window listening in when she showed me the fragment."

"Here's another puzzler, Drayco—why did Oakley never mention he had a mother? Why all the secrecy?"

"Short of Oakley coming back from the dead, the answer will remain with him in his grave. My guess—he didn't want anyone prying into his past because it might ruin his plan for revenge."

Sailor rubbed the back of his neck. He'd apparently been having headaches, too. "I've got the who, what, and where, but not the why, or I guess I should say, the why now?"

"That one will have to wait for a confession."

"If we get one. At least now I understand the meaning of the 'G' part." The sheriff regarded Drayco with a hint of a smile working its way across his face. "Sure does make Oakley's college genealogy project look like a stroke of genius. Can you think of a better cover to track someone down?"

"Oakley wouldn't have made a bad sleuth. At least with his writing skills, he'd make short work of that FBI paperwork I hated."

The sheriff took a couple of aspirins out of his desk and swallowed them dry. "Speaking of paperwork. I'll get a warrant to search the house for that other Webley, possible blood traces, and shoe treads to match our cast from the woods. But it's a Friday evening, and you've seen those tabbies and poodles it's raining out there. I'll let you know as soon as I get the go-ahead. Keep me posted on your end."

"I'm heading down to Norfolk."

"Harmon Ainscough? The address you used Tyler's computer to research?"

"Turns out, he lives within a half-day's driving distance, lucky for me. I don't think my bank account could handle last-minute plane tickets."

"Safer for you out of town anyway, until we get this all nailed down, with that bull's eye on your back."

"Keep me from pestering you and adding to your migraines. How many calls are you up to?"

"Dozens. Injured drivers, people without power, live wires down on roads, trees toppled onto a couple of houses. And one terrified cat that won't come out of an underground drain pipe."

"Sounds fun. Wish I could help, but. .."

"Yeah, yeah, go practice scales."

"I might do that. I should check on the Opera House to see if it's still standing."

"Hopefully, it'll get blown down. I'll put in a good word with the weather gods for you."

"Thanks. I think. By the way, Sheriff, did you know the word *klucze* means 'keys' in Polish?"

45

The small cottage was such an archetype of a traditional English dwelling that it was like stepping across the Pond. But this was Norfolk, Virginia, not Suffolk, England. He'd take the time to admire the architecture if it weren't for the thirty-knot wind gusts.

A man wrapped in a plaid flannel shawl sitting in a wheelchair greeted Drayco's knock. Harmon Ainscough was molded into his chair as only one who is chronically ill can seem. He was bald, shriveled, with oxygen tubes wedded to his nostrils. But his still-blue eyes were bright and his voice clear. He sized up Drayco. "Got any smokes?"

"Sorry, no."

Disappointed, Ainscough folded himself farther into his prison of a chair. "They won't let me have any. Doctor's orders. Never hurts to ask."

Dozens of signed photographs perched on tables and hung on walls. Drayco stopped to examine them and recognized several musical artists, including a picture of Konstantina, wearing a red carnation. He asked, "Clients of yours?"

Ainscough motioned Drayco toward a chair. "All clients at one time or another. I had my share of stars, but as you can see," he made a sweeping gesture around the humble room, "I didn't get rich off of them. I did all right, but no winter home in the Riviera. But I've got all I need here. A small plot of land, my daughter, grandkids, my bulldog Winston and memories. Lots of memories. .." He dozed off.

Drayco raised his voice slightly. "It's one of those memories I've come to discuss."

Ainscough perked up again. "Sorry about that lapse. It's all the bloody meds they have me on."

"I need to ask about a former client, a pianist who died in the 1950s. Konstantina Klucze."

At the mention of her name, Ainscough's jaw dropped open, and his whole body froze. He answered with a quaver, "One of the most promising talents I came across. Lost after the war."

"She was murdered."

"That's what the police said."

"You don't agree?"

Ainscough tried to steady the spasms in his hands, from what was likely Parkinson's, and wrapped the shawl tighter around him. "They never found who did it. It was a difficult time for everyone in Europe, citizens, soldiers, the police."

"Was she threatened in some way?"

Ainscough again hesitated. "Curious timing of yours. It was so long ago." He coughed. "She's one of the reasons I moved here, you know. I liked the area when we went on tour together." He coughed again and wiped his sleeve across his lips. "Now, what did you say your interests were about Konstantina?"

"I'm acting on behalf of someone with reason to inquire into her death."

"Her son? She had a baby before she died. Never heard what happened to him." Drayco didn't contradict him, and Ainscough sighed. "If it's her son looking for answers, he should have some. I can't tell him who murdered her. But I do know she and Filip had many arguments beforehand."

"Filip? Would that be her stepson?"

Ainscough's eyes widened in surprise. "That's right. Filip Gozdowski. He was Edmund's—her husband's—son from his first marriage. One of those sad family disputes. The Nazi invasion forced them out of Poland, and they lost most of the family fortune in the process. Filip was embittered at the prospect of being poor. Felt the manuscript his father gave Konstantina rightfully belonged to him. Been in the family for a few generations. I think Filip made Konstantina's life miserable after Edward left to join the resistance."

"This was the Chopin manuscript."

"A piano sonata."

"The one in B-flat minor?" B-flat, written as b-b in certain musical notation. Phonic, an anagram for Chopin. Oakley's tree carving, the paper from the dropped file. All the puzzle pieces were fitting together. Oddly, it was a snippet from Reece's carousel tune that popped into Drayco's mind, *Is the sound of distant drumming just the fingers of your hand?. .. Like a circle in a spiral, like a wheel within a wheel ...*

The older man's voice was a whisper. "Yes, yes. An original copy Chopin intended for a publisher. Filip thought it would be worth a small fortune."

"What happened to it after Konstantina's death?"

Ainscough's spasms grew more agitated, and Drayco reached over to hold his hand. "Mr. Ainscough, at this point, nothing you say would be held against you. It's a relief to tell the truth, don't you agree?"

Ainscough calmed down though his breathing remained labored. "I've had a few ethical crises. Konstantina was the innocent object of one. Filip came to me before Konstantina's American tour, knowing I'd be with her the whole time, and asked—no, demanded—I keep an eye on the manuscript. He was just shy of twenty, but he could be a formidable fellow. He learned she was going to take it with her for safekeeping. Told me if I could find a way to steal it, he'd give me a share of the profits."

"You tried to sell it?"

"Konstantina carried around a black satchel with the manuscript and its jeweled case inside. After she caught me trying to steal it in New York, she never let it out of her sight. I'm sure she figured out I was acting on behalf of Filip. I never had a chance to sell it."

"What happened after the last concert in Cape Unity?"

"I hurt my arm. Konstantina drove me to a clinic and dropped me off for a couple of hours. When she returned, she no longer carried the satchel. You're too young to remember, but there were few transatlantic flights in those days. We rushed back to New York to catch the one we'd booked."

Ainscough paused, twisting awkwardly in his chair, the constant shaking of his body making it difficult. "Back in London when I told Filip about the satchel, he was livid. Grew violent. Accused me of making the whole story up. Taking the manuscript myself. I convinced him it was the truth. He left me alone, but stole a few of my possessions, out of spite I guess. Never heard from him again. I think he left the country."

"How does this fit, time-wise, with Konstantina's murder?"

"This was right after we got back. Konstantina found out she was pregnant, had the baby a few months later, and was killed not long after. She fired me when we returned. I didn't have a chance to see her again before her death."

He coughed so hard, Drayco went to the kitchen to pour him a glass of water and waited for the other man's attack to subside. "Do you personally believe Filip was involved with her murder?"

"He had a pattern of violence. But to kill his own stepmother?"

Drayco sized up Konstantina's photograph. "Why did Konstantina wear a red carnation in that picture?"

"People gave her those in bouquets after concerts instead of roses. It was her favorite flower."

Oakley's research into his mother's past was thorough. A mental snapshot of Oakley's body on the Opera House stage came to Drayco's mind, and the sad carnation in his lapel. In a way, it was more fitting than any of the flowers that would be heaped on Oakley's grave.

"Have you lived in the States long, Mr. Ainscough?"

"I moved to New York around 1960. I retired here a few years ago to be near my daughter, the main reason I'm here now."

"Do you have a middle name, sir?"

Ainscough looked confused. "It's Horatio."

How Shakespearean. H-A-H, the monogram of Harmon Horatio Ainscough. Drayco took pity on the old man who looked even older than when he'd arrived. "As you say, it's ancient history, isn't it?"

Drayco rose to leave. "You do have a nice home here, cozy and peaceful. I'm sorry I didn't get to meet Winston, but you'll give him my regards, won't you?"

The old man nodded, and once Drayco was outside, he saw through the window that Ainscough was once again asleep.

Drayco made a quick call to Maida. "Everything good there? Is the power still on?"

Maida reassured him. "Everyone and everything is hunky-dory. To prove how optimistic I am, I've got the makings of a Smith Island ten-layer cake in the oven. Major had to run errands and said he wouldn't be back for a while. He was cagey and said he wanted to surprise me, but it was something he had to take care of. You'll be here for dinner?"

"I wouldn't miss it—your smiling face or the cake. I'm going to check out the Opera House first, but I should be back by meal time, sooner if I can manage it. You can count on me."

46

The Opera House was still standing although Drayco had to dodge flying debris and ice pellets as he ducked inside. Seth still followed Horatio Rockingham's mandate with the furnace turned down to sixty degrees. Drayco pulled his coat tighter around him. He'd waited until after five when Seth would be through with his rounds and watched the door to make sure Seth left. Drayco wanted to be alone for this.

He turned on one bank of Fresnel lights on the downstage lighting pipe. Then, he opened his briefcase and pulled out the blueprints from Reece.

Konstantina was virtually alone in an unfamiliar country, not knowing anyone except her agent, whom she'd come to distrust. She knew when she returned to England, Filip would get the manuscript by any means possible. Confused, tired from the tour, the stress of the war's aftermath and her husband's death, she must have made the decision to hide the manuscript in Cape Unity. That would explain why it hadn't turned up at some auction house before now.

Since she didn't have much time alone—two hours by Harmon Ainscough's reckoning—the only place in town she knew was the Opera House. Drayco didn't believe the manuscript made it back to England. Certainly, the murderer didn't think so.

Ainscough's injury gave Konstantina an opportunity she hadn't considered. For the first time in months, she was free from the double threat of her agent and her stepson. It was impossible to determine whether she was trying to find a way to hide the manuscript during her entire tour or whether she seized the moment.

Where would she have spent the most time in the Opera House? Drayco studied the blueprints. There was the wide-open stage and the public lobby. Neither a good hiding place.

The greenroom was a possibility, but nothing in the blueprints indicated a potential cache site, unless Konstantina stuffed it inside furniture, long gone. That would be ironic. A valuable manuscript inside a faded fifty-year-old armchair, lying in someone's basement among the broken stereos and unused stationary bikes.

But what was it Reece said? A pipe burst in the greenroom right before Konstantina's concert. Drayco walked to the back of the stage and looked up at the curved staircases. One of those side rooms at the top could serve as a temporary greenroom.

He flipped through the blueprints for a detail of the catwalk and headed up the old stairs for the second time since he arrived in Cape Unity, hoping they were climb-worthy. He celebrated when he made it to the top unscathed.

The larger room on the left of the landing looked more promising. After flipping on the one dim bulb in the room, Drayco carried the blueprints inside. A faded rug with burn marks in the center was the only object in the room, moved from the office long ago after an incident with a cigar.

He examined the walls and thumped around in various places, but the walls were solid. The blueprints indicated a straightforward architecture, four walls, no attic or closets. Except. .. there was once a crawlspace under the wooden plank floor, an overflow area for storing props.

A crawlspace would make a perfect hiding place. But would a woman even as desperate as Konstantina entrust an irreplaceable manuscript to a dark hole where someone could find it?

Konstantina's recital was one of the last at the Opera House before Rockingham closed it down. And Konstantina, as she had explicitly mentioned to Reece Wable's mother after that 1955 concert, made plans to return to the States as soon as possible.

Drayco tried to place himself in Konstantina's mindset. Filip Gozdowski's relentless and threatening bullying, the loss of Edmund, the horrors of the war and uncertainties of post-war Europe. Did it generate so much fear and confusion she decided she'd rather lose the manuscript altogether than have it fall into Filip's hands?

Perhaps she believed it would be invisible among the other props stashed in the crowded space. If someone did find it, she could still lay claim.

All hypothetical. But as he researched Konstantina's life, he formed an emotional, intuitive bond with her. They shared a mutual passion for music, for the piano, a shared feeling of pain and loss.

He believed she didn't want to lose the manuscript, but her instincts about her stepson were correct. Filip would have found a way to take the manuscript from her in London. Better lost forever than in the hands of a cold-hearted demon with no respect for life or art.

Drayco scanned the flooring. If the crawlspace was in use at the time of her concert, there must be an access point, but the floorboards looked seamless. He walked off the footage indicated in the blueprints to where the edge of the crawlspace should be and rolled back the rug.

The wooden floor pattern looked typical, some boards tight-fitting and others sporting slight cracks between. Taking out his Leatherman knife, he poked around the edges of the nailed boards, but they wouldn't budge. *Please don't let this be a dead end.* He had no way of knowing when the crawlspace had stopped being used, possibly sealed off long before Konstantina arrived.

He decided to try the area that would have marked the other end of the crawlspace. This time, the faint outline of a circular indentation looked promising. An old liquid stain? Or the site of a former pull ring?

He tried jiggling the board with the ring outline. This time, the plank moved a fraction of an inch.

Buoyed by that success, Drayco slipped the knife deeper into the crack and jiggled the board harder until one edge moved a fraction.

He worked on adjacent boards, and an entire section of the floor flipped up and fell over with a loud "thunk." The opening was barely big enough for his arm and shoulder.

Whipping out a flashlight from his coat pocket, he peered into the dark aperture. He grinned as props appeared like vampires in their coffins, each illuminated in turn—a wig, swords, crowns.

He reached the flashlight farther into the hole where the light hit an object the size of a coffee table book, covered in black leather with handles. He lay on his stomach, reaching as far as he could until his fingers clasped around the piece, and maneuvered it out of its coffin.

Thin and lightweight, it hardly seemed the vessel for anything valuable. He imagined his disappointment when he opened it to find more yellowed invoices. He tried to pull the zipper on the pouch, but it stuck. Struggling with it for a few minutes, he coaxed it open. Then, he held his breath as he peered inside to get a look.

Afraid the oil on his fingers might contaminate a possible rare Chopin manuscript, he took his time. The light in the room kept flickering as the storm took its toll on power lines. But there was enough light to see a smaller portfolio inside covered with glints of gold embroidery and glass. Red glass, like rubies. It was like the pouch Harmon Ainscough described, the one that vanished after Konstantina's murder.

A moment later, the lights in the Opera House winked out.

47

It was the third time Sheriff Sailor banged on the door, but still no answer. He tried the knob, and the door swung open. Turning toward Nelia nearby, he motioned with his head in the direction of Nelia's gun. "Just in case," he said.

They were startled by a loud crack behind them and swirled around to watch as the force of the winds broke off a branch the size of a telephone pole from an oak tree in the yard. Sailor shook his head, and they entered the house, keeping their guard up. Paddy could be unpredictable. He'd been known to start fights in a drunken stupor, been found stone cold on public benches, ticketed for public urination, and of course the thefts and marijuana, but he'd never before called the sheriff to say he was committing suicide.

Sailor pointed for Nelia to check one of the bedrooms while he checked the other, but they were empty. Sailor paused in the kitchen to examine a bottle on the counter. Cayenne pepper capsules. A low moan rose from the living room, and the Sheriff and Nelia approached the back of the sofa from different sides, converging in the front where Paddy lay outstretched on the floor. Nearby were a couple of empty tequila bottles and one empty bottle of sleeping pills.

Nelia knelt beside Paddy, and Sailor called the dispatcher to send out EMTs. He glanced over at a TV tray, where a cardboard file box was sitting, the label scratched off. Still, he recognized it. The missing Opera House box. Also on the tray lay several papers. He picked the one on the top. It was an unsent love letter to Nanette Keys from Seth. Next to it was the missing library manuscript.

Paddy stopped moaning and started mumbling, low and unintelligible. Sailor got closer and shook Paddy gently. "What is it, Paddy?"

Paddy lay there, his mouth moving wordlessly. Then he licked his lips and uttered in a low, hoarse voice, "We were searching for it. All those years. We never found it in the Opera House. So we searched all those houses. Then he came and messed everything up."

"Searching for what, Paddy? You mean those break-ins years ago, don't you?"

"But we never found it. Just never found it."

His voice was getting weaker, and the sheriff hoped the bottle of sleeping pills hadn't been full. A siren faint in the background grew louder, and Sailor headed to the door to point the way for the medical crew. As they rushed in and worked with Paddy, Sailor's radio crackled on. A dispatcher forwarded a call through, and he was surprised to hear Maida.

"I expect you're busy, Sheriff, and I hate to bother you. But I haven't heard from Scott. He's an hour late. That's not like him."

"Drayco told me he was meeting someone in Norfolk. Probably got caught in traffic due to the lousy weather."

"He would have called. You know that."

Sailor did know. In the sheriff's dealings with Drayco, he was usually early, never late. "Was he stopping anywhere else, Maida?"

"The only place he mentioned was the Opera House."

"The Opera House?" The sheriff looked at Paddy who was on a stretcher, hooked up to oxygen and an IV. But apparently, Paddy was listening to the sheriff's end of the conversation and was sufficiently aware to gaze back at Sailor, a wide, unblinking stare. The look in those eyes said more than enough to make Sailor's blood run cold, and he jumped up and darted out the front door. The rain pelted his uniform, soaking his shirt, and the wind picked up his hat and launched it into the sky. But Sailor hardly noticed. This was shades of his younger brother all over again, and this time, he hoped he got there in time.

48

Drayco waited a few moments and was relieved when the lights came back on, although dimmer, bathing everything in a sepia glow. He opened the satchel as wide as possible to get a better look at what he was now certain were rubies on the smaller case hidden inside. He walked toward the stage and its brighter lighting.

If he were the type to believe in ghosts, he'd swear the spirit of Konstantina was near him now, her presence palpable. This innocent-looking case he held was both what she lived for and what she had died for, and it felt like lead in his hands.

Yet it could also contain a priceless manuscript. Drayco was so absorbed by an overwhelming eagerness to glimpse notes possibly penned by Chopin's own hand, it took him a moment to realize he wasn't alone.

A piece of railing caught his sleeve and pulled him around toward a figure perched in the middle of the catwalk, just as his practiced ears heard the unmistakable click of a revolver being cocked. He instinctively twisted toward one side simultaneously with the discharge of the gun, falling against the railing. He stopped short of slipping down the stairs but banged his head hard on the catwalk floor.

He tried to raise himself up as the figure approached, but a wave of dizziness washed over him, and he fell back again. He knew who it was by the apricot conical-shaped wheezing. Through a thick swirling fog, Drayco watched the man scoop up the pouch with his left hand and peer inside. In his right hand, he clutched a Webley.

Drayco managed a wan smile. "'G' is for Gozdowski. Hello, Filip."

Seth Bakely stood silently over Drayco at first, then stooped down and opened Drayco's coat, looking at the red stain spreading over his right shoulder.

Seth's accent was thicker than Drayco had heard it before, with more hints of Polish than Tangier Island, as if the past fifty years had never happened. "Thanks for finding my heritage, Drayco. Been looking for this all my life."

Drayco tried to raise himself once more, but he fought a losing battle as another wave of dizziness hit. No way he'd be able to reach the gun in his shoulder holster. His own voice sounded far away, as he said, "And it only took three murders to do it, right Filip? Konstantina, Oakley, Nanette."

"You're right about the murders." Seth stepped back. "But I'm sorry to say you're not right about the numbers. It took four." He raised the gun and pointed it at Drayco's head. A shot rang out, but Drayco didn't feel any pain.

He heard a small cry and turned his head far enough to see Seth's body tumbling through one of the gaps in the railing. Seth fell to the floor at the back of the stage, wearing his own badge of red from the bullet hole in his chest.

From below, Sheriff Sailor lowered his gun and ran up the stairs. Drayco fell back against the catwalk one last time as he watched the ceiling continue to swirl until the light slowly faded to black.

49

The first sunny day in Cape Unity in over a week felt like a mistake. The storm left litter strewn in its path—a grate from a charcoal grill hanging on a tree, a garbage can dropped on one of the defiant boats still moored at the pier—but it also left behind deep blue skies, sucking out the clouds and pollution.

"Thought you might like to see this view at its best, for a change." Sailor had opted for the short-sleeve version of the uniform and didn't seem to mind the goose bumps. The sunlight glinted off ripples in the water, a golden tide heading toward shore. They walked along the pier basking in the warmth radiating from the planks.

"Like a postcard," Drayco adjusted the sling on his arm.

"Cape Unity isn't such a bad town unless you're obsessed with fifty-year-old grudges."

"Between half-brothers, at that. How's Oakley's nephew Paddy doing?"

"Physically, okay. Emotionally, not so much. He only decided to start talking to us last night, but he's devastated at losing Seth. Despite doing everything he could to prevent such an ending—warning you with that last letter, throwing what he thought was the murder weapon off the pier. Unfortunately for him, he didn't know the story behind the HAH cane or that mask he sold to Squier. Or that Seth had two Webleys."

Drayco stopped to examine a post covered in carved initials and dates and ran his finger over the splintered surface. "Paddy was an innocent victim. Like Nanette."

"Ironic, isn't it? Seth uses her to blackmail Oakley into silence but ends up falling for her. Yet he winds up killing her after she confronts him about what she read in Oakley's testament."

Drayco watched a rockfish splashing through the water, finding its obliviousness to human concerns oddly soothing. "So in the end, Seth's sense of injustice drowned out everything else. Paddy, Nanette, his own chance for happiness."

The sheriff clapped a hand on Drayco's back, avoiding the injured shoulder. "Guess the lawyers get to sort out what happens to that manuscript. But I have it on good authority it may come down to finders, keepers. Whatever will you do with all that money, your highness?"

"Sotheby's sold some rare manuscripts, Chopin and Beethoven, for several hundred grand. There's also the leather case with the rubies, which might fetch a penny or two. Not enough to retire on," he added with a small smile, "But possible seed money for matching grants to restore one aging Opera House."

The sheriff looked at him in amazement. "Thought you were going to dump the place."

"I was. I may still. But then I think of what it's meant to the community. And all the people who have performed there, including Konstantina's last concert. Might be more of a fitting tribute to her than Oakley's shrine."

The sheriff squinted at the full sun. "Have to admit, I'm grateful you were a musician in your former life. Not sure anyone else would have drawn the same conclusions. Makes me want to believe in Kismet."

"Have you been talking to Reece? He's on a Kismet kick."

"Guess it's in the air. Or barometer fluctuations squeezing those little gray brain cells."

Drayco leaned against the post and looked in vain for the rockfish to make a reappearance. "You do know why I left you in the dark, don't you?"

"I get it." Sailor turned his head to glance at a car pulling up, but Drayco didn't have to see him to hear the scowl in his voice. "Just don't do it again."

The car didn't turn off its engine, and the Starfire's window rolled down as Nelia's head poked out. "You ready?" Drayco had protested he could drive his own car back to D.C., but he was outvoted.

Sailor held up his hand. "He's coming." The sheriff turned to Drayco. "It was nice of the potentially soon-to-be-single Mrs. Squier to visit you in the hospital."

Drayco shrugged, then wished he hadn't, forgetting about the shoulder. "So did the Jepsons, Reece, you, and Tyler. It's a friendly town." He smiled, remembering the flowering plant Nelia brought him, with a tiny toy piano on top. It was she who'd offered to drive him in the Starfire back to D.C.

"Squier could get one to twenty for the embezzlement."

Legally, yes, likely, no. If Reece had a betting pool on that one, Drayco would lay wagers on Squier avoiding jail time, with restitution. He said, "You know, I wasted a lot of time believing Squier was our murderer. I'm embarrassed to admit I couldn't get past that repulsive voice of his."

The sheriff flicked a pebble on the dock railing into the water. "So, you got some new hot case waiting for you to invoke your consultant magic?"

"Would you believe it's a decade-old blackmail case?"

Sailor grinned. "Let's hope it doesn't include a burned letter. And Doc, next time you're in town, why don't I treat you to some of that Wachapreague flounder."

"It's a deal, Sheriff."

Epilogue

Friday 26 March

Unlike his last visit here, it was Nelia who was waiting in the car across the street watching from afar, not him. She went along with his request to stop at a florist first after they arrived in D.C., understanding his need to do this. And to do it alone.

The late afternoon sunlight cast a crisscross pattern of shadows on the ground as fallen leaves swirled around like mini-vortices in the wind. Drayco knelt down and placed one red carnation on each of the tiny graves marked by tombstones with the names Callie Cadden and Calvin Cadden.

The nightmares were less frequent in the past few days, but they hadn't stopped, and he didn't want them to. He needed them. Needed the reminders that he should never let his guard down, never be complacent. There were no universal truths, no fate, no Kismet, no God's will, no sense, in any of this. He hadn't been so much a conduit of death as merely a bit player.

He straightened up, taking one last look at the graves. Tomorrow would mean a new case, a new day, and like all new days, there would be beginnings and endings and ways in which some things would never be the same.

CPSIA information can be obtained
at www.ICGtesting.com
Printed in the USA
LVHW031204040420
652211LV00007B/1976